Silence of Murder

Silence of Murder

Carolyn Abner Gaston

TATE PUBLISHING
AND ENTERPRISES, LLC

Published by Tate Publishing & Enterprises, LLC
127 E. Trade Center Terrace | Mustang, Oklahoma 73064 USA
1.888.361.9473 | www.tatepublishing.com

Tate Publishing is committed to excellence in the publishing industry. The company reflects the philosophy established by the founders, based on Psalm 68:11,
"The Lord gave the word and great was the company of those who published it."

Book design copyright © 2013 by Tate Publishing, LLC. All rights reserved.
Cover design by Allen Jomoc
Interior design by Jake Muelle

Published in the United States of America

ISBN: 978-1-62902-552-0
1. Fiction / Mystery & Detective / General
2. Fiction / Thrillers / Crime
13.11.06

Acknowledgments

Special thanks to family and friends for their love and support.

Table of Contents

Introduction 9

Hit and Buried 11

Road 15 Investigation 34

Alan's Alibi 46

Silences of Secrets 57

Richard's Remains 76

Richard's Secret Lover 83

Change of Heart 105

Looking for Love 116

Guilty Conscience 119

The Love of Family 129

Fire Station 139

Breeze of Brookville 149

Family Gathering 160

Morally Corrupted 169

Furious of Fear 177

Mr. Johnson's Service 186

Richard's Service 195

Vows of Silence 205

Richard's Repast 213

Alan's Secret Lover 223

Quotable Women's Dress Shop 232

Lisa's New Date 242

Cousins Investigate. 251

Soul Mates 256

Engagement Plans 266

Engagement Party 278

Dupree Meets His Fiancé's Family. 285

The Love Nest 294

Wedding Ceremony 304

Alan's Mortality 311

Family Mourners 320

Alan's Assets. 330

Move Forward 336

Dupree's Court Date 342

House for Sale 347

Destiny Arrives. 351

New Edition. 357

Brother's Death. 362

Dupree Solves the Case 366

The Fatal Truth 378

The Great Sense of Humor Story. 381

Introduction

I'm in love with my writing and in a relationship with the work my writing gives me to do! A high-motivation state and a thirst for knowledge determines my attitude in seeking my goals to think better, act better, feel better, and get better!

Hit and Buried

"Alan, my boy! How was the poker game?"

"I've won $200!"

"That's great!" his uncle Patrick said, feeling tipsy from drinking his gin and juice. He then walks over to his black-top leather bar stand and pours a shot of Jack Daniels. He smelled chicken or duck coming from the kitchen where his wife Joanna was pouring red wine over the stuffed duck. She placed the medium duck back into the oven, and she walked out the kitchen with appetizers of fruit and crackers. She was wearing her new light green dress with red sparkles that smoothly outlined her curves.

"How was the rest of your day dear? Good," her husband replied. While pouring a quick shot of Jack Daniels that he quickly swallowed down, he slams his empty shot glass on the bar. "Let's make a toast to Fourth of July!" His grin had widened to cheer with the clink of their glasses. Joanna had placed the plate of appetizers on their wooden living room coffee table. Joanna's family bloodline is mixed with Creole and Indian with a little darker complexion, with a haircut that favors, Nia Long, who lights up the evening with her dazzling smile. He quickly walks over to his wife, who stands 5'6, and wrapped his strong arms around her medium waist, hugging her gently and compressing her soft body. He begins pressing his face against her right cheek and neck. "Control yourself," she'd whispered in his ear, hoping that their guest wouldn't notice. "I really miss that feeling of love and passion, baby."

"Let's go and light our flame.' His speech was sounding a bit slurred and the stench of the whiskey on his breath was stronger than the way he tried to persuade.

"The only thing you're going to feel is your pillow." She managed to wiggle her way out of his strong grasp. "That whiskey you're holding smells awful." She had turned around and walked back toward the kitchen.

"Hey, nephew!" Patrick's slurred.

"Do you mind going to the store and getting some more beer and more red wine?"

"I'm afraid we're all out!" Patrick's deep voice slurred. The fifty-five-year-old American Indian, who stands five eight with his black and silver hair, smirked, wearing his black-framed reading glasses that sits on his round nose and above his wild eyebrows and his large ears.

Patrick began swinging the neck of the empty Cabernet wine bottle while Alan was going through his pants pocket for his keys "Uh, sure, Uncle. I'll be right back." And he walks out of his round wooden front door and jumps into his dark blue 1998 Lincoln Navigator and drives slow out of his driveway, feeling a little tipsy. Alan decided to turn left on Road 15; it's a dark curvy back road that's surrounded by fields with dim street lights that he follows to the city limits.

And as he arrives at the 7-Eleven in Brookville he parks a bit crookedly in a small parking space, where he begins stumbling toward the store and leans on the side of the building to catch himself.

"That was a close one." He then walks casually into the store and walks toward the back and grabs a red wine bottle and a six pack of beer. He then walks toward a couple of customers, while trying to keep his balance.

A couple of minutes later, he walks back to his vehicle with his liquor.

From a distance, he hears loud arguing and stands up more erect, although a bit off balance. He is now yelling into the dark, where the arguments continue echoing from across the way.

"Happy Fourth of July all!" He yells into the air. The echoing continues. "Posh!" He blew them off and stumbles toward his vehicle where he drops his keys on the pavement by a small puddle of water. He starts shaking his head back and forth. "*Snap out of it!*"

He grabs his keys from the wet pavement and unlocks his car door. At that point, he jumps into his 1999 dark blue Lincoln Navigator and starts the engine and immediately drives over to the gas pumps to get ten dollars of unleaded gas.

He then hears a loud echo of laughter on the side of the Liquor and Market, that's adjacent to the 7-Eleven store, where he notices a middle-aged white construction worker, wearing ripped blue jeans and a white dusty T-shirt.

The man apparently decided to stop at the liquor store to get him a six pack of beer for the evening. When the construction worker parked his jeep he notices three rough-looking bikers, who were hanging out on the side of the liquor store. As they started walking slowly towards him, the construction worker gets out of the car. The man begins to feel a little fear.

"Get away from the car, punk!" the heavy-built biker yells, while the other two bikers, that have pale rough skin that you could spot in the darkest areas of the night, were laughing. The tall rough-looking biker points a pistol at the working man, who tries rushing to jump back into his 2000 silver Jeep Compass.

The rough-looking biker, wearing dark shades, grabbed the worker and pushed him down with the assist of his two rough biker buddies wearing blue bandannas over their heads with dark shades and black leather gloves. One biker held a silver lead pipe in his right hand while the other biker held an aluminum bat "Please! I won't say anything!"

"We're taking the car, punk!" the big heavy biker said.

"Just let me go home to my family!" the helpless worker nervously began sweating. With his dark brown short hair, small beady eyes, and his thin weight and wearing faded jeans standing near his vehicle, he was begging with his piercing brown eyes that the rough bikers let him go.

"I hate wimps!"

"That begs with weakness!"

"Get away from the car, punk! I don't want you! I want your freaking vehicle!" The 250-pound biker grabs the helpless man by his collar of his blue uniform shirt and pushed the man hard down on the ground and grabbed his keys aggressively from his right hand. The heavyset biker jumps into the man's silver Compass Jeep and snickers with laughter.

"That wasn't so hard!" the heartless biker said. The helpless man quickly got up and punched him on the side of his face, causing a bruise.

"Oh! So you want to play Mr. Big Shot!" His buddies jumps off their motorcycles and begin surrounding him. One of them grabbed the helpless man from behind, holding his arms back, while the other two bikers began to pistol whip him and kicked him in the stomach—*plow!*—hard with his left right foot. The three bikers were to beat him mercilessly, punching him in his face hard, and they kicked the man hard in his ribs and back. *Slug! Biff!* The helpless man fell to the ground. *Clump!*

"Who's the tough guy now, punk?" the main biker chuckled with laughter. "Oh, wait! I have to take a piss on your face, coward!" the cruel, vicious biker said roughly. The fearless biker unzipped his black worn faded pants and whips his privates out and begin urinating all over the helpless man. A few seconds later, the rough biker zips up his worn-out jeans and jumps into the helpless man's 2000 silver Jeep and drove off while his rough buddies follows behind on their motorcycles.

"You're a wimp!" the mean bikers yelled.

"I need my car, punks!" the helpless man felt his pride hurt more than his physical body. He started stumbling toward his residence that turns off Road 15. Alan had finished pumping gas and jumps into his blue Lincoln Navigator. It's less traffic on Road 15 since most of the townspeople was in the south area at the baseball stadium watching the fireworks. He began feeling a little intoxicated from the gas fumes.

He turns on his car stereo to keep the vibe going. His cell phone began vibrating. *Buzz, buzz.* He reaches for his cell phone out of his right side pants pocket. His cell phone slips from his fingers and falls underneath his seat. He reaches for his cell phone with his left hand and reaches lower to the floor.

His right leg began reflexively pushing harder on the gas pedal while his left hand began bracing the steering wheel to the right. *Pow! Slam!* He felt something hit hard against the car, and he slammed on his brakes.

"What the hell was that? An animal? Shit!" he yelled and put his car in park and immediately jumped out of his vehicle. He then rushed over to the passenger side, and he noticed a man that looked homeless, wearing dirty clothes. His victim's ribs were crushed from the right side front tire. Alan's mind was devastated, and his soul felt shattered with a bleeding heart of panic. He then began feeling sympathy for the victim. He couldn't stop staring at the blood pouring out of the victim's mouth; he was rubbing his brown eyes to visualize. With a wave of shock rushing through his reckless nerves, it led to an outburst!

"Oh, God! What the hell have I done?" His heart was throbbing while he was pacing and gripping with rage.

"What am I going to do? I-I don't want to leave him on the side road dead!"

He began wiping his forehead fast with sweat dripping on his dark blue long-sleeve shirt. Alan's fast thoughts remembered a small garden shovel in the trunk. He rushed back and grabbed his keys from the ignition and turned his headlights off and rushed to the truck of his car and opened the trunk and grabbed his small garden shovel out of his trunk and rushed back to his victim and noticed the tire mark across his victim's chest that looked crusted. Suddenly, his guilt began crawling through his conscience watching his victim's blood flowing fast on the dry dirt while his victim was grasping for air. His nerves began racing with more panic. Alan began kicking his vehicle to let out more anger. He then began loosening his blue tie to release pressure from this disastrous moment; he began pulling his victim's body from underneath his car, heavily breathing with anxiety. As he began rolling his victim down a dried field, his victim's weight felt over hundred and seventy-five pounds. The victim's body had stopped rolling down and landed by a weeping willow tree. He started looking around nervously to see if anyone was watching him.

He then decided to take full advantage of the bright fireworks that lit up the night sky, and he started digging a shallow hole of two feet or more. He then began smelling his victim's body odor, which smelled like he'd been playing sports.

Alan continually dug a shallow hole that seemed like a lifetime. He'd finished digging three feet of dry grass and dirt. Alan continued rolling his victim's body into a small hole. The helpless man landed flat on his back in the small hole. Covering his victim's bloody body with a couple of swings of dry dirt and grass looking around nervously, not noticing his victim's boots were sticking out from the dry dirt, while he rushed back up the hill, eager to get back to his residence. His heart began thumping harder, as he watched an old farmer's truck coming down Road 15 with bright headlights. He'd ducked behind a large tree with mortal fear; his heart felt like lightning striking with extreme pressure, while he watched the slow vehicle disappear into the darkness. His nerves continuous trembling, feeling even reckless, shaking like a windy leaf. He rushed back to his vehicle and grabbed a cold beer and drank it down with three gulps.

"It seems like hours. Oh, God! I'm daunted for life!" He then turns on the ignition and pulls off fast, feeling a chill up his spine. A couple of minutes later, he pulls into his brick-carved driveway and takes a deep breath to collect his unraveled nerves. He then turns off the engine and stumbles out of his Lincoln toward his front door. He then stood at the front door for a moment, hearing the laughter and clinking of dishes. His conscience corrupting his thoughts from his horror experience, looking at his victim lying underneath the tire. He began puking up in the bushes by his front door; his wife heard coughing and then opened the door. "Sweetie, what happened?" She helped him into their home.

"You seem a little out of it! You've been gone over an hour."

"I called you earlier, but it went to your voice mail." He gave his wife a dazed look and his thoughts were confused. His spirit was climbing faster with guilt.

"You're looking a little tired, dear. What happened to you?" He stumbled past her; he drops the beers on their front table, mumbling under his breath, "I'm not feeling too well. My head hurts."

"You've probably had too much to drink!" his Aunt Josephine said. His wife had a curious look on her face.

"Are you hungry, dear?" His eyebrows arched down, feeling lifeless.

He deliberately ignored his wife and continued his way to their bedroom. He lands on their king-sized bed and lays his worried head on his pillow, grasping with fright.

"I have to try to calm myself down but more pressure is consciously nagging and picking at my brain." He buries his head into his pillow.

"How do I get rid of this constantly nagging guilt? I'm a firefighter! I save lives! My mind can't stop feeling aggravated and angry, and my spirit feels damaged and my thoughts are out of control. I've killed an innocent man! Should I tell my secret to everyone and end it all or keep silent?" His thoughts were confused as a white Lexus pulls up into their driveway with low-beam headlights.

"Lisa just arrived!" Josephine shouted, feeling excited to see her niece. She gets out of her car dressed in a short silk red mini dress that matches her large round red earrings and a black leather belt wrapped around her small waist. Her red pumps, swinging her long blonde hair, and her suntanned thin face, with her glazing bright smile.

"Hello, Auntie Josephine. I'm just in time for some dinner!" Lisa said.

"I'm glad you decided to join us this exciting evening?" Josephine said. Joanna looks at Lisa with her brown squinty eyes, feeling a little jealous of her sister-in-law. The family sits around the dining table.

"Mm! The duck smells like turkey!" Patrick said. He was feeling his big round stomach. Lisa started giggling at her uncle Patrick and gives him a kiss on his rough face. Everyone began eating the delicious stuffed duck dinner. Joanna looked confused.

What's going on with my husband? Maybe, I'm just making a big deal, she thought. *He was gone too long just to go to the store down a few blocks.* She was determined to find out.

"Excuse me everyone, please!" Joanna stood up from her chair and walked past her company.

She could feel their eyes staring as Joanna left the room in silence. She started walking through the hallway into their bedroom. Alan was lying down in their bed, feeling guilty and confused. She spoke into the dark softly, but she didn't get responses at first.

"Alan!"

"Yes?" His voice was weak.

"Please! Tell me what's going on with you!" She tried to keep her voice stern, but her curiosity took control of her soft voice that sounded more worried than angry. He buried his face once again into the pillow and tried to dry the guilt from his eyes.

"I ran into a friend and we went to the bar for a couple of drinks." Joanna felt a slight sense that he was lying. "Who? A female friend?"

"What a stupid question, Joanna."

"I think something else's is wrong with you," she angrily said.

"I just don't feel good, Joanna! I really…"

"Okay, honey! I'll just bring some warm milk and call the doctor!

"All right, whatever!" Alan said with a guilty attitude. She walked out the room, and he gets up to take a hot shower and he starts getting undressed and noticed a little of his victim's blood and dirt on his hands and underneath his fingernails. His heart began to race uncontrollably and his mind began quivering with panic and fear. He rushed to rinse off the blood, watching it swirl down the small drain along with dirt. He couldn't stand looking at himself in the mirror. He felt nothing but reckless and confession. *My spirit feels dark as the late night with guilt that's growing wider within me.*

"I'm nothing but a cowardly murderer!" he'd had spoken quietly to his reflection with rage and fear. He then turned the hot water on and stepped in the shower, feeling the hot beads of water softly beat down on his guilt. Staring down at the tub, he noticed more of his victim's blood, and he watched the dirt and small traces of blood swirling down the drain. He was having aggravated thoughts while in the shower. "Alan?" He thought it was his wife so he ignored her. "Alan? I know you hear me? It's your sister!" And she stood at the door with her right hand on her right hip, patiently waiting for his response, but he still didn't reply.

"It's time for you to get out! What, I'm not thirteen years old!" He was feeling annoyed. "I'll be out the shower in a few! Go away!" he yelled.

"Dr. Thorne is here!"

"I need to talk to you, brother. I miss you!" she shouted.

Whenever she used that sad tone of her voice, it always gets to me.

Alan closed his eyes, still feeling the guilt like a bad dream. His sister Lisa walked out the bedroom and back to the living room where Joanna was having a conversation with the doctor.

"What did Alan say?"

"I guess he didn't hear me."

A few minutes later, they heard the shower turned off and he stepped out the shower. Drying his brown curly hair and face to his chest and the rest of his body wrapped in a towel, he opens the bathroom door. He gets his night clothes out of his brown dresser drawer. Joanna left his dinner plate hot on the nightstand.

"I don't want dinner. Put it in the microwave oven!"

"What's your problem? This isn't like you."

He gritted his teeth. "My problem is that I can't freaking think around here! You won't leave me the hell alone! I can't even take a damn shower without one of you coming to brothering me about the damn doctor's here!" Lisa looked at him in shock. His wife rushed into their bedroom.

"Why are you yelling at Lisa?" He felt an anxiety attack. "I don't need a damn doctor!" He spit the words at her with such anger. Lisa rushed out of her brother's bedroom feeling disappointment. His wife looked at him with her squinted eyes, feeling confused.

If she only knew the truth about tonight, and I now realized what I've done. I can't stop feeling so damn angry with myself. He paced to her slowly and placed both his hands on her shoulders.

"Tell my sister Lisa I apologize for my outburst all right? Just let me get dressed, and then the doctor can come in...all right? He took a deep breath, trying to control his temper.

"What has he had to drink and how much?" Dr. Thorne asked. He's short and overweight with gray sideburns.

"About four shots of Jack Daniels with ice and Samuel Adams and beer. He's acting like a stubborn child! He won't drink the milk or eat the soup. He's always handled his liquor even when he was younger," Lisa announced.

"I don't understand why he's acting like this." Joanna looked at the doctor with her brown eyes full of confusion. A couple of minutes later, he gets out the shower and puts on his boxer shorts. Dr. Thorne walked into the bedroom. "Hello, Mr. Jones!" He gave the doctor a weak smile.

"I hear you aren't feeling well!" Alan looked at the doctor and nodded his head.

"So I've heard that you have been drinking a little too much tonight?" The doctor pushed up his clear reading glasses.

"I just want to make sure you didn't go over the limit. Let me check your heart and lungs."

"I'm pretty sure if I could take a shower and dress myself, then I'm not over the legal limit, Doctor," Alan said with a sarcastic attitude.

"Well, I still need to check your blood level, and certainly, your behavior isn't one of the best tonight," Dr. Thorne replied. He sat down next to him and pulled out the scope to check his blood pressure. "You're just over the limit. Your blood pressure is a little high.

A couple more drinks and you would've been more than sick! Alan looked up at the doctor, feeling depression and fear.

"Is there anything that's hurting you like your stomach or your back?" Alan placed his right hand over his heart and replied, "My spirit." Dr. Thorne widened his eyes and was bit surprised by his response. He looked a bit puzzled.

"Well, the only cure I have for that is prayer! Take a couple Advil and get some rest now!" Dr. Thorne replied. The doctor gets up and walks out the bedroom.

"How is he, Dr. Thorne?" They both asked.

"He's fine, he just seems to be a little over the limit. Just make sure he gets plenty of water and that delicious chicken or duck I'm smelling."

"Oh, thank goodness! I thought it was something serious," Lisa said.

"Thank you so much, Dr. Thorne!"

"He's just a little depressed, about what? Don't worry, he'll come around after he gets some rest."

"Good night, Dr. Thorne!" Joanna closed their front door for the evening. Joanna turned around and went into their bedroom while Lisa went into the kitchen.

His wife walked into their bedroom while he was cuddled up under the sheets. She felt clueless and she closed their bedroom door and he took no notice to her. Joanna sat next to him on their bed, and finally, he looked up at her for a second, avoiding her brown eyes. "What's wrong? I think it's more than the drinking, Alan! Because when you drink, you're always in a good mood!"

I wish that she wouldn't touch me. I'm not in the mood to be touched. He felt chills like a bad storm. *I had just killed a man and have nothing but a mixed whirl pool of guilt and bad memories.* He kept his thoughts to himself. He tried to make himself sound a bit happier with his slurred words.

"It's nothing, baby! I'm drunk and tired!" he yelled.

"Uh…yeah. Sleep it off, dear!" she said with an attitude. He held his weary head down. *I'm feeling like a big weight is sitting on my heart.* He was keeping silence to himself. She then took one last confused look at him and got up and walked toward the door. "All right, dear! Let me know if you need anything, sweetie."

Just turn off the light, turn off the light! he shouted in his mind. She then turned the light switch off.

"It's a little chilly in here. I'll leave the door open for some heat!"

"No!" he yelled.

"I've never heard you scream like that!" his wife shouted a little.

He then lowered his eyelids. "I'm just feeling a little weird…" he said in his low voice.

My husband is losing his mind! she thought and gawked at him and closed their door.

"Lisa, I'm going to close the evening early. Alan's not feeling well. I'm sure he'll feel a lot better tomorrow. He needs his rest."

She walks back into the living room where Bill and Patrick were still enjoying the evening.

"I apologize for my husband's behavior, he's just not feeling very well this evening."

"I understand. Thank you for your hospitality!"

Bill tasted the last sip of his drink from his glass and handed it to Joanna and gives Patrick a handshake while Lisa generously opens the front door and Bill walked in the loud smell of lit fireworks in the air, hearing *boom*, and the crackling of the bright fireworks.

"I'll see you later."

"Good night, Patrick!" Bill went staggering to his car, yelling, "*Happy fourth!*" Patrick waved from the front door and closed it.

"Well, good night, dears!"

"Good night, Josephine and Patrick! I'll see you both tomorrow!"

"Good night Lisa!" Joanna softly spoke while closing her front door. She turned out the lights for the evening and walked into their bedroom. Alan was in his confused mind of depression, feeling like he was sinking more into his misery rather than trying to find his way. She started getting undressed and changed into her nightgown. Once again, it feels airy in the room. She stood at the edge of their bed. Her curiosity began to build up her thoughts and the embarrassment she'd felt from his behavior that brought out her furious words out between her thin lips. "What's wrong with you tonight? Why are you acting so damn depressed!? Everything was fine until you went to the damn *bar* when you were supposed to go straight to the store? And I know that's where you were!" Her last words dripped with sarcasm.

Her soft voice was awkward to hear yelling. He looked up at her with anger, and he quickly got up from the bed and walked toward her and he stood a couple inches to her face. "All I asked for you is to leave me the hell alone! You can't even understand simple instructions!" Alan bellowed.

"I'm really worried about you! It's not usual for you to come home depressed, not wanting to socialize with anyone!" He grabbed his feather pillow and a small blanket and walked out their bedroom door.

"Sleep with anger if you want!" he shouted. "You can keep asking the same damn question over and over!" He slammed the bedroom door behind him, making his way to the couch for the rest of the evening. While he tossed and turned in his sleep, feeling unpleasant fear in his heart and spirit. Early Monday morning light of dawn beams into his restless eyes. He listened to the early birds tweeting in the trees and the horn of the neighbor's car blowing their loud motor. It seemed to run louder and the neighbor's horn blowing feels like it's cracking his skull.

"*Beep! Beep!* We're going to be late!" His neighbor yelled. Alan was glad his neighbor finally drove off. He tried to continue listening to silence. *Buzz, buzz*, he heard the 7 am alarm go off in the bedroom. He was feeling lack of sleep with guilt. He'd jump off the couch to take his shower. A few seconds later, his wife was stepping out the shower with a towel wrapped around her thin body. And she walks out into the bathroom and gazes at him with her brown Creole eyes that quickly filled with silence as he tried hard not to look at his wife with the guilt flowing in his heart. He got his undergarment out of the top drawer and sat down on their bed.

"How are you feeling this morning?"

"All right I guess." His voice was groggy and hoarse.

"Could you next time advance your sociability status better?"

"Not this morning, Joanna!" He rubs his left eye while he sits on the edge of their bed, trying to collect his nerves. *This guilt is killing me, it's worse than this hangover*, he thought to himself.'

"I hope you're not going to act weird this morning, like you were last night!"

"Please I don't want to hear your bitching this morning! I have too much on my mind!" He got up quickly and walked into the bathroom, closing the door behind him while she rolled her brown eyes. He turned on the hot water and steam covered the walls and mirror. Seven minutes later, he got out the shower and dried off his muscled body and gets dressed for work. "Coffee is ready!" His aunt Josephine yelled from the kitchen. Josephine and Patrick come over in the mornings to help cook and clean. It's like their second home. "Thanks, Auntie, I'll see you later!" Alan grabs his case with his keys and walks out the front door wondering what the day is going to be like while his heart was crawling slowly with fear.

How am I going to face the volunteer firefighters this coming weekend? I hope to God they don't notice that it was me that killed that man. I really enjoy being a volunteer, which is one of my projects, and I'm a professional financial investment banker. Thinking while he opened his car door and noticed the morning paper thrown near his 1969 dark green Mustang; he grabbed the morning newspaper and threw it into his green leather interior seat on the passenger side and slammed his door. He then looked into his windshield mirror for a second and started his Mustang engine to let it run for a second, fighting his feelings of guilt. Fifteen minutes later, he arrived to his employment after fighting the heavy traffic. Driving down in an underground parking stall, feeling awkward and strange, he can't control the terrified feeling in his soul. He grabs the newspaper from the passenger seat and walks to the elevator and pushes eighth floor while other employees entered the elevator behind him. Alan tries to control his emotional guilt that he carries in his heart and soul. "Good morning!" an employer said while the elevator doors where closing. "Morning." He was feeling like he was going to explode if he had spoken any louder. *The fears I'm feeling in my heart and soul are corrupting my thoughts even more.* He takes a deep breath and walks off the elevator feeling fearful.

"Good morning, Mr. Jones!"

"Morning! Could you please get me a cup of black coffee?"

"Right away, Mr. Jones!"

A couple of seconds later, Richard walks in a good mood.

"What's up, buddy?" Richard closes the door behind him.

"We need to meet around noon."

"I'm ready to transfer twenty thousand into your account until—"

"I'll open up another account in a new username next week. I promise."

"I will remove the money next week!"

"This is embezzlement, Richard!"

"I'm not looking for any prison time. Oh! Now you're afraid? And just remember how you got this job!" Richard whispered. Alan stares at Richard like he wanted to hurt him right at that moment, but the fear he carries pulls his anger back.

"All right, Richard, but the percentage stands?"

"Yes, of course!" Alan left with a little attitude while feeling even guiltier.

While he was looking through his office files stacked on his desk, he heard a ringing. The receptionist walks in with a hot cup of coffee.

"Thank you," he said in a low voice.

"What is it, Joanna?"

"I called to see how you're feeling."

"I'm fine!"

"I also called to tell you that a detective came by the house this morning, asking about your job location!" Alan kept silent for a moment and felt his heart jump into his throat.

"And what did you tell him?" Alan replied nervously.

"That we were having dinner around that time."

"What time did he say?"

It happened Saturday evening after eight p.m. That's when it happened. He was keeping his thoughts silent from his wife.

"Do you have a hangover this morning, dear?"

"I'm feeling a little better."

"I'm sorry we argued last night, dear."

"I'll see you after work." They both hung up. He took a deep breath, feeling heavy pressure on his mind. *I forgot to ask Joanna what's the detective's name. And I have all these accounts on my desk.* While looking at his desk clock, he was thinking, *It's only eight fifty-five a.m.* while his office phone rings.

"Jones!"

"Mr. Silva is on line 1, sir!"

"Thank you." Alan clears his throat to answer the call.

"Mr. Silva, what can I do for you today?" Alan tried to change his voice to be more cheerful. "Yes, I've checked your credit and I can start the transfer of your mortgage loan to your account. I already have your signature and your account number!" *Beep.* "Could you please hold for a sec, Mr. Silva? Yes?"

"Mr. Terrace Louis is on line 3, sir."

"Could you tell Mr. Silva I'll be with him in a couple of minutes."

"Also there's a Lieutenant Theodore here to see you, sir!" He freezes for a moment and his heart started pounding with fear.

"Give me a couple of minutes!"

"Yes, Mr. Jones."

"I'll get right on it, Mr. Silva"

"Thank you!"

He nervously hangs up the receiver and takes a deep breath.

"Mr. Terrace Louis! What can I do for you today? Yes, sir!"

The pounding of his heart begin to riddle his quivery nerves.

"The loan will happen today!"

"Thank you. Good-bye!" Alan hangs up his office phone.

"Lieutenant! Mr. Jones is off the phone and you can go right in."

"Thank you." He gives her a smile. Detective Theodore stands up with his unlit cigar. Wearing his stylish brown suit with a dark green tie and brown dress shoes with a light brown overcoat, he walks into Alan's office. Detective Theodore clears his throat.

"Mr. Jones, I'm Lieutenant Theodore!" He starts walking toward Alan's wide brown desk and gives Alan a handshake.

"I'll be as quick as I can with this."

"What can I do for you, Detective Theodore?" Alan asked nervously.

"This is a nice office, lots of space better then my office." He takes his unlit cigar out of his mouth.

"No smoking in here, Detective!"

"Oh, I'm not going to light it in here! See, that's the thing. It's just the flavor that helps me think things out!"

He showed his expressive ways by waving his hands when he gets excited with his thoughts.

"I went by your place this morning, just a routine check with everyone on the block and those that live in that area." Detective Theodore was taking his time talking, trying to get the feeling of Alan.

"Oh, may I have a seat?"

"Yes, of course!" Alan said nervously.

"Myself and a couple of officers are going around the area, trying to get much information as fresh as possible and I'll get out of your hair. Mr. Jones, did you see or hear anything unusual Saturday evening around eight thirty p.m.?"

"Sorry, Lieutenant, I've heard nothing," Alan replied nervously.

"Umm, I also spoke to your uncle Patrick and he tells me that you went to the store for him Saturday evening! Could you tell me what time that was, sir?"

"It was still daylight around six p.m." He began clearing his throat, trying to keep his guilt hidden by crossing his nervous hands, rocking back and forth in his black leather chair while trying to compose his nerves.

"Well, I think that will be all for now." *Knock.* Richard comes walking into Alan's office. "Hey, Richard! This is Lieutenant Theodore of Homicide!" Alan announced with great fear.

"Homicide!" Richard said as they shake hands. "Is everything all right?" Richard looked a little surprised that a detective was visiting Alan. Theodore curiously looks at Richard with his swinish dark eyes and his thick hairy eyebrows.

Theodore decided to put his unlit cigar back in his pocket.

"I didn't catch your last name?"

"Mr. Oxford. Everyone calls me Richard!" He stands five nine and was wearing a gray and black striped cashmere light shirt and pressed black pants. His brownish hair combed back to where you can see the comb lines, with his light brown unshaved faded bushy mustache above his small lips, and his light blue eyes, and long nose that fits his face with his straight sparkling teeth and short hairs on his Caucasian arms.

"Do you live in the area of Road 15?"

"Just a few blocks from that road."

"Did you read the morning paper?" Detective Theodore asked.

"Yes. Is this about the victim that was killed on Road 15 where a man's dog found the victim buried?"

"Yes, it is!" Detective Theodore answered.

"Do you know anything about Saturday evening around eight thirty p.m.?"

"No! I was out at the Bam club where I'm always at!" Richard had a little smirk with his smile.

"And can you verify that?"

"Yes, just go to the Bam club and ask the bartender Randy or Pete! I was there from 6 p.m. till closing time, which is at eleven p.m. then I went home and slept all night and came to work this morning!"

"Sounds like you have an alibi! Well, I'll let you gentleman get back to work. Have a good day!" Detective Theodore walks out of Alan's office and closes the door behind him and walks towards the elevators while the receptionist was on the phone. Detective Theodore walks in the elevator and pushes the ground floor button. A few seconds later, he walks off the elevator and toward the parked cars till he recognized the name Jones and noticed a dark green 1969 Ford Mustang. Reserved for Alan Jones. He walked around Mr. Jones's vehicle. *This must have cost him a pretty penny.* Detective Theodore continued walking around the Mustang. *Nice dark green color too and nice rims. With the salary I'm making, I couldn't afford this. Why would he drive this car to work after his wife said he has a Lincoln that he parks in their driveway! I need to go look at that car again! Maybe this is his second car? Or maybe his wife's second car!* Detective Theodore leaves the building with his unlit cigar and walks back into his vehicle while Alan and Richard were planning to transfer twenty thousand dollars into Alan's account before any other surprises come up.

"I'll be in Mr. Oxford's office. I need to help him with an account!"

"Yes, Mr. Jones."

"You want to go to lunch after this, buddy?" Richard asked in a swift way.

"Sure! All right, give me your account number, buddy!" Alan reads his account numbers. Richard transfers the money into Alan's business account as Alan stands nervous with Detective Theodore on his mind.

"Are you finished?" Alan asked nervously.

"Now, I hit send and the money is in your account."

"When you pull from my business account, leave my percent in there! You only take ten million, not the whole twenty million!" Richard looked at Alan in the corner of his eyes. "Come on, trust me! We've been friends too long for me to dog you out. You should know me better than that, buddy!"

"Don't be nervous, partner. It's all good!"

"It's almost twelve and I only have two appointments this afternoon!" Alan said and puts his wallet back into his pants pocket, and they both walk out. Richard throws his left arm over Alan's shoulders, while Alan's head was up with a fake smile, feeling that something finally went right today. Richard walks up to the receptionist and leans toward her and gives her a flirty smile.

"Hold all my calls," he said romantically to her.

"Yes, Mr. Oxford." The receptionist flirts back at him with a smile. "Let me grab my keys!" Alan walks back to his office.

I need some air! I've got to pull myself together! or someone or all are going to notice the changes in me! His mind was racing while he grabs his car keys and locks his office door. They both walk toward the elevator while Richard turns his head, winking his right eye at his receptionist before he steps into the elevator on their way to lunch. Meanwhile, Detective Theodore parks his car across from the Jones residence. In front of a brick home that sits with a two-car garage, a stylishly designed home with a perfect green lawn that's cut in a fashion design with a small garden that follows the walkway to the front door. He then looked to the right and noticed Alan's Lincoln and decided to take another look at Mr. Jones's vehicle. Detective Theodore gets on his car dispatch and calls an officer at the station to bring a Kodak camera to Twenty-Three Twenty River View Drive.

"Yes, Lieutenant, right away!" The detective walks around the 2000 Lincoln navigator and spots a little dent and scratch on the passenger side while Josephine was looking out the kitchen window and noticed someone was looking at her nephew's vehicle in the driveway. She walks out the side kitchen door where there's a walkway to the driveway.

"May I help you, sir?" Josephine was wiping her hands with an apron that's around her waist.

"I'm Lieutenant Theodore." He shows his badge with his identification. "I'm here to investigate the incident on Road 15 on Sunday evening."

"I'm Ms Josephine, this is my nephew's residence," she said in a curious way.

"Oh, I don't mean no harm miss, but we have to check everyone's car in the area, and I noticed here on the right side that there's a long fresh dent on the passenger side. Josephine looks at the mark on the vehicle. While her husband came out the front door with a lit pipe in his mouth and stepped toward his wife.

"Hello, Detective!" They shook hands. "What's going on?"

"I was just showing your wife the dent on this vehicle, and I noticed it looks fresh and you told me earlier that your nephew went to the store last evening and he tells me that it was still daylight. Do you remember what time was that?"

"I wouldn't remember the time, Detective. I was drinking with my friend Bill and my wife was cooking and talking to Lisa!"

"Who is Lisa?"

"My older sister daughter, Alan's sister."

Couple of seconds later, a police vehicle drives up and parks in front of their residence. They both looked surprised. The officer gets out with a camera and walks over to the detective and hands him the camera.

"What are you doing, Detective?"

"I just want to take a couple of pictures of theses marks on this vehicle."

Patrick begins looking really curiously at the detective, as he began taking pictures of Alan's Lincoln Navigator and also his licenses plates. "Okay, that's all of it!" Detective Theodore walks toward the officer and hands him the Kodak camera.

"I want this film developed right away, Officer! Call me immediately when they finish developing, and I'll be here or at another location nearby." The officer leaves right away to his vehicle and drives off.

"Lieutenant, you don't think it was Alan that hit that victim, do you? You're making a big mistake thinking that! We were all here with our nephew. His wife Joanna was cooking around the time of the accident!"

"Oh really. Was he drinking last night?"

"Yes, a little, because Alan wasn't feeling well and he went to go lie down."

"Was that before he went to the store for you or after he came back?"

"I don't remember, I was drinking and watching the pre-games," Patrick said with his slow deep voice. "That's right!"

"I understand," Detective Theodore said.

Road 15 Investigation

"**W**ell, thank you for the information, I'm just trying to do my job!" He then gives Patrick a left handshake and turns around and walks to his 1989 light blue Victoria Chrysler vehicle, waving to them both. Josephine and Patrick just stood there, staring at Detective Theodore until he drives off.

"He's a strange man! I have to get dinner on. Let's go into the house."

Detective Theodore was making a U-turn toward the corner stop sign and turns his left blinker on to turn left toward Road 15. He then turns on his radio to hear the news.

"It's earlier in the afternoon. The weather is warm where you don't have to carry a jacket around!" the radio announcer said. *It's past my lunch hour. One more stop on Road 15 to check out those tire marks again!* He was chewing on his lit cigar. He then makes a left and drives toward the area of the accident and makes a call to the station.

"Hello, Sergeant."

"Detective Theodore'. What can I do for you?"

"Who's in charge of the tire cast that was done yesterday?"

"Um, Officer Dune!"

"Can you contact him and see if those casts are ready?"

"Yes, Lieutenant!"

Detective Theodore arrived at the incident area and gets out of his vehicle and walks over to the tire marks.

"They look like Firestone tire marks, I need those tire casts!" His cell phones rings at that moment.

"Lieutenant Theodore, I have the pictures."

"Where are you located?" He then walks back to his vehicle while talking on his dispatch radio. "I'll be there in ten minutes."

"Roger that, Lieutenant!" The officer was talking army code. Detective Theodore starts his vehicle.

"I normally forget to put my seat belt on while my mind is wondering about the investigation." He pulls off the road, following behind another car to the city limits. Both vehicles yield and stop by the red signal light, waiting for it to change to green. Detective Theodore makes a call to the station.

"Is Officer Dune around?"

"This is Officer Dune."

"Did those tire casts come back yet?"

"Yes, Lieutenant Theodore. They should be on your desk. Would you like for me to check, Detective?"

"No, That's all right. I'm on my way to the station, but first I'm going to make a quick stop and get something to eat first!"

"Okay, Lieutenant!" And Officer Dune hung up his receiver.

"I also need to talk to his sister, Lisa Jones, who's another witness that's going to give her brother an alibi. If it takes all my breath, I'm going to prove that Alan Jones is the responsible party for the hit and burial of Mr. Johnson."

Lieutenant Theodore was thinking while driving up to the 7-Eleven store, and he locks the car doors. He's carrying his 57 magnum gun in his holster across his right shoulder, looking really handsome with his brownish dark hair and pressed beige dress suit pants and his shining black shoes.

"Hello. I'm investigating the robbery that occurred last night."

"Oh yes! You're here for that robbery Saturday night?"

The lieutenant looks straight at the Chinese man behind the counter.

"I'm Lieutenant Theodore. Could you tell me what happened last evening?"

"A couple of men robbed another man wearing a silver hat and orange boots, a construction worker that works just across the way," the Chinese man was explaining. "What time was the robbery?"

"It was dark around eight or eight thirty p.m. when the fireworks had started."

"Oh, one more question. Did a tall man named Alan Jones come in here that night?"

"I see a lot of people, Detective. I don't know," the Chinese clerk said.

"Maybe he did die Saturday between eight or eight thirty p.m. I won't know until the autopsy comes back." He then turned around and went to the ice box to grab a sandwich and some grape juice and walked back to the counter. "How much?"

"Three dollars and seventy cents please, and thank you very much!"

"If you have any more information about that evening, give me a call and here's my card. Call me anytime if you remember anything else!" The Chinese man was smiling hard. Lieutenant Theodore was rushing out the store carrying a plastic bag and was reaching for his keys in his right pocket. *I'm going to confront Mr. Jones about the time of the accident. If he had seen a robbery or heard something Saturday night around the time he went to the store. I have a feeling he's hiding the truth about the time.*

All the while, Alan was trying to concentrate and finish his work without stress.

"Hey, buddy, after work, you want to stop by the Bam bar tonight and play a couple of games of poker and drink a couple of beers? How about it, buddy?"

"I can't tonight. I have to get home and make up with my wife!"

Richard starts giggling. "If that's what marriage is about, I hope I don't ever get into that situation. I'll see you later, buddy!"

Five forty-five p.m. and Alan was still feeling confused and stressed. He gets up and walks out of his office while carrying his brown leather briefcase.

"Good night," Alan said to his receptionist.

"Good night, Mr. Jones and Mr. Oxford," the receptionist said softly. Alan and Richard walk toward the elevator.

"Where did you get that new briefcase?

"My wife got it last week at the famers' market," Alan said with his weak voice of unwanted guilt.

"Really! If I ever get a wife! I'll make sure she gets me a nice briefcase like that! That case looks like real leather! It wasn't too expensive?" Richard started feeling the leather case. The building elevator had stopped to the garage floor.

"I'll see you tomorrow, buddy." Richard continues walking to his vehicle and pulls his keys out, jumps into his car, and starts his vehicle. He then puts the gear in reverse and backs up. Richard then puts it in drive, blowing his horn, driving out the garage. Alan was sitting in his 1964 dark green Mustang with the motor running, and he fastens his seat belt, reverses, and then puts the gear into drive and pulls off slowly with the sound and vibration of the heavy motor. *Vroom! Vroom!* He came to a stop while his cell phone rings and he looks at the caller ID. The light turns green, and the five o'clock traffic is heavy.

"James, what's up?"

"The Monday night game is what's up!"

"Sure! Do you mind if I drop by around seven p.m.? That would be cool, man, and I'm rolling in traffic now, so I'll see you tonight, buddy!" And he hung up to pay more attention to the traffic, trying to get on the north freeway, taking a cut off near his area. With the bumper-to-bumper traffic, he noticed a motorcycle officer going through the traffic with both yellow blinkers rolling by. *It looks as if there's an accident ahead. Vehicles are slowing down. I better change lanes to get closer to the next right exit. I've just had a thought. Eleven Street exit freeway runs into Road 20 close to my neighborhood to where I don't have to drive down bad memory Road 15.* And he then turns the radio on the maxi soft jazz station and tries to remove the pressure off his mind. He then turns left onto Road 20 from Eleven Street exit. Taking a deep breath in his adjustable Mustang seat, he was cruising the speed limit, feeling the cool breeze in the air and he comes to a stop sign, puts his left blinker on, and makes a left turn on Road 20. Just a couple blocks to his home, he was thinking while he made a right turn on his block where the neighborhood looks like it should be in a home magazine. Trees in full bloom with pink and white spring flowers with green leaves in front of the neighbors homes. Even the birds sang in the trees while making their nest for their families. He then turns into his driveway. *What a nice ride to clear my head.* He then raises the motor. Joanna hears his vehicle and comes quickly, walking out the door.

"Hello, dear." She gives him a kiss on the lips. He then turns the motor off.

"We need to talk, Alan." Alan stares at his wife with fear in his face.

"You know that Detective Theodore has been hanging around here this afternoon, asking more questions about your Lincoln and that he noticed a dent on the top of the car."

His mood went back to reckless.

"How did that dent get there?"

"I've told you I hit a pole! You're starting to sound like that detective." He gets out of his vehicle slowly and locks it with his alarm key while his wife was beginning to be suspicious. While they both walk into their home, holding hands, he closes the front door behind them and locks it, feeling fearful. He noticed his uncle Patrick was looking a little intoxicated. Alan then walks over to his bar in his living room and pours a little brandy with three ice cubes and sits with his uncle.

"Alan, that detective was hanging around your car again this morning and a police officer came with a camera and started taking pictures of the passenger side of your Lincoln." *Ding dong.*

"Detective!"

"Sorry to bother you, but is your husband home?"

"Yes. Come in, Detective!"

"I just have a couple of questions if you don't mind, sir? Something has been nagging me all day about that dent on your hood. Where did it happen, sir?" Detective Theodore was looking straight into his lying eyes.

"It happened at the Bam Club downtown on Hostel Street. A coworker and I went downtown for a drink last weekend and someone was parked close to my car and I didn't want to hit their car and so I hit a side pole."

"But the dent is more on top of the car." Joanna was sitting in the dining area, listening to their conversation while cutting up vegetables and cleaning corn on the cob. Alan's expression of fears appeared.

"I've told you how I got that dent on my car, Detective!" Alan wanted to desperately run at the spur of the moment from his fear.

"Well, I think that's all for now! Good night!" Detective said while walking out the front door.

"I've told you about that nosey detective around your car today! He frightened me today till he showed me his badge!" Josephine said. "He kept asking us about what time you went to the store Saturday evening and Patrick told him that he was too drunk that evening that he didn't know exactly what time it was!" Alan gives a little laugh, holding his drink as they join laughing. Even his wife had a little smile on her face.

"What time did he come around today? I wasn't feeling too well."

"That's right!" Joanna said. "When you came home, you went straight to bed. Then I called the doctor! Alan just had a hangover, drinking too much last Saturday, the doctor said."

Alan was trying to cover his guilty feelings by acting like his old self, trying to keep his thoughts silent. "What time is it?" Alan grabs the remote to his wooden trim-model wide fifty-inch color screen television and changed the channels to the preview football games. "It's now six nineteen p.m." Alan was feeling protected in his home around his family. *I'm not going to let this guilt control my emotions or the distress and fear in my heart and soul.*

"James will be coming over soon," Alan announced. Both sit on the long leather black couch drinking cold beer while his wife gets up from the table and walks into the kitchen.

Ding dong. Josephine gets up from the table to answer the door. "Hello, Lisa!" Josephine said, excited. "I got off work kind of late tonight. Football fans in the living room," Josephine said cheerfully. Lisa then walks over to the living room and sits on the right side of the couch beside her brother and puts her right arm around his shoulder.

"Alan, can I ask you a favor?"

"What is it, Lisa?" he said while he was looking at the football previews.

"Can I borrow some money until whenever?" she asked with a little sarcastic attitude.

"How much?"

"Two hundred for my car insurance."

"I'm not the bank of Brookville."

"I promise to pay you back Friday," his sister replied. Alan reaches for his brown leather wallet from his back pocket after and stuck his tongue at her, and she smiled as he pulls out his dark brown leather design wallet and hands her two hundred dollar bills. *Ding-dong.* Lisa walks out the living room with a smile and walks into the kitchen. Alan gets up to answer the front door.

"Hey, James, come on in!" James enters with a black plastic bag holding a six pack of cold beer.

James stood 5'9, an African American with dark complexion with trim wavy dark hair and dark shaped eyebrows and his slant brown eyes and his Nero nose and black trimmed mustache like Tiger Woods'. He was wearing his light blue sport short-sleeved shirt with blue small buttons going down the front that matches his blue jeans and black dress shoes, looking sporty.

"I'm glad you made it, man!" Alan was feeling secure around his friend. James pulls up his left pants leg like a gentleman and takes a seat on the couch. Alan takes out the cold beer and sets it on his bar. Alan introduces his friend. "Uncle Patrick, this is my friend James!"

"Nice to meet you, James," and they shook hands. Alan hands James a cold Coors beer while Patrick was drinking gin and orange juice. Alan also was sipping on his gin and juice, standing behind the bar.

"Yes, touch down!" They were watching the pro football game with the Rams and the Cowboys.

"The Rams have a good quarterback," James said.

"Jerry Rice was a good player back in the days!" Patrick said. Lisa enters the living room wearing her white sleeveless short dress that shows her knees and thin thighs with a brown sway belt around her small waist. As James noticed her, she said, "Introduce me to your company. Don't be rude!"

"First, you want my money, now you want to meet my company? James, this is my spoiled sister Lisa!"

"Hello!" James said in a polite way.

"James is a firefighter down at the station number 5. We go back in high school," Alan announced.

"Wait! You're not that little black boy who used to play football in the middle of the streets playing with my brother?" Lisa asked in a surprised way. He gave a small giggle. "That's me!"

"You're all grown up!" She gave him a flirty smile.

"It's nice seeing you also," James said. She goes and sits next to her uncle and crosses her thin legs.

"Do you remember Jimmy and little Charles and his brother Ronnie? We used to just run him over in our football practice!" James felt a little excited talking about their childhood.

"Whatever happened to Gary?" James asked.

"Gary?" Alan repeated.

"You know that boy who was kind of heavyset with reddish hair."

"Oh yes, I remember him. Gary!" Alan said. "Think he had moved or got transferred for fighting. I'm surprised you remember him!"

"He had made a lot of touchdowns for our team when we were in school. That's right!" Alan said.

"We were playing against each other." James laughs.

"Gary was a good runner!" Patrick and Lisa were listening to their conversation.

"The game starts in five minutes," the announcer said while Patrick gets up for a refill on his gin and juice. James was drinking slow, flirting with Lisa without Alan noticing.

"Alan, you're out of ice," his uncle Patrick said. Lisa grabs the ice bucket and keeps her wandering eyes on James with a small smile as she leaves the room to get more ice.

"What's that smile about?" Josephine asked.

"Did you see James?" Lisa whispered.

"Yes, he's very handsome," Josephine said. "I saw him when he came in."

"I'm going to fill the bucket with ice, so I don't have to leave the living room! He's very handsome, Auntie!" She rushes back to the mini bar where Alan is sitting on the bar stool. Alan gets the bucket of ice from her while she grabs a glass and some ice.

Her wandering eyes capture James's appearance and she began flirting with him. James gets up for another beer, trying to pay attention on the football game.

"Listen to this, when I was driving over here, a police unit was on Road 15. He was standing with yellow tape tied around the trees that says Police/Crime. Maybe something happened earlier?" James said. Alan got nervous and drops his glass on the carpet. "Damn it!" Lisa grabs a small towel from behind the bar and hands it to her brother. "Thanks, Lisa. My hands are wet from the ice. Did I get any on either of you?" Alan asked in a nervous way.

"I'm okay," James said.

"None is on me either," Lisa replied.

James grabs another Coors beer and winks his right eye at Lisa while Alan was bent over wiping the wet carpet.

"Touchdown! The score is 18 to 22. The Cowboys win!" Patrick yelled.

"I've should have betted with you, Alan!" James said. Joanna walks in the living room with cold cuts. Alan was pouring himself another drink of gin and juice.

"Damn it!" Alan began feeling frustrated for a moment. "Joanna, bring a towel out the kitchen!"

"You all right, man?" James asked.

"I just still have a little hangover from last night!" Alan said.

"Run! Run! Cowboys!" Patrick yells! Alan tried to focus on the reruns of the game, but his mind and heart is too heavy with guilt, feeling corrupted as if his nerves were going to drop to the floor.

A couple of hours later: "Good night, all!" Lisa said.

"That's the game! 36 to 24, the Cowboys won." James was finishing his cold beer and getting ready to leave, and he gets up and walks over to Alan. "Thanks, man, for your hospitality," he said while they shook hands.

"It was nice meeting you, Patrick!"

"Come again," Patrick said. James was walking out the front door.

"Good night, ladies!" Joanna and Josephine were sitting around the dinner table. James walks outside behind Lisa.

"Can I walk you to your car?" James asked her in a polite way.

"So are you single?"

"Maybe?" James answered.

"Are you single and available?"

"I wouldn't have asked if I wasn't single," Lisa answered.

"Then can I get your number? Maybe we can go out this weekend?" James said. Lisa grabs her cell phone as they exchange numbers.

"I'll call you tomorrow!"

"That would be cool!" Lisa said.

"Good night, Lisa."

"Good night, James!"

"Alan, I kept your dinner warm," his wife said.

"What did you cook?"

"Fried chicken with baked potatoes and corn on the cob with crab salad and juice!"

"Make me a plate please!" he said under his weak voice.

"Patrick, your plate is also ready," his wife Josephine said.

"After we eat, we are going home and get some good sleep tonight," Patrick said to his wife. And he gets up and walks to the kitchen to wash his hands. Josephine walks behind him and turns the microwave on for a few minutes. Patrick was trying sneaking a kiss from his wife and she pushes back from him while placing their dinner plates on the counter as she was reaching for a glass for some orange juice.

"You're smelling like liquor. Get back!" his wife said. Patrick goes and sits down at the dining table.

"That was a good game!" Patrick said. Joanna looks at her husband with an attitude while having their late dinner and conversation.

"I enjoyed myself tonight," Patrick said. "And now it's time to go home and get some good sleep tonight! Do you need help with the dishes, Joanna?"

"No, I can handle it!" And Joanna gets up and takes the dishes into the kitchen.

"Well, good night, Alan!" And he gets up and helps his uncle to the front door while Josephine goes and grabs her purse from the back bedroom.

"We'll see you both tomorrow, and, Alan, no more drinking for you tonight and get some sleep!"

"Don't worry, Auntie. I'm not drinking anymore tonight. I'll walk both of you to your car."

"Thank you, Alan," Patrick said in a generous way. Alan opens the front door and walks them out to their car. He watches them drive off, and he then decided to walk around his Lincoln to the right side and touched the top of the dent of his car with a cracked headlight. *I've got to get this fixed right away*, he was thinking. He got the keys out his pocket and parks his Lincoln Navigator into the garage with his remote, and he locked the garage door with a panel lock. He rushed back into his house.

"Where were you?"

"I walked Aunt and Uncle to their car!"

"I'm finished with the dishes. Come on, let's go to bed. It's nearly eleven p.m." She then turned off the television and the lights in the living room and left on the night light by the bar and went to the bedroom. His wife hears the shower running and gets her nightgown out the drawer and walks into the bathroom to get undressed and to join her husband in the shower. Joanna opens the shower curtain and steps in and starts caressing her husband. They begin kissing and feeling each other's nude bodies.

"Alan, did you pick up the newspaper this morning?"

"I forgot about the newspaper. It's in my office!"

A couple minutes later, they both get out the shower, and they both went to bed nude and turned their nightstand light off and got under the covers, feeling passionate. Fifteen minutes later, they were sweaty, and they both turned over to get some sleep.

"That was great lovemaking," Joanna said. Alan mumbled and fell asleep. Joanna gets up and goes to the bathroom. A few minutes later, she comes out and gets into the bed and falls asleep beside her husband.

Alan's Alibi

Tuesday Morning, seven a.m. *Buzz*. Alan reached over to his right to turn off the clock alarm.

"Good morning! I'll get breakfast ready!" Alan lies in bed trying to fight his unwanted fear that now grows in his heart, and he gets up and puts on his robe and walks to the bathroom; fifteen minutes later, he gets out of the shower and dries off and walks to the closet and grabs his gray suit and lays it on the bed and gets his gray tie to match. He smells bacon cooking and he finishes dressing. His wife walks into the bedroom to get dressed for work.

"Breakfast is ready!"

"I hope that detective doesn't come around snooping today," Alan said.

"And if he asks me once more! Because he always asks, 'What time was that?'" Alan was imitating Detective Theodore. "And I wasn't feeling well that night!"

"No drinking tonight with Patrick! And I knew you went to the bar that night, probably with Richard because you were gone more like an hour and a half." Alan began thinking about that horror nightmare evening. She gave her husband a kiss and slips her feet in her white high heels that matches her white loose dress that shines with her blond hair and her perfectly shaped eyebrows. She puts on a little mascara, and she powders her thin nose and red lipstick on her thin lips.

"Did you get the newspaper?"

"It's on the chair by the front door!" she yelled. Alan was rushing his breakfast.

"How are things going at the Lila Beauty Shop?" He was trying to have a quick conversion with his wife without her noticing the fear he carries.

"The hair shop is doing well, Alan. It helps pay the mortgage!" she said sarcastically. He jumps up from his chair and rushes to grab the morning newspaper and his leather case with an little attitude that his wife carries with her morally corrupt attitude. Alan opens the front door and both grab their car keys from the key holder that's hanging on the wall next to the front door and they both walked out. And he locked the front door while his wife gets into her 2000 Tahoe Hybrid. Alan decided to start driving his classic dark green 1968 Mustang while his wife was looking into her rearview mirror and noticed a man walking up to their driveway with the smell of a lit cigar. He walks up to Joanna's car.

"Mrs. Jones?" She rolls her car window down right away.

"Yes! Who are you?"

"Do you remember me from last night?"

"Oh, yes. What can I help you with, Lieutenant?"

"I didn't get chance to talk to you yesterday! Did you get the chance to read yesterday's newspaper?"

"No, my husband took it to work with him! What's this about, Lieutenant? I'm in a rush to work!"

"Did you hear about an accident out on Road 15 on Saturday evening around eight thirty?"

"Sorry, I didn't!"

Alan was watching in his green Mustang rearview mirror. His nerves begin rattling, and he decides to get out of the vehicle.

"Detective, is there a problem?" Alan asked nervously.

"I just want to ask her a couple of questions, if you don't mind! I'll be quick about it. Mrs. Jones, do you remember what time your husband went to the store last Saturday evening on the fourth?"

"Alan didn't go straight to the store that evening, Lieutenant! I found out he went to the Bam bar before he went to the store evening and that's what caused us to argue and he came home sick from drinking too much from the bar that evening."

"Mrs. Jones, may I ask you what time that was?"

"It was still early, like around six thirty to seven p.m."

"What's the name of the bar again?"

"The Bam Club!" Alan shouted with his fear.

"That's right. The Bam Club on Main Street. That's the only bar he goes to with his friends." She gave Alan a serious look.

"That's my alibi! Now will you leave us alone?" Alan replied with fear. "Is that all, Lieutenant Theodore?"

"Yes. Oh, one more question? I wanted to ask you, Mr. Jones, about your Lincoln? Where is it?" the lieutenant asked in a surprised way. He felt more nervous.

"It's in the garage so my wife can park her Tahoe Hybrid in the driveway!"

"You know something keeps bothering me about that broken headlight on the same side of the dent that's on top of your vehicle!"

"I thought we've been through this, Lieutenant! I hit a pole because someone at the Bam bar had my car squeezed between another car and I hit the concert pole."

"But the dent is on top of your vehicle! You see what I'm saying?"

"I've told you what happened! Now I'm late for work! Good day, Detective!" Alan said nervously with frustration in his voice.

"Oh! One more question!"

"Good-bye, Detective!"

Joanna rolls her tinted window up. Alan rushes back to his Mustang and drives off. While Joanna follows her husband out their driveway, the lieutenant was watching them both drive off and he had walked back to his patrol car. Lieutenant was looking at the time with his silver watch that his wife bought for him on their tenth anniversary. "It's five after eight a.m. I don't think the Bam bar opens till nine a.m. and I need to go find this address." He grabs on his seat belt and starts his car and drives toward downtown. Five minutes later, he starts looking for an address, Two Seventy-Five Payton Avenue. Lieutenant Theodore puts his lit cigar in the back into his mouth for taste, thinking hard about his case. "I don't believe a pole is going to jump on top of a vehicle! It looks like a body landed on top of his vehicle and with a broken headlight also! And then he hides his Lincoln in his garage and started driving his '68 or '69 Mustang? He's really trying to hide the evidences and I have a little proof with the photos." Detective Theodore had dropped a little ash on his white cotton shirt and on his dark green tie and his black leather belt, also on his gray polyester pants, and he pulled a white designer cloth napkin from his left pants pocket and starts wiping the ashes of his shirt and his green tie as he was watching the busy traffic. He put his white cloth napkin back into his back left pocket while continualyl driving toward Lisa's employment in the city limits. A couple of minutes later, Lieutenant Theodore arrives to 275 Payton Street Quotable Women Dress Shop. That's the address with the large sign hanging from the building. Detective Theodore then parks his vehicle away from the fire hydrant and red paint on the concrete curve and gets out of his car and walks down the sidewalk and opens the door to the Quotable shop, looks around, and sees there are five females, Caucasian and Asian. The ladies noticed a man standing by the front counter.

"Good morning! May I help you?"

"Lisa Jones, please?"

"Right over there!" An Asian lady pointed north. Detective Theodore walks toward Lisa. "Are you Lisa Jones?"

"Who wants to know?"

"The police." He showed his badge. "I have a couple of questions, if you don't mind? On the fourth of July, Saturday evening, there was an accident on Road 15."

"I've read it in the paper," Lisa replied.

"Were you over at your brother house that evening?"

"Yes, I was over there. Why?"

"Do you remember what time your brother went to the store that evening for your uncle Patrick?"

"It was early, like maybe six thirty, maybe seven, because my sister-in-law was cooking dinner and I remember my brother was in a bad mood that evening and didn't go anywhere else but to bed!"

"Are you sure? Because his wife said he'd went to the Bam bar that evening with a coworker!"

"That's right, and he came home, feeling sick from the liquor. Joanna had to call the doctor. 'It's just he was drinking too much that night,' the doctor said."

"Umm, they didn't tell me that a doctor came over. Do you remember the doctor's name?"

"Dr. Thorne, our family doctor."

"Well, thank you for your time."

"Lieutenant, if you ever want a manicure, come back!" Lieutenant Theodore smiled and walked out the front door. Detective Theodore walks back to his car and puts his seat belt on and starts his car while he looks in his rearview mirror to see if there was any traffic to get back to the headquarters to see if the DNA came back from the forensic to see if Mr. Jones had left any hairs or skin from the deceased. Lieutenant Theodore was thinking hard. He parks his car in a reserved law enforcement pavement and rushes into the police station. "Lieutenant!" an officer yelled and rushed toward him. "A missing person report was filed about an hour ago. Her husband has been missing since the Fourth of July." "Thanks!" the Lieutenant said as the officer gives him the report.

"I need to check the deceased identification in his wallet." Detective Theodore walks toward the coroner's office, reading the report of a missing person: Mr. Jerry Johnson, thirty five years old, his height is five seven, his weight is one hundred sixty five pounds, with dark brown hair and works for Smith's Construction Company. He walks into the coroner's medical examiner office. Detective Theodore noticed the victim's corpse lying on the examiner table.

"Oh, Lieutenant! Is this the deceased who got hit and buried out on Road 15?"

"Yes, I have a missing report here that says he's been missing since July 4, and that's the evening he was killed!" Detective Theodore said.

"I assume the time of death was around eight p.m." the medical examiner said.

"Do you have his belongings in here?"

"Yes, over there on that table, Lieutenant." He walked over and looks into a clear plastic bag. "Here we go. Let's see who you are? And I bet money that this is the missing person." The detective pulls out a brown wallet and pulls out the deceased driver's license. "Mr. Jerry Johnson! Seventy-Eight Twenty-Two West Court Drive. And you say the time of death was eight p.m. on the fourth?"

"Yes, I'm positive!"

"I'll contact the family today," Detective Theodore said.

"Well, thank you, Doctor!"

"Sure, anytime!" the medical examiner said. Lieutenant Theodore walks out the coroner's and rushes to his office where Kodak pictures were on his desk with a note.

"Here are the pictures from Mr. Jones's vehicle that you wanted. Now, let me take a look!" Lieutenant Theodore whispered to himself and takes a seat in his short leather office chair with his unlit cigar in his mouth. Two knocks!

"Lieutenant, here are the files from the tires marks and foot casts as well!"

He jumps up from his seat to take a closer look. "Size 10 shoe prints." He picks up the tire casts and looks at the brand. "I knew it! Mr. Jones's tires are Firestones. He sure is hiding the truth from me." Detective Theodore grabs his jacket and puts it over his shoulders with his unlit cigar and walks out his office with the Kodak pictures of Alan's 2000 dark blue Lincoln Navigator while he walks back toward the coroner's office. "Then I have to go tell the family about their loved one who is lying in the morgue. And I'm going to need Detective Ken with me to explain what happened to her husband!"

"Detective, you're back?" the coroner said.

"I need to check the victim's shoe size. You know where his items are."

"This is a crying shame. When he got hit, he was unconscious and breathing at the time!" "What?" Detective Theodore said, surprised.

"Yes," the coroner said slowly.

"Mr. Johnson died from suffocation. Dirt in the lungs is what killed him! But he was still breathing before the person or persons buried him!" Detective Theodore was in shock from the results.

"Damn it! He didn't even check to see if the victim was still alive! Thanks for that piece of information. That's considered murder!" Theodore walks out the swing doors. "I am going to get this guy, Mr. Jones! Detective Ken, I need you to take a ride with me."

"What's up?" Detective Ken asked.

"I'll tell you on the way. Let's take my car!" Lieutenant Theodore said with his unlit cigar in his mouth, walking out of the police headquarters. Detective Theodore was giving Detective Ken the details of the hit and buried victim, and he feels that it's his job to tell the victim's family. Fifteen minutes later, Detective Theodore arrives at 7820 West Court Drive. They both get out the vehicle with their badges and walk toward a wooden brown front door and knock. A short Mexican female looks out her living room window and rushes to the front door.

"Mrs. Johnson?"

"Yes."

"We're Detective Theodore and Detective Ken!"

"Did you find my husband?" Mrs. Johnson asked.

"May we come in?"

"Yes, of course," she said in her nervous voice. They both stepped in and was looking around.

"Is anyone here with you, Mrs. Johnson?"

"Only my two children are in the backyard playing."

"Is your husband named Jerry Johnson?"

"Yes!"

"We have some bad news! He's dead!"

"What! How did it happen?" Mrs. Johnson was yelling with tears.

"He was hit by a car and someone buried him down in the park on Road 15 on Fourth of July evening. Where was your husband coming from that evening? Do you know?"

"Um, he was coming from his friend's place who he worked late with sometimes till seven thirty or sometimes eight p.m.," Mrs. Johnson replied with tears. She began wiping her tears with her fingers. Detective Ken hands her a napkin from her coffee table.

"Thank you! How am I going to explain to our children that their father is never coming home? Do you know where my husband's 2000 four-door silver Jeep is?"

"We didn't see his Jeep that evening," Theodore said.

"My husband's Jeep is missing?"

"Oh, I just had a thought! He must be the guy that got robbed that night near the liquor store. It's all coming to me now!" Detective Theodore whispered.

"Do you have a picture of your husband's vehicle?"

"Yes, I'll get it."

"Mother, can we have some juice?" Her young children came into the house from playing outside.

"Go wash your hands first, kids," she said gently.

"Here's the picture of my husband standing by his new Jeep. He's Italian and a hardworking man for his family!" the wife said with an accent.

"Sorry for your loss, Mrs. Johnson. Can I keep this picture? I'll bring it back later."

"Yes, of course." Detective Theodore puts the picture into his right shirt pocket.

"I have to get my kids some juice!"

"We'll let ourselves out," Detective Ken said. "Are you going to be all right?"

"I'll be all right. I'm going to make some calls to the family."

"Mrs. Johnson, I hate to ask you this, but is it possible you can come to the coroner's and identify him?"

"Yes, I'll have my family bring me tomorrow." Her three children walk to their mother. "What's wrong, Mother?" Tears were rolling down her wide cheeks.

"We are sorry about your loss." Detective Theodore politely said good-bye. And they walk out her front door and close it behind them.

"There's a stolen vehicle out there, and we are going to put an APB out and have the units do a search around the area."

"Its eleven a.m. almost time for lunch," Detective Ken said. They both get into the patrol car and put on their seat belts and drive off.

"We're going back to the station and put an APB out on Mr. Johnson's vehicle. I've figured it out! This man gets off work after he went his friend's place and stops at the liquor store and got jumped and beat up for his vehicle. Then he started walking home around eight p.m. when Mr. Jones was driving intoxicated and he didn't see Mr. Johnson on the right side of the road walking, and he hit Mr. Johnson with panic, and the horrifying thing about it is Mr. Jones didn't check his pulse to see if he was still breathing and he decided to roll his body down the hill and buried him!"

"How you know he was still alive?"

"The coroner told me!"

"Wow, that's murder!" Detective Ken shouted.

"Do you know who did it?

"Yes, his name is Mr. Alan Jones, a big finance adviser banker and he works downtown. I need to check something out!" Lieutenant Theodore said.

"Mr. Alan Jones's alibi that he was at the Bam club that evening around the time of the robbery. I also need to find out who took the report of the robbery? That's the missing piece to the puzzle: the time of the robbery! So it was Mr. Jerry Johnson that got robbed that evening for his vehicle and buried alive the same evening of the fourth."

"You have it! Wow."

"Mr. Johnson had some unexpected bad luck on the Fourth and sounds like Mr. Johnson was a hardworking man for his family also," Detective Ken said. A few minutes later, they arrived at the police station. "This case is getting better each time," Lieutenant Theodore said, as he parked his dark blue patrol car in the reserved area. He got out of the vehicle, where he rushed into the police headquarters, and walked to the front desk.

"Officer John, who was there taking the report on a robbery on the Fourth, around 8 p.m.? Who arrived on the call?"

"Let me take a look here," the front desk officer said.

"Here it is! The call came a little after 8 p.m.' and it looks like Officer Dunn went to investigate."

"Thank you very much!"

While the detective was digging deeper into the case, Alan's office phone rings.

"Yes, Joanna?"

"Why is Detective Theodore so interested about that dent in your car? What really happened that evening, Alan?"

"I told you I hit a pole that night from the bar. Why are you questioning me like this?" Alan asked with anger. "Don't call questioning me!"

"I'm just curious about that detective coming around."

Alan started getting more frustrated with her questions. "I have another call on hold. I'll see you later." *The frustration is climbing into my thoughts.*

Silences of Secrets

"I pray that Lieutenant Theodore doesn't go to the bar and start asking questions about that evening with Pete. I should drive by there after work. Or maybe around lunch, I can swing by there. It's eleven fifty." Alan gets up from his office chair, grabs his keys, and walks out of his office.

"Alan! Where you off to, buddy?"

"Going out to lunch!" Alan said with worry.

"Maybe I'll join you."

"No, I have to make a stop first."

"Well, I'll be at the Joe's Crabs. See you, buddy! Oh yes! I forgot to tell you I'll be transferring the money into another account Friday," Richard whispered to Alan.

"Good, and don't forget the deal. And I'll be there when you make the switch," Alan said to Richard.

"That's cool. See you, buddy." Alan jumps into his 1969 green Mustang and looks into his rearview mirror and sees a coworker walking behind his vehicle that's parked next to his. He waves to Alan. He then puts it into reverse and backs up and puts it into drive and spins off with his heavy engine. *Vroom!* Alan starts driving faster to get to the bar before detective gets there to ask Pete questions. Two minutes later, Alan gets to the Bam bar and parks his car in the back parking lot and steps out and walks around the front and opens the bar door. "Hey, Pete! Where are you?" Alan yells out as he looks around at the customers sitting at their tables having lunch.

"Hello, Mr. Jones. What can I get for you?" the bartender, Pete, said.

"Do you remember when I came here on the Fourth?"

"I don't recall. Why?"

"Because there's a detective going around asking questions if I've seen an accident that evening around my area. I told him I was here most of the evening." Alan slips Pete a hundred dollar bill. "Remember! I was here till 8 p.m."

"Yes, sir." The bartender Pete winked his right eye. "Can I still get you something?"

"Sure you can get me a ham sandwich please!"

The bartender Pete came back with a ham sandwich.

"Would you like something to drink?"

"Yes, you can get me a Coors beer please," Alan asked right away. "I'm going to sit over here and watch the basketball game."

"Yes, sir. One Coors beer coming up!" Pete the bartender said. As soon as Alan sits in the back of the bar area, Detective Theodore walks in.

"Can I help you, sir?" Pete the bartender asked.

"Yes! I need some information on one of your customers on the Fourth of July evening." Alan was watching from the back table.

"Do you recall, if Mr. Alan Jones was here on evening of the Fourth of July between eight p.m. till nine p.m.?"

"Let me think," Pete the bartender said.

"Yes, he was here that evening from eight till nine thirty p.m."

"Are you sure?"

"Yes, I'm sure." The bartender was trying not to ogle his brown eyes over in the dark corner of the bar. Detective Theodore writes down the information.

"Thank you very much." He walked out the bar and to his vehicle. Lieutenant Theodore decides to sit in his patrol car and wait for a few minutes and starts eating his lunch that he picked up at the grill sandwiches on Main Street. While Lieutenant

Theodore was eating his lunch couple of minutes later, Alan came walking out the Bam bar.

"Mr. Jones was in there all the time and I bet he paid that bartender for his alibi."

The lieutenant starts his vehicle and notices Alan pulling out from the back parking lot and put his right blinker on, then turned right. The lieutenant makes a U-turn and follows Alan's green 1964 Mustang. Alan pulls into a gas station to get some gas for his car. Detective Theodore parks across the street from the gas station, watching Alan go in to pay for his gas. He walks back out the mini market to pump the gas into his tank. A couple of minutes later, Alan put the gas pump back and gets into his green Mustang and starts it. *Vroom! Vroom!* Lieutenant Theodore was listening to his engine and he pulls out fast, then slows down, driving the speed limit, and turns right from the gas station.

This car drinks up gas like a speedboat in the water.

A few minutes later, Alan makes it back to his job and drives into the underground parking and parks into his reserved lot. *Vroom!* He turns off the engine and gets out the vehicle and locks it and walks toward the elevators as he rushes into the elevator as the doors were still open with a couple of workers standing in the elevator. Alan pushes the fifth floor button. As the lieutenant missed the elevator, he pushes the down button to the next elevator. Detective Theodore walks on the elevator and pushes button number 5. He was watching the numbers of floors on the elevator and arrives on the fifth floor and he walks off the elevator toward the reception.

As if he didn't know, "Is Mr. Jones back from lunch?"

"Do you have an appointment with Mr. Jones?"

"No, not really. Do you remember me?" Detective Theodore asked the receptionist.

"Yes! The detective! Mr. Jones just got back from lunch. I'll let him know you're here, sir." She buzzed his office intercom.

"Yes?"

"Detective Theodore is here to see you, sir."

"I'll be out in a minute."

"Yes, sir. He'll be right out, Detective," the receptionist said with a smile.

"Thank you."

Alan walks out of his office.

"Detective, what can I do for you this time?"

"Well, I still need a little more information. Can we talk in your office for a brief moment?"

"Detective, I have a lot of work to do," Alan said aggressively and walks to his office and closes the door hard behind him. "What is it this time, Lieutenant?"

"Well, I've noticed around lunch you were coming out the Bam bar, and I didn't see you there when I was talking to the bartender." Alan started getting more nervous.

"The bartender tells me that you were there from eight till nine p.m.? I also know you paid him to say that." He felt he was ready to confess, but he couldn't bring it out, thinking about the consequences. "Did you see a robbery across from the 7-Eleven store that evening?"

"No, I didn't."

"Well, the man that got hit that night around eight p.m. on Road 15 was robbed, and his gray Jeep was stolen. Are you sure you didn't see or hear anything that night around eight thirty?"

"I told you I was home in bed, so how am I going to see or hear anything?" The lieutenant looks through Alan's fearful eyes.

"There was something more surprising about the victim. He was still alive. As a matter of fact, he was unconscious when the driver buried him. The driver never checked to see if he was still breathing. He hit the victim and rolled him down the hill and started digging a small hole and covered him in the dirt that was found in his lungs and he was breathing. He had suffocated from the dirt! He didn't die from the hit of the vehicle."

"Why are you telling me all this?" he asked with frustration.

"If you just tell me the truth, you would feel a lot better and I also know the guilt is eating you up."

"Just get out! I've done nothing wrong!" he shouted. The receptionist heard the yelling. "Okay, I'm leaving!" he said while walking over to the door. "Mr. Jones, it's not over because I can see the guilt in your eyes. You're trying to hide something!" the lieutenant said feeling angry with him, not coming clean with the truth, and he walks out of Alan's office while Alan's receptionist was watching Detective Theodore leaving. Alan was trying to calm his nerves, and at that moment, his cell phone rings. And he looks at the caller ID.

"What is it, Joanna?" Alan answered with an attitude.

"I just called to tell you to meet me at the Water Breeze Restaurant when you get off work because we need to talk."

"Where?"

"The Water Breeze Restaurant on Ocean Drive. Do you remember where we went on your birthday?"

"Oh yes!"

"I'll see you there at five thirty all right?"

"Sure!" he said pitifully. And he closed his cell phone and dropped it on his desk and looks at his round gold-trimmed wooden clock sitting on his desk that his wife give him for his office as a gift. He picks up a file folder and he tries to concentrate, but he feels very agitated. He looks at the file and clears his throat and just sees words while his thoughts are corrupted of his fear! Alan stands up and walks to Richards's office just a couple of feet away. *Knock.*

"Alan, you look troubled. What's up?"

"I'm trying to focus on my work, but that Detective Theodore keeps disturbing me with his damn questions!" Alan was feeling scared; frustration was climbing to his brain! "What kind of questions are he asking?" Richard asks in a concerned way.

"He even went to Bam club, asking the bartender Pete if I was there on the Fourth of July evening."

"And what did Pete say?" Alan looked at Richard.

"He told him I was there that evening."

"Why would he keep asking you these questions?"

"I told him I had stopped at the 7-Eleven Store, and he thinks I've seen something unusual that night, but I was at the bar at eight p.m. that evening and he said that's the time the incident happened."

"So what are you worried about?"

"It was a robbery that evening and the man that got robbed was the same man that got hit and buried. His car is missing. That evening at the store, I did hear some yelling, but I thought it was just kids messing around, and that detective said the man was still alive when the driver buried him."

"What? That doesn't make any sense. Well, it wasn't you, buddy, so don't worry about it!" Richard said.

"But how can I stop that detective from coming around asking questions?"

"Don't worry about it. I'll make a call to my lawyer!"

"Thanks, Richard."

"If that detective comes around again, call me and I'll have a word with him!" Richard said.

"I yelled at him today about harassing me with his questions," Alan said in a nervous way. "I have some files to work on. Thanks again, Richard!"

"No problem!" Richard picks up his office phone to call his lawyer.

"Mr. Stewart is on line 2."

"I'll take it in my office." Alan walks into his office and picks up his office phone.

"Mr. Stewart! What can I do for you today?" Alan asked in a more cheerful way. "Yes, your account is updated for a loan." As the time rolls by, Alan looks at his clock;

it 3:50 p.m. Alan finally gets off the phone after two hours with a business meeting.

"And now I have to meet my wife at the Water Breeze Restaurant in thirty minutes." He gets up and grabs his keys and case and locks his office door.

"Good night, Mr. Jones," the receptionist said.

"Good night!" Richard was still in his office on his phone. Alan then walks on the elevator and pushes the garage floor button. His cell phone rings. "Hello!" Other employees were walking in the elevator from another floor.

"I just got off the phone with my lawyer and he said he would look into the matter for you."

"Thanks, Richard," Alan whispered so the other employees wouldn't hear his conversation. "I'll give you call when I hear back with results. Thanks, buddy," Alan said and hung up his cell phone with a smirk. *I hope that Detective Theodore will back off with his investigation!* Alan was thinking while he walked off the elevator to his vehicle, feeling less frightful. He makes it to his vehicle and opens the door and gets in and starts it up with his 8.5 heavy motor. He puts it into reverse and then into drive. *Vroom!* Alan drives out the employee's garage into the heavy traffic and drives on Freeway 12. *What a relief. Traffic is not backed up today.* Alan changes lanes, going toward the south to get to his location. Ten minutes later, Alan arrives at the Water Breeze Restaurant and parks close to his wife's Tahoe hybrid car and walks toward the restaurant door while he turned his head, looking at a pretty lady that walked past him, and he opened the restaurant door and walks in, hearing soft music playing in the background. He then walks over to his wife and gives her a kiss on the cheek and takes a seat. A waiter, wearing a dark blue shirt that says Water Breeze printed on the right side and his name tag on his left side shirt, approaches them. "Hello. Welcome to Breeze's, are you ready for your order?"

"Yes, we would like two shrimp cocktails and crab patties with two iced teas please!" Joanna said while Alan kept quiet. the waiter walks away. Joanna looks right into her husband's face with both her hands together like she is praying with both her elbows on the table to talk closer to her husband. "Now, we've been married eleven years, and I know you to your bones! And I can see the fear in your eyes, so come out with it!" Joanna whispers with concern. Alan keeps quiet as he looks at his wife and took a deep breath; just then, at that moment, the waiter came with their iced tea just when he was ready to tell his wife the truth.

"We need to talk privately," he whispers to his wife.

"I know you very well and I need to know the truth!" she whispered.

"Was it you who killed that man on Road 15?" He kept quiet for a moment and looked straight into his wife's eyes.

"Yes! It was me who accidently killed that man, but it was an accident! When you were calling me on my cell phone, it slipped out my hand and landed on the passenger side floor, and when I went to reach for it, the wheel was pulling to the right. By the time I looked up, I felt something hit hard! I went into shock when I discovered a homeless man who I thought was dead at the time!" he whispered loud.

"Hush! People will hear you!" she said in a low voice.

"Then I pulled his body down the hill where there were lots of trees, and I got my small shovel and I dug a hole and buried the man who I thought was dead. But I heard he was still alive at the time! Detective Theodore said so."

"Oh my god!" Joanna quietly whispered.

"And I ran back to the Lincoln, feeling nervous and rushed home! And that's the reason I felt sick with fear and guilt about that guy and that's the truth!" he whispered while tears began rolling down her face, and she grabs a napkin and wipes her tears while the waiter arrives with their dinners.

"I lost my appetite." She felt disappointed in her husband.

"It's unprofessional and disappointing!" she whispered aggressively. His head dropped down, feeling the guilt chewing on his heart and soul.

"I'm really sorry!" he whispered sorrowfully with his head down. Joanna's cell phone rings while she was crying. "Hello. Where are you?" her friend ginger asked.

"I am having dinner with my husband. Why?"

"Did you remember Cindy's birthday party tonight at six p.m.?"

"Oh, I forgot! Could you tell her I couldn't make it tonight and I'll bring her a birthday gift Tomorrow?" Joanna said in a confused voice.

"Are you crying?" her friend Cindy asked.

"I'm okay. I'll talk to you tomorrow." She hung up, feeling disappointed, and wipes her nose with a napkin she was holding in her right hand.

"That's why that detective kept asking about the time you went to the store?" Joanna whispered.

"It happened around eight p.m. on the Fourth of July weekend. I wish I never went to the store that evening! I'm feeling guilty every moment."

"Did you really go to the Bam bar that night?" she whispered.

He took a deep breath. "No! I was lying about that too!"

She looked at him with more anger. "You're so fucking damaged!" she said with anger. He couldn't look at his wife without the guilt chewing him up. She gets up, grabbing her purse, and leaves toward the casher to pay for their dinner that neither touched. Alan gets up from his seat and followed her to the cashier.

"Joanna?" She paid no attention to him and walks out the restaurant. "Please don't do this! I can go to jail and lose you!"

"I lied to the police, thinking you were speaking the truth, Alan!" she yelled with aggravation. Both were standing by her Tahoe Hybrid, arguing.

"Please don't leave me."

"We will work it out later! I'm not going to lose anything!" She looked at him strangely with anger. "Just act normal around everyone. Don't act nervous, or they will notice something isn't right. Be more relaxed by the time we get home."

She gives him a kiss on the cheek and unlocks her Tahoe Hybrid and gets in while he walks over to his dark green Mustang, feeling confidence in his wife who gives him unconditional love with her greed. Alan starts his Mustang and waits for his wife. He then pulls off behind her car. As they drive out the parking lot of the restaurant, Alan turns his radio on, listening to soft music.

While he was following behind his wife as she drives on the northeast freeway, Alan speeds up to get on the freeway. As he passed his wife's vehicle, he blew his horn, waving at her to follow him. He was driving 68 mph, and a police car was behind him with red and blue lights and the siren. Alan pulls over to the right while she pulls up behind the police vehicle. His luck just keeps getting worse! She sits in her car a couple of feet away and waits.

"Hello, may I see your license, sir?" Alan reaches for his wallet and pulls out his license and hands it to the officer.

"Be right back." The officer walks back to his vehicle.

"I don't have to worry about paying the ticket. It's my first ticket I've ever received and I can get a lawyer to fight it. I would be better off if I just pay the ticket. That would give Detective Theodore another reason to come around."

"Okay, Mr. Jones, just sign your name here at the bottom and you can be on your way." Alan signs the ticket.

"Drive carefully!" the officer said while he walked back to his police vehicle and pulled off, then Alan pulled off slowly. Joanna continued to follow him back on the freeway. Ten minutes later, they both arrived, driving up in their driveway. She parks her car on the left side of the driveway and gets out with an attitude, slamming her car door, walking up steps to their front door, and opens it with her key. She walks to their dinner table and sets her things in the chair and walks over to the bar and starts pouring her a brandy with ice. As Alan walks in and looks at his wife with pity in his eyes, he throws his keys on the table and goes sit on the couch, feeling worse.

"I asked you to be cheerful!"

"It seems more bad luck keeps hitting me!" he yelled with more frustration. "Can you make me a gin and juice please!"

"I hope you don't have any more skeletons you would like to come out with? Or should I say skeletons in your closets!" she said with a sarcastic attitude. His heart fell low and his spirit went numb. She was pouring his gin and juice in a clear glass and walks over to her husband and hands him his drink and sits next to him.

"Just don't let the guilt show so much when your family comes over." He listened to the anger in her voice.

"It's nearly seven p.m. We didn't eat at the restaurant. That was a waste of money!" she shouted and walked to their bedroom, feeling disappointed. He began feeling his liquor and grabs the remote to watch the news to see any new leads to the hit and buried investigation. His wife walked past the dining room and into the kitchen. Joanna was feeling awkward with anger. "I'm not the one to lose everything because of him." She then decided to put her feelings behind for a moment and move forward. It's seven thirty p.m. Joanna was fixing leftovers while she was thinking the worst. *What if he does get arrested for the murder? I'll lose everything and I can't make the mortgage on my salary. I would have to sell the house if he goes to jail for the rest of his life.* She was thinking hard. *I'll have to cash in our joint account of four thousand dollars and our life insurance policy is worth fifty thousand dollars, but I can't collect that money till he's dead. Maybe it could happen accidentally.* She gets two plates from the cover, the microwave stops, and she begins making their plates and walks over to the dinner table. He gets up from the couch while trying to concentrate on the news, but his conscience had control of his thoughts. He walks over to the dining room table, wishing things were back to normal by putting his guilty feeling behind him. They both sit down to eat with fear and panic. *Ding-dong.* They both jump a little. His wife gets up slowly with fear to answer the door.

"Gail, what is it?" Gail was breathing with panic.

"Alan, your friend, the one you worked with? Richard?"

"Yes! The one that lives on East Lake Drive!" Gail was breathing hard. "The police and coroner are at his place!" Alan jumps up and grabs his shoes from the living room and puts them on. "Are you sure it's his place?"

"I'm sure it's his place!" Gail was breathing hard, feeling excited. "Come on!" Gail yelled. Joanna locks their front door and they all jump into Gail's dark blue 1998 Land Rover and she begins driving north toward Richard's, which is five blocks away. They were driving closer to his friend Richard's place and noticed the flashing lights from the police cars. "It must be real bad and the press is here!" Alan said. Gail makes a right turn on East Lake Drive and parks her vehicle across from Richard's place and Alan rushes out of her car and begins walking faster toward Richard's front lawn. The crime scene tape was wrapped around two brown trees. Alan rushed under the yellow tape.

"Hold it!" an officer yelled. "You can't go in there, sir."

"My friend Richard lives here! What happened?" Alan asked in a panicky way. Lieutenant Theodore arrives at the scene.

"Mr. Jones, may I ask you a few questions?"

"What happened, Lieutenant?" Alan asked in a caring way while the neighbors were hankering to find out what had happened.

"When was the last time you talk to Richard Oxford?"

"Today in his office!" Alan replied.

"Do you have any idea if Richard was supposed to meet someone this evening?"

"No, I wouldn't know, Detective!"

"I hate to tell you this. Mr. Oxford was murdered!"

Alan looked surprised.

"Where were you between five thirty till six?"

"My wife and I were at the Water Breeze Restaurant from five thirty till six p.m. That's right, Lieutenant!"

"Hello, Mrs. Jones. I didn't see you standing there! And who is this young lady?"

"This is my cousin Gail Salina!"

"Hello, Gail. did you see or hear anything this evening?"

"No, I didn't, sir." Gail said with her low voice. Detective Theodore walks over to a police officer and whispers, "Ask questions to see if there are any witnesses." The officer walks over to a crowd of neighbors who were watching.

"Excuse me, if anyone saw or heard anything, please come forward."

"I saw a man jumping from Mr. Oxford's back gate earlier," a neighbor said.

"Lieutenant!" He comes rushing over to the officer. "What is your name, miss?"

"Mrs. Bailey!"

"I'm Lieutenant Theodore," he said while reaching into his coat pocket and showing his badge.

"Tell me what you saw tonight?"

"Well, my eyes are poor, but I heard the dogs barking, then I saw someone climbing over Mr. Oxford's brown wooden gate, wearing all black, and then I didn't see the person anymore. Then the dogs kept barking, so I sat back into my rocking chair and grabbed my phone and called the police."

"Where do you live, Ms. Bailey?"

"Across the street from Mr. Oxford."

"Thank you, Ms. Bailey, and if I have any more questions, I'll contact you!"

"Get her information and her address," he whispered to the officer.

"Lieutenant Theodore!" He rushed into Richard's residence.

"The killer has an imagination."

"Why do you say that?"

"I hope you haven't eaten dinner yet?"

"Not just yet. Why?" he asked, as they both walked into the front room, where they noticed the body was lying between the kitchen floor and the dining room floor.

"This man has multiple stab wounds in the chest and the groin area. The killer also castrated his penis and stuffed his own penis into his mouth, which could be a message," Detective Ken said.

"He looks like he recognized the killer before he died."

"Officer, did you take a lot of pictures?"

"I have Detective Theodore."

"The coroner is going to have a ball with this one!" Lieutenant Ken whispered.

"The coroner has arrived!" an officer shouted.

"What a mess," the medical coroner said while pulling the deceased's penis out of his mouth. Both detectives had sensitive expressions on their faces.

"Who's mad at you, Richard Oxford?" Lieutenant Theodore asked the deceased.

"He steps out of the shower nude and puts on his robe and walks toward the kitchen and the killer surprised him and started stabbing him and cuts his private off and stuffs his penis into his mouth while he was dying slowly. We're all finished here, Lieutenant!" the coroner said.

"Okay, you can take him out!" As the coroner lifts up the gurney and picked up Richard's bloody body with the bloody penis in the black plastic body bag and rolls his body out to the coroner's van. While both detectives were investigating around in Richard's place to see if it was a robbery. Detective Theodore noticed his wallet was missing, but not his watch and keys that were on the nightstand.

"Where is his wallet?" Detective Theodore accidently kicked something by the nightstand and looked down; it was a brown leather wallet on the floor that looks like someone took all his cash out and left his credit cards where they wanted it to look like a robbery.

"I have this feeling it was someone he knew who tormented him for a reason," Detective Theodore said to Detective Ken.

"I think you're right. Because nothing is really missing but the money that was in his wallet, and there are a lot more expensive things here than the amount he probably had in his wallet and he kept his place clean," Detective Ken said.

"Well, we have to get to the coroner's and do the report," Detective Theodore said.

"So let's lock the place up and try to get rid of these neighbors hanging around." As they both walk out to the front lawn toward their patrol car, Detective Theodore noticed that Mr. Jones and his wife had left the scene.

"Okay, folks, it's over. You all can go home now!" the police officer announced while he was removing the crime scene yellow tape from around the trees.

Gail drops them both off in front of their home.

"Good night, Gail, and thanks, we'll see you later!" They both walk up to their home while they both were still feeling frightened and devastated.

"Who would want to kill your friend like that?" his wife asked.

"I don't know who would do that to him."

Joanna walks into the dining room.

"Feel like finishing your dinner?"

"Not really!" Alan was even more frightened, waiting for the police to come to arrest him, and walks to the bathroom to wash his hands and face. While Joanna was nervously thinking about losing everything she's worked so hard for all these years. He can't look directly into his wife's brown eyes, quietly holding his head down while trying to eat his dinner.

"What if that detective arrests you for murder?"

"What!"

"And what am I supposed to do after you're gone?"

"You selfish greedy bitch! Stop thinking about is yourself!"

"Someone may try to kill you next," his wife said in anger and frustration. Alan throws his fist on the table and throws both of his hands over his face. Joanna gets up with more anger and walks into the kitchen, feeling disappointed. *How could he let this happen?* She brushes her left hand across her forehead. *If he didn't drink so much, he wouldn't be in this situation!* She walks back into the dining room. Alan had gone to the bedroom to take a shower. Joanna clears the table and puts the dishes into the dishwasher, thinking too herself, feeling disappointed in her husband, and looks at the kitchen clock. *I'm so glad his family didn't come over tonight. He would have shown his guilt like a wimp.*

She hung her kitchen towel over dish rack and turned off the kitchen lights and walked to their bedroom as she heard the shower water turning off.

She was thinking of protecting herself when worst comes to worst, wondering when the police were coming. She had different thoughts running through her fearful mind. *I don't feel like worrying all night.* Alan walks out the bathroom, wearing his light blue robe, and walks over to his side of the bed. Joanna jumps up and grabs her nightgown out of her dresser and walks into the bathroom. Alan turns his night light off and rolls over to his right side and tries to close his eyes to hide from his worst nightmares. The house phone rings Alan turns the light on and reaches to the phone.

"Hello?"

"Alan, I just heard about your friend Richard who was murdered in his home!"

"I was just going to bed, Lisa, and I'm tired and I feel devastated about Richard. I'll call you tomorrow! Good night."

His sister felt a little confused.

"Good night, Alan!"

Joanna was still in the shower.

My wife feels disappointed in me. I just want to die! Things are not going to be the same between us since I've told her the truth. She gets out the shower and brushes her teeth while Alan was lying down with his corrupt conscience. His wife came out the bathroom in her nightgown and walks over to her side of the bed, not feeling sexually affectionate. She then turns her nightstand light out.

Wednesday morning, the clock alarm went off and they both wake up without saying good morning. He felt like he hadn't slept all evening.

I can't wake up from a nightmare, he thought to himself. She puts her slippers on and gets up to get dressed for work.

"No breakfast this morning?" Alan said in his weak voice. She kept silent, still feeling angry and disappointed and began dressing in her dark green short skirt and a white long-sleeve blouse as fast as she can to get away from him with the anger she was feeling at the moment.

"Good morning! No conversation this morning?" He was feeling more neglected from his wife. Joanna continues getting dressed, keeping silent while she slips on her high white heels and walks out their bedroom and slams the door behind her with more anger and walks into their kitchen to make fresh coffee and toast for the both of them. Alan gets up to get dressed, feeling like a dark life has fallen on him. *She's supposed to stick with me through thick and thin with the marriage vows. That's a joke!* While getting dressed in his black pants and white cotton sleeves shirt and his black silk socks and slips on his shining black dress shoes and walks into the bathroom mirror, hoping to see a whole new person. *I want to wake up from this nightmare that I see and feel differently, but it's not going away, no matter how many times I wash my face and look into the mirror.* Alan grabs his matching suit jacket and gets his wallet and walks out their bedroom while his wife was drinking a cup of coffee. Reading the morning newspaper, Alan pours a cup of coffee. "Are you going to speak to me this morning?" He gets angrier and throws an empty cup against the wall.

She looked at him with anger. "You damaged our marriage!" she yelled. "Why are you letting it get to you!" Alan was breathing hard with anger and tries to get rid of that guilty feeling that he carries in his soul and heart. Alan takes a deep breath to relieve his anger. He grabs his keys and walks out to his car.

Ten minutes later, Alan parks in his reserved space and locks his car and walks onto the elevator to the fifth floor and walks off and toward the reception and notices Detective Theodore sitting down.

"Are you waiting for me, Detective?" Alan said.

"Not really, I am waiting for your supervisor, Mr. Looms, to see if I could look around in Mr. Oxford's office. Maybe I'll find something that may help me in this new case!" Detective Theodore was anxious and eager to learn about Richard's past. Alan started feeling furiously nervous with Detective Theodore who wanted to investigate Richard's office, hoping he doesn't look into Richard's computer and see the transfer of the association funds that was transferred into my account.

It seems even more frightening with Richard not around any longer. The receptionist answers a call, "Detective Theodore? Mr. Looms will see you now!"

He gets up from his seat and walks to Mr. Loom's office, which is the first door on the right.

"Thank you very much!" Alan was watching Detective Theodore walking to his supervisor's office. Mr. Loom and Detective Theodore were having a conversation.

"Richard Oxford was a good hard worker for many years after he went to college to became an executive for our cooperative finance company. I'm so sorry to hear about Richard Oxford, and I will be going to his service to give my condolence to his family. You're welcome to anything that will help Richard's case."

"Thank you!"

"And it was nice meeting you and good luck," Mr. Looms said. The lieutenant walks back to Richard's office to find something that will give him a lead on the killer. Detective Theodore begins looking around Richard's office and notices a letter to Richard from a female named Susan Ross. Detective Theodore sits in Richard's office chair and begins reading the letter.

Richard's Remains

The following Wednesday morning, Lisa calls James.

"Hello! Good morning, James!"

"Hi, Lisa. How you doing?" James asked in an exciting way.

"I'm doing well, sitting at work. I thought I would give you a call and see if you want to meet this evening?"

"Where would you like to meet?" James asked.

"Downtown at the Oak Brooks Restaurant at 6 p.m. tonight."

"I'll be there," James said. "I'm driving to the fire station now and I'll meet you at six."

"Have a good day." She closes her pink cell phone while customers came walking into the shop. Lisa had a smile on her face while standing by the cash register.

"Welcome to the Quotable Women Dress Shop!"

"Thank you," the customers said.

"Look at these lovely dresses? We also have reasonable prices!" At the same time, Detective Theodore was passing Lisa's employment, driving toward the Oxford's residence. Lieutenant Theodore was reading the address on a piece of paper: 836 East Lake Drive, holding his unlit cigar in his mouth, while driving in the city limits. A couple of minutes later, he arrives to the Oxford family house and parks his car in front of a light blue house with white trimming. The green grass was trimmed and the hedges were cut perfectly. Lieutenant Theodore gets out of his car and walks up to the Oxford's residence and knocks on the front door.

A Mexican-Caucasian female with golden blond short hair and thin eyebrows with small squeaky brown eyes answers the door.

"Hello, may I help you?"

"Are you Mrs. Oxford?" He was surprised by her appearance. She was wearing her black short-sleeved velvet dress that's above her knees and was wearing yellow house shoes. She looked about the age of fifty.

"I'm Mrs. Oxford? Who are you?" He grabs his badge out of his front jacket and shows his badge to her.

"Lieutenant Theodore, Homicide!" He spoke with clear English. "Can we go in and talk?"

"What's this about?"

"Do you have a son named Richard Oxford?"

"Yes! He lives on the north side of town," Mrs. Oxford said with a worried look on her face.

"Are you alone, ma'am?"

"No, my husband is upstairs, getting ready for breakfast."

"Could I have the both of you in here please? Because this is not good news!" He grabs her right hand. She hurries and calls her husband. "Jimmy! Come down here!" He comes rushing down the stairs. "Breakfast ready?"

"I'm Lieutenant Theodore, Homicide!" They shake hands.

"I'm here because I didn't want you to find out from the evening news that your son Richard was brutally murdered last night!" They both went into shock, grabbing each other. Richard's mother was holding her hand across her mouth and sat down on their couch. "Oh my God! My son! He was killed in his home last night!"

"He was stabbed multiple times and one other thing happened, which I think I believe it was a message."

"What is it, Detective?" Jimmy asked.

"I think I better tell you in private, Mr. Oxford." They walk into the hallway.

"I hate to tell you this, but his private part was in his mouth when we found him!" the detective whispered.

"Oh my God!" Jimmy shouted.

"I'm so sorry to tell you this way, but I think its best that I get some information from you as fresh as possible. When was the last time you saw your son Richard?"

"It was…um…last week. He stopped by for about an hour." Liz breaks out with a loud cry. "Our firstborn son! Who did this?" she asked with emotions of heartbreak and agony. "Our other son is going to be devastated when he hears about his brother!"

"You both have another son?"

"Our youngest son."

"Is he here?"

"He hasn't come home yet! He went over a friends to watch a game. He's twenty-one, and he look up to his older brother, Richard," Mr. Oxford said.

"He loves his brother more than anything. Richard kind of spoiled Dupree. It's going to break his heart when he hears about his brother!" Mrs. Oxford said while they both were feeling devastated. A few minutes later, Dupree walks into their front door.

"Mother, what's going on?" Her eyes were puffy and red from crying. Dupree rushed over to his parents.

"What happened?"

"Are you Dupree Oxford?"

"Yes! Who are you?" Dupree asked in a concerned way.

"I'm Lieutenant Theodore." He shows his badge.

"Someone murdered Richard!" his father said emotionally and dropped his head down while he sat next to his wife.

"How did it happen?" Dupree asked nervously. Lieutenant Theodore began looking in his small tablet. "Someone broke into his place around seven or eight p.m. When the intruder entered, he began stabbing him, and there's another thing that's not pleasing to say, but someone deliberately castrated his private part and

I also think someone intentionally wanted payback," Detective Theodore said. Dupree was feeling confused with shock.

"May I ask you where you were last night?" Dupree's mother stands up from her seat.

"I told you, Lieutenant."

"Wait, Mother! I went to my classes, then I was out with my friends."

"Can you verify that? It's just a routine check."

"I was with my friends, watching a game on cable and stayed the night."

"What's your friend name?"

"Larry and Anthony. They're brothers who live at 902 Chase Street."

"It sounds like you have an alibi." Dupree stares at Detective Theodore with his piercing eyes.

Caucasian stands five six wearing his black jeans pants and a blue shirt.

"I'll be all right!" Mrs. Oxford said.

"Detective, do you have any suspects?" Dupree asked. "Not yet?"

"Did Richard have any enemies?"

"Not that we know of." Dupree started clearing his throat with worry.

"Poor Richard. He had a wonderful life and a good job, and he never got into anything bad!" Mrs. Oxford said with grief. "Did he have a girlfriend?"

"He had lots of female friends, but no one special. Oh, wait a minute, he was seeing someone, but I don't know her name," Dupree said.

"If you remember her name, give me a call."

"I will Detective," Dupree said.

"I think that is all for now, and I'll leave you my card, if you think of anything or need to contact me. And I'm truly sorry about your loss. Good-bye," Detective Theodore said and walks out their front door.

Dupree watches Theodore walk to his vehicle till he drove off. "We need to contact the families and make arrangements also," Mr. Oxford said. Then he broke out, crying aloud.

"Oh, Richard!"

Dupree hugs both his parents, sobbing and trembling, traumatized, broken up over the tragic news. His father walks over to his black leather recliner and drops his body in the chair, feeling shocked and devastated, while Lieutenant Theodore drives over to the Bam Club for more information on Richard Oxford's mystery death.

Fifteen minutes later, Lieutenant arrives at the Bam club once again and walks into the club with his right hand in his pocket.

"Can I get you a drink?" Pete the bartender said.

"That's all right. Just a couple of questions about Mr. Oxford. Did he come here often?" "Yes! I'm sorry to hear about Richard. Did Richard Oxford have any enemies?"

Detective, Richard was a bachelor and a hard gambler. Richard would sit and play poker from eight p.m. till eleven p.m. or till closing time. One late evening, over a weekend, Dupree would come into the bar and watch his brother Richard playing poker. Like last month, on a weekend, Dupree came in and walked up to his brother Richard and whispered something in ear. Richard then got up from his seat and yelled at Dupree about a money situation, then I heard Richard saying, 'I don't owe you shit' and started laughing at Dupree and calling him a piece of shit!

"Dupree was feeling embarrassed when Richard grabbed Curtis, his gay friend, and started kissing him on the mouth, and *everyone* was watching how Richard was acting that evening, and the way Dupree was looking at his brother was like he wanted to kill Richard that moment!

"Dupree's face was full of anger, and he had slammed his glass down on a table. The contents splashed on the floor. He was feeling mad as hell! Excuse my expression," Pete said.

"Do you have an address on Curtis, or his last name?"

"I have his address." Pete goes to the back room. Couple seconds later, he was back. "Here's Curtis's address, Detective!" And Pete hands him a piece of paper.

"Thanks!"

"I hope I was some help." Pete was feeling a little guilty helping Alan Jones. Detective Theodore walks to his vehicle and drives off. Lisa's cell phone rings.

"Hello, Lisa!"

"What's up, twins?"

"We've heard about your brother's friend! It's all in the news, Lisa, and this is the second murder in this town! First, that guy was killed on Road 15 and now your brother's friend was murdered last night!" Diana said.

"I remember him. He was that older guy that was at your brother's birthday party last year!" Dana the twin said.

"Did you read this morning newspaper in the back column?"

"No, what's it's about?"

"I'll read it over the phone," Dana said.

"It's called the Guru of Greed! It occurs when a personal property has been stolen and used without your knowledge to commit fraud. I've always wanted to be a crime writer. It's in my blood to snoop around when my investigation was on when I received several letters from the Internal Revenue Service saying that I owed five thousand dollars, plus civil penalty for filing frivolous tax. I've have not filed taxes in ten years or more. So I started doing my own investigation when I came back from my vacation in January 2000. I had received another letter from the Internal Revenue Service and I decided to go to the main office to give them all proof of my last filing year. The ten forty was filed in my name and Social Security Number so I called the police to file a report and a phone call to the IRS and I was told some information that put a shock on my mind that the address where the check went to was my son's ex-girlfriend. A person of interest and that she was using that address for mailing purposes only;

she had stolen my identity. I was in shock because something like this has never happened to me. On a January evening, she came over without her son and she wanted me to help her with some paperwork. I did not realize at the time that she really came to see if I have received any letters from the internal Revenue Service. She did not say that, but she had seemed a little nervous at the time, and I had no clue that she came to see if her scam had worked. It took me two long suffering years that I have proof that this person of interest has five or more Social Security Numbers to scam the Internal Revenue Service. There's no stopping me on this investigation. This person of interest doesn't have morals and values for herself; she's just a scam for money. After getting calls saying the charges were removed, I still received more letters to finish my investigation in October 2000. This person of interest is still at large. Now the IRS have proven that I was a victim identity theft, and now, I can put a close to it. If the law doesn't get her, God will take care of it and that's a promise. Written by unknown author."

"Wow, that is deep! This is in the today's paper?" Lisa asked.

"Yes," Dana said.

"I have a customer. Talk to you both later!"

"Bye, Lisa!"

Richard's Secret Lover

ieutenant Theodore arrives at Curtis Leonard's residence and parks his vehicle in front and gets out and walks up his driveway. Curtis notices him coming to his door and opens it. "Are you lost?" Curtis asked.

"Are you Curtis Leonard?"

"Yes, who are you?"

Lieutenant Theodore shows his badge.

"What can I help you with?" Curtis asked.

"Well, I need to ask you about Richard Oxford."

"Sure, come on in!" Curtis said in a sweet way. Lieutenant Theodore walked in and noticed a real tiger fur rug with the head and teeth across his living room floor, which matches his furry tiger robe. Curtis begin swinging his curly black hair like a girl while the detective noticed his drawn-on eyeliner and red lipstick on his shaved face, feeling something with him wasn't right. Lieutenant noticed a tiger fur blanket covering his couch and mirrors on his living room walls and ceiling like the funk dales styles. Curtis was pouring himself a brandy with ice.

"Would you like a drink, Lieutenant?"

"No, thank you! Now, how long did you know Richard Oxford?"

"About two years!" Curtis replied.

"When was the last time you saw him?"

"A couple of nights ago!" Curtis said in a girly way.

"Can you tell me about his personality?"

"Richard had an unusual addiction, if you know what I mean, and he had his dark secrets that he kept to himself. He was selfish with greed and a coward inside his soul! But I loved him!" Curtis begin twitching like a female, walking toward Lieutenant Theodore.

"But he would turn a woman's heart and a man's head!"

"Do you mean Richard was romantically involved with you?" Lieutenant Theodore was a little shocked for sure.

"All the way," Curtis said in his girly way. "We've were dating for over two years, and he would give me money, love, and attention always, then there came the drugs, cocaine, pills, and the gambling. Richard did it all! Richard was even messing with another man's wife and that would get anyone beat up or threaten or killed." Curtis was swinging his hands with his red fingernails like a woman.

"Can you tell me about his brother Dupree?"

"Dupree is Richard's younger brother, and he always followed Richard around, no matter what! See, Richard was six years older than Dupree. He would blow Dupree off by embarrassing him around his friends. He told his brother to stop being his bodyguard and following him. Until a couple of months ago, Richard decided to take full advantage of Dupree by making him sell drugs for him, like last weekend at the Bam club! Dupree went to collect his earnings from his brother, but he would blow him off and give Dupree nothing but a hard time! Then, Richard started using his own products! Well, it doesn't matter now, he's deceased." Curtis was pacing back and forth. Detective Theodore was relaxing and listening while smoking his half cigar.

"Richard made a lot of broken promises to his brother Dupree! Dupree wanted to make him some quick cash, so Richard would have his brother Dupree delivers his drugs for him."

"What kind of drugs?"

"Pills and crack whatever Richard had, he gave Dupree to sell. Richard told his brother that he would give him ten percent out of fifty percent, which Dupree had no choice really because Dupree wanted a car at the time!"

Detective Theodore was relighting his half cigar wearing his dark brown overcoat, while sitting on Curtis's tiger-skin covered couch crossing one leg up over his knee.

"Dupree is the quiet type, and he wouldn't hurt a fly."

"One more thing... Can you tell me what happened at the Bam bar?"

"Well, Dupree came in and walked up to Richard and whispered in his ear, then Richard had got up from his seat and yelled at his brother who left out the Bam bar pissed off!"

"Well, thank you for your help, Curtis!" Theodore stood up and walked toward the front door.

"Anytime, Lieutenant," Curtis said in his soft girly voice.

"I'll be in touch!" Detective Theodore said, walking out Curtis's front door and giggling a little.

Meanwhile, Jimmy was calling his brother.

"What's wrong, Jimmy?" his brother Louis asked.

"Have you heard the bad news?"

"What happened?"

"Our son Richard was murdered last night!"

"Oh my God, Jimmy! I'll send Donny over there right away to be with you both!" he said nervously and he had hung up from his brother Jimmy.

Louis began dialing his firstborn son and daughter-in-law.

"Hi, Dad."

"I have bad news, Son! You're cousin Richard was killed last night!"

"Calm down, Dad!"

"I need you to go over to your uncle's place today please, son!"

"Of course, Dad. Susan, come in here!" His wife comes rushing from the kitchen.

"Uncle Jimmy's son Richard was killed last night!"

"Oh god, how?"

"I don't know, dear. We're going to go over to my uncle Jimmy's place!" Susan takes her apron off and grabs her purse and keys. "Give him our condolences!"

"All right, Dad! And call me when you get over there!"

"I will, Dad!" And he hangs up with his father.

"Let's go, dear!" And they both walk out their front door and lock it. "You drive, Susan, while I call Cousin Brian on my cell phone!" Donny was rushing to call his cousin while he puts on his seat beat.

"Hello! Brian? Did you hear the bad news?"

"No! Uncle Jimmy's son Richard was killed last night!"

"I heard about that but no name was released!"

"It was my cousin Richard who was killed last night! We're on our way to Uncle Jimmy's place!"

"Oh my god, Angel! You're not going to believe this!"

"What is it?"

"Do you remember hearing about a man that was killed in his home last night? And no name was released?"

"Yes!"

"It's my cousin Richard that was killed last night!"

"What?" Angel shouted. "I'll call you tomorrow, Brian!"

Jimmy gets the Yellow Pages, feeling devastated and confused with tears.

"I thought we were never going to make this call!" he said to wife.

"Jeffrey Mortuary, may I help you?"

"Yes, my name is Jimmy Oxford. I'm calling to make an appointment for arrangements of Richard Oxford?"

"Yes, of course, sir. I have an opening tomorrow at ten o'clock a.m. Would that be a good time for you?" the mortuary man asked.

"That would be just fine," Jimmy said.

"Thank you for calling Jeffrey Mortuary." Jimmy hangs up. *Ding-dong.*

"Hello, Donny and Susan!" Jimmy said as they all give each other a hug. Liz breaks down in tears even more.

"We came to help, Uncle," Donny said, standing five nine tall and slim with brown wavy hair a clean shave with no facial hair. He hugged his firstborn nephew.

"Uncle Jimmy, don't worry we're here to help you and Auntie Liz." Susan was giving Liz a hug also.

"We have appointment tomorrow at ten in the morning at the Jeffrey Mortuary!"

"I'll go with you if you want, Uncle."

"Please, that would be nice, nephew," his uncle said with sorrow.

"Would anyone like something to drink?" Liz asked.

"Yes, please, if it's no trouble?" Susan said. Tears run down Liz's face as she walked away.

"We have cola and iced tea."

"Iced tea would fine!" Susan said. "Thank you. Do you need help getting the tea?"

"You can get the glasses and get the ice from the freezer for me," Liz said, wiping her tears. Susan then follows Liz into the kitchen.

"Uncle, do you know why he was murdered?" Donny whispered with concern.

"No, just that he was stabbed and that the killer—" Jimmy began crying harder.

Donny was rubbing his uncle Jimmy's back to make him feel better.

"The detective that was here said that the killer cut his private part off and pushed it in his mouth while he was dying," Jimmy whispered and he broke down, crying with sorrow. "Take a deep breath, Uncle!"

Susan and Liz walks out with four tall glasses of iced tea and sets the iced tea on the table and sits next to her auntie-in-law and hands Liz a glass of iced tea.

"Is it okay if we'll stay the night, if you both don't mind?" Donny said to Auntie.

"Yes, we would like that!" Liz said.

"Knock, knock, Liz are you home?" A neighbor was yelling at the front door.

"Excuse me." She gets up and opens the front door.

"Liz! I just heard the news. I am so sorry to hear about your son!" And she gave Liz a hug. "My daughter Julie called and told me it's your son that got killed last night and how are you holding up?"

"It's very devastating!"

"Uncle Jimmy, we'll be right back. We're going to go home and get some change of clothes so we can stay a couple of nights and help out!"

"Thanks, Donny!"

"Come on, Susan."

"Oh, excuse me. This is my neighbor June!"

"Hello, nice to meet you," Donny and his wife said. "We will be right back, okay?" "That's fine," his uncle Jimmy said in sorrow as their neighbor was sitting with them, feeling sad and confused.

Thirty minutes later, Donny and Susan return to stay a few nights.

"Liz, Donny and Susan are back!" Donny comes walking in with some food and their change of clothes.

"Donny, you can put your things in the guest room down the hall on the right," Liz said sadly.

"Aunt Liz, would you like me to help cook lunch and dinner?"

"That would be very nice of you, Susan, there are chicken wings in the refrigerator ready to be cooked!" Liz said, feeling too depressed to cook. "And there's also salad to be made."

"I'll get lunch started," Susan said.

Donny walks back into the living room and sat next to his uncle Jimmy and gives him a big hug while their next-door neighbor June was giving Liz comfort and support.

"I better go before my husband starts wondering about me," the neighbor said. "I'll see you tomorrow, Liz! And God bless you both!" June gives Liz a long hug and walks out the front door.

"Where's my cousin Dupree?"

"He had to leave to get his car fixed. He was devastated hearing about his brother's death. Dupree hasn't been staying home lately. I think he has a new girlfriend!" Liz said.

"I haven't seen my cousin in a while! When they were young, Dupree and Richard would always be together as brothers, and they loved each other even when they used to fight a lot over that blue football!" Liz had a small grin on her face from memories.

"Yes, these were some good times and Richard used to tell his brother he was too young to play with his friends! Dupree would follow Richard and his friends around, and I remember they used to ride their bikes in the streets and race each other." Liz had a little laugh from the memories her beloved son.

"When Dupree used to wear Richards's clothes that were too big for him and Richard would come home and take his clothes off Dupree! One other time, Richard came home from school and starts a fight with his brother about wearing his clothes and plays with Richard's toys and Dupree always wanted to be like his big brother. Yes!" Jimmy said with sorrow in his heart.

"Remember Dupree wanted to sleep with his brother, but Richard would make him sleep in his own bed and they would fight about that, so Richard decide to let Dupree sleep with him till he fell asleep and then Richard would carry Dupree to his own bed!

"It was so funny because when Dupree woke up and noticed he was in his own bed, he would jump up and get into Richard's bed after he went to school," Liz said with a small grin on her face while trying to hold up her tears.

"Dinner is almost ready!" Susan said, walking out the kitchen.

"Thank you, dear!" The memories continued through the evening. The next morning, they all got ready to go to the mortuary. Thirty minutes later, they arrive at the funeral home.

Donny parks his vehicle while Jimmy and Liz were trying to compose themselves. Jimmy gets out and walks around the car and opens the car door on the right side to walk with his wife Liz; they all walked toward the mortuary front door while Donny holds the door open for them and they walk in, looking around and feeling how peaceful it felt.

"Hello, I'm Mr. Jeffrey White, the funeral director."

"We're the Oxfords. This is my nephew and his wife!"

"Yes, Mr. Oxford, this way please," They followed into his office. "First, we give you our condolences."

"Thank you," they all said.

"What's the deceased's full name?"

"Our son, Richard Oxford!"

"Here is a book you can look through for the obituary and full services and also the casket prices!" Jimmy and Liz started looking into the book that Mr. White handed to Jimmy gently.

"We have general price listing for embalming that costs four hundred and the casket prices are five thousand to seven thousand," Mr. White said. "What kind of life insurance do you carry?"

"State life insurance," Jimmy said.

"And how much is the life insurance policy for?"

"We have fifty thousand dollars full coverage policies for our family!" Jimmy said sadly. "May I take a look at the policy?"

"Yes, of course, and here's the state life insurance policies." Jimmy pulls out the paperwork from his pocket and hands the insurance policy to Mr. White who started reading through the policy.

"Thank you," Mr. White said.

"Which day next week would you like your son's services?" Mr. White asked.

"Um, next week would be fine!" Jimmy said.

"We have an opening next Thursday at one p.m." Mr. Jeffrey White said.

"Is that fine, dear?" Jimmy asked his wife, who was not taking it too well.

"Now one of you or all can come and pick out the casket for your loved one, and will you be bringing his suit or do you want us to handle it?"

"We can bring one of his suits!" Jimmy said.

"If you just follow me again," Mr. White said. Liz was feeling very depressed and devastated. "Here we go." They all walked into a room full of different color caskets.

"Does this include the burial and the hearse?"

"Yes, everything in one package," Mr. White said.

"Look at all these caskets!" Donny said as they walked into the room, looking around. "What's the price for this one?" Jimmy asked.

"That's for five thousand dollars."

"We'll take this one with white and silk all around with gold trimming," Jimmy said. "That's a NE7 Gold Cross casket." They all walked out the room while Mr. White closed the door from behind him. "Okay, I'll pull up the paperwork, and will there be a wake before the service?" Mr. White asked.

"Yes, that would be fine."

"The wake would be from nine a.m. till five p.m." Mr. White said. "All right, let's go back to my office and get started with the paperwork!" Jimmy and Liz walk into Mr. White's office. "The visitation wake for two days cost two hundred and twenty-five dollars and the casket will be five thousand dollars! The service will be seven thousand and thirty five dollars with the hearse. We also have a nice cemetery five miles from here," Mr. White said. "And the hearse will be at your residences one hour before the service. Alone with the repast dinner at the Oxford Residences, is that correct?"

"Yes, that's fine," Jimmy said.

"And how would you like the program in loving memory of Richard Oxford?"

"With a picture." Jimmy then pulls out his wallet and hands Mr. White a picture of Richard on his birthday, smiling and cheerful.

"All right, everything is set for next week," Mr. White said.

"And this is my nephew Donny and his wife Susan."

"Nice to meet you both, Donny." They shake his hand.

"Well, thank you coming and for choosing Jeffrey's Mortuary. And we will be seeing you next week." They all walked out the funeral home to the parking lot toward their white four-door Nissan, holding each other.

"Donny, I need a favor!" his uncle Jimmy said.

"Sure, anything!"

His uncle Jimmy was looking depressed as he was helping his wife Liz into Susan's white 1999 Nissan car. "I need you to go to the morgue and get Richard's belongings? And we need to get a suit from his place! I can't do it! We can't take any more heartache right now!"

"No problem. I can do it today and let my wife Susan cook for you both some lunch, and try to relax, Uncle, while I'll go and handle that!" Donny said.

"Thank you, nephew, for helping us." He gave his nephew Donny a long hug and they both got into Susan's car and put their seat beats on, and she starts the car and puts it into reverse and then into drive to get to the main streets as they all stayed silent all through the ride. Liz was sniffling with tears.

Twenty minutes later, they arrive to their residence. And they both take off their seat belts and open the car doors. Jimmy helps his wife out the car and starts walking toward their front door. Jimmy pulls out his house keys and unlocks the front door, so everyone can walk in and take a seat in the living room to relax. Donny asks Susan to come into their guest room for a couple of minutes.

"Susan, there's something I have to go do for my uncle really quick."

"What is it?" Donny began rubbing his wife's arm with his right hand.

"My uncle Jimmy asked me to go get Richard's property and keys so he can pick out a suit for Richard!"

"So you have to go to his place too?"

"Maybe tomorrow, okay?" Donny said in a quiet voice, trying to stay strong.

"We are here to help." They gave each other a hug. "When this is all over, we'll go out to dinner and go somewhere special, the two of us, okay?" Donny said to his pretty wife. "That sounds nice," Susan said. "Just stay by my side, and after that, you want to get remarried?" Susan starts laughing, holding her husband.

"Oh, you want to get married again?" He was playing with his wife; they both grinned while holding each other tightly. And he slaps her on the butt cheek and gives her a kiss. "Now I have to go and I need you to help Auntie Liz with lunch, and I will be back as soon as possible. I love you!" They both walk out the room, holding hands for a moment, and close the door behind them and Susan walks to the kitchen to wash her hands and start cooking chicken for lunch. Susan feels that hot passion from her husband who always had been in love with each other since they met.

"Nephew, I wanted to give you this money for gas!"

"I have gas money, Uncle, don't worry about it!"

"Donny, you're a good man, and God bless you for helping us." Liz grabs his hand and gives him a hug.

"I love my family in good times and bad times," Donny said.

"How is my brother Louis really doing? He's still working at the plant! I've talked to him earlier and he sounds good, his uncle Jimmy said. "He just has been busy."

"My wife Susan is cooking you both lunch and I'll be back real soon."

"Thank you, nephew!" Donny walks out the front door and walks to his wife's white four-door Nissan car and starts it up and drives off going south to get to Main Street. Donny began thinking, *Who would murder my cousin Richard?* Donny turns on the radio. *I remember partying with Richard last year, and it was cool for a moment, but then when I noticed he was also doing crack, I quit hanging with him. There's no telling what else he was into and it will all come out soon!* Donny was thinking. *I haven't seen Cousin Richard since last year, and now I'm going to go see him dead! This is devastating to our family.* Fifteen minutes later, Donny arrives at the city morgue and parks. He sits there for a few seconds, opens the car door and steps out.

He walks toward the morgue building down the street from the police department and walks in and notice the pointing arrows to the morgue. Donny starts following the arrows to a door that has Morgue on it. Donny starts clearing his throat and starts getting a little nervous as he opens the door to the morgue. "May I help you?" the coroner asked.

"Yes, I'm here for Richard Oxford's belongings and to identify the remains," Donny said in a nervous way.

"Yes, of course, over here." The coroner opens a large drawer with Richard's body. Donny walks closer to his cousin's frozen body and just stares at Richard.

"Are you all right, sir?" the Coroner asked.

"Yes! I just never had seen a dead person before and the smell is awful," Donny said in a nervous way. The coroner closes the drawer of Richard's deceased body and picks up a sheet of paper to read.

"And here are his belongings, and could you sign here please!" the coroner asked.

"Yes, of course!" Donny stood still in shock and gets Richard's belongings and walks out the morgue, releasing a deep breath. He was bent down against the morgue building wall to pull himself together for a moment and begin walking toward the front door.

"Hello, are you here for Richard Oxford?"

"Yes, who are you?" Donny asked.

"Detective Theodore, I'm working on the case of Richard Oxford." Detective Theodore shows his silver badge.

"May I ask who are you to the Oxford family?"

"I'm his first cousin Donny Oxford."

"Oh, all right. Sorry about your cousin Richard." He was holding his lit cigar in his left hand.

"When was the last time you saw Richard alive?"

"That's funny you asked that question because on my way here, I was just thinking about the last time I've seen him!"

"Oh really, when was that?"

"Last year, we went to his friend's house, and let me tell you, I decided not to hang with my cousin Richard. May God rest his soul."

"What happened?" Detective Theodore asked in a surprised way. Donny walks up closer to Detective Theodore.

"Well, it doesn't matter now, but Cousin Richard was into some serious drugs."

"Oh really, what kind of drugs?"

"Different types of drugs and liquor of course. The last time I saw my cousin was at a party across town and I loved and cared for my cousin Richard because we grew up together! Detective, can I ask you a question?"

"Sure!" Detective Theodore said.

"I heard that the killer castrated his private part off."

"I'm afraid so, Donny, and I think it's the killer's message."

"What's the message, Detective?"

"I have to find out who is mad at him first and why," Detective said.

"And that would be the motive," Donny said.

"And I have the motive," Detective Theodore said.

"What's the motive?" Donny asked. "Let's go have a seat over here." They both walk over to a wooden bench in the building and they both sat down.

"Richard Oxford was gay!" Detective whispered.

"What? No way, man!" Donny yelled.

"Yes, and that's the motive of why his private was cut off and put into his mouth. Now I know this is hard for you. But you being his cousin, you should know the truth and you seem like a nice guy!" Detective said.

"Well, the only reason I'm here is because my uncle asks me to pick up his belongings and I've seen my cousin Richard dead a few moments ago! I'm glad I ran into you, Detective, and now I know the truth!

"What about your cousin Dupree?"

"I don't know. I haven't seen my cousin Dupree since Richard's birthday party and that was January of this year," Donny said.

"Well, it was nice meeting you," Detective Theodore said. They both shake hands.

"Thank you, Detective, and I'll keep this to myself about my cousin." And Donny walked out the building to his wife's car and gets his keys out his pocket and unlocks the car door and opens the door and gets into the car and starts it up and sits there for a moment with more shocking and surprising news. He lays his head back in the driver's seat, taking a deep breath before he decides to drive off. He puts his seat belt on and puts the car in reverse and looks behind him and reverses and then puts the gear into drive and drives to the main street.

"I like that Detective Theodore, and I got my answer right away about Richard. Thank you, God!" Donny drives toward the north area. "I can't believe my cousin was gay! And that the killer put his private in his mouth while he was still alive! Maybe his last gay lover killed him for messing around. Or maybe he was messing with another man's wife? That would be the reason the killer put his private in his mouth and stabbed him many times, my poor cousin lying in the morgue. Wow, what an afternoon this has been!" Donny was thinking. "Just a couple of blocks more to Uncle's house and I have Richard's belongings. I'm glad it's my day off from work. I wonder why he was asking about cousin

Dupree? I hope my cousin is back from getting his car fixed. I would like to see Dupree. It's been about six months since I've seen my cousin like I told the detective. I know he's upset about his brother Richard when he heard the news." As Donny turns right and parks his wife's car across the street from his uncle's house and turns the motor off and takes off his seat belt and opens the car door and gets out and locks it with the alarm. He walks toward his uncle Jimmy and aunt's Liz house, and he knocks on the door.

"Come in!" they both yelled softly. Donny walks in, wiping his eyes.

"It was him. I identified Richard and brought back his belongings," Donny said sadly. "Donny! Are you sure it was Richard?"

"I haven't seen him since his birthday this year, but I recognized him, and I'm sorry to say it was my cousin Richard. I only saw his head. The sheet was covering the rest of his remains, and here are his belongings." Donny hands a big yellow envelope to his uncle and Jimmy opens the envelope and sees his son's robe, no underpants and no keys!

"You have to remember he was killed in his home," Donny said.

"Oh, that's right! I forget that detective told me!"

"I like Detective Theodore!" Donny said.

"Yes, he's on top of this crime!" his uncle said.

"I met him about forty-five minutes ago!"

"Where?"

"At the morgue when I was leaving. He seems cool."

"What did he look like?" his uncle asked.

"He has dark brown hair and tall, maybe five eight, wearing a brown suit with a brown jacket and dress shoes. And an unlit cigar! Why? Did he come by already?"

"No! Did he ask you anything about Richard?"

"Yes, but I told him the truth! The last time I've seen my cousin Richard was his last birthday. I was hoping Dupree was here before I got back."

"No, we haven't heard from him since we told him about his brother Richard!" Liz said.

"I know he is very upset right now and he just had to get away for a moment! He'll be back!" his uncle jimmy said.

"Well, I need to call that detective to get into Richard's place to get that suit over to the morgue." Susan walks out the guest room. "Hey, baby!" And they kiss for a moment. They both had lunch with pork chops with cabbage and corn bread.

"I thought you were cooking chicken?"

"Liz changed her mind and your lunch is still warm. Are you hungry?"

"Oh yes, and I'm going to go wash my hands and eat lunch before I do anything else! Where is Auntie Liz?"

"She's lying down!"

"Oh okay." Jimmy was calling the detective to get the keys while Donny was washing his hands in the bathroom. Susan was getting his lunch on the table and pouring him some Gatorade in a glass and sat his lunch on the table. Donny walks out the bathroom. "Susan, come here for a second!" As they both walked into their guest bedroom, he closes the door behind them. Donny looked a little worried.

"What's wrong?"

"Susan, I ran into a Detective Theodore and he told me something!" Donny whispered. "Now we can't let my uncle or auntie know about this!"

"What is it?"

"Detective Theodore had told me that my cousin Richard was gay! And I know about the drugs he used! My cousin was into a lot of things and we can't let the family know about this?"

"You're right!" his wife said. "Are they a religious family?"

"They go every Sunday and they think their kids are angels! And they could never find out the truth! It would kill them! Dupree is living a good life, but Richard was living a totally different life!" Donny then gets up to go eat his lunch and spend time with his uncle.

Meanwhile, Joanna was still upset about the incident and couldn't concentrate at work for her heart was changing for the worst. Thinking about what to do about her husband Alan, that he may be going to jail for the rest of his life! *And I would lose everything.* She didn't even hear the phone ringing.

"Oh, hello! Yes, your order is here, Ms. Hopper. I'll be here till six p.m., then we'll close. Thank you." Joanna hung the phone up. *It's one thirty. I need to think hard and fast about my future! This job is not going to pay all bills and a house note and car note. Let me call this fool!* Joanna picks up her cell phone and calls her husband. *Ring.*

"Yes, dear!" Alan answered.

"I just called to see if you were all right!" Joanna said.

"I'm just trying to do some work," Alan said in a slow voice.

"That Detective Theodore coming around doesn't help?" Joanna said.

"Not seeing him is a big release to me."

"I'm sorry about your friend Richard."

"It feels strange with Richard, not seeing him here or in his office," Alan said.

"Yes, I'm sure!"

"I'll see you after work," Alan said.

"Well, I have to go do something, then I'll be home to make dinner."

"All right," Alan said in a low voice, and he hung up his cell phone.

"Let me call Lisa and see if she got paid yet!" Her cell phone rings.

"Hello!"

"Lisa! You get paid yet?" Alan asked his sister.

"No, brother, you'll have to wait till tonight!" Lisa was shouting at her brother. Alan started laughing.

"I'm just playing with you," Alan said.

"Well, I also have a date tonight!" Lisa said.

"With whom?" he asked with curiosity.

"None of your beeswax," she said.

"I'm so glad it is Friday!"

"Why? So you can go spend my money on some clothes and shoes?" Alan said.

"Yes, and I'm going to be looking good tonight, brother, with my date!" Lisa was teasing her brother over the phone.

"Lisa, we have to talk. It's serious!"

"What's going on, Alan? You know you can talk to me anytime, brother!"

"Yes, I know, little sister, but this is serious! How about tomorrow when you're not on one of your dates?" Alan said.

"That will be fine. I'll be home in the morning, you can come over for breakfast!"

"And you can give me my money!" Alan said.

"Yes, brother. I have my check. I just need to get to the bank to cash it! I'll take you in the morning about nine, so we can talk!"

"That's cool! We need to spend time together!"

"Have you heard from Mom and Dad?"

"Yes. They're back from Cactus Lake, and they are staying on their second honeymoon for a week!"

"I hope someday I meet someone that loves to travel and keep me happy!"

"Now be careful, little sister, for what you ask for it may come true!"

They both laughed. "I'll see you in the morning," Alan said as he hangs up. Lisa was still laughing as she closed her cell phone. Her phone rings again.

"Hello, James!"

"Are you ready for tonight?"

"Yes, I'll be ready," she said with a grin on her face.

"I'll pick you up around seven this evening?" James asked.

"Yes," Lisa said in a slow voice.

"You sound so sexy," James said.

"And so do you!" Lisa said.

"I will see you tonight!" James said and they both hang up. Lisa looks at the clock on the wall of her job. "It's a quarter till two p.m. please let this day go by fast," Lisa said to herself as customers walked in. "Welcome!" Lisa said to the customers. "May I help you with something?"

"Yes, I'm looking for something to wear to a wedding."

"What size, miss?"

"Size 10 in the waist. I'm looking for a long blue and yellow dress," the customer said. "This shop is nice," the customers said.

"Thank you," Lisa said. "I'll be right with you," she said to another customer. While Lisa was serving her customers, her two friends Diana and Dana, the twin sisters, walk in, laughing with each other. While the twins begin walking around, looking at the new fashioned outfits. Her two best friends Dana and Diana noticed Lisa with a customer. Lisa then noticed her best friends.

"What are you two doing here? What a surprise." Lisa gives them a hug.

Both were wearing their matching black vest and black low-cut blouses and gray pantsuit with a black belt around their small waist with thin legs with their matching black high heels.

"Let's check out the new outfits!" Dana said. "So you're going out tonight with your new friend?"

"What's his name? James?" Diana asked.

"Have to find something sexy to wear tonight and James is very handsome!"

"What does he do?" Diana asked while her twin Dana was checking out all the new outfits.

"He stands six feet and he's African American and he works for the Brookville fire department!"

"Does he know you're a white girl?" They both laughed with the joke.

"Yes, I told you both over the phone how we met over my brother's place," Lisa said. "Excuse me, is this dress on sale?" a customer asked.

"Yes, its five percent off sale."

"Thank you," the customer said.

"So are you guys going out to dinner and a movie?" Diana asked.

"We're going over to his place for a drink and have sex all night!" They both were laughing hard.

"Diana! Buy me these sparkling short pants outfit for twenty bucks?"

"Dana, you have some money!"

"Who was born first?"

"I was born first and then Dana came out trying to kick me in the head." They both laughed.

"How are your parents doing?

"All right. They're still working from paycheck to paycheck!"

"And you both are still spoiled!"

"Of course, they had us and they are proud parents," Diana said. Lisa walked behind the counter to the cash register. "That would be nineteen dollars and eight one cents please! Thank you come again!" Lisa said.

"How old are you both now?"

"Twenty years old," Dana said.

"Remember hanging together in school and flirting with the boys and they were afraid to talk to us. Those were the fun school days."

"You both going out tonight?"

"We are going to hang out at the frizzy club with your cousin Gail who loves to flirt!" They both laughed.

"Have fun tonight, twins!" They give each other a big hug.

"Call me in the morning and let me know how it went!" Lisa said.

"Bye!" The twins left together, walking out the Quotable women store.

Detective Theodore returns to Alan's employment and rushes up to the reception desk. "Mr. Jones in today?"

"Do you have appointment?"

"No, but it will be just a second. I just want to show him something." Detective Theodore was holding a large yellow envelope in his right hand.

"I'll let him know you're here."

"Mr. Jones!" Detective Theodore walks straight into Mr. Jones's office.

"I have a theory!" Alan looked surprised with fear.

"Lieutenant!"

"This would just take a minute. It's very important, sir!" Detective Theodore pulls out one large ten by twelve photo.

"I just want to bring something to your attention about the marks and dent on your Lincoln?"

"What about it, Lieutenant?" His heartbeat began beating faster.

"What I noticed here on the hood of your vehicle. It looks like a body landed on top rather than a concrete pole." The detective was pointing at the picture.

"The front top of your vehicle keeps bugging me to where I can't sleep last night!" Detective Theodore was showing his emotions, putting his hand up to his right temple. And he was thinking, *Mr. Jones, that's the only way the victim's ribs got broken. Is that Mr. Johnson's body that landed on a vehicle that was going to fast or weren't you paying attention to the road?*

"What do you think, Mr. Jones, about my theory?" Alan begin looking pinkish in his face with frustration burning through his fear.

"Now look, Lieutenant! I have work to do while you're coming in here without an appointment! Please leave, Detective, and take your damn theory with you!" Alan was furiously aggravated with frustration that hit his unraveled nerves.

Detective Theodore stares at Alan while chewing on his unlit half cigar.

"Oh, there's another thing! The tire and foot cast from the ground by the scene, but I'll talk to you another time about that!" Detective Theodore turns around and walks out of Alan's office and walks past the receptionist smiling. The detective pushed the elevator button to the garage floor and walks fast to his vehicle to rush to his captain. Lieutenant Theodore jumps into his police vehicle and drives toward Brookville police department. *I wonder if this picture is enough evidence to arrest him on suspicion of hit and bury and and murder! I'm going to keep him under pressure and I'm on to his fear of lies also.* Ten minutes later, he arrives at the police station and parks his vehicle and gets out and starts walking toward the door of the Brookville police department and walks into his captain's office.

Change of Heart

"Hi, Captain, I have a question if you have a moment?" Lieutenant Theodore said.

"With this photo and the tire and foot cast, do I have enough evidence to arrest Mr. Alan Jones for suspicion of murder?"

"No way, This won't hold in court. It's just a picture of a dent on a car. Maybe the tire cast that match the shoes he was wearing that evening. Just get me more proof!" his captain yelled.

"This is not enough to even pull him in court. The judge would let him go. That's not enough evidence!"

"I'll keep on it, Captain." He walks out his captain's office for more evidences. "I'm going back to the scene of the crime. Maybe I missed something, also I need to find the shovel or other object tool that he used to bury Mr. Johnson. Maybe it's still in the trunk of his vehicle. That would be proof enough to stand in court! So I would need a search warrant to his vehicle and his property." The detective snaps his two right fingers and turned around, walking back to his captain's office.

"Lieutenant Theodore, I though you left the building!"

"Captain! Can I get a warrant to search the vehicle of Mr. Jones?"

"What do you have, Theodore?"

"I just had a thought about the tool he had to used to dig a hole to bury Mr. Johnson with. And it hit me, a shovel or another tool? I would like to look inside of the trunk of his vehicle that I never checked out, and I have a hunch, Captain, that the evidence is right there just waiting!"

"I'll get you the warrant! It sounds like you're on to something just bring me more evidence!"

"Yes, Captain." Lieutenant Theodore rushes out of his captain's office once again, feeling confident while walking to his office to wait for the warrant. "I got him now!" While he sits behind his desk waiting, his office phone rings.

"Theodore speaking!"

"Detective Theodore, this is Mr. Jimmy Oxford!"

"What can I do for you?"

"I'm calling you to see if you have the keys to my son Richard's place so we can get a suit for his service and send it over to the funeral home?"

"I think we do have his house keys for fingerprints and you can meet me there in about fifteen minutes!"

"That would be fine, Detective," Jimmy said in a polite way.

"By the time I get there and back, the warrant should be here by then." As he gets up from his seat, he grabs his keys from his desk and walks out with his unlit cigar. He walks to his car and drives toward north. Fifteen minutes later, the lieutenant drives up to Richard's residence and notices Donny and his uncle Jimmy sitting in a four-door white Nissan. Detective Theodore gets out his vehicle and walks toward Richard's residence.

"Hello, Detective!"

"Well! Hello, Donny. Good to see you again."

"Thank you, Detective, for the keys," Jimmy said.

"Detective Theodore, I haven't said anything to my uncle Jimmy."

"One other thing: when is your cousin Richard's services?"

"It's next Thursday at eleven a.m. at Jeffery's Funeral Home!"

"Okay. Thank you." They shake hands.

"I'm going to sit and wait for Uncle Jimmy!"

"I don't blame you, you're a good man! I'll see you around," Detective Theodore said and he starts his car while he waves at them, driving off. Donny was standing there, watching his uncle carrying his deceased son's dark pressed blue suit and walks out and locks the front door while his tears drop.

"His place smells really bad. It needs to be aired out!" Jimmy was coughing from the smell.

"Are you all right, Uncle?"

"I'm all right. Let's get out of here!" They both jump into Susan's car and start the motor and drive off slowly.

"I want to know who and why they castrated his private part," Jimmy said.

Donny started driving toward his uncle's place.

"Where are you going?"

"To your place?"

"No! We have to drop this suit off at the funeral home."

"Let me turn around and get back on Road 15."

Detective Theodore then drives back to the police station to see if the warrant came, so he can go to Alan's residence. Fifteen minutes later, he arrives at the police station and parks his vehicle and gets out and locks it and walks into the police station toward his office. "Lieutenant! I put that warrant on your desk from the judge!"

"Thanks, Officer!" And he rushes to his office and picks up the warrant and walks to the front desk.

"Sergeant! I need a couple officers to come with me on a search warrant. Officers Brine and Whaley, I need you both to come with me!"

"All right, Lieutenant!" Both officers repeated.

Wearing their pressed beige uniform shirts with their silver badges on their left sides And wearing their gun holsters on their left side of their pressed black pants uniforms.

"Where are we going, Lieutenant?"

"We are going to do a search on Mr. Alan Jones's property and vehicle!" The officer starts his police unit and follows behind the lieutenant's vehicle, and they drive out the parking lot of the Brookville police department, which turns on Highway 21 to the north beachside. Fifteen minutes later, the lieutenant arrives to 2323 River View Drive and parks in front of the residence and gets out of their vehicles and walks toward Alan Jones's residence and rings the doorbell. Its three fifteen in the afternoon'. The detective hears a radio in the kitchen window and a police officer knocks hard on the front door. Josephine rushes to answers the door.

"May I assist you, officers?"

"I have here a warrant to search Mr. Alan Jones's Lincoln Navigator. Is it still in the garage?" Lieutenant Theodore asked politely.

"Patrick, come out here!" Lieutenant Theodore walks to the side garage door.

Josephine rushes out the kitchen to the back door that leads to the side garage door.

"What are you looking for?" Josephine asked with panic. Lieutenant Theodore started looking for a shovel in the garage.

"Do you have the keys to this Lincoln?"

"No, Detective!"

"Alan has his keys with him!" Josephine said with anguish and anger.

"Officer! I want you to look around in the backyard for a shovel or any other big object that digs or has dirt on it!"

"Yes, Lieutenant!" The officers walk into their backyard while Patrick came outside by the garage.

"I've called Alan and Joanna, and they both are on their way home! Detective, what's all this about?" Patrick shouted.

"What are you looking for?"

"Can I have you both stand back please?" Lieutenant Theodore said in a polite way as they both take a step back.

"So you said Mr. Jones is on his way here?"

"Yes, I've told him you were here with a search warrant, and I told him to come home right away!" Patrick said in his deep heavy voice. Lieutenant Theodore begins looking around all in the corners of the garage.

"Detective Theodore! There's a locked tool shed in the backyard!" an officer yelled.

"All right. I'll ask him to open it, and if he refuses, we will cut it open!"

"Lieutenant! What is this really all about?" Josephine asked anxiously.

"Well, do you remember the accident a couple of weeks ago on Highway 15? Well, I think it was your nephew that hit and buried Mr. Johnson, who was breathing at the time, and he buried the victim alive and that's murder!"

"Oh, that's a lie!" Patrick burst out with anger! Josephine felt devastated, faintish, and began fanning herself.

"You are lying, Detective! Our nephew would never do anything like that! You have him all wrong!" Patrick shouted in anger. "Alan would have told us if something like that had happened! Why don't you go find the real person that did this crime?" Patrick was furious and angry. Fifteen minutes later, Alan drives up with anger.

"What the hell is going on here, Detective! What are you doing here?" Alan yelled! He slammed his car door while Joanna drives up, parking her dark blue 1999 Tahoe Hybrid vehicle and gets out, rushing toward Josephine.

"Are you all right?"

"We're fine, dear!" Alan begins shouting at Detective Theodore and walks into their home through the kitchen sliding door and close it behind him. He already knew why they were there!

Alan was fussing at the lieutenant about coming on his property, "Mr. Jones, I have a search warrant to search your vehicle." Lieutenant Theodore hands Alan a piece of paper. Alan begins reading the warrant: a shovel or object.

"I have done nothing! But you keep hounding my ass! I'll open my vehicle and you can search all you want! Then you get the hell off my property! Before I call my lawyer!" Alan shouted.

Alan opens up the driver side of his dark blue Lincoln Navigator and pops open the back hitch.

"Take a good look, Lieutenant! There's nothing in there, all clean, so whatever you're looking for is just your imagination!" Alan said with anger. "Is that all, Detective?"

"No! I also need to take a look in your tool shed in the back."

"Why? What do you think you're going find, Lieutenant? I have nothing to hide," Alan said with anger.

"I think you used a shovel or an object to dig a hole that night and I think you are hiding that shovel or object…and I'm going to find it to prove I was right!" Lieutenant Theodore said with confidence.

"I have this warrant to search your property, so can you please open your tool shed?" Detective Theodore said. Alan then walks to his tool shed, looking through his keys to open the tool shed, and opens the single wooden painted white door as the lieutenant walks into the tool shed and started looking around, and but he didn't find a shovel or a digging object; the tool shed was clean, just an edge tool and a chain saw and a electric drill and a lawn mower. Lieutenant Theodore felt a little disappointed. "Well, Mr. Jones! You win! I thought I had you this time! Unfortunately, I didn't find what I was looking for, so I'll be on my way." And the detective started walking toward the driveway. The other officers approach as they are leaving. "We didn't find anything, Lieutenant," "Yes, I know!" Detective Theodore said with a little attitude. "Well, maybe next time, I'll catch him in his lies." Detective Theodore walked to his car and sat in his vehicle. "I'm on my way back to the office and try to explain to the captain that I didn't find any shovel with the warrant. He's going to be disappointed at me," the detective said to the officers. The officers drove off going to south toward Highway 15. Alan walks into his house angry. "That goddamn detective keeps coming around causing problems!"

"Alan, you know what that detective told us: he really believes that it's you who killed that man out on Road 20 and I told him he was a liar to even think it was you!" Patrick yelled.

"He just doesn't have anyone else to blame!" Alan said with fear in his eyes.

Joanna was looking straight at Alan and how he could stand there and lie with guilt.

"You look a little tired," Patrick asked.

"I'm going to my room to change my clothes and lay down for a while." Joanna follows her husband to their bedroom.

"I'll be right back, Josephine!" Alan and Joanna walked into their bedroom together and closed the door behind them.

"This is not how to control your paranoid feelings!" his wife yelled.

"What are we going to do about this situation?"

"I don't know. Let me think. I'll come up with something! First, I'm going to put the Lincoln in the shop and have it fixed."

"Great! That would make you look guiltier!" He sits on the edge of their bed with both his hands over his face.

"What was that detective looking for in the Lincoln?" Joanna asked with frustration. Alan gives Joanna a sad look.

"He was looking for the shovel I used that night, but I got rid of it by throwing the shovel in the ocean the next evening." Joanna takes a deep breath with anger.

"Sooner or later, Detective Theodore is going to figure it all out!"

"I would be disappointed and devastated if he's already figured it out that it was me that hit and buried that poor guy that night," he said sadly.

"And when you get arrested, I'll lose you and everything we've have built in this relationship for eleven years!"

"That's all you think about?" Alan raised his voice to her.

"Yes! I lose you and this house, our cars, nothing will ever be the same again! You destroyed our marriage for what you've done!"

"Stop it!" Alan yelled. Josephine and Patrick were listening from the living room; they started getting their things together to leave for the evening.

"Joanna and Alan! Um, we're leaving!" Josephine yelled while holding her purse. Patrick was standing by the front door, looking confused. Joanna tries to say bye in a gentle way, feeling fearful with silence while she hears the front door closes. He was breathing nervously.

"I have to take Lisa to the bank to cash her check tomorrow, and I'm going to tell her everything!"

"Oh great! The whole town is going to know!" Joanna shouted. "You'll be in jail real quick. That's what you want?"

Alan held his head down. "This feels like a nightmare!" Joanna starts changing her clothes she was feeling more aggressive with anger.

"This is a total nightmare!" Joanna said.

"I won't say anything to Lisa," Alan said quietly.

"That would be wise! Till I figure something out," Joanna said. "Don't say anything to Theodore. He's so perspective and determined to get the truth out because that's his daily life!" The house phone rings.

"Hello."

"Hi, Joanna, you're home early."

"I called to remind my brother that the bank opens at nine a.m."

"Yes, I'll tell him Lisa."

Lisa was excited for her date with James.

"Good night, Lisa!" Joanna was trying to feel excited for her young sister-in-law, but no thrills entered her feelings. Lisa was rushing to close the shop for her boss lady who had a meeting to attend and turns on the alarm and locks the shops door and walks to her Lexus and unlocks the driver side and gets in and puts her seat belt on and starts the car and starts northeast. A few moments later, she parks her silver Lexus in her driveway and rushes to her front door to unlock it and she walks in her living room. Lisa then rushes to turned on the shower and walks to her bedroom to find something sexy to wear. Just seconds later, Fluffy the cat walks up to her and she picks her cat up and gives her a kiss and puts her back on the floor.

"Meow!"

"You want some milk, Fluffy?" She pours a little milk in a small bowl; Lisa walks into the living room and picks up the remote to her stereo and turns some music on and walks to her bathroom and gets undressed to get into the hot shower. Five minutes later, she gets out the shower and grabs her yellow towel hanging for a towel rack and dries herself off and looks at her Mickey Mouse clock hanging on her bathroom wall.

It's six twenty-five p.m. She puts on her pink robe and walks to her bedroom with her hair dripping wet. She walks over to her dresser with a round mirror and grabs her hair drier and plugs it up and turns it on. Lisa has her white with greenish flowered cotton mini-dress laid out on her bed with her white high heels pumps and her white stockings. "You're listening to 93.3 rock and roll station," the announcer said. Lisa then started doing a little dance when she can barely hear the music while drying her long golden blonde hair that's past her shoulders. A couple of minutes later, her hair was dried and starts combing her hair back and then puts her mascara and red lipstick to make her smile brighter. "Looking good, Lisa," she said to herself. Then she puts her deodorant and lotion on while she sprays her perfume all over her body. Fluffy comes in licking her gray paws and gray hairs and watches Lisa get dressed. Her cell phone begins ringing with a tune.

"Hello!" James said in his deep voice.

"I'm just about ready, James."

"I'll be there in fifteen minutes," James said.

"I'll see you soon!" Lisa said. Lisa started rushing to get her dress on and her stockings and high heels on and rushed to put more mascara on to see more of her bright brown eyes. Seventeen minutes later, her doorbell rings.

"He's here, Fluffy! I'll get the door." She walks to front door and opens the door with a smile.

"Hello, James!" And he walks in smoothly like a gentleman.

"Hello!" he said smoothly.

"I'll grab my purse and we can go!" James was feeling good and smelling wild with Axe aftershave lotion, with a clean shave, standing proud, looking nice in his cashmere brown sweater, wearing his gold watch that was shining on his wrist, while wearing his pressed blue casual tailored dress pants. A few seconds later, they walk out the front door.

"Good night, Fluffy." She locks her front door and walks to James's car. James, as a gentleman, unlocks the passenger side and opens it for her and gets in and closes her door and rushes around to the driver side and puts his seat belt on and starts his gray 2000 Infinity Qx4 sport utility with tinted windows and drives off putting the radio on with soft music. His right arm was over the passenger seat, looking into his rearview mirror.

"It feels so cozy inside." Lisa starts a conversation about dreams. "Everything we can imagine is possible and plausible."

"That's true!" James said.

"So what do you dream about, James?"

"Well, I dream about going on a cruise as soon as I get all my bills caught up! I'm thinking about taking one this summer like in the next three months," James said.

"That's cool, and are you going alone?" Lisa asked.

"My son who is only seven years old from my first relationship!"

"Do you work tomorrow Saturday?"

"Yes, for a few hours and I'll be thinking about you!" James said while grinning hard. They arrived at the Oceanside

Restaurant that's on an old ship. James parks his vehicle in front of the restaurant and turns his engine off and opens his car door and walks over to Lisa's side and opens the door for her. As he closes the car door and pushes his alarm on, he then grabs Lisa's right hand and walks the restaurant and makes it in as they both hear music and a waiter walks up to them. "How many?" the waiter asked.

"Two please," James said.

"I have a corner table ready," the female waiter said as they both walk to their table and take a seat as the waiter hands them both a menu.

They both started looking through the menus to order.

"Has anyone taken your order yet?" a waitress asked.

"Yes, we would like the crab salad with shrimp and two well done steaks with buttered potatoes and sour cream and a daiquiri please."

"And I'll have a Collins with gin on ice please," James said.

"All right, it will be about fifteen minutes," the waiter said.

"So what do you do at your job?" Lisa asked James.

"I work in the shipping and handling of the FedEx company and I work for the Brooksville fire department. What do you do every day?"

"Well, I work at the Quotable Women Clothing Store. It's been four years now since I finished college! I don't have any children but Fluffy, and I'm single and a very positive person and aggressive in a fun way!"

"What's your sign, Lisa?"

"I'm a Capricorn, the go-getter and has some patience and very wise with ambitious and a humorous personality."

"Very well said!"

"What do you like to do?"

"Go to the beach and watch the waves and feel the sand with my bare feet!" They both laughed while their dinners arrive.

Looking for Love

Forty five minutes later, they finished their dinner and decided to drive over to his place to watch a movie to get more acquainted. Fifteen minutes later, James drives up to his driveway and turns off the engine And then he gets out of his car and walks over to Lisa's side and opens the car door and Lisa gets out of his car and they walks up to his front door. He then opens his door and lets Lisa walk in first, and he closes the door behind him and turns his hall light on.

"You can have a seat on the sofa and I'll turn some music on or would you like to watch a movie?"

"A movie is fine!"

"But after the movie I am going to drive you home so I can get up early for work tomorrow!"

"Are you ready for the movie?" She asked.

And a little while later, James has brought Lisa home, but before she exits the car she inquires. "Will you be going to Alan's friend's service next week?"

"I'll be busy working!"

"All right, give me a call. Good night," Lisa said in a sweet voice. She steps out of his car and starts walking toward her front door while James blows his horn while he was driving off.

Lisa had a big smile on her face while she opens her front door. Fluffy meets her at the door.

"Fluffy baby!" She picks up her calico cat and walks into the kitchen to feed her cat. She then walks to her bedroom to call her friends about her date with James. She starts changing her clothes into her night clothes and turns on her cable television as Fluffy jumps on the bed. Lisa gets her remote control and grabs her cell phone to call her friends Diana and Dana. Lisa turns the channel to a romantic movie.

"Hello, Lisa! So did you go on your date?" Diana asked.

"Yes, and it was nice. First, we went out to dinner, then to his place to drink some wine, and then we watched a movie!"

"Oh my, I hope you used protection!" Diana asked with concern.

"We didn't need it. We didn't do anything!" They both laughed.

"Good for you!" Diana said.

"We're going out to breakfast with our parents, and I'll call when we get back and it's almost eleven p.m.!"

"Good morning to you too, brother! You're looking casual this morning, and you had a haircut. It looks nice," Lisa said with a smile.

"Come on, let's get there before the line gets too long," Alan said.

And a short time later, she exits the bank and reenters the car where she hands her withdrawal. "Thank you. Here is your two hundred dollars!"

"Thanks, sister!" He then puts the money in his back pocket.

"By the way, are you going to your friend Richard's services?"

"Yes! Why? Do you want to go?" His phone suddenly rings and he answers it.

"What is it, Joanna?"

"Where are you?"

"I'm at the bank, is there a problem?"

"I just wanted to tell you Detective Theodore called. He has one more question to ask you!"

"I'll call you back, Joanna!" Alan rushes her off his cell and his fears hit once again. He didn't want to start facing his fear again.

Lisa is watching her brother and queries, "What's wrong, brother?"

"Nothing!" He tries not to look at his sister with the fear in his face as he proceeds to pull into traffic.

"Where are we going now?"

"To my house, I have to get ready to go the fire station."

The signal light turns green, and not long after, he turns off the city streets and onto the freeway.

And a short time later, he reenters the city's traffic system and heads towards his neighborhood, where he pulls his Mustang into his driveway.

Lisa grabs her purse, opens the passenger door, and closes it.

Alan turns off the motor and sits there, thinking it may get a lot worst, worrying that he might get arrested soon.

Guilty Conscience

"Good morning, Joanna!" Lisa said.

"Good morning!" Joanna repeated.

"What's wrong?"

"Nothing!" Joanna said with an attitude. Alan looks at his wife and walks to the living room to pour an early drink.

"So how was your date last night?" Joanna asked.

Lisa begins looking around for her brother. "Let's go into the kitchen." They both walk into the kitchen.

The doorbell rings. *Ding! Dong!*

"Alan, would you get that?" Joanna yells. Alan walks to the front door, feeling fear in his soul. *I'm so tired of this corrupted feeling. I fear it won't go away no matter how hard I've tried. God, please don't let this be that Detective Theodore! He opens his front door.*

"Good morning, nephew!"

"Hi, Auntie Josephine and Uncle Patrick. What a surprise. Come in!" What a release of fear and panic!

He took a deep breath to calm down but before he closes the door he recognizes someone sitting in a gray Victoria with tinted windows seating across the street from his place. But he felt relieved when he notices that it wasn't Detective Theodore.

Lisa, at the same time, was helping Aunt Josephine with their things.

Alan walks away from the door and walks behind his bar to make himself another gin and juice on ice. Uncle Patrick notices what appears to be a strange behavior for his Nephew. "Alan, my boy! How are you feeling?"

"Better now, thank you."

"Isn't it too early to be drinking," his Uncle Patrick said.

"It only eleven forty-five a.m. Oh, what the hell! Make me the same, nephew!"

Josephine gives her husband a harsh look about his drinking.

"What did you say, Patrick?"

"Nothing, dear!"

"What's that about?" Lisa asked.

"He knows we just got out of a prayer meeting at the church!" Josephine yells.

"And Patrick knows better to start drinking this early!"

"That's what's up, Auntie!"

"I have to keep my husband in line every day!"

Lisa started laughing at Patrick as she starts removing food from containers.

"All this food, Auntie. I'm not hungry."

Josephine asks, "Why not?"

"Alan and I went out for breakfast after I had to pay him back the money I borrowed last weekend. I want to tell you about my date with James last night, Alan's friend."

Alan gives Lisa a dashing look and turns his eyes back to his uncle, listening to him talk.

"I'm sorry to hear about your friend Richard!" Patrick, who was standing near the bar, says. "That was a mind blow. Isn't he one of your coworkers and good friends?"

Alan takes a deep breath. "Yes, he was a good worker, it's a devastating mind blower.

I've had just talked with Richard at work this week, and then, cousin Gail came rushing over to tell us that the police and the coroners were at Richard's place; and I went into a little shock when I heard he was murdered!"

"I would have been in shock too if my friend was murdered!" Patrick said while sipping on his gin with ice in his clear glass.

"The killer had to be a psychopath to cut his private off! When is his service?"

"Next Thursday at eleven a.m. at Jeffery Mortuary. I called his family to get the information and I also know his cousin Donny will be there!"

"It's a shame, a murderer is in our town! Oh, I wanted to know if Detective Theodore stopped harassing you?" Alan suddenly becomes silent while trying to ignore the question.

Lisa and Josephine are busy in the kitchen, while Joanna walks down the hallway to the restroom. She is praying that Alan's family wouldn't recognize the fear in their faces.

She walks into their bathroom, feeling more scared, and turns the hot water on and bends over the sink with fright.

"I'm so scared they're going to arrest him." But her obstinate nature won't let her drop a tear. "I have to think of something fast before that nosey Detective Theodore comes and arrests my husband!" Her thoughts were roaming while she was looking in the mirror. "That detective knows Alan did it! That's why he keeps hanging around to put the fear in him! I love him, but I can't lose everything and start at the bottom again!"

"Joanna?"

"What is it, Alan!" she said with no remorse.

"The restroom, please!"

She walks out, looking at him with an attitude, while Alan walks in and closes the door. Patrick continues hiding his gin and juice from his wife who is in and out of the kitchen. Patrick takes a sip of his gin and juice and sets his drink on the side of the end table. Alan walks back into the living room. Joanna looks kind of worried.

"Anything wrong?" Patrick asked.

"Nothing's wrong, Uncle!" Alan said while clearing his throat. Patrick gets up and walks over to his nephew. "Do you have finance problems? If you ever need some money, call me. I can see what we can do for you because I know bills eat our money up too! And with more money, the bills seem to become even larger.

I have a little change in my savings account from my retirement and I can loan you some money to help you out,"

Alan tries to placate his Uncle's concern.

"I just remembered Richard transferred twenty thousand dollars two weeks ago and it should still be in a safe box in my personal account, but how would I explain that money to Joanna? I can't touch that money yet, especially, with that lieutenant around and his smelly lit cigar. He would think I skipped town if he knew about that twenty thousand dollars, and with Richard dead, he would definitely think I've killed Richard for the money. I better not touch it just yet and hope my job don't start snooping around in my accounts." He starts feeling more frustrated.

"Nephew, do you hear me?"

"Oh, yes, Uncle, I hear you and I appreciate that! Thank you for the offer." Patrick then pats his nephew on the shoulders with his heavy right hand and walks back over to the couch and grabs his gin and juice from the side of the couch. Alan looks curiously at his uncle Patrick. "Why do you put your drink down there, Uncle?" He gives a little laugh. "Because I'm afraid of my wife. She will get me while I'm asleep on the sofa. She might be a small-sized woman, but she will punch me hard!"

Alan was laughing hard at his uncle while Josephine walks back to the dinner table to get something and was looking at Patrick with an evil look. She then returned to the kitchen to finish cooking. Alan was laughing even harder, trying to keep his fear out of his thoughts.

"I'll tell you about my wife. She has her mean ways too! Patrick whispered. Alan continued laughing at his uncle. "Man! You give us guys a bad name! Being afraid of a size 4 female, who stands 5'2," while laughing at his uncle.

"She hit me with a skillet once in my head for talking smart to her." Alan was cracking up laughing.

"Uncle, you've made my day!" Alan said while still laughing. Lisa walks out the kitchen. "What are you drinking, and what's so funny?" Lisa asked.

"Uncle is making me laugh. This is too funny!" She turns and walks down the hallway. Patrick gets up for another drink.

"Hurry before my wife comes out!

"That's a shame, Uncle, don't let a woman run over you?"

"Well, when I said I do! I did! And she took control over me since and my money also, and I am stuck with her till death do us apart!" Alan continued laughing, trying to hide his worst fears. The house phone rings. Joanna answered the phone in the kitchen.

"Hello, is Patrick there?"

"Yes, just a minute."

"Bill? It's your friend Patrick!"

"Hey, Bill, what's going on with you, man?" Patrick was on the phone, talking loud, feeling his gin and juice. "Well, come on over and have a drink with me!"

"I'll be there soon," Bill said.

"Come here, Patrick. Come close to me and let me smell your breath," his wife said. Patrick rushes back into the living room. "Patrick, you are terrible! Just can't stop drinking." Alan continued laughing while trying to hide his fear. "Uncle! You're bigger then her. You can take her anytime." His wife Josephine stands up with her hands on her hip. "You try me if you want! And see what happens to you!" she said aggressively. Alan started laughing even harder. Patrick grabs his liquor when Josephine turns her back and walks back into the kitchen. Patrick hides it back on the side of the couch. Joanna walks out the kitchen and to the living room to see what Alan was doing; she hears him laughing.

"It's good to see you laughing for a change! What time do you have to be at the fire station tonight?"

"Not till six p.m."

"Don't worry. I'm not drinking heavy."

"You better not! You still have to drop me off!"

"The fried chicken is almost ready!" Josephine said while Joanna picks up Alan's drink and turns it up to her lips. "The taste that's not strong," he said to his wife. Joanna walks out the living room over to the dinner table.

"The mashed potatoes and brown gravy is ready just waiting for the fried chicken to finish cooking!" Josephine said. Lisa walks back to the kitchen on her cell phone, talking to a friend.

"Alan, do you have to go work for the fire department tonight?" Patrick asked.

"Just for a couple of hours from seven to nine, then the other firemen come on duty." "That's great!" Patrick said. *Ding-dong.* "That's Bill! Let me get the door!"

"Bill, my friend. It's about time. Come on in!"

"I smell chicken cooking!" Bill said.

"Yes! my wife is cooking as usual!" They both walk into the living room. Josephine comes out of the kitchen. "Now, don't let your best friend Bill get you into more trouble!" His wife Josephine walks back into the kitchen. Alan started laughing at his uncle Patrick once again.

"What's going on with your wife this afternoon?" Bill asked.

"Curiosity kills the cat!" Alan starts laughing again, trying to hide his enormous fear that's chewing him up inside!

"Please pour me some gin and juice," Bill asked.

"What's so funny?"

"Oh, my nephew has been laughing at me all afternoon because I don't want Josephine to find out I've been drinking tonight!"

"That's not the reason!" Alan shouted. "Bill? How long have you've known my uncle?" "About twenty years," Bill answers.

"Did you know he's afraid of his own wife!" Alan kept laughing. What's this about?"

"I told Alan about that time Josephine hit me in head with a light skillet." Alan broke down, laughing harder at his uncle.

"It's good to see my brother laughing again. The past week he's been acting quiet! Maybe, it's that detective that's been coming around here," Lisa said.

"Upsetting them both," Josephine said.

"That detective came to my job yesterday asking about that accident last weekend, but I haven't seen him since," Lisa said, getting prepared to cook fried chicken with mashed potatoes and green salad. "Auntie! You're an expert when it comes to romance, you just don't go about it the way most people do."

"Well, when you set out to be irresistible to someone, you don't just grab a pizza and beer. You intimate them in the most stylish and fashionable way. Have a great dinner and tickets to the ballet. If you can't afford all that, don't despair. If anyone can make a pizza and beer romantic, then that man loves you," Josephine said.

"That's quite idealistic, Auntie."

"Just enjoy yourself and keep smiling!"

"Thanks for the advice, Auntie!" She gives her auntie Josephine a big hug.

"That means take a leap of faith. The fried chicken is ready to eat," Josephine said. She sets a full jug of lemonade on the table with six blue swirled-design tall drinking glasses and with six matching blue plates and sterling silverware. "Lunch is ready!" Lisa yells. "Let's go wash up, Uncle." Alan walks into the kitchen to wash his hands to sit at the head of the table. His wife comes out of their bedroom and into the kitchen to help Josephine with the food, while Patrick and his best friend Bill came and sat at the table, ready to serve themselves. Josephine comes out the kitchen carrying a plate full of fried chicken while Joanna walks out the kitchen with fresh green salad with tomatoes, also avocados and uncooked shrimp and with the ranch salad dressing. She takes a seat. Josephine takes her seat and puts her hands together. "Let's thank the lord for this lunch," Everyone bows their heads while Josephine says the Lord's Prayer. "Amen!"

Everyone begins to eat their chicken and salad. *Ding-dong.* Alan's joyous laughter turns into enormous fear! Joanna gets up from the table and walks to the front door and opens it. "Detective!" she said surprised.

"We're just having lunch! Is there something I can do for you, Detective Theodore?" Joanna asked nervously.

"Is your husband home, Mrs. Jones?" Detective Theodore asked politely.

"Um, come in, Detective!" Joanna said nervously. Detective Theodore steps in and notices everyone sitting around the table, having lunch.

"Hello, everyone!" Detective Theodore said, waving his right hand.

"Well, I won't disturb your lunch. I just have one question for Mr. Jones, but I'll come back another time!"

"What this about?" Bill asked.

"Everything smells good," Lieutenant Theodore said with a smile.

"Detective! What's this about?" Bill repeated.

"Oh! It's about the incident last weekend on Highway 15 when a man got killed!" "Lieutenant, we are trying to eat our lunch, do you mind!" Alan shouts with an attitude. "Oh, I'm sorry. I'll just come back another time!" Lieutenant Theodore walks to the front door. "Oh, one more thing, Mr. Jones, what size of shoes do you wear?"

"If you must know, size 10 in shoes, Detective!" Alan says with frustration.

"That will be all for now. Enjoy your lunch!" Detective Theodore said. Detective Theodore leaves in his black trench coat and his unlit cigar. Joanna stares at Alan with a grieving look in her eyes. Alan was feeling a little paranoid as everyone continued eating their dinner in silence.

"Why does that Detective Theodore keep coming around here? I thought he was just checking out the neighborhood," Patrick says. "He came the other day, checking your vehicle in the garage, but what he really is trying to do is put the blame on someone, so he can close his case. He can't find the real person that killed that man! So he comes around here to find someone to blame!"

"I agree with Patrick. That's how they really do it!" Bill says.

"Oh, stop it the both of you!" Josephine shouts.

"He came to my job yesterday, asking questions if I saw something!" Lisa said. "Maybe the other neighbors won't talk to him and that's why he comes here!"

"This lunch is good," Bill says.

"Bill? How's your wife doing?" Lisa asked.

"Oh, she had to go to a meeting for our church this morning and she's happy and doing well," Bill replied. Alan finishes his lunch and takes his plate to the kitchen, takes a deep breath for a few seconds, and walks back to the dining table to finish his lemonade. Joanna stares at him with hatefulness as he walks back into the living room to pour another drink of gin and juice on ice.

Patrick and Bill return to the living room to finish their drinks.

Josephine takes the empty plates into the kitchen, while Joanna sits there, picking at her chicken and salad with her fork, keeping silent, not realizing her left elbow was on the table, feeling feared, trapped, and confused.

"I'm so full now," Lisa said. While rubbing her small belly, she gets up to take her plate in the kitchen.

While drying her hands on a kitchen towel. Lisa walks back into the dining room to get Joanna's plate. "I'm not quite finished," Joanna said in sadness.

"What's wrong?" Lisa asked.

"Nothing's wrong!" Joanna replied and glances at Alan with envy. *You make me cringe now*, she said in her thoughts,

"I need to calm down before someone notices something's not right.

Detective Theodore parks across the street, looking at his watch. "I should be at home with my family," He was thinking as he starts up his car.

Alan looks out of his wide living room window and notices the detective as he leaves. He looks over at Joanna and puts his head down, feeling dreadful.

Bill and Patrick were laughing about something in the past. "Do you remember that, Patrick?"

"I sure do, Bill."

"Alan, pour me another gin and juice with ice, please." Bill demanded in a polite manner. The house phone begins ringing. Josephine answers. "Hello? Lynn, where are you?" Josephine asked her older sister, Lisa and Alan's mother, feeling excited. "We just finished lunch," Josephine said. "Are you coming this way?" Josephine asked. Lisa rushes into the kitchen and grabs the phone. "Hello, Mother! I miss you!" Lisa said, feeling excited from hearing from her mother who lives out of town. "We were thinking of driving out there this evening," Lisa's mother said. "All right, Mother, about what time?"

"Around three or four hours," her mother said. "Or sooner. I called your place, but I see you're at your brother's place."

"Yes, Mother! Alan took me out for breakfast this morning," Lisa said.

"That's nice of him, where is he?" Mother asked.

"Alan! Mother wants you on the phone!" Lisa yelled out the kitchen. Alan walks to the kitchen to get the phone. Lisa hands the phone to him. "Hello, Mother, how are you?" Alan said in a low voice.

"Hello, Alan! It's good to hear your voice, son! Is everything all right?" his mother asks.

"Yes. Everything's fine," Alan said sadly.

"We'll be there soon."

"How is dad doing?"

"Still working hard as usual."

"All right, Mother, can't wait to see you and Dad," Alan said. "I hope to see you both before I go to work tonight at seven!"

The Love of Family

"I'm pretty sure we'll be there before then, son," his mother said.

"All right, here is your spoiled daughter!" Lisa takes the phone from her brother Alan. "Mother, I can't wait to see you and Dad," Lisa replied.

"Just as soon as your father gets back from putting the gas in the car and comes and picks me up! And we'll take the freeway and be there in no time, my spoiled daughter."

"Okay, I love you and can't wait to see you both," Lisa said.

"Let me talk to my sister real quick!" Lisa hands the phone to her auntie Josephine.

"What time will you both coming?"

"We should arrive by two or three p.m.," Lynn said.

"We'll all be here waiting for you, guys!"

"I'll call you when we get into town!" Lynn sounds excited. "We'll be on our way as soon as Joe drives up. We will jump on the freeway."

"All right, see you when you both get here." Josephine hangs up the house phone.

"They will be on their way soon," Josephine said.

"It will be good to see my mother again," Lisa said.

"Yes, it will!" Josephine says as Alan walks back behind his bar. His wife's feelings were growing with aggravation, but she is determined to remain silent.

Lisa was feeling exuberant, "Isn't it great! My parents are coming to visit!"

Joanna, momentarily, breaks her silence. "Yes, I haven't seen my mother-in-law since Alan's birthday party a year ago."

Lisa and Josephine walk out of the kitchen and sit down at the table.

"I remember when we were kids playing in the backyard trying to build a doll house together. We argued all the time and played and work together till our doll house was built!" Josephine was like in a daze. Lisa and Joanna started laughing at Aunt Josephine. "You kids will never know what I'm talking about! It was fun and hard growing up in our days. Laugh all you want and then ask your mother when she gets here!" Lisa still had the giggles. Joanna just sat there listening with a small glum grin.

"Well, I'm going to take a nap till your mother gets here!" Josephine says. "And let that fool get drunk and then I can beat him up in his sleep!" Lisa and Joanna starts laughing. She gets up from the table. "You get drunk if you want and I'll get my skillet out," Josephine said to her husband. Alan started to laugh at his uncle. A couple of hours later, Lisa and Joanna hear a car door close. Lisa jumps up to look out the dining room window. "They're here!" Lisa runs to open the front door while Lisa rushes outside to her parents, feeling excited! Joanna looks at Alan, rolls her brown eyes at him, growing an attitude. Joanna gets up from the table and walks to the front door. "Hello, Lynn!" Joanna said. And she gives her mother-in-law a hug and her father-in-law also. Lisa walks in hugging her father Leroy.

The older man walks up to his son and they both give each other a handshake and a hug while Patrick walks up to Leroy and gives him a handshake. "You look good, Leroy!" Patrick said.

"Where is my sister-in-law Josephine?" Leroy asked.

"Auntie Josephine is lying down! I'll go tell her you both are here! She can't wait to see you!" Lisa said while she walks to the guest room to wake up her auntie. "The house looks good, son!" his father said. "Thank you, Dad!" Alan said.

"Oh, forgive me, let me introduce you to Bill Andrews, my old army buddy."

"Nice to meet you!" Leroy said.

"And that's his wife Lynn over there sitting at the table with Joanna," Patrick said. Bill waves his right hand to Lynn. "Nice to meet you, Lynn!" Bill said with a smile.

"So how's the company job been going, son?" his father asked.

"Doing good, Dad, as a matter of fact, I have to work at the fire station 52 on Main Street this evening for a couple of hours," Alan said in his normally deep voice.

"That's exciting work. I'm proud of you, son! How did you get that job?" his father asked.

"Through an old friend. Do you remember the only black family that used to live on our old block by the gram school, Dad, where we used to go to when we were young?" Alan asked.

"Yes! I remember when you and the other boys on the block put a team together to play football in the streets. Yes!" his father said while a smiling.

"We had one colored boy on my team and his name is James. He hooked me up for the volunteer fire fighter job, if there's a big fire or not!" Alan said.

"That's great son! I'm happy for you, you're doing well!" Alan looks at his father with a guilty conscience, wanting to pour his heart out to his father about his incident but afraid of the disappointment to their spirits. *A big disappointment to a successful businessman that they see in me and my father is really proud of me. I can't wait to go to the fire station tonight! Maybe I'll feel a lot more safer and it makes me feel independent again and escape this guilt of betrayal,* Alan was thinking hard while holding his glass of less gin and more orange juice and four ice cubes. He was looking at the time! *It's four fifty-five p.m. I am hoping that damn Detective Theodore doesn't come through tonight while my parents are here!*

"Son, turn on your big screen television on to the sports station!" his father asked.

"All right, Dad. Hand me the remote in front of you, Uncle Patrick." Alan gets the remote and changes the channel to the sports station.

"Who's your favorite team, Leroy?" Bill asked.

"The Lakers and the cowboys," Leroy said with his deep strong voice.

"What would you like to drink, Leroy?" Patrick asked.

"A Coors beer would be fine! Thank you," Leroy said.

"So you guys made it!" Josephine said, walking into the dining room.

"Lynn! It's so good to see you!" Josephine puts her arms out and gave her younger sister a big hug!

"You are still the same, you never gain any weight! I need to feed you some greens so you can gain some weight, Liz! How much do you weigh?"

"One hundred and twenty eighteen pounds! I look good with my burgundy curly hair and my matching hazel eyes and trimmed eyebrows with my lovely smile!"

Lynn was talking to her older sister. "How much do you weigh now, sister?"

"I'm one forty five and still looking good!"

"And how old are the both of you?" Lisa asked with a grin.

"Old enough to know better not to tell my age!" And they both laughed. "Are you hungry from that long trip?" Josephine asks.

"Just a little hungry, sis!"

"Well, you need some meat on those bones," Josephine says to her sister.

"There's fried chicken and green salad," Lisa replies, as she sits next to her mother.

"I'm glad you all are doing well!" Lynn replies with a smile. "It's been eleven years now and look how successful you both have become! I'm proud of all of you for taking good care of each other! And my son looks good!"

If she only knew the truth about her loving son! Joanna struggles within herself to avoid revealing the truth.

"So, daughter, how's the business going?"

"It's doing good, selling more outfits. Dana and Diana came by the shop yesterday!"

"How are the twins?" Lynn asked, feeling excited!

"They're still spoiled as ever!" Lisa said.

Lynn started laughing. "I remember my daughter played a big joke on me! Lisa invited her little girl friend over to play in her room! About five minutes later, the doorbell rang, and it was the same girl in different clothes!" Josephine was giggling. "I thought that was the same little girl? Wearing blue jeans and a white summer short top!" Lynn was laughing while telling the story.

"Then I saw the girl again about two minutes later with white jeans and a blue top on and I thought to myself, *Are my eyes playing tricks on me? Or do I need a new pair of reading glasses.* Then I yelled for Lisa. She slowly walked from her bedroom smiling hard! And the two twelve-year-olds twins walked together behind Lisa, I started laughing hard, thinking I lost my mind! They played a good trick on me!" Clapping her hands, enjoying the lovely atmosphere of the story, they were laughing and giggling having a good time. They were sitting around the dining room table, spending good time together. Ten minutes later, Josephine walks out with a hot plate with fried chicken wings,

potatoes, and salad with ranch dressing and sits the hot plate in front of her sister.

"I'll bring a glass of lemonade," Josephine said.

"Thank you, sister!"

"Oh, Mother, I have so much to tell you. First, I want to tell you that I'm dating one of Alan's friends and his name is James! And he's African American and really nice, and he knows how to treat a lady, like he opens the car door for me, and you don't get treated like a lady often," Lisa said. Josephine walks back into the dining room with a glass of lemonade and sets it in front of Lynn.

"Who is James?"

"Girl! Your daughter has been moon dating like we used to do!" Josephine said, excited. They were all grinning, even Joanna gave a little laugh, sitting next to her mother-in-law. "Does Alan know you're dating his friend?"

"Yes! And I told my brother that I'm a grown young lady and I can take care of myself," she said with a little attitude.

"You've have become a very independent young lady. I'm very proud of you, daughter!"

"It sounds like the guys are having a good time!" Lisa said. The men were shouting loud about the all-star baseball while they were watching the Saturday previews.

"What kind of excitement goes on around in town?" Leroy asked.

Alan just stares at his television, ignoring his father's question.

"Well, things haven't been good lately in this town, um," Alan clears his throat, trying to keep that pressure of fear away.

"What's been going on?"

"Well, your son's friend was killed last weekend, and before that, a man got hit by a car out here on Road 15 two weeks ago and the poor guy died and it was in the papers. Whoever did it has no shame or remorse," Bill said.

"Well, I better go take a shower and get ready for work," Alan said, feeling nervous listening to his uncle and father. Alan walks out from behind the bar and walks over to his mother and gives her a kiss on her cheek. "I have to get ready, excuse me," Alan said. Joanna gets up from the table to follow Alan to their bedroom and closes the door behind her. "How you are feeling?" Alan takes a deep breath and sits on the end of their bed with his head down for a moment.

"I'm so sorry about what happened, and people just keep talking about it," Alan whispered to his wife Joanna.

"Let's not talk about it while your parents are here!" Joanna whispered.

"And that damn detective just keeps coming around, even on the weekend," Alan said.

"I don't want to hear this right now!" Joanna whispers with an attitude. "Just stay calm till your folks leave tomorrow night." She gives him an unwavering stare, like a crawling bug that needs to be squished! Joanna walks out their bedroom and closes the door behind her. Alan gets up to get his clothes out of his closet to take a shower while he's hearing his family talking loud.

"This is going to be a long weekend for me, and I keep trying to hide my horrifying fear. It's eating my conscience alive!" Alan walks into his bathroom and turns the shower on and gets his towel. "Oh, God! Take this guilt and fear out my heart and soul. Show me the way, God!" While looking into the steamed mirror from the hot shower, he gets undressed to get into the shower. "Alan! Are you in the shower?" Joanna yelled through the bathroom door. "Yes, what is it?"

"I'm going to drive Lisa and your mother to the market, I just wanted to let you know!" Joanna shouted.

"All right, we will be back before you leave for work!" Joanna shouted. Alan was under the hot shower with lather soap running down his body. Five minutes later, Alan steps out of the shower and grabs his dark blue towel to dry himself off. "Joanna!" She comes walking back into the bedroom.

"Yes, Alan."

"Can you drop Lisa off to get her car on your way for me please?"

"Sure, I'll see you later," Joanna said with wide hazel eyes staring at his nude body.

She then closes the bedroom door, still feeling nervous and shivery.

Alan walks out of their bedroom to the living room, where his father was sitting on the couch, watching a baseball game with Patrick and Bill.

"Who's winning?"

"The game's just starting," Patrick said.

"I think I better go in early, Dad! So I can come back in a couple of hours."

"That's fine, son." Alan walks out to the garage, while his father was standing by the kitchen door, looking out at his son's dark blue 2000 Lincoln Navigator.

Alan decides to drive his Lincoln to the fire station to see how it runs after the accident. *It's been two weeks. I'll get up early Monday morning and drive the Lincoln to the shop to test the brakes and get the front hood fixed. Maybe Detective Theodore will get out of my freaking hair!* He was feeling frustrated, while he jumps into the driver side and starts pulling out of the garage. But now he honks the horn twice.

Driving west toward road fifteen he was driving the speed limit, and momentarily feeling the cool breeze of the evening. *I'm feeling no pressure of stress at this time.* Suddenly he realizes where he is at. *Oh, no! This is the area where I accidently killed an innocent guy. Sometimes I just want to give it all up and come clean, because this stress and fear Is like a growing disease that sticks with me forever. It's an awful dishonest feeling. But then there are consequences in my marriage, where me and my wife have gone through a lo*t *together? I promised her that I would treat her like a respected woman. She's always was a person with a greed for money. I don't think she married me for my heart. She's too aggressive and wants only for herself. She doesn't care about my feelings. She'd always focuses on the future and that's why I had to tell her the truth! Because I thought she was the love of my life! But she is so greedy for money and not my feelings.*

He arrives at the fire station and parks beside James's silver 2000 Infinity qx4 sports utility and turns the engine off.

He, then, walks in the front door of the Brookville fire station. "Hello!" Alan says to the Fire Chief, who is standing at the front entrance.

"Mr. Jones, how have you been?" the Fire Chief asks. "Okay," Alan says with a little excitement. "So you're on tonight?" the chief asks.

"Yes, I'm a little early!"

"That's fine, you can hang out with the others tonight."

"I'll see you there," Alan said, walking away while his chief answers the phones. Alan walks into the locker room, hearing hysterical laughing.

"Alan! You made it!" one of the fire workers said.

"Hey, buddy! Good to see you. How you doing?"

"Good!" Alan said in a low voice.

"Well, are you ready to go do some heavy work?" James asked.

"Sure, I'm ready!" Alan said, feeling a little excited.

"Relax, man." James puts his left hand on Alan's right shoulder. *Ding! Ding!* The loud fire bell rings! Alan started rushing, opening his locker and grabbing his yellow rubber uniform, and puts it on fast and grabbing his yellow fire hat and runs and jumps onto the fire truck, drives onto the heavy traffic, blowing the horn with the siren. Alan and James holding on the back of the fire truck heading south. The fire truck makes a left turn down Alpine Street and noticed smoke coming from a house with lots of trees in front. Alan and James jumps off the truck, pulling the hose closer to the fire, and turns it on! James yells! "The water pressure's pushing hard."

Alan stands behind James holding the hose as tight as he can.

People were standing around watching the fire blaze and coughing from the smoke.

A police officer was standing with his arms out, so the people won't cross the caution tape, while Alan and James and the other fire fighters continue to put the fire out.

"This house is damaged!" James said to Alan, both coughing from the black smoke. Alan gets a stick and starts poking through the burnt things.

When the fire inspector walks in to start his investigation on what started the fire. "Did everyone got out?" the fire inspector asks James.

"I'm sure they did. We didn't find anything yet, sir."

Alan was feeling a little nervous around the inspector, as he starts looking around for anything that looks suspicious of arson. He then starts following James to different rooms, looking for wires and loose plugs." A half an hour later, they jump back on the truck to get back to the station. Ten minutes later, they returned to the station and jump off the truck and walk to their locker room to take showers. Alan walks to his locker and started getting undressed like the others and opens his locker and looks at his cell phone: two missed calls, and looks at the missed calls. "The house number. When I get out the shower, I'll return the call."

"We all smell like black smoke!" All the guys laughed, changing their clothes, getting out the showers as Alan had a white towel around his waist showing his chest with no hair, walking to the showers with his hairy legs and his white feet. Few minutes later, Alan gets out the shower and dries his body off in front of all males and wraps the towel around his body and walks back to his locker to get dressed. Few minutes later, all the guys walk to the backyard to play basketball till the next fire bell rings.

Fire Station

*J*ames walks up to Alan. "Now that wasn't too bad of a fire," James said.

"Not bad at all! Alan replied.

"Good thing that old house didn't fall on us," James said.

"You're right about that, man! I heard you and my sister went out together!"

"We did! She is nice and smart, like you!" James begins grinning hard.

"I'm glad she enjoyed herself!" Alan said.

"Oh, we just went out to dinner and I've drove her back home that evening."

"Hey, guys? The news is on!" one of the workers yelled. James and Alan walked fast to the recreation room. "This coming week for the funeral service of Richard Oxford, who was murdered in his home a week ago and the authorities have no suspects yet. Also another Brookville resident, Mr. Johnson, who was killed on Road 20 two weeks ago. The Johnson family has arranged his funeral service Monday at one p.m. at the Christian Church on Main Street."

Peer pressure is a bitch! I just want to burst out my fear and frustration and my paranoia building up all at once. I feel like yelling without anyone noticing the anxiety attack. The guilt in my soul feels like exploding.

"Alan, you worked with that guy Richard before," James said.

Alan's heart was thumping. "Calm down, man, you look like you're ready to explode!"

"Yes, I've known Richard for years," Alan said, nervously clearing his throat.

"Just a robbery gone badly that night," one of the fire fighters said.

"And that poor man who got hit and the driver buried him and there are some sick mental people out there!" one of the volunteers said while they continued watching the news.

"My mother and father are here for the weekend." Alan tried to change the subject, sitting next to James. "I remember your folks, how are they doing?" James asked. "Getting older." They both laughed. "Well, my poor body is going to bed as soon as I get home! I sure hope there are no more fires tonight!" James said.

"What time do you get off tonight?" Alan asked.

"Twelve midnight!" James said.

"And in sports tonight, coming right up after these commercials."

Their captain walks in. "You guys did very well out there tonight! The fire was put out in ten minutes and cleaned up in thirty minutes. It's ten p.m. You volunteers can go home now for the next shift." He walks back to his office, Alan gets up and gives James a handshake. "I'll see you next week!" Alan said.

"Maybe I'll stop by next week!" James said.

"See you later, James!" Alan follows the other volunteer workers out to the parking lot.

He grabs his keys and opens his car door and jumps in and snaps his seat belt on and starts his Lincoln, then calls his wife on his cell phone. *Ring!* "Hello!" Joanna answered. "Hey, it's me. Are you on your way home?"

"No, I have to go see something first. Just tell my folks I'll be home soon!" Alan said.

"I'll keep your dinner warm and your parents are still up waiting for you and your mother cooked dinner tonight," Joanna said.

"Good! I miss her cooking. I'll be there soon." He closed his cell phone and drove off in his dark blue Lincoln Navigator. "I should check out a couple of repair shops and put this vehicle early Monday morning."

Alan stays on the right lane and turns right off Main Street on to Creek Road and noticed bright lights at a car shop. Alan continued driving down Creek Road and noticed the lot was full of vehicles needing repair. Alan turns his Lincoln Navigator around. "Yes this is where I'm coming Monday morning. I'll just call in to work and tell my boss that I'll be a little late." Alan was thinking and he drives back through Creek Road, a dusty street. Driving slow, he makes a left turn when the light turned green to get back to Main Street. Alan feels a little excited for his car to be fixed, and he turns his radio on. "It feels good to drive my Navigator again," Alan said to himself while his cell phone rings. "That's how that happened that evening! And that's how I killed that poor guy that night. Lord, forgive me," Alan said and just lets it ring. "It's true you can cause an accident and kill or get killed," Alan was thinking to himself. *Beep!* "Someone left me a message." Alan turns back on Highway 15 in the same area the accident happened. He tries not to pay any attention to his guilty conscience.

"I can't get rid of this guilt feeling. What can I do? Turn myself in and lose everything, even greedy Joanna? I can't do that!" He takes a deep breath, listening to the song, "Urgent" by the Foreigners Greatest Hits. Driving 15 mph, ten minutes later, he pulls into his driveway to get his remote control from his sun beam. The garage door opens, and he drives in slow and opens the glove box to put something in it and locks it back and push the remote to close the garage door and opens his car door and steps out and locks it and walks into the kitchen door.

"Hello, Aunt Josephine."

"Everyone still up and enjoying the game?"

"Yes! And your plate will be ready in a few minutes, and I can't wait to eat her cooking!" Alan said and walked into the dining room, where his wife and his mother were sitting.

"Hey, baby! You seem to be in a better mood," Joanna said.

"Because it was an exciting evening. We've put a house fire out tonight!"

"Are you all right?" his mother asked with concern.

"I'm all right, Mother. I'm good."

"Son! You're home!" his father yelled.

Joanna looked at him with a curious expression.

"Don't worry, everything is fine," Alan said, feeling positive energy, and he walked into the living room.

"Alan! How was it tonight?" his father asked.

"There was a house fire on the west side tonight! Feeling self-confident around my family."

"Ready for a drink, son?"

"How you feeling, Dad?" Alan asked.

"A little drunk, but happy!"

"I'm not driving tonight," his father said. "But I'm feeling happy. Your mother is in the back room, resting!"

"Pour me a little gin, Dad, and some orange juice with ice, please, and I'll be right back!" He rushed to the bathroom and closed the door behind him.

Lisa came into the guest bedroom and heard the toilet flush. She walked into the dining room and noticed Joanna and her auntie Josephine were sitting at the table, drinking coffee and talking.

"Who's in the bathroom?" Lisa asked.

"Alan," Joanna said. "Look at my dad, just drinking away!"

"Hey, Dad! Are you on full?" Lisa laughed, teasing her father. "What time is it?"

"It's 9:40 p.m."

"I'm watching a good movie. It's a comedy movie. I better get back in there before I miss the movie," Lisa said.

"Are you going to stay the night, Lisa?"

"No, Auntie. I'm going home in a little to Fluffy," Lisa said.

"God knows this house is big enough!" Josephine said, while Joanna drank her coffee, keeping silent.

"I'll be back at movie-time," Lisa said. She walked out the dining room and back down the hallway and into the bathroom.

Alan and his mother were having a nice conversation about the fire tonight.

"So what did you cook tonight, Mother?"

"Pork chops, sweet potato pie, Chinese greens with neck bones, cornbread, and green salad," his mother said.

"Yum! I'm hungry for my mother's cooking!" he shouted, and they both laughed. Alan gave his mother a kiss on the cheek.

Lisa walked out the guest room and returned, closing the door behind her brother to finish watching the movie with their mother.

Alan walked into the dining area. "Where's my plate of food?"

Joanna got up and walked into the kitchen while Alan sat down at the dinner table, ready to eat. Josephine laughed at her nephew.

"What?" Alan asked with a grin.

"The more you eat, the more you thin out. Where does all your food go? You never gain weight anymore," his auntie said.

"I sprout up, not round." They both laughed.

Joanna walked in with Alan's hot plate from the microwave and sat his plate in front of him. He started eating his dinner.

"Alan, your mother has always been a good cook. She even outdoes my cooking sometimes," Josephine said.

Alan just looked at her with a small grin and continued eating his dinner.

Leroy walked over to his son. "Do you have any plans for tomorrow?"

"Nothing, really. Just relaxing and watching the Sunday-night football games. Why, Dad?"

"I want to go to the gun shop before we leave tomorrow."

"It may not be open on Sundays, Dad!"

"Oh, that's right. I want to check out the new hunting rifles."

"Dad, you're still hunting ducks after all these years?" Alan was trying to feel normal.

"Why, yes. And I'm still fishing by the lake near our home too! You remember that small lake when I used to always carry you out there?" his father asked.

"Yes, Dad. I remember, but I didn't think you were still shooting ducks," Alan said, surprised.

"One weekend we could go together, and I'll show you all around that beautiful lake." "Sounds good, Dad! Well, that's it for me tonight," Alan said. He then stretched his arms out and got up from the couch and walked to the kitchen. Joanna was finishing up the dishes. He handed his wife his empty plate. He then noticed she hadn't said anything to him. She had an attitude like that. He walked out the kitchen, keeping silent.

His father watched him walk to the living room, and his father got the remote and turned off the late-preview football games. "It's 11:30 p.m. Bill's wife came and picked him up, and your uncle Patrick went to bed."

"Oh, good. I can get some sleep tonight," Alan said.

They both walked to their bedrooms.

"Good night, Dad. Talk to you in the morning!"

"Good night, son!"

Oh, my poor feet! Alan starts taking off his shoes and stretches his legs. "Good night!"

It was Sunday morning, and the first football game was coming on in thirty minutes.

"Who's playing?"

"I think the Packers and the Raiders," Alan said.

"They're both good teams. This nice-looking home, son, is comfortable. I may never leave."

Father and son both smiled.

"Thanks, Dad!"

"What time are you guys planning to leave tomorrow?"

"Oh, in the evening. I'll be all resting up to drive, and no drinking for me today. Your mother will have a fit and start fussing about my drinking and driving."

"Dad, you don't drink and drive, do you?" Alan asked.

"No, son! Your mother hides the car keys even if I look at a drink!"

"Well, I don't blame her. Drinking and driving don't mix. Trust me, Dad."

"Go! Go, Raiders!" his father yelled.

And the game was over. The Raiders won!

His father, Leroy, was cheering. Alan sat down as his mind wandered off somewhere else for a moment.

"That's the game!" Leroy said. "Well, good morning, Bill!" Leroy was feeling happy. "Good morning, Bill. You missed the first half previews this morning," Alan said.

"Good morning, Lynn!" Joanna said with her low voice.

"Good morning! Did Lisa go home last night?" Joanna asked.

"Yes. After the movie was over, she left, and she said she would be over here this morning for breakfast. But it's still early."

Josephine walked into the kitchen. "Good morning! I see you cooked breakfast.

I was just talking to Alan last night about your cooking, that you have always outcooked me."

"That's because Mother kept me in the kitchen while she kept you in the books. That's the truth!"

They both laughed.

"I'll get the plates and the milk out," Josephine said.

"Like my mother kept me in the kitchen also," Joanna said, grabbing the bread to be toasted.

"I think that's how we were raised in the kitchen," Lynn said.

"That's why we have husbands who love to eat." Josephine laughed.

"I hear you there!"

"That's breakfast, lunch with snacks, and then their dinner. That's our job," Lynn said.

"It's going to be hard on Alan even more this coming week," Joanna said.

"Why do you say that?" Lynn asked.

Joanna took a deep breath. "His friend and coworker Richard's funeral service is this coming week."

"What happened to him?" Lynn asked.

"He got murdered last Thursday evening in his home."

"I didn't hear about this! Are you going with him to his friend's funeral service?"

"Yes, of course," Joanna replied.

"Alan is going to need you by his side," her mother-in-law said.

"That's right. We've always been there in times of need like this," Josephine said.

Fifteen minutes later, Alan came out his bedroom, yawning. "Good morning, everyone!" He was looking restless wearing his white T-shirt, brown dress pants, and black leather slippers. Patrick came up behind Alan.

"Good morning, Alan!" all said at the same time.

"I smell breakfast," Patrick said.

Ding-dong!

"Come in!" Alan shouted.

"Good morning!" Lisa said, while closing the front door.

"You're up early on a Sunday morning," Josephine said.

"Oh, Auntie, it's 8:30 a.m." Lisa sat down for breakfast.

"Good morning, everybody," Leroy said.

"Good morning, Dad!" Lisa and Alan said.

"Breakfast smells good!"

Alan grabbed the coffeepot off the table and poured his father a cup of coffee. He then poured himself a cup and set it down while Patrick and Leroy passed the pancakes and sausage and eggs to Alan. They were all quiet, eating their breakfast.

"We'll be leaving at around 6:00 p.m. this evening and get on the two-hour drive," Leroy said. "Son, when are you coming up to visit?"

"Soon, Dad."

"I'll help you drive, brother."

"If I let you drive, we may not make it," Alan said.

Everyone laughed. Lisa smirked at Alan. "Very funny, brother."

"Your brother has always picked on you." Their mother gave Lisa a hug and a kiss. "Don't worry about your brother. He's just teasing."

"Sister Lynn, how about you going to church with us?" Josephine asked.

"That would be nice. I brought my new dress! I've been dying to wear it," her mother, Lynn, said.

"I'm coming also, and after breakfast, I'll go home and put on my blue-and-pink sleeveless dress with my pink shawl over the dress, and my blue pumps," Lisa said while eating.

"We better get up and clean these dishes and get ready for church," Josephine said.

"Would you like to come with us, Joanna?" Lynn asked. "It's an All-Girls' Day! Come on! We'll have some fun before I leave. We don't spend much time together, and it's time."

They both smiled at each other with care.

"Okay. I'll come to church with you," Joanna said.

Lynn and Joanna both got up and started taking the breakfast plates into the kitchen and started cleaning the table off, while Alan and his father started making plans to go into town and look around for a couple of hours.

"That sounds fine, son!"

They all were rushing to get ready for the day. A few minutes later, the guys got into Alan's white 1964 Mustang. He put the top down, showing his red leather interior. Alan started his car.

Vroom!

"The engine sounds great," his father said, sitting in the passenger seat with his seat belt on.

Patrick was feeling young again.

Breeze of Brookville

Alan parks in front of a gun shop that's open on a Sunday morning. Alan parks his Mustang in front of the shop and turns off the engine and his father opens his car door and steps out. Patrick follows, closing the passenger side door. Alan walks behind Patrick and his father while they all walk into the gun shop. "Hello," a tall man said. "Can I help with all with something?" the old Caucasian man said. "We're just looking around," Alan said. Leroy and Uncle Patrick felt like they were in hunting heaven, looking at all the hunting rifles, deer and moose heads hanging from the walls, bows with arrows, golf bags and balls, and sport hats and caps. Leroy picks up a riffle with no bullets.

"You ever go hunting, Patrick?" Leroy asked.

"No, not lately, but I would love to go someday," Patrick said.

"Well, maybe next time you come up to visit, we can go hunting. I live in the forest where you see the deer and the other animals we can shoot for dinner. I have my hunting license for a year, and when you come to visit, I can get your hunting licenses for a day or two," Leroy said. Alan was just looking around and feeling calmer.

"So you gentlemen like hunting?" the old man asked. "Yes, I hunt sometimes up in my area," Leroy said to the old man as another customer walks in to look around. Alan's father Leroy decides to duy some bullets for his rifle for the next time he goes hunting. "Thank you, sir!" They all walk out the gun shop. "There's a lot of buildings downtown," his father said. They noticed a coffee shop open. "Let's walk over to the coffee shop and get a cup of coffee." Leroy looks at his watch. It's eleven a.m. They then cross Main Street and walk to the open coffee shop. They walked in together and began looking around, smelling fresh coffee. Meanwhile, Josephine and her sister Lynn were holding Lisa's hands, walking to church together. Joanna followed behind them, feeling kind of fearful about knowing the truth about her husband's incident and not reporting it. *I'll pray that he don't get arrested,* Joanna was thinking while following Josephine and Lynn to their seats. They began listening to the preacher telling the story of Noah's ark. Two hours later, church was over, and they decided to go to the market in Joanna's car. And she drives to the J&S market on Main Street while Josephine picks up a pack of pork chops and rice with salad for dinner later. Joanna grabs a bottle of red wine. They were standing at the checkout stand and paying for their purchase and they walk out the market and walk back to Joanna's car and they all get in, and Joanna starts her car and drives to her place. "What time is it? The men should be back by now," Lynn said. Joanna kept silent, driving down Road 15, thinking about her husband's incident on that road; she then turns right into her block and parks into her driveway. Lisa and Josephine were admiring Alan's Mustang that's parked in front of the garage. Joanna walks into the house and noticed Alan staring at her with a little grin, standing by the bar, and his mother and Josephine walks in with Lisa holding a couple of brown groceries bag.

"I'll put the bags in the kitchen."

"You ladies back from church?" Leroy said while he was looking at the time. "It's almost noon!" his father said, standing tall in the living room with Patrick who was making a drink of gin and juice with ice. "Starting already, Patrick?" his wife said with her hands on her small hips, looking at her husband Patrick and turns around and goes into the kitchen to help Joanna get lunch ready. Josephine turns around, walks into the kitchen door, and smells a hot skillet with cooking oil getting warm. Joanna was rinsing the pork chops off and puts six pork chops in a bowl and pours flour over the pork chops with seasonal salt with a little black pepper and gets a fork to lay the pork chops into the hot skillet. Lisa and her mother was getting the rest of the lunch ready. Alan walks into the kitchen to get some orange juice out the refrigerator; he then comes walking out the kitchen and to the living room bar. "I forget the ice. Be right back, Dad," Alan said, walking back into the kitchen. "What did you forget, Alan?" his mother asked, standing by the sink with the ice. Alan opens the top freezer of the refrigerator and gets the ice tray and walks over to the sink where his mother stands making a green salad, while Alan grabs a bowl for the ice. "Don't forget to refill the tray," his mother said. The house phone rings. Joanna answers. "Hello!"

"This is Bill. Are Patrick and Leroy still there?"

"Sure, just a moment. Patrick, the phone! It's Bill!" Patrick puts his drink on the table, gets up from the couch, and walks to the kitchen to get the phone. Alan walks back to the living room with the ice and hands the bowl to his father. "It's beginning to smell like pork chops!" his father said. "Joanna is cooking pork chops for lunch, Dad. What's the plan when you get home?" Alan asked. "I'm going to turn on the television and relax while your mother starts dinner." They both laughed. "We have it made, son, we have good wives that like to cook and clean and stay by our side for many years and treat us like kings while we work hard and keep a decent, respected life. We've never hurt or killed anyone, so we look forward for the best part of life ahead of us," his father said. Alan takes a deep swallow of his drink and clears his throat, looking down at the floor. I remember the enormous horrible fear I've felt that evening, and I regret it all. *It feels like a bad curse! If my father knew the truth about what I did that night, I've buried an innocent man! I need to snap out of this! Before my hair-raising fear appears,* Alan was thinking to himself. "You're right, Dad," Alan said. Patrick walks back into the living room. "Bill will be arriving soon! And he's going to bring more liquor after lunch," Patrick said, feeling excited.

"That's very nice of Bill. He must like to drink a lot!" Leroy said with sarcasm.

"Yes, he's an alcoholic! He started drinking when he was twelve when they made moonshine back in Mississippi where he's from," Patrick said.

"Oh yes, back in the days when they called it corn whiskey," Leroy said.

"Yes! Have you ever tasted it, Alan?" his father asked.

"No, Dad! I hear it tastes like gasoline! That would blow you miles from here," Alan said. "That's what it tastes like, but it puts hair on your chest!" Patrick said as they all laughed. Leroy was shaking his head.

"No, son! Don't ever even want to taste moonshine!" Fifteen minutes later, Lisa and Josephine was setting the dining room table with plates and silverware and napkins.

"Why are you shaking your head, Dad?" Lisa asked.

"Oh, we were talking about moonshine whiskey," Leroy said. "Back in the days before your time," her father said.

"Moonshine! Our folks used to drink moonshine and Lynn and I and our cousins used to follow our parents to the blues bar back in Georgia and watch them drink moonshine. It was the only hard drink back in those days," Josephine said. Joanna comes out the kitchen with the smell of pork chops and sets the plate of pork chops on the dinner table while Lynn comes out with the green salad and ranch dressing.

"We better go wash our hands for lunch, Dad," Alan said.

"Oh, all right," his father said, watching the news. "And here on the news today. Mr. Johnson was a family man that was hit and buried two weeks ago out on Road 15. The funeral service will be held Tuesday at the Family Christian Church on Second Street at ten a.m., and in the news today, the Oxford family is asking for any information on the murder of their son Richard

Oxford and that there is a reward for any information. Please contact the police department. Now in sports today..."

"Come on, Dad, let's go wash our hands for lunch." Alan begin feeling that spine chilling fear from hearing the news, while walking down the hall to the bathroom, feeling disappointed, trying to get that guilt and shameful feeling to leave before sitting down in front of his family.

"Everything smells and looks good!" Leroy said.

"Yes, it does," his wife Lynn said.

"Come on, let's all sit down and say a prayer before we eat," Josephine said.

"Patrick, don't eat anything till I finish saying a prayer," Josephine yelled.

"Yes, dear." Everyone sits around the table and bows their heads.

"Lord, we want to thank you for having Lynn and my brother-in-law Leroy in front of us today and thank you for this special lunch. Amen!" Josephine said.

"Amen," they all said in their low voices. Alan still had his head down and his hands together, praying for forgiveness while everyone started eating their lunch.

"Amen."

"Well, son, you must have something to tell the Lord in that long prayer," his mother said. Alan stared with more fear at his mother for a moment.

"Can you please pass me the pork chops and the salad," his mother said. Joanna wasn't speaking much and hands her husband the salad and the pork chops. *Ding dong!*

"That's the doorbell." Alan gets up to answer it nervously and stopped for a moment with fear that it may be that relentless Detective! "Who is it?"

"Bill!" His fear drops quickly and opens the front door happy to see that it's Bill and not that Detective Theodore; he then rushes to take another look out the door before he close the door. Feeling relieved, he walks back to his seat and continues eating.

"You've made it!" Patrick said.

"I sure did."

"Would you like some lunch, Bill?" Joanna asked.

"No thanks! I just had a big lunch with my wife. She cooked spaghetti and corn bread," he said with his deep voice.

"That's sounds delicious," Patrick said. Josephine give Patrick that mean look again.

"I'll just make me a drink at the bar while you good people finish your lunch," Bill said. "Before you both leave this afternoon, I'll pack a couple of sandwiches and a couple of soda for the road," Josephine said.

"That would be nice, sister! Thank you," Lynn said.

"How long does it take to get out there at Mountain Lake City?"

"That's about two and a half hours, driving straight through, no stops," Lynn said.

"And you can go fishing anytime and hunting out there just in the hunting season," Leroy said.

"Maybe Josephine and I will take a trip up there before winter comes. That would be nice. Let's do it, Josephine!" Patrick says. "I have a vacation time coming up next month, and the workers gets a bonus. It may be a small bonus, but it's a blessing."

"That's right and we can pack up the mobile home."

"You guys still have that old mobile home?" Leroy asked

"Oh, I traded that old thing in two years ago," Patrick said. "And got a new model I'm now driving a 1999 Fleetwood mobile home."

"So we'll see you two next month?" Leroy asked.

"Yes, for sure that would be a prize winner." Josephine comments.

Leroy turns to his son, "Hey! Why don't you and Joanna take the trip with us next month?"

"I don't know, we'll see!" Alan said.

"See if you can take a week off, Alan!" Joanna said.

"Maybe," Alan said with his low voice as Joanna rolls her eyes with fear at him, feeling more disappointed.

"Well, I'm finished with my lunch, excuse me." Alan gets up with his plate and walks into the kitchen and turns the hot water to wash his hands and face before going into the living room.

"I'm full. Thank you, ladies." He was wiping his hands on his napkin and drops the napkin on his empty plate.

"I'll get your plate when I go into the kitchen," his wife Lynn said.

"Thanks, sweetheart," Leroy replied and winks from his right eye and walks into the living room.

"Lunch was delicious," Lisa said.

"Yes, it was," her mother replied. Pouring a glass of iced tea that's still cold from the refrigerator, Josephine gets up from her chair and picks up the empty glass.

"This was a nice visit, Mother, and I'm going to miss you both," Lisa said.

"It turned out to be a nice visit," her mother said.

"Do you have to leave so soon, Mother?"

"Yes, your father has to go to work tomorrow morning early, and I have to get his breakfast and lunch ready."

Her mother gave her a little kiss on her face with a smile. "Are you coming up next month with your auntie Josephine?"

"I hope so, I mean to." Lisa begins feeling sad.

"I better get up and start getting our things together, daughter! Come help me with our suitcase, baby."

"Yes, Mother." Lisa and her mother get up and walk toward the hallway to the guest room while Joanna and Josephine get the table cleared. Alan watched a Western movie with Clint Eastwood.

"He may walk slowly, but Clint Eastwood was a fast shooter," Patrick said. While Joanna answers their front door.

"Hello, Detective Theodore!" Joanna said nervously while clearing her throat.

"Oh, sorry to disturb you on a Sunday afternoon. I just have to finish my report by tomorrow morning or my captain and I'll tell you that he's one tight character from the navy."

"Come in, Lieutenant!"

This is it, he's coming to arrest Alan. I just know it! Her thoughts with fear raced against her frightened thoughts.

Alan had a look on his face!

"Detective! What can we do for you this evening?" Alan began feeling a lump in his throat and the blood rushing through his veins. "So, Detective Theodore, you believe in working twenty-four hours a day?"

Meanwhile Lisa and her mother enter into the dining room, Alan's blood pressure rose with panic when he saw his mother walking towards them.

"Mr. Jones? I just want to ask you!"

"Hello, who are you?" his mother asked.

"I'm Lieutenant Theodore, and you're related to?"

"I'm Alan's mother, Mrs. Jones."

"I just stopped by for a moment to talk to your son about something important!" Lisa and her mother walk into the dining area.

"Why is that detective here talking to your brother?"

"He came to my job, asking about Alan."

A look of fear starts appearing on Joanna's face. "God, please don't let that detective arrest him in front of his family!" She begins praying in her thoughts.

"I just want to ask you about your friend Mr. Oxford? Do you know if Richard knew a man named Curtis Leonard?"

"Sorry, I never heard the name before. Will that be all, Detective?" Alan said with fear. Trying to rush the detective out the door before his father walks in and starts asking questions.

"One more question I have for you, Mr. Jones. The night of the hit and bury case, I call it, I can't understand if you came down that road, how you didn't see or hear about a robbery that evening if you were at that 7-Eleven store around the time of the robbery and the cashier remembers you that night because you bought gas there and he can verify that with a receipt from the Fourth of July and you bought wine and a case of Coors beer and you used your credit card that evening around the same time of the robbery?" Alan was ready to burst out with anger but he held control of his thoughts! He opens the front door slowly. "I was not feeling well that evening, Detective Theodore! And I don't remember any robbery that evening, and I don't have any idea what you are trying to do, Detective! Now, would you mind leaving so I can enjoy my family on this Sunday evening," Alan said with an obnoxious look on his face while he was shaking like an earthquake, feeling like a heavy storm coming over him! "There you are, Alan!"

His father walked toward the front door, looking for his son.

"Hello, are you one of my son's friends?" his father asked.

"Um, no, sir. As a matter of fact, I'm Lieutenant Theodore!" He shows his badge. "I'm just out investigating an incident. Did you hear about it on television? The accident that happened a couple of weeks ago and also about the murder of his coworker. I'm just going around asking if anyone saw or heard anything?"

"No, we haven't, Lieutenant!" Alan said nervously.

"It was nice meeting you!" his father said and walked over to his wife and daughter while Joanna was drinking iced tea, feeling nervous, trying not to stare at Detective Theodore with her head turned toward the kitchen.

"Well, I think that will be all for now! Have a good evening," Detective Theodore said. And he opens the front door and walks out, putting his right hand in his right pocket walking to his light blue 1965 Mustang. Grabbing his keys out his right pocket to unlock the driver side door and jumps in and drives off. Alan walks to the den and looks at Joanna and his parents.

"What did that detective want?" his mother asked.

"Oh, he's just doing his routine around the area," Alan said, looking kind of worried.

"How come?" his mother asked. "Oh! About your coworker! I'm sorry to hear about your friend! Does he have any idea who killed him?"

"No, not yet," he said in fear. "That is so scary. He got killed in his own home! "Really," her mother said.

"I'm going to his service with Alan and Joanna Thursday. I'll just work half a day."

"That's right, Lisa, and be there for Alan."

"Well, it's almost two p.m.!" their father Leroy said.

"I better go put some gas in the car before we hit the road! Alan, come show me where the gas station is in this town."

"Sure, Dad!

"Let me get my keys, and I'll be ready!" Alan said with that lump of worry going down in his throat.

"Alan, you ready?"

"I'm coming now, Dad!" He then walks out his bedroom, feeling little more relieved that Detective Theodore left.

"Son, are you all right?" his father asked in a concerned way.

"Sure, I'm fine, Dad!"

"We'll be back," Leroy said while Patrick and Bill continued watching a Western movie drinking their liquor.

Lisa was sitting quiet with her thoughts wondering, *why that same detective keeps coming back…after Alan maybe? Either Alan saw something that night or he knows something about his friend's murder!*

"What's wrong, Lisa, with that deep look on your face?"

"Nothing, Mother!"

Maybe Alan's afraid to say anything and that detective mentioned there was a robbery that night and that the same man got killed. I just hope to God that it wasn't Alan that hit and buried that man. No, not my brother! Lisa, maybe he had seen what happened that night and don't want to get involved.

Joanna stands up and walks into her bedroom and closes the door behind her. *What's going on, Lord? Detective Theodore keeps coming around having Alan nervous every time.* She walks into the bathroom and closes the door behind her. Lynn still talking about crimes all over the world.

"It's a shame people have to kill for money or just out of anger, and I can't stand a theft."

"I don't blame you, sister! I feel the same way!" Josephine said.

"I remembered Mr. and Mrs. Douglas's son Ben broke into his own parent's house and they put him out again! Because he was using drugs and he tried to steal everything out his parent's house and they called the police."

Family Gathering

"**O**ur mother started packing things to move that same day!"

"That was funny because our mother was afraid of your grandfather's guns and he kept his guns loaded in their bedroom closet! And it wasn't a bad neighborhood, just a lot of kids on the block, but your grandfather had trust issues. He would stand in the yard, watching the neighbors, thinking they're stealing from him and he could outdrink anyone and come home and to pass out. And our mother would hit him in the head with the broom and make him get up and take a shower and eat some dinner, then bed." They all laughed.

"But your grandfather would never miss a day at work. I don't know how he did it! I would have not made it to work with a hangover like your grandfather had every morning. And he would come home from work and start drinking his whiskey every day!"

"Didn't that bother grandmother?" Lisa asked.

"Oh! Yes, she would cook and clean all day, waiting for dad to come home, so she could feed him, but he came home to drink, not to eat, and that's when the arguments started and our mother used to fuss at him and make him eat at the dinner table and he would eat a little and then go back to his drinking!" Lynn laughed. "I think Dad loved his drinking more than anything else, except he had to support his drinking habit because our mother would not give your grandfather any money because she knew where that money was going: to his whiskey! But he was a hard worker every day! Our father would work seven days a week! That's was so great about your grandfather."

"What did he do for a living?" Lisa asked.

"Detailed cars, even went to the rich neighborhood to detail cars every weekend," Lynn said. Ten minutes later, Alan and his father drove up into the driveway and his father parks his white 1997 Lincoln Continental pushing on the gas pedal and turns his V6 motor off.

"The engine sounds good, Dad!"

"Thanks, son! I keep the motor in shape. That vehicle is my joy!" Alan puts his right arm around his father's shoulders while walking into the front door together.

"The vehicle is all gassed up and ready to roll!" Leroy said. Leroy then walks into the living room and gives Patrick and Bill handshakes.

"Now don't forget to come next month and bring your hunting gun, brother-in-law," Leroy said to Patrick. "And it was nice meeting you, Bill!"

Lynn was giving her son and daughter a hug and a kiss on the forehead.

"It's three forty-five p.m. Let's leave now and get on the 88 freeway before the five o'clock traffic hits! They were hugging and giving handshakes as Joanna opens the front door, giving her in-laws a hug. Alan was standing next to his wife Joanna while Lisa was looking sad. Joanna gave Lisa a hug.

"Well, this is it," his father said, opening his car door and gets in, talking to his son about coming up to visit. Lisa and Josephine walk Lynn to the passenger side while Lynn opens the car door and gives her sister and her daughter a big hug.

"Call us when you get home, Mother!" Lisa said.

"Yes, dear." She gets into their vehicle, and they drive off waving. Patrick and Bill were standing in the front doorway, watching them leave, both waving. His father blowing his horn, driving to the corner, putting his left blinker on to make a left turn while they all turn around and walk back into the house.

Patrick and his friend Bill walk into the living room to finish their drinks.

"Well, I better get going too for work tomorrow!" Lisa grabs her things. "I'll see you later!"

"Wait a second, Lisa, I'll make you a plate to take home," Josephine said. "And give your tiger the bones to chew on."

"Thanks, Auntie!" She walks over to her brother.

"Let me get a drink of soda first! It was good to see mom and dad again!" Lisa said while drinking 7 Up.

"Yes," Alan said.

"Good night, all." Lisa then walks out the living room.

"I have it all wrapped in aluminum foil to keep warm."

"Thanks, Auntie! See you all tomorrow." Her auntie Josephine opens the front door for Lisa. Josephine stands at the door and watches Lisa walk to her vehicle using her car alarm beep to unlock her car door and jumps in and starts her white Lexus and snaps her seat belt on while her car warms up for a second. She then drives off going east, driving fifteen miles an hour the speed limit. Lisa turns her radio on, listening to soft music, taking shortcuts to her place; fifteen minutes later, she makes it to her place to call her friends.

She now walks up to her front door and opens it to a familiar sound. "Meow!"

"Hello, Fluffy." She puts her plate of food on in the refrigerator and kicks off her shoes in her living room and turns her television on and walks into bathroom and puts on in her pink Betty Boop shorts and grabs her toothpaste to brush her teeth. She then brushes her golden blond hair and walks back into her bedroom and calls her friends.

"Hello!"

"Diana?"

"Hi, Lisa! It's me, Dana! Diana went to the store with our mother!"

"I was calling to see if you both want to go to the mall?" Lisa asked.

"About what time are you planning to go?" Dana asked.

"Around six p.m.?"

"I'll ask Diana when she gets back from the store."

"Dana, do you remember I told you both about that Detective Theodore coming to my job asking questions about that accident on Highway 15."

"Yes, I remember," Dana answered.

"Well, that same detective showed up at my brother's house while our parents were there!"

"That detective came again?" Dana asked.

"That accident happened two weeks ago and he was asking my brother about his coworker also!" Lisa said.

"They have to ask everyone those questions, Lisa! Nothing to worry about! The police do that. It's their job," Dana said.

"Well, I guess so," Lisa said. "I think my brother saw something that night because he hasn't been acting like himself lately. Did you hear about a robbery that same night, Dana?"

"I'm not into watching the news."

"Our parents watch the news all night."

Dana said, "I'm into flirting with the good-looking guys."

Both laughed.

"Are you still dating James?" Dana asked curiously.

"He hasn't called back. I guess he's busy with his job. He's a firefighter, and he got a bank account!"

Dana said, "You better keep him. Is he a homeowner?"

"No, he lives in a one-bedroom apartment. And he treated me so nicely that night! It was so romantic."

Lisa's thoughts drifted to her memory with James while Diana and her mother walked in with two brown paper bags. Dana got off the couch, and the book she was reading fell on the floor. She picked it up and dropped it on the end table. She helped her mother carry a bag into their kitchen.

"Diana! Lisa's waiting on the phone!" Dana shouted.

Diana put the groceries on the dinner table and walked over to answer the phone. "Hello, Lisa."

"Hi, Diana. Ready to go the mall around 6:00 p.m.? I want you to see that outfit that will turn every young man's head."

They both laughed.

"I thought you were dating that good-looking guy, James?"

"I haven't heard from him in a couple of days. Maybe when he's not busy, but it's time to move forward," Lisa said. "And you know what worries me the most?"

"What is that?"

"We have a killer in town," Lisa said.

"Now that's scary," Diana said.

"But we will keep our eyes out when we're at the mall. Are you still going to your brother's friend's funeral service?"

"Yes. My brother is going to need support, Lisa."

"Is his wife going?"

"I'm sure she's going, but the last time we went to a funeral was when our grandfather passed away last year, and he did not look the same," Diana said with sadness. "I better go help in the kitchen. Call us when you're ready. And we'll meet at the mall."

"See you then." Lisa got off the phone. She got up from her bed to find something fashionable to wear.

Meanwhile, her auntie Josephine was looking at the time.

It's 5:00 p.m. My sister should be home another hour, Josephine thought. She decided to go take a nap and wait for her sister Liz's call. Patrick and Bill were watching Western movies as Alan and Joanna walked into their bedroom and closed the door. Joanna gave her husband a noxious look.

"Don't start with me, please. I just want to try and relax from this entire weekend, so could you leave me alone, please?"

"What's wrong with you!" his wife yelled. "You better get it together, because I'm not losing anything. We have a history together, Alan!"

He then wanted to slap her at that moment.

"That's all you care about, Joanna! Yes, our lives together! You're not thinking straight!" Joanna rushed into their bathroom in anger. *Slam!*

"Bitch!" he yelled and laid down in the middle of their captain's bed. He laid his head back on his pillow. *Why did this have to happen? My heart and soul are trapped with a big secret that I need to release.*

Joanna walked out their bathroom with frightened tears.

He gave her a noxious look. "After Richard's service, I'm going to turn myself in and get rid of this awful, guilty feeling of the annoying fear. It's for the best! Whatever happens, I'll go to prison the rest of my life."

He was feeling shivery and nervous.

"And you get to keep the house and vehicles and my money. And you'll probably get married again while I sit in prison! That's why you married me in the first place? You bastard! That's what you think of me? You go to hell, bastard!" And she slammed their bedroom door shut.

Pissed off, her blood began rushing through her head. Joanna grabbed her car keys, walked out her front door, and got into her 1999 Tahoe hybrid. She sat there to cool off before she started her vehicle. She took a deep breath to calm her nerves and rolled her windows down.

She drove out their driveway, turning left, toward downtown. *I hope roaster still goes to the Rig's bar where my old friends hang out.* She drove into town, making a right on Lincoln Street. She parked her vehicle and looked into her mirror before she went into a bar, where all the rough bikers party. She grabbed her purse and locked her car door and walked toward the front door. As people were coming out of the club, she heard loud rock-and-roll music blasting out the bar. She walked in, noticing the disco lights flashing different colors. People were on the dance floor. Joanna then walked up to the bar to get a beer. She then started looking around to see if Roaster was around.

"Hello, pretty lady," a tall man with a long red beard, who can hardly see walks up and sits down on a bar stool next to her.

"What's your name, pretty lady?"

"My name is Promise."

"Well, Promise. I like that name." The tall drunk man's breath smelled like old beer.

"What kind of promises do you give, pretty lady?"

"Do you know Roaster?" she asked the drunken man.

"Everyone knows Roaster!

"I'll give you five dollars if you can tell me where Roaster lives."

"Just up the road, in the trailer park, number 9. You'll find him there."

Joanna gave the drunken man five dollars. She walked out the bar and got into her car and drove down the road to the trailer park. She looked around for address number 9, driving slowly down the rocky road. *There it is.*

Joanna parked her car in front of the number 9 trailer. She stepped out of her car. *It's dark around here.* She walked to the front door of number 9 and knocked.

A big guy opened the door.

"Roaster, is that you? It's Joanna."

"I'll be doggone. Where have you been hiding your pretty self? I thought you got married and moved away." Roaster gave her a big hug.

"I see you're still wearing that cheap cologne. I'm still Roaster!" He laughed, showing a few missing teeth, and he closed his front trailer door.

Meanwhile, Alan fell asleep on his bed, tossing and turning, feeling his guilty conscience. Patrick and Bill were watching Western movies and drinking.

"You may have your wife pick you up later," Patrick said to Bill.

The house phone rang, and Patrick jumped up and rushed to the kitchen phone. "Hello?"

"Is Joanna home?"

"No, she's not in. May I take a message?"

"Tell her Jenna called."

"All right, I'll tell her." Patrick hung up the phone. His wife walked into the kitchen. "Was that Lynn?"

"No, it was for Joanna. Her friend Jenna."

"Where's Joanna?"

"She left. It looked like she was in a hurry," Patrick said.

"And where's Alan?"

"He's gone to bed."

Thirty-five minutes later, Joanna walked out of Roaster's place with a serious look on her face. Roaster heard Joanna driving out of the trailer park. Joanna looked at the speed limit, driving out the trailer park to the main streets. She then made a right turn to Main Street to the signal lights.

I'll take the city streets to Road 15. It's the fastest way home. I'm really not that much in a rush to look at Alan. Thank God for Mondays. And roaster was trying to get me drunk, telling me he still loves me! I'm feeling a little buzz from his gin. She was feeling dispirited with greed. *And that stupid bastard husband of mine!*

She had her left arm out the car window, feeling the warm breeze, while another car passed her, going south. She turned up the stereo, cruising past the speed limit. She checked the rearview mirror to see if she looked high. A couple of minutes later, she put on her right blinker and turned into her street. She pulled up into her driveway and parked next to Josephine's vehicle. She turned off the engine and left on her stereo, listening to an Aretha Franklin song.

If you love me! Joanna turned up the volume, not caring if the neighbors heard the music. *The way I feel right now, I just want to leave him. I married the bastard, and our relationship hasn't been trustworthy for a long time since he cheated on me with Ashlee or Alexis, whatever was her name. That was when we first dated, then after two months, I found out he had cheated. I should have left him then, but I was deeply in love with him at the time! I just don't feel the same love I used to have for him.*

Joanna began singing while she drove into her driveway. "It's no way for you to love me! Sing it, Aretha Franklin!" Joanna shouted.

"Joanna, are you coming in?"

Joanna ignored Josephine. She went on sitting in her car, singing, not caring about anything at the moment.

Josephine closed the front door to grab the phone. "Hello?"

"Just a minute," Patrick said.

Josephine picks up the house phone. "Lynn! I'm glad you made it home safe." She was feeling excited talking to her older sister.

Morally Corrupted

"We just walked into the door. Let the good Lord do the driving," Josephine said with laughter. "Is Lisa still there?"

"No, she went home a little while ago."

"I'm sure she made it home!" Josephine said.

"Tell her don't worry. Everything is going to be all right. They're just a little depressed about Alan's friend," Lynn said. "And they're going to the service next week. Alan wasn't acting himself and he's usually the life of the party!"

"Remember that, Josephine, just as happy as he could be!"

"I remember that!"

"But I guess people change," Lynn said.

"I'm glad you both made it safe!"

"The freeway wasn't too bad, well, I'm going to get out of these clothes."

"I'll remember to tell Lisa to call you later."

"She changes her numbers too much for me to keep up!" her sister Lynn said as they laughed.

"All right, you get some rest and call me tomorrow!" Josephine said.

"Love you, sister, talk to you later, bye!" Lynn said. Josephine hangs up and walks back into the dining room and sits down. "Where's Joanna?"

"She is sitting in her car, listening to music."

Alan walks out to his wife. "Where have you been the last couple of hours?"

"You know what, Alan? You are an idiot! I feel everything is ending because of your drinking and driving!" she yells with tears rolling down her face, feeling disappointed in their marriage. He walks back into his house and slams the front door hard! And he walks over to his bar, looking confused with anger.

"I need a drink!"

"What's wrong, Alan?" Patrick asked.

"She pisses me off!"

He grabs the fifth of gin bottle and quickly takes a drink with no chaser.

"What happened?" Patrick whispered.

"She's talking stupid! Smelling like she's been in a bar drinking with someone."

"It's time for us to go home for the evening and let them work out their problems." Josephine gets up from the dining table and goes down the hallway to the guest room to get her purse.

"It's time to go, Bill. We'll drop you off on our way home."

Alan walks in. "Where are you all going?"

"Good night. We'll see you two tomorrow!" Patrick said. Josephine had her purse over her shoulders. They were walking out the front door and down the two steps on the porch. "Good night."

Josephine gets into the driver side, waiting for Patrick and to get in and get into their seatbelts. Josephine drives off slowly. Joanna gets out her car and locks it. She then walks into their bedroom and slams the door. Alan turns out the lights in the house and lies on his couch and falls asleep.

It's six thirty a.m. He realized that he fell asleep in his clothes and gets up looking at the television was still on from last night. He gets up and turns the television off and grabs his empty glass and puts it into the kitchen sink. Alan then walks out the kitchen to his bedroom to get ready for work. He continues with his plans to take his Lincoln Navigator to the shop this morning.

I'll just wait till she leaves for work so she won't start any arguments, he was thinking to himself. Alan looks at his wife and then he grabs his pressed suit out their closet and lays it on the bed and walks over to their white gold-trimmed five dresser and pulls out his undershorts and a clean white T-shirt. She walks into the bathroom and turns on the hot shower. Joanna finished dressing, and she walks out the bedroom and goes into the kitchen to start the coffee pot and makes some toast and eggs and gets two plates from the cabinet, rolling her eyes, thinking about her damaged husband but still carrying the memory of their best times. *Alan used to keep me smiling, just looking at how handsome and charming he used to be. He opened the car door for me all the time. He used to show me love and respect that I deserved. He used to treat me like a lady! He would always ask me about love and never disappoint me till now!*

She then pours herself a cup and puts butter on her toasts and makes sunny-side up eggs. Alan was stepping out the shower and dries himself off to get dressed. He puts the towel around his wet body and starts brushing his teeth and brushing his brownish short hair, and putting aftershave lotion on. *I can't wait to get the car fixed today, and I would have to leave it there for a day or two, but it will be fixed then. Maybe that detective will stop coming around, and if he had something on me, he would have arrested me. That detective has no proof by taking those pictures of my car. Anything could have happened, but he seems not to believe my alibi.* He then opens the bathroom door and starts smelling coffee and eggs. Alan then he puts his light blue two-piece suit and his white long-sleeved cotton shirt with his light blue pressed suit pants and then he put some nylon light blue socks on and his black Stacy Adams shoes. Looking clean with his dark blue tie, he puts on last his matching light blue suit coat. Walking out the bedroom toward the kitchen, he looked at Joanna standing there cooking eggs and toast. "Would you like some breakfast?"

"I'm a little hungry this morning."

"There's your plate and your toast!" she said.

"Do we have any jam in the refrigerator?" he asked in his soft deep voice.

"There should be a jar of jam in there," she yelled.

She then looks at the time. *It's ten after seven a.m.,* thinking to herself.

"Alan, I just want to say you let me down and you let yourself down by drinking alcohol too much! And that's why you're in trouble now!"

"Joanna, I don't want to hear no shit this morning!"

"Then what, Alan? We can't even have a decent honest conversation together! Because you can't think straight anymore! And you were acting weird around your parents!" she shouted. "Lisa even noticed the change in you also!" While she was eating her toast and drinking her black coffee, she takes a deep breath and finishes her coffee and puts her empty cup on the counter. "I'm going in early!" she said with an attitude. He just looks at her and says nothing more. *Just waiting for you to leave for work so I can continue with my plans this morning,* he was thinking. Joanna grabbed her purse and turns and walks out the front door and slams it behind her and walks to her 1999 Tahoe Hybrid with tinted windows and unlocks her car and opens the driver door and gets in and starts her car and drives out the driveway and noticed Alan come out the front door and locks the door. Watching his wife drive toward the corner, putting her right blinker on and makes a right turn as Alan walks to his light green Mustang, and he unlocks it to get the remote to the garage to drive his 2000 Lincoln to the shop this morning. He gets into his Lincoln and drives it to a shop and puts his left blinker on and drives on Road 15, the same direction where the accident happened. Trying not to remember the accident. he turns left to the city limits, driving down Main Street to get to the auto shop early. A few minutes later he arrives to Mark's auto shop and steps out of his Lincoln to talk to the auto repair worker, leaving his car running. A guy walks up to Alan, "May I help you?"

"I need an estimate on my front hood."

"Sure! I'll take a look." The auto repair guy started looking at the hood and side for an estimate. "Yes, it can be repaired," the auto man said, holding a writing pad and doing the estimate.

"I can have it ready for you Friday!

"That would be fine. What's it going to cost?"

"Well, from the estimate, it's going to cost you 925 dollars all together," the auto repair man said.

"Okay thanks, where can I get a cab?" Alan asked the repair man.

"You just fill out this paperwork and I'll call a cab for you." Alan sits in the auto shop office and fills out the paperwork. A few minutes later, Alan gets into the cab and drives off.

And a half hour later, he makes it to work.

"Mr. Jones, you're late!" his receptionist said.

"You have three calls to return," the receptionist said.

"Has my wife called?" Alan asked.

"No sir," the receptionist said, walking behind Alan to give him his messages. The receptionist walks back to her desk while the phones rings.

"Could you hold please?" the receptionist said to a caller. "Mr. Jones! Mr. Terrie is on line 1."

"Thank you!" He picks up his office phone.

"Mr. Terrie! How are you?" Alan tried to sound excited. *Buzz!* "Could you hold for just a second please?"

"There's Lieutenant Theodore! He's waiting in the lobby for you." He gets a little nervous.

"Okay, I'm on a conference call for the moment! It will be a while before I get to him!" Alan started getting nervous and panicky.

His receptionist said, "Lieutenant, he's on a conference call. He will be just a few minutes!"

"That will be fine, I'll wait!" Lieutenant Theodore whispers to the receptionist. Forty-five minutes later, Alan gets off his conference call.

"He's off the phone, you can go in now!"

"Thank you very much." *Knock*!

"Lieutenant! What can I do for you?"

"Well, I came by to show you this photo of the road."

"Detective, why would I want to see a picture of a road?"

"Oh, because I'm still working on the case of the hit and buried man, and you know what? I think it's the tire marks from the accident that evening, which was two weeks ago!" the lieutenant said.

"Lieutenant! I'm very busy today!" Alan said with a little attitude.

"Oh, I'm sorry, but I waited to show you this picture!" He walked closer to Alan's desk to show him the photo. "Now you see here in this area? This tire mark it looks like someone drove in reverse, and then he gets out of a vehicle and then walked around the car where the body was! The driver put a lot of time in to pull the body down the hill of this park! It's just a theory of mine, Mr. Jones! And in your right mind and soul, you want your conscience cleared!"

"I'm very busy, Lieutenant! So why don't you take your theory someplace else!" Alan yelled as his phone rings.

"I have to get this. Do you mind?"

"N,o go right ahead, I'll just leave. Thank you! Oh, I almost forgot!" He snapped his fingers.

"What is it, Lieutenant?" He begins feeling more fear.

"Well, you know tomorrow is Mr. Johnson's service, the victim that got hit and buried on Road 15." Alan looks at him with a lump in his throat and he felt he couldn't swallow.

"This is not a convenient time, Lieutenant!"

"I just want to let you know that the investigation is going fine!"

A look appears on Alan's face as Lieutenant Theodore abruptly walks out of Mr. Jones's office, with his unlit cigar, without further explaining his comment.

Alan rolls his eyes and answers his office phone.

"Mr. Morris, how are you doing?"

He had buzzed his receptionist. "Hold my calls for a few minutes please?" Alan was feeling a little fidgety from Detective Theodore coming around again, Alan was breathing a little hard, trying to calm down his nerves and puts his left hand over his face.

Is this ever going to stop? Alan was thinking. *I need to send the Johnson family some flowers but anonymously! I'll do that after work and send it to the church from the flower shop, saying it's from a friend with no name. That would be a good deed for the day, and it's still early. Richard's service is this week, and I hope my wife still plans to go with me. If not, it's okay. I can handle it myself. But it's feels so weird how a casual friend can just go like that. It suddenly makes me realize just how much we had in common beyond the obvious. Nothing ever happens until it happens! This is draining my energy!* Alan was thinking. *I feel so guilty that I took a life! This guilty feeling is eating me up inside.* A couple of hours later, Alan goes to lunch. He closes his office door. "I'm off to lunch," he tells his receptionist while she was on the phone. Alan walks to the elevator to the garage, where he has a dark green Mustang with red interior parked in his reserved space. Alan gets the keys out of his pocket and jumps into the car, and he then puts his car in reverse and drives off going to a flower shop. Alan was driving slow looking around for the lieutenant's car and he noticed a flower shop on Main Street and parks in front of the flower shop. He then walks toward the flower shop and opens the door that swings out. He walks around, looking at different flowers till he notice the yellow roses and picks up a bouquet of yellow flowers with long stems and thorns. He then walks up to the counter with the yellow roses.

"Would you like a box with these?" the lady asked.

"Yes please and a card to go with it."

"Sure," the lady said behind the counter as Alan started to fill the card out.

"Where would you like to send these?" the lady behind the counter asked.

"190 Main Street Christian church. Can you send them out this evening?"

"Yes, sir! And that will be twenty dollars and eighteen cents." Alan takes some the money out of his wallet and gives to the cashier.

"Keep the change."

"Thank you and come again," the cashier said.

Alan walks out the flower shop and gets into his green Mustang and drives down Main Street and makes a stop at Jack in the Box and parks and walks in.

"May I help you?"

"Yes, I would like a double cheese burger with large fries."

"And what would you like to drink with that?"

"A large Coke please."

"That would be five eighty."

Alan gets his wallet out and pulls out twenty dollars as the young man gives Alan a cup and his change. Alan walks over to the soda fountain and pours his Coke into his cup and stands there till his food is ready. He looks at his cell phone. "No call yet from my wife." "Number 17!" the young man yells. Alan walks back up to the counter and gets his food and walks to his vehicle and unlocks it the driver side and gets in and puts his food on top of the glove box and starts his Mustang and grabs some fries before driving off. *Everything is taken care of,* he was thinking. He waits for a car to pass him. He then puts the Mustang in reverse and then he puts it into drive while eating fries and drives to the signal light.

Furious of Fear

Alan was eating his beef sandwich while the signal light turns green. He makes a left turn toward his job on the corner of Fifth and Main Streets. It's ten to one p.m. Alan continued eating his meal while driving back to work. A couple of minutes later, Alan arrives back to his employment building and parks in his stall. *Vroom.* Alan was enjoying the feeling of the engine and finishing his meal before he turns the engine off and grabbed his meal bag and gets a napkin to wipe his face and hands and grabs the keys out of the ignition and gets out and locks the door and walk to the elevator. Few moments later, Alan arrives and walks into his office and notices messages on his desk and picks up his messages. "Mr. Oxford's clients were assigned to you till we get a replacement."

"Great! More work," he thought to himself and sits at his desk and started reading the names of Richard's clients and gets up and walks out of his office to Richard's office to get the files of those seven clients he was assigned to. He walks down the hall and opens Richard's office door, turns on the lights, and walks toward his desk and notices nothing been touched. Alan then walks slowly to Richard's file cabinet and opens it, looking for seven clients' names. Alan turns his head and looked around for a second and closed the file cabinet drawer. "Poor Richard! You left too soon." Alan walks toward the door and turns out the lights and closes the door. *It felt creepy going in there without Richard!*

Alan was thinking and walks back to his office feeling weird!

"I sure do miss him walking into my office with his outgoing happy personality. I don't think I have ever seen Richard mad or sad out the couple of years I've known him. He was like an inspiration to me. Let the good times roll, and don't worry about the bad times, he used to say to me.

Alan was like in a daze, thinking of Richard swinging back and forth slowly in his black leather office chair, taking a deep breath.

Ring, ring. Alan then came out of his thoughts of Richard and grabs his cell phone and looks at the caller ID. "Joanna." A surprised look on his face. "I didn't think you were going to call me today."

"I've been doing some thinking!"

"About what?" he asked his wife.

"About sticking together for our marriage," Joanna said with a little aggressiveness. "Did have lunch?" Joanna asked.

"Yes, and you?" he asked.

"Yes, I had a crab salad and some coffee."

"Will you be going with me to Richard's service on Thursday?" Alan asked his wife.

"I suppose so! But we will talk about it when we get home!" Joanna said. "How are you feeling? I know you were kind of close to him!"

"I'm okay," Alan said. "I'm glad you called, Joanna, you make me feel better! You know you are my better half. I don't think I can go on living with you!"

"Well, I'll see you later!" Joanna said.

"All right, baby!" They both hang up. The rest of his day and evening went nervously.

Tuesday morning, Alan gets up at five thirty a.m., rubbing his eyes, feeling like he couldn't sleep a wink. He tries to lie back down, but couldn't like there's a block around my heart and my soul, feeling restless. Alan takes his right hand across his face, feeling awkward with fear, thinking about the man he killed and his family. Alan gets up from his side of the bed to go wash his face while Joanna sleeps soundly. Alan turns on the light in the bathroom and closes the door. A few minutes later, Alan was walking back into the bathroom. Joanna looks at the time clock on their dresser. It's ten minutes to six a.m. Joanna turns back over, pulling the covers over her chest to get a little more sleep while Alan steps into the shower to start the day.

A few minutes later, Alan gets out the shower and gets dressed and walks into the kitchen to make the coffee, trying to keep his mind together. *I hope those flowers for Mr. Johnson arrived. I should drive by there. Maybe I'll feel a little better or just feel guiltier as hell.*

I can't feel any worst then. I don't know why this had to happen to me? Alan listening to the coffee maker dripping and poured himself a cup of coffee, adding sugar and creamer too, and starts to drink his coffee, looking out the kitchen window, listening to the birds singing and the sun rising. "Lord? Where do I go from here?" He was looking out the kitchen window at the sky. "Lord, I'm still feeling guilty. I feel it's my responsibility to face my troubles, but how, without going to prison for the rest of my life!" He was looking at the sky, talking to God.

"No, I can't do that. I'd rather die first than to face prison, God! I feel agitated and guilty as hell." He was nervous, shaking and feeling panicky, breathing hard. "Forgive me, Lord God, please. It's six twenty-five a.m. I need to calm down my nervous self. He pours himself another cup of coffee and opens the refrigerator, and he get out the ham and eggs. He grabs the ham and eggs out slowly and grabs a skillet. He turns on the fire to the stove and started mixing his eggs and takes two slices of cut ham and pours a little cooking oil in the skillet and makes breakfast for his wife also. He hears the shower water turned on. "Joanna must be up!"

He begins rushing to cook breakfast and have it on the table before she walks out the bedroom. "Let me get two plates ready and have her cup of coffee ready."

Alan sets the two plates on the dinner table and walks back into the kitchen to turn the ham over and get the four eggs in a bowl to scramble and pours the eggs in a hot skillet. While Alan was cooking, Joanna walks out the shower and started drying her hair, wondering how her day was going to go.

I hope this day goes by fast so Thursday will get here because I don't like funerals, but who does? If it wasn't Alan's coworker and friend, I would talk him out of going because all this depression is going to hit him and Detective Theodore doesn't make it any better by coming around often, Joanna was thinking, and she turns off her hair drier. She was brushing her hair and puts on her makeup and walks out the bathroom and puts on her short dark green dress and her black high heels and puts on her far away perfume and walks out the bedroom toward the dinner room and notices two plates sitting on the table with silver ware and the smell of ham and eggs coming from the kitchen. His wife walks into the kitchen. "Good morning!"

"Good morning," he repeated.

"I see you cooked breakfast. Thank you," his wife said with her soft voice.

"I want to ask you something," Alan said. "Did you decide to go with me to Richard's services Thursday?"

"Yes, of course. Isn't that's what the wife's supposed to do: stand by her man?" she said with her smart attitude. "The ham and eggs look good."

"Thanks." They both walk into the dining room and sit at the table and begin eating their breakfast and drinking their coffee, keeping silent from each other, feeling a little down, wondering if the police is ever going to come through the front or back door to arrest him. Alan was wondering the same every morning and evening.

This fear I'm feeling for him every day and I didn't do the crime! I shouldn't be feeling this way and it won't let go! They both just look at each other, finishing up their breakfast, and get up and take their plates into the kitchen.

"Alan! I don't want to lose faith in our marriage, but I feel this guilt that you're feeling because I am a part of you, and I feel things you feel and it's not something you want to

keep inside of you!"

"Don't go there, Joanna, not this morning! What's done is done!" Alan shouts.

"Then what? We live with your guilt?" Joanna yelled.

"You know what you're asking me to do, Joanna? I'm not going to do that! And lose you and my future?" he shouted. "I'm going to work early. It's better than standing here and fighting with you!" He grabs his keys and she grabs her purse, and they both walk out the front door toward their vehicles. He jumps into his green 1969 Mustang with red interior and drives out their driveway. *Maybe I should go by the church at eleven and say a forgiving prayer. This indescribable guilty feeling sticks to me like glue. I feel so bad for this man that I killed! I hope they received the flowers I've sent anonymously!* Alan was thinking while he was driving into town on Main Street, with his right hand on the wheel and his left on his lap on his way to work thinking about going by a church. *Damn! I don't even feel right about this day! I wish I was more careful that night! I've learned not to drink and drive. Wow, I truly understand what the law is saying! And I'm so sorry. I just feel awful about this!* Alan was wiping his small tears with his left hand and then reached in the glove box for a napkin while driving slowly toward his employment on the busy main street. The signal light turned red. He slowed down and stops sitting in his '69 Mustang, looking at other drivers, thinking that everyone notices his guilt that sticks in his soul. *Beep, beep.* Car horns blow; the light turns green. *Just three more blocks to my job!* A few minutes later, Alan drives down in parking garage and he stopped to get a ticket to put into the windshield. Alan parks his dark Mustang while listening to his music, having a moment of silence to collect his thoughts before going upstairs. *It doesn't feel the same with Richard gone. This whole thing has gotten on my nerves. I'm hoping Detective*

Theodore isn't waiting for me in my office because he's really getting on my damn nerves! I don't know what to do to make things right! Turning myself in isn't going to make this terrifying guilty feeling go away. Oh, God! What can I do? What can I do to make things right again? I've killed a man by burying him alive, not realizing he was alive! I've could have saved him. I just panicked, thinking he was dead. And I thought I could hide the body where no one would ever find him. Fifteen minutes later, he returns to his employment. Alan noticed the elevator door was closing. He rushes on the elevator and arrives to his office on the fifth floor.

"Good morning," Alan said in a low voice as he walks by his receptionist with his head down.

"Good morning, Mr. Jones!" Alan walks into his office, feeling a little relieved that the detective wasn't sitting there and closes the door behind him with less fear. *I'm really thinking about going by there around lunch. Maybe I'll feel a little better than I did earlier. I want to go pay my respect or something for the victim! I'm trying to do something about this guilt that I carry day and night and all through my restless nights! This intense distress is sticking to my conscience like glue! It's called guilt of sin, and I'm so afraid I'm going to go to hell for the silence of murder, which means I'm a coward! I can't face the crime I've committed and hope Joanna sticks to my silence till death do us part.*

"Here are the new clients' files, Mr. Jones." She hands him Richard's files.

"Thanks."

Alan lets out a deep breath and buried his face into both his hands. *My life seems completely different now for worse!* He stands up from his chair and walks over to the large window and looks out and sees the sun has risen and people rushing to their responsibilities. *And that's what life is about. I can't even feel that normal life, living anymore like I used to feel. I remember the first time we got drunk together at a party ten years ago, and we woke up together on the beach. I fell in love with Joanna. She was the reason why I wanted to graduate from college to show her I was the best at everything and that I liked her and I won her heart and she returned her love for me! She's a little insecure and jealous, but ambitious and an aggressive personality, and she sticks by my side like a wife. We both bring in great incomes to keep the bills paid and we're homeowners together. I don't want to lose what we built in our relationship, the trust and devotion. I promise to keep her happy and that keeps me happy. I still remember when I cheated on my wife when we first got together and she's been faithful to me and all the guys wanted Joanna in our senior school years.* He then looks at the time. It's only fifteen after nine in the morning.

"I should drive by the church where his family is having the service." Just waiting for the time to move on, he sits back at his desk and starts looking at the new client's application and clears his throat and takes a deep breath.

I try to concentrate on my work, but my thoughts won't focus on my work. It's like I just can't seem to focus! Alan slams his right fist to his desk.

Buzz!

"Yes!"

"Mr. Jones, Detective Theodore on line 2!"

"Thank you." He waits a second before he picks up the phone. "Mr. Jones speaking!"

"This is Detective Theodore. I just wanted to know if you are going to be busy around noon today. I have a couple of more theories I would like to go over with you."

"Um, Detective, I'm sorry I have plans at noon!"

"Oh, okay, maybe later then," Detective Theodore said. "Good-bye!"

What is that Detective Theodore up too? Alan was thinking. The hours went by while Alan still trying to figure out if he should drive by the church. *I will feel so ashamed and so remorseful.* It's bugging him where he can't concentrate on his new client's files.

So he stands up and walks out of his office. "I'm going to lunch, hold my calls!"

"Yes, Mr. Jones," his receptionist said. Alan walks toward the elevator; he makes it to his green Mustang and gets in and starts it and drives out the parking lot and drives on Main Street, turning right. The street light turned red; he puts his left foot on the breaks! Seconds later, the street light turns green. Alan drives slower just a few blocks down toward Beaver Street and turned left off Main Street on to Beaver Street to the church on the corner were the black limo and the black hearse sits. He drives slowly down the block of the Christian church and notices two men were standing outside by the black limo talking in front of the church. Alan drives down past the church and turns his green Mustang around with his heavy engine. *Vroom.* He parks across the street four buildings down from the Christian church with a big golden cross on top of the white church building with two large brown doors that opened at that moment. Alan was looking hard through his windshield and notices five males were carrying the white and blue casket with flowers. Alan was looking even harder at the casket, feeling heavyhearted and deprived of courage! *I just want to run out there and tell his family it was me that killed your family member. It was me that caused his death! And that it was an freak accident! And I didn't mean for any of this to happen! This is a heavy burden that's sinking my heart.* Alan continued looking at all the mourners walking out the church to their vehicles with bright orange stickers on their windshields that read Funeral to the Interment. *I'm going to wait till they all leave so no one will notice me driving by.*

Two minutes later, the black hearse and the black limo begin to drive slow from the church with their headlights on while all the mourners follow. Alan was watching the hearse drive slowly passing him. Alan was looking at the open side window with curtains. He just stared hard at the casket while the hearse drives by. "I am so sorry, Mr. Johnson!" Alan said aloud to the deceased while the hearse drives off slowly and the black limousine with his family members and other vehicles follow.

Alan looks at the time: a quarter to one p.m. Alan starts his Mustang. Three more vehicles drive by slowly. About fifteen cars went by. Alan noticed one more car pulled out from a couple cars parked headed for him and he recognized Detective Theodore. Alan was surprised. *He didn't notice I was parked here. He would have walked over to me and that would have given me away!*

Mr. Johnson's Service

*A*lan takes a deep breath. *I noticed Detective Theodore driving off following the mourners. I'll wait a few minutes before I drive off to make sure everyone left, even Detective Theodore! I'm really surprised! That kind of shocked my nerves even more. This week is not so easy for me, but once Mr. Johnson's buried, gods bless his soul, then I can feel more relaxed, but when my time comes, God is not going to be happy to see me! I'm a coward in my crime I committed.* Alan drives back to Main Street. He stops at a stop sign and looks around to see if Detective Theodore was parked somewhere watching him. He turns right and drives to a restaurant just a couple of more blocks away to get something for lunch. He turns into an IHOP restaurant and parks his green Mustang.

He turns off the engine and opens the car door and locks with the remote and walks into the IHOP restaurant and stands in line looking at the menu board above, holding his car keys, feeling a little nervous, looking around for that detective, wondering if he really went to the graveyard or was he just watching him?

"May I help you, sir?"

"Yes, I would like a ham toasted on white bread with everything on it," Alan said to the man behind the counter.

"And what would you like a drink with that?"

"Of course, some tea with lemon please!" A few minutes later, Alan gets back into the car with his sandwich. It's five after one p.m., a few minutes late doesn't matter.

He drives down on Main Street and drives through town and gets back to the job two minutes later and parks in his reserve. Alan turns off the engine and opens the car door and steps out and locks it as he walks back toward the elevator and walks on it and pushes the fifth floor button standing with two other employees. A few seconds later, he makes it to his office.

"Mr. Jones! Mr. Sanders wants you to call him back as soon as possible." The receptionist hands Alan a piece a paper with messages.

"Thank you." He walks into his office and closes the door and walks over to his desk and takes a seat in his chair and takes a deep breath while he answers his office phone and calls his client, Mr. Sanders.

"Hello!"

"Mr. Sanders, this is Mr. Jones returning your call."

"Yes, Mr. Jones. I called to see if my wife and I could get a mortgage loan on our home?" "Well, let me pull up your files and we can go from there! I'm going to put you on hold for a few minutes." Alan gets up and walks over to his file cabinet. His cell phone rings, sitting on his desk. Alan lets it go to voice mail while he concentrates on his client's file. "Yes, Mr. Sanders. I see that you paid all your payments and things look okay to start the process." Alan's cell phone begins to ring again. Alan looks at the caller ID. *It's Lisa calling. I'll call her back later!* Alan began talking to his client on his office phone for one hour and twenty minutes. Alan looks at the time. *It's two twenty-two. Let me call Lisa back.* Alan picks up his cell phone and he calls Lisa back.

"Lisa, what's going on?" Alan asked.

"I just wanted to know: should we take some flowers to your friend's services Thursday?"

"I don't know. Let me think about it and I'll call you back," Alan said in a sad voice.

"Is anything wrong, Alan? You sound so down," Lisa said.

"I'm fine," he replied in a low deep voice. "I'll call you back," Alan said.

"Okay." He hangs up. *Buzz.*

"Yes!"

"Detective Theodore is waiting in the lobby," the receptionist said. Alan gets nervous and begins breathing a little hard.

"Yes! Tell him I'm on the phone with a client and I'll be with him in few minutes."

"Yes, sir," the receptionist said. "Detective, he's on a call right now and he will be with you soon."

"Thank you!" Detective Theodore was sitting on a long black trench coat and gets up to take off his coat and onto his lap. The receptionist noticed his gray suit and his black Stacy Adams shoes and his smell of aftershave lotion.

"Detective, he's off the phone now. You can go right in."

"Thank you!" He gets up and walks into Alan's office and closes the door behind him.

"Detective Theodore, what can I do for you today?"

"I just want to see if you made it back from lunch yet?"

"What do you mean?"

"Well, I've called your office around eleven a.m. and your receptionist said you had gone early for lunch and that's why I asked!"

"Okay, Detective! What is that you want?"

"Well, I went by the church where they had Mr. Johnson's services today to see if I can spot the killer, but I didn't notice anything strange, except I did notice a dark blue '68 Mustang just like your car parked, and it looked like someone was actually sitting in the car about four or five buildings down, but I couldn't recognize the driver. It could have been a friend or the killer not trying to be noticed," the detective said. Alan swallows and feels more nervous.

"Detective! I have a lot of work to finish, and if that's all you come by for, then I'm really busy, Detective!"

"I noticed that, sir," the detective said.

Buzz.

"Yes!"

"You have a call on line 4."

"Thank you," Alan replied nervously while Lieutenant Theodore was trying to stare hard in his teary eyes.

"Well, I better be on my way," Theodore said and walks out of his office, closing the door behind him.

"I can see the guilt is eating him alive, and sooner or later, he's going to make a confession, and I'll be ready to hear it all! Or I'll just use the little evidence I do have, which may not hold in court, but his confession will." Theodore was thinking hard while stepping onto the open door of a elevator and pushed the ground floor button for parking. As the detective steps off the elevator couple of seconds later and walks toward Mr. Jones's parking space, he noticed the same dark blue Mustang that was sitting down the street from the church. "It's him because I noticed the sticker at the back of his window, 'Let's roll in my '68.' In my heart, I feel it was him sitting in this car watching the service of Mr. Johnson, the man he killed. He was feeling guilty, and I feel Mr. Johnson needs justice and closure for his soul to rest in peace, and I'll be the one to give it to him, that peace." Detective Theodore was feeling that for Mr. Jones to confess the truth. it looks like I'm going to have to push the truth out of him or the guilt is going to eat up his heart and soul alive! The detective walks back to his car and drives down Main Street to Lisa's job. A few minutes later, he arrives and parks in front of Quotable Women's and gets out, looking aggressive, feeling more serious about this case. And he walks into the hair salon smelling of hair spray and curling iron!

"Lisa Jones?"

"Yes! Hello, Detective!" Lisa said with a happy attitude.

"How are you?" Detective asked.

"What questions do you have today? I haven't seen you since you came by my brothers place." She was combing her client's brown long curly hair with a hot comb.

"Sorry to bother you, but I need to ask you about Thursday."

"What about it?"

"Well, I wanted to know how your brother was taking it and if he was going to be all right with his close friend deceased now."

"Why don't you ask him?" Lisa replied.

"Well, I've tried, but he seems very busy working. I didn't want to keep bothering him too much, feeling all depressed and so forth!"

"You should understand that, Detective, we plan to go to his friend's services Thursday at eleven a.m."

"Oh! You're going also," Theodore asked in surprise.

"Yes, I feel I should be with my brother on occasions like this. He was close to Richard as a good friend for five years. Remember, they worked together, and I know his heart is broken about his friend and my brother wants me to be by his side like his wife, Joanna.

Joanna will give her husband comfort and support," Lisa replied. Detective Theodore smiles at Lisa, holding his lit cigar.

"Does your brother seems a little nervous lately about his friend getting murdered?"

"I would be if it was my close friend, wouldn't you, Detective?" Lisa replied.

"Yes, I probably would be," Theodore said, shaking his head yes, standing behind Lisa looking around at the pretty ladies.

"So you're a lady's man," Lisa said curiously noticing Theodore smiling at the ladies in the hair shop. "You married, Detective?" Lisa asked.

"Just browsing," Detective Theodore said. "Well, I better get going, Mrs. Jones, may I call you that?"

"I prefer Lisa."

"Sure!" He smiles, admiring Lisa's honesty and walks toward the front door slowly, continues smiling at the ladies, feeling good that changed his attitude. Theodore walks with a grin on his face to his car and unlocks it and gets in and starts his vehicle and drives off smiling.

"I'm glad I stopped by there! Seeing all those pretty ladies now. I need to get back to the office and write down my report on how I noticed he showed up at Mr. Johnson's service today, and I need to talk to the captain, and I'm going to Mr. Oxford's services and I have a theory that the brother of Richard Oxford may have killed him or had him killed! I'm going to watch him very closely, but I need the murder weapon, and when I get a chance to look closer in his trunk of his car or maybe just possibly, he hid it in the back of something. I just could feel it! To be certain I need to go really quick and see a close friend that can help me with these two murder cases." Detective Theodore drives into town, looking for a street named Crane Brook Court. The detective drives till he finds the street and turns right and drives, looking for the address: 920. *There it is!* The detective parks his car and gets out and walks to a wooden door and rings the doorbell. His mystery friend comes to the door.

"Detective! Good to see you!" his mystery friend said, holding incense.

"I need your help," the detective said to his mystery friend. The detective steps in and closes the door behind him. Fifteen minutes later, the detective walks out of his mystery friend's place, rushes to his car, jumps in, and drives off, rushing to the police station to get a warrant.

"From what my mystery lady told me that the murder weapon is somewhere dark, wrapped in a bloody rag or towel! Now I need to look in his backyard in the tool shed and look around for a bucket! No, she said somewhere closed in, under the spare tire in his trunk where he wouldn't think the police would look! Maybe he buried the weapon in the ground. I need to get another search warrant!" The detective drives faster to the station and arrives a couple of minutes later and parks his vehicle and rushes into his captain's office and knocks on the door. "Captain! I have an idea where that murder weapon is!"

"What do you have?" his captain asked in a curious way.

"I went to see a friend, and while I was talking to my friend, it hit me, Captain, the murder weapon is buried in his backyard."

"Whose backyard?" his captain asked.

"Dupree Oxford! He murdered his brother. Captain! If I could get another warrant to serve his parents' home and dig up the backyard, and I think I should do it after the service Thursday because the family wouldn't understand why I would start digging in their backyard! And for what reason! And I would have to tell them for a murder weapon!" the detective pours his feelings out to his captain.

"I see your point, Theodore!" his captain said. "I'll have the warrant first thing Friday morning after I talk to the judge. Now what's going on with the Jones's case?"

"He's almost ready to turn himself up! I'm almost certain, Captain."

"Oh, how do you know this, Theodore?"

"Because I can feel it, Captain! I am riding him hard to where he can't take it anymore." "Good job, Theodore!"

"Thank you, Captain!" He walks out of his captain's office and walked to his office to write down his report for the day. Two days later, the morning of Richard Oxford's service. It's nine a.m. two more hours before Richard's service. Alan was looking at the clock sitting behind his desk. "I have to pick Lisa up and Joanna can drive her car from work. Let me let me call her to make sure.

"Alan!" Joanna said.

"Are you going to drive your car to the service this morning?" Alan asked his wife.

"Yes, from my job."

"I'll have to meet you there and you know where it is?" Alan asked.

"Yes," his wife said.

"Why don't you follow me from Lisa's place," Alan replied.

"Sure. I have a customer coming in. I'll see you at Lisa's at ten forty-five."

"All right."

They both hang up. He was still trying to concentrate on his work for an hour and gets up and grabs his keys and walks out his office.

"I'm leaving for Oxford's service. Hold all my calls?"

"Alan Jones," his boss yelled.

"Yes, sir!"

"Are you going to Mr. Oxford's services this morning?"

"Yes, sir! I was just on my way sir!" Alan said.

"See you there!" his boss said.

"Yes, sir."

"And what time does it start?" his boss asked.

"At eleven a.m. this morning, sir!" Alan was feeling nervous.

"Richard was a good, respectable, and hard worker," his boss said.

"Yes, he was, sir."

"Well, I better get going myself," his boss said. "Oh, did you finish going through the new clients' files?"

"Yes, sir!"

"They're your new clients till I hire someone to take over Mr. Oxford's cases," his boss said and walks back to his office. Alan turns around and continues walking to the elevator and walks on and pushes the button for ground floor, feeling very nervous. He walks fast off the elevator and to his white Corvette and gets in and starts it and backs up and then puts it into drive without warming the car up and drives to the main streets to get home for a few minutes to relax his nerves before he faces Joanna and Lisa.

I need to calm down. I though my boss was upset today about Richard, but that was a release. Alan drives down Main Street and turns off on Highway 15 and started driving a little faster. Seven minutes later, he drives up to his driveway and parks and turns off the engine and just sits there for a few minutes to collect his nerves. Alan gets out of his car and locks it and looks at the time from his cell phone. "It's ten forty a.m.," Alan said to himself and walks to his front door and noticed how quiet it is. *It feels peaceful in here without anybody here. Let me change my clothes and get something to drink real fast.* Alan walks into his bedroom and changes his pants and shirt, wearing a black suit and a black long tie and a white dress shirt with the buttons in front and his black Stacy Adams shoes and splashes black Suede aftershave and walks out his bedroom and into the kitchen to get something to drink. His cell phone rings.

"Hello? Where are you?" Lisa asked.

"I'm on my way. Be ready. Are you at home or work?" Alan asked.

"I'm just leaving work. I'll be home in ten minutes. I'm riding with you, so I don't have to drive."

"All right, Lisa, Joanna should be on her way to your place also. I've told her to meet us there!" Alan said. "And I'm on my way to your place in about five more minutes, so you better get there before me or I'll leave you," Alan said, playing with his sister. Lisa hangs up and rushes out of her work place and jumps into her car and drives off to her place.

Richard's Service

Alan drinks some tea that's in his refrigerator and walks out the kitchen and grabs his keys and walks out the front door and locks it and walks to his 1968 Mustang and gets in and starts the engine and drives off going north toward Lisa's place. Ten minutes later, he arrives to pick up his sister, Lisa, and Joanna follows in her car to Richard's funeral services. Alan drives off Lisa's block and turns left to get back on Road 15, driving toward town to Main Street.

"Before we get there, can we stop at a flower shop. I'll feel better if you walked in there with flowers and a card." Alan looks at Lisa like she was crazy.

"We don't have time!"

"Please, Alan! I would feel better! I have never been to a funeral service before, and I want us to bring some flowers and a card. It's respectable," Lisa said.

"All right, really quick! We'll stop at the flower shop."

"Thank you, brother!" Alan pulls into the same flower shop where he came in a couple of days ago. Alan parks his '68 Mustang and walks in with Lisa to pick up some flowers while Joanna sits in her car, waiting for them.

"Hello, Mr. Jones," the woman behind the counter said.

"Hello! Alan said.

"Need more flowers?"

"Yes, for a funeral service today. My sister wants to buy. Give her whatever flowers she picks out," Alan said to the cashier.

"Yes, sir," the lady behind the counter said.

'Come on, Lisa, it's five minutes after eleven. Hurry up!" Alan was rushing her.

"All right, brother, here are a few red and white roses. They look nice," Lisa said. Alan gets his wallet out of his back pocket and pays for the flowers that Lisa had picked out for Richard's services, and they both walk back to his blue Mustang and they both jump in. Alan starts his car and puts it into reverse and backs up and puts it into drive while Joanna starts her car and follows Alan to Jeffery's funeral home just a few blocks away. Sixty seconds later, they arrive at Jeffery's funeral home parking lot in the back. Joanna parks next to Alan's 1968 Mustang as they turn off their engines and open their car doors at the same time. Joanna gets out of her Tahoe Hybrid and walks toward Alan and Lisa. As they walked up to the front door of the service, a man opens the doors for them. They looked around and noticed a lot of people have arrived for Richard's services and they take a seat in the last row. Everyone in the church was listening to the pastor talking about Richard's days and how he lived a short life.

"If there is anyone who'd like to come up here to the altar and say a few words?" One of Richard's family member steps up and says a few words about Richard. Richards's mother and father had tears running down their faces, holding each other's hands.

"Thank you, anyone else would like to read their cards or say anything?" the pastor asked. Everyone was looking around. "I have something to say," Richard's friend Curtis steps up, wearing black pants and a white shirt and also lipstick and makeup. Everyone was looking at him weird. "Richard was a good friend of mine for two years, and I just have to say I'm going to miss him dearly." As Curtis walks down from the altar with a twitch, everyone began gazing at him strangely. While Curtis takes his seat, Dupree was looking at him like he wanted to hurt Curtis for showing up today.

"Anyone else has cards to read for the service of Mr. Oxford?" the pastor asked. A heavyset woman walks up to the altar to read her condolence cards and prayers while mourners where sitting there, wiping tears and crying, feeling remorseful and devastated. Alan sits and starts looking around for Richard's brother Dupree, who's sitting between his parents to give them comfort and support for his brother's death. Lisa began feeling sad and Joanna just kept her head up, listening to the mourners reading their cards aloud. Alan looks at the time on his cell phone while sitting in the backseat of the church with Joanna and Lisa.

"And now we are going to a say prayer. Everyone, please bow your heads. Lord, we give you this comfort of this grievous day. May the Lord bless the Oxford family and give them courage to carry on with their lives and to heal their hearts with love. Bless the soul of Richard Oxford, and may he watch over his mother and father and his only brother. *Our father, who art in heaven…*" The pastor finished praying a few seconds later. "Now we will be reading the obituary, the homecoming of Richard Oxford." He takes a moment to look at the mourners. "Now we will view the remains of Richard Oxford."

Two men walk up and open the casket and uncover Richard's face with a white silk cloth.

His mother and father look at the casket noticing his hands were folded and looking good in his blue suit and wearing a lot of makeup. Mrs. Oxford had heavy tears in her eyes; her makeup was running.

The Pastor looks at another part of the viewing room. "Now those sitting on the left side of the back, please stand and walk to the front." Alan stands up and starts walking. Lisa and Joanna follow Alan to the front of the church toward the casket, and he stands there for a moment and gives Richard's mother a kiss and Richard's father a handshake.

"I'm sorry, he was a great man," Alan whispers to Mr. Oxford.

"Thank you," Mr. Oxford said. Alan walks over to Richard's body and just looks at him with Joanna and Lisa. "He has a lot of makeup on, he don't even look like himself," Alan said. Other mourners walk up behind Alan and Lisa and Joanna. "I'll miss you, buddy," Alan said and walks away from the body with his head down. Joanna grabs Alan and walks outside. Alan was feeling devastated and depressed after reviewing Richard's body. "That was hard on me," Alan said. Alan notices his boss walking up to the church.

"Alan Jones, are you all right?" his boss asked in a concerned way. "You look pained."

"I'll be all right. You're just making it?" Alan asked his boss.

"Yes! Is the service still going?" his boss asked.

"Yes, it is, sir." Alan looks at his boss.

"You look like you need the rest of the day off, I understand."

"Thank you, sir. I would like that, sir." He pats Alan on his back.

"I'm going to go in now," his boss said. "And you get some rest! And that's an order," his boss said. Joanna looks at Alan. "He's right. You don't look so good, dear, maybe we should leave." Lisa has another concern. "I thought we were going to the repast after we leave the cemetery?" Alan was speechless.

"Let's wait in the car till it's time to go," Lisa said.

"All right." While they walk to their vehicle, Alan recognizes Detective Theodore sitting in his police vehicle, watching everyone coming out of the Jeffery's funeral home. Everyone coming out the entrance was giving their condolences. The mourners' vehicles had bright orange stickers on their front windshields that say Funeral. "Please turn on your lights on when you get to your cars to get through the traffic and to the cemetery," the driver of the hearse said to everyone walking out the church, except Mr. and Mrs. Oxford and their only son Dupree, spending a couple of last minutes with their deceased son and brother. Three minutes later, the director closed the casket for burial while Dupree and five family male members lift up the casket and carry the casket to the hearse while the Oxfords follow their deceased son's casket out the doorway and into the black hearse. The driver closes the back door of the hearse and starts driving slow to the cemetery with the headlights on. The black limo follows with Mr. and Mrs. Oxford and their only son Dupree holding his mother's hand as she lays her head on her husband's shoulders. She was holding a white napkin, wiping her runny nose.

"It will be all right, Liz," her husband said. "We will get through this, I promise." Alan gets into his car with Lisa while Joanna follows Alan out of the parking lot while Theodore is following close behind Joanna's vehicle to the graveyard.

Joanna, initially, doesn't realize that his car with no orange sticker displayed on the windshield is following close to the other mourners behind the Hearse.

She then notices and watches the street lights as the drivers following the Hearse pass through the red lights.

We don't have to stop on a red light. We have a sticker, but the car behind me doesn't have a sticker on their windshield and it doesn't stop at the red lights, either. I see a motorcycled police officer driving on the left side of my car and passes all the cars to get ahead of the traffic. I have a headache. I'll be happy when all this is over!

Five minutes later, they arrived to the graveyard following the hearse to where they see the chairs sitting out next to a green cover over the dirt and a green tent for family members to sit close to the casket. The pastor say a few words and the last prayer for Richard Oxford as Mr. and Mrs. Oxford sit and look at their son's grave while Dupree sits next to his mother and father.

Detective Theodore gets out of his car and walks closer to the mourners that's standing close to the grave. He stands by someone's headstone to where he hears the pastor and looks around at the mourners.

Ten minutes later, Richard's service was over.

Everyone turns around and starts to walk back to their cars. Alan started back to his car with Lisa and Joanna. He noticed Detective Theodore was standing by a tall headstone, watching everyone leaving the cemetery.

"Detective, thank you for coming," Mr. and Mrs. Oxford said.

"Well, I thought I would look around, maybe I missed someone."

"Do you have any clues who killed my brother?" Dupree asked in a sarcastic manner.

"No, but the case is coming along just fine. I'm putting the pieces together, but I'll catch the killer. He can't hide too long because his conscience will bring him out and then we will make an arrest."

"Well, I need to get my family in the limousine, but it was nice talking to you!" The limo driver opens the door and his parents gets in the limo, while Dupree climbs in the other side. Alan and Lisa walk to his Mustang and unlock the doors. Alan rushes to get into his Mustang while Joanna gets into her car to follow her husband to Richard's family home for the repast. They noticed the detective was talking to Dupree and his parents for couple minutes. Alan follows other cars out the cemetery and on to the main street while Detective Theodore gets into his vehicle and follows behind the other vehicles leaving the cemetery. All the family members and mourners followed the limousine to Mr. and Mrs. Oxford's home for the repast. Fifteen minutes later, Alan drives up in his 1968 Mustang and parks it across the street from the Oxford's residence.

A couple of seconds later, Alan notices the detective driving up and parking a few houses down from the Oxford family. Alan gets a little nervous and gets out of his Mustang and walks normally toward the Oxford's residence, so he won't have to talk to Detective Theodore. Alan walks up to the front door of the Oxford's house and knocks on the door. Dupree answers the door and gives Alan a handshake. "Come on in." They step into their hallway and into the living room where there where people sitting on the couch and love seat and the smell of that country cooking of fried chicken and pot of spaghetti and garlic bread and an apple pie sitting next to the stove. Lisa walks up to Mrs. Oxford to give her the flowers and condolences card.

"I'm sorry for your loss," Lisa said.

"Did you know my son Richard?" Liz asked Lisa nicely.

"I've met him through my brother, Alan Jones."

"Oh, yes! Richard's friend who he worked with! Thank you for the flowers," Mrs. Oxford said. "You're welcome," Lisa said.

"You're more than welcome to eat something and socialize while I'll put these yellow flowers into a vase," Mrs. Oxford said.

"Thank you," Lisa said. Dupree was in the kitchen, making himself a brandy on ice, feeling kind of awkward. Dupree's mother walks into the kitchen. "I'm just going to put these flowers in a vase," his mother said. "Are you all right, son?"

"Yes, sure, Mother." His mother puts the vase down and gives her younger son a hug and walks back into the living room. Dupree walks behind his mother, and he notices the crowd in the living room and the dining room. Some people were standing while Alan and his wife and his sister Lisa was sitting on the couch, and Dupree noticed Lisa with her pretty legs crossed. Dupree smiles at Lisa as she smiles back at him.

"Dupree baby, could you get ten glasses from the cabinet and set them on the table for our guests please," his mother Liz asked. Dupree walks back into the kitchen. Lisa gets up from the couch and follows Dupree to the kitchen to help him.

"May I help you?" Lisa asked.

"Sure," Dupree said and just looks at her. "You're very pretty."

"Thank you! My condolences," Lisa said. Dupree didn't say a word and put his head down for a moment.

"Give these to me, and I'll take them to the guests," Lisa said. They both walked back into the dining room where most of the guests were sitting. They both set the tall blue glasses on the dinner table. Dupree was looking interesting to Lisa.

"Would you like to get some air?" Lisa asked.

"Yes, that would be nice." They both walked outside together.

"So are you single?" Dupree asked Lisa.

"Yes, I am. I date once in a while and yourself?" Lisa asked.

"Yes, I'm also single," Dupree said. "So how come I've never seen you around before?" "Well, I've been living in this town since I was born," Lisa said. They both grin at each other. "Would you like to go out sometimes?" Dupree asked. They both were walking out the driveway to the sidewalk. "Yes, that would be nice," Lisa said.

"How about next weekend? We can go to dinner and a movie."

"Yes, that would be nice," Lisa said.

"So can I have your number?"

"Of course. Let me program my number in your cell phone," Lisa said in her sweet soft voice. He hands his cell phone to Lisa and touches her hand. She dials her number into his cell and hands it back to Dupree as they both turnaround from their short walk on the block and returned back to his place. Dupree opens the front door like a gentleman. Alan and his wife were looking at Lisa and Dupree walking back into the house together. Twenty minutes later, Alan and Joanna were ready to leave. Alan walks up to Mr. and Mrs. Oxford. "Well, I think it's time for us to leave."

"Thank you for coming," Liz said in her teary voice.

"You're welcome," Alan said and gives Richard's father a handshake.

"Thank you for coming," he said with sorrow in his voice. Alan and his wife and sister walk out the front door. Dupree was standing by the front door and gives Alan a handshake and watches Lisa walk out.

"Give me a call this weekend," Lisa said.

"I sure will." Lisa gave Dupree a sweet smile as he watches her walk to her brothers 1968 Mustang while Joanna walks to her car and unlocks it and gets in and starts her vehicle. Dupree still had a small smile on his face, watching Alan drive off slowly. Dupree closes the front door and walks over to his father. "How are you doing, Dad?" Dupree asked calmly.

"Not so good, son. I'm glad we still have you here." His father grabs Dupree's left hand. "Just relax, Dad." Dupree grabs his father left hand with his right hand with his head down standing.

"I'm so sorry, Dad!" Dupree said in sadness.

"Who would do this to my oldest son?" his father yells.

"Dad, calm down. Everyone is looking at you."

"I don't give a damn! Your brother was deliberately murdered! And the killer might be just around the corner! Who killed my son!"

"Dad? Do you need a drink or something?" Dupree asked calmly.

"Pour me a rum on ice please, son," his father asked with sorrow. The doorbell rings and his father gets up and walks to answer the front door.

"Here's your drink, Dad! I'll put it on the table and go help mother with the guests in the backyard," Dupree said.

"Thanks, son," his father said as he answers the door. "Detective?"

"It's Theodore, sir!"

"Come on in, Detective Theodore! Liz!" Jimmy yelled.

"I just came by to see if everything was all right with you folks," the lieutenant asks.

Liz walks in the hallway by the front door.

"Hello, Detective! Did you need to talk to us in private?"

"No! I came by to see if everything was all right like I told your husband." Dupree walks from the kitchen with a paper towel, wiping his hands.

"Detective? You remember my son Dupree?"

"Yes, Richard's younger brother. How are you holding up, Dupree?" the lieutenant asked while giving him a handshake.

"It's tough, but I'm hanging in there," Dupree said surprised.

"Good, can we talk a little, Dupree? I know it's a bad time, but I may need your help in this case, Dupree, because you know about your brother's background and I would hate to bother your parents at this time of sorrow and grief." The lieutenant puts a sad face on. "That would be fine, Detective!" Dupree said slowly.

"I think that would help," his father said. "Just don't put too much stress on him about his brother Richard. Remember, Detective, he's really hurting inside about his only brother. You know, Dupree and his brother were close!"

Few minutes later, Alan drives around the block and notices the detective walking out the Oxford's front door. "What did you and Dupree talk about outside?" Alan asked his sister Lisa.

"We just talked and I tried to cheer him up and give him my condolences," Lisa said. "Well, it takes time to heal from a loss," Alan said.

"Are you all right, Alan?"

"Yes, I'm okay." He gives Lisa a fake smile.

"Then why are we driving around the block?" Lisa asked in a curious way.

"Are you going back to work today, Lisa?"

"I don't think so. You can take me back home to my car," Lisa said in her low sweet voice. "And I'll come by later. I just want to get out of these shoes."

"Did you get enough to eat?" Alan asked Lisa.

"No, but I bet Auntie Josephine is at your house cooking," Lisa said. "Let me call on my cell to make sure." Alan gave a little laugh.

"You're so spoiled," Alan said.

"Hello, Auntie."

"Lisa, my love! Are you guys on your way?" Josephine asked.

"I called to see what you cooked for us?"

"I cooked some green beans and pork roast with potatoes. You all on your way back?" Josephine asked.

"Yes, and I'm so hungry," Lisa said with a little laugh. Joanna just drove up in the driveway. "All right. I'll be there, Auntie!" Lisa hangs up. Joanna just made it home. Lisa begins stretching her body.

Fifteen minutes later, they all arrived.

Vows of Silence

Alan drives up to Lisa's driveway. Lisa opens the car door. "I'll see you in a few. I have to feed Fluffy and change my clothes, and I'll be there soon, brother." Lisa walks up to her front door, watching her brother drive off. Thirty minutes later, Lisa drives over to her brother's house and parks her white Lexus and walks into her brother's house. "Where is Alan? Isn't he here? He dropped me off thirty minutes ago."

"Call him on his cell, Lisa."

"I did call him, but there was no answer," Joanna said.

"Don't worry. Maybe he just needs a little time to himself. He'll be okay, don't worry," Josephine said. "Maybe he went back to work."

"Maybe he did."

"Lisa, you can make a plate, it's ready."

"Thank you, Auntie Josephine." Lisa walks into the kitchen and washes her hands and makes her plate. A few minutes later, Lisa walks back to the dining room where her auntie Josephine and Joanna were sitting.

"You're not hungry, Joanna?" Josephine asked.

"Not at the moment. I've eaten a little when we were there," Joanna said. "Well, I'm going to go change my clothes and get out of these shoes!"

She gets up and walks to her bedroom. "Where is Uncle Patrick?"

"He was still at work and then he's going to go to the hardware store on his way home. I'll call him when he gets home to come over for some dinner. So tell me how was it?" "Just a sad day for the Oxford family," Lisa said. "He didn't even look like himself in the casket, and I've met Richard's brother Dupree! He is so cute and fine looking." Lisa takes a deep breath. "He has golden brown hair with lips that look like they have never been kissed. And ready to be kissed." They both laughed.

"He must be special for you to flatter him," Josephine said with a grin. "Where is James?"

"He hasn't called me lately, and I have been thinking about him. I just don't want to rush into anything yet, and I'm not ready to have a baby. I was thinking about giving Dupree a call to see how he's holding up, but I'll wait till tomorrow." Josephine just sat there listening to Lisa with a grin. "That's right, baby, take your time in romance."

Joanna walks out after changing her clothes.

"Alan hasn't come back yet?"

"No, not yet," Lisa and Josephine said together. Joanna seemed worried and calls Alan again. Alan was driving over to a friend's house, not answering Joanna's calls while talking to his old girlfriend.

"Hello! Alexis? I'm on my way to please your sexy emotions," Alan said. Alexis began laughing over the phone. "You know where I am, sexy, just park in front and walk in. The front door is open," Alexis said in a sexy soft voice. "I'll be waiting in my white see-through gown smelling of timeless perfume."

"I'll be there in five minutes." Alan hangs up, and Alan starts driving a little faster.

"I just need a break from everybody, especially Detective Theodore, so I can try to relax and figure things out! That's where Alexis comes in. She is so sweet and fun to be with, but I can't let her see the guilt that won't shake off." Ten minutes later, Alan arrives to Alexis's place and parks his Mustang. "I can't wait see Alexis again. It's been awhile." Alan was thinking to himself. Alan was looking around to see if anyone would notice him, but no one was around on her quiet block with green trees with a little breeze with the sun shining bright. Alan walks into Alexis's place, a light blue-trimmed two-bedroom house where she and her sister lives. "Hello! I'm here!"

"Come in here!" Alexis said with low sweet voice. Alan walks into her bedroom and starts taking his clothes off as he felt at home, feeling more relaxed. But before he can go any further in his adulterous affair his cell phone rings.

Buzz!

And now he turns to Alexis with regret. "Oh, I forgot to turn my cell phone off."

"Who is that interrupting us?" she asked in a low voice.

"Forget it. Let's just continue what we were doing," Alan said.

For the next couple of hours, Alan begins feeling more relaxed as he reaches for the remote to Alexis's television to see what time it was.

It's five thirty p.m., I got here at two p.m. It's still early. I'm not ready to go home yet, too depressed about Richard. And Joanna knowing the truth about it just doesn't seem the same, he was thinking to himself.

Alan was feeling that all his troubles had gone away being with Alexis. *She just makes me feel confident again. Joanna can't make me feel like that anymore. She doesn't even hold me in our bed anymore like she used to do. There's no passion of love between us or even love making anymore, and that's where Alexis comes in with her soft and sweet personality, I should have married Alexis. My life would have been different. Maybe I wouldn't be in this mess I'm in now. It feels like my life has ended because this fear never goes away no matter what I do,* Alan was thinking to himself.

He kisses Alexis on her soft forehead while she sleeps. He then grabs his cell phone out and checks his messages. *I have four voice messages, five missed calls.* Alan begin listening to his messages.

"Alan, I'm calling to see if your all right, call me please."

Next message: "Alan! I just want to know where you are?" Delete!

"Alan, please don't be out there drinking, baby. I'm worried about you!"

Why is she so worried about me if it isn't about money! Joanna doesn't give a damn about anyone but herself. I've given her everything she asked for throughout the years we've been together. New car, new outfit once a week, I give her half of my paycheck every two weeks, but that's about to stop. I've spoiled her too much through the years. Maybe she thinks I'm gone for good and that's why she's calling, and if I do leave for good, she gets half of everything in the divorce. I'd rather give everything to Alexis, but that's not going to happen. Let me stop thinking like this.

Joanna was feeling something wasn't right. *I hope he isn't drinking. That's what I'm afraid of him accidently killing someone else or he's cheating on me because we have not been making love as often,* Joanna was thinking while sitting at the table with his family. *And he's not even here. Let me try to call him again.* She gets up from the table and walks toward the kitchen. "I like that outfit you're wearing," Josephine said.

"Thank you, I got this outfit at the mall," Joanna said.

"It's nice." The women are talking about a yellow blouse with white flowers.

"That's what we need to do: go shopping, walk around the mall, it's refreshing and we can buy something. Do you mind, Joanna?"

"You're right, Auntie, it's still early. It's only five forty-five p.m." Josephine gets up from the table to use the bathroom. Joanna walks out the kitchen.

"Come on, Joanna, get your coat on. We are going to the mall and window-shop and buy something nice."

"Oh, I'm not in the mood, Lisa," Joanna said.

"That's why we've decided to go to the mall to feel better. Get out for some air. It would help you to stop worrying about Alan," Lisa said.

"Okay, I'll get my coat," Joanna said without a smile.

"Oh, wait a minute. Uncle Patrick is supposed to come by to eat some dinner when he gets back."

Josephine walks into the dining room.

"Auntie, what about Uncle Patrick?"

"Oh, let me call the house and tell him that I'm leaving." Josephine walks into the kitchen and calls her husband. "Hello, what are you doing, Patrick?"

"When are you coming home?" her husband Patrick asked.

"I'm not coming home right now. We ladies are going to the mall for a couple of hours," Josephine said.

"Where is Alan?" Patrick asked.

"He's not here. We don't know where he is. But don't worry, Patrick, he's a big boy!" "Don't be so sarcastic," Patrick said to his wife.

"I cooked over here, so if you want to, wait till I get back to bring you dinner and there's also some leftover pork steaks and fried rice you can warm up. I'll call you when we get back." Josephine hangs up the phone.

"Is everything okay, Auntie?" Lisa asked.

"Yes, Patrick's at home, babysitting the television, just let me get my purse," Josephine said.

"And let's be on our way," Lisa said in a happy mood as they walked out the front door. "Whose vehicle are we taking?" Lisa asked.

"Let's take my car," Josephine said. Joanna's worried look carried all through the evening. Joanna walked around with fear, looking to see if she can spot Alan around with anyone. *I'm feeling insecurity in my heart and soul. Alan has lost my trust now. I'm afraid that he'll leave me and then a warrant would be issued for his arrest!*

I'll lose everything. Joanna was lost in her thoughts, walking with a curious look on her face. Detective Theodore and Dupree take a ride in his unmarked car.

"Thank you for the help," Detective Theodore said while getting into his car. Dupree puts on his seat belt and clears his throat while the detective drives off in his unmarked vehicle.

"Do you drink coffee, Dupree?"

"Sometimes in the morning," Dupree said, feeling nervous. "So where are we going, Detective?"

"It's okay. You don't have to be nervous with me, but I would like to ask you these questions while it's still fresh in my head. Have you ever met your brother's friend, Curtis, the queer guy?"

"Of course, I've seen him before. He showed up at my brother's service today looking like a damn fool," Dupree said nervously. "What about him? Or her?"

"I've met Curtis the other day and he tells me that you and your brother did a little business together." Dupree looks at the detective strangely.

"He was just teaching me the ropes, you know how it is out here, to make fast money. It was just to make a little money to try to get my own place and move out of the nest! Richard told me that's what I needed to do."

"You and your brother were close!" the detective asked.

"Let's just say he showed me a few things to protect myself. Things that a big brother should," he said with a little attitude.

"How did you feel about your brother having a gay friend? And to be so close with each other? Like telling each other their secrets," the detective said.

"Like what, Detective! What are you trying to say?" Dupree said aggressively.

"How do you feel about that?" Detective asked.

"That was Richard's personal business." Dupree started feeling uncomfortable talking about his brother's personal business.

"Dupree, I feel you're a quiet and ambitious person and willing to get what you want out of life. But sometimes, things get in the way, like our conscience. You can try to do the right thing in life, but some people just put their problems behind them and try to move on and live with their guilt!"

"What's your point, Lieutenant!" Dupree said.

"I was just making a point!" Detective Theodore said with a little laughter. Dupree takes a deep breath and lays his head back for a moment.

"Are you all right?" Detective asked.

"Yes, I'm okay. This death of my brother's is still a shock to us all!" Dupree said. "Can you drive me back to my parents?"

"Are you feeling sick!" The Lieutenant asked with concern.

"It's my stomach."

"Do I need to pull over for a minute?"

"No, just get me home please."

Lieutenant Theodore turns his car around and starts driving north. "Do you need air?" Detective asked and rolled the passenger side window down remotely.

"Lieutenant, that's too much air!" Dupree shouts.

"Oh, I'm sorry." Detective Theodore felt like laughing, but he held it in. Dupree rolled his eyes at the lieutenant.

"Oh, I was thinking," the detective said.

"Oh," Dupree said.

"How are you feeling?"

"A little better." Dupree was holding his stomach.

"We'll be there in a moment! I didn't mean to put so much pressure on you!" Dupree kept silent. Detective Theodore pulls into the Oxford's driveway, and Dupree gets out of the detective's vehicle and closes the door and walks toward his front door when his mother opens the front door. Dupree was watching Detective Theodore wave good-bye and drives off and closes their front door. Dupree notices some of the guests left.

"Where did you and the detective go?" his mother asked.

"Oh, just around the area. He was asking about Richard's friends, and I told him I didn't know too many of his friends."

"Maybe one of his friends killed him?" his father said.

"I don't know, Dad, maybe he owed someone money and Richard didn't pay! That could be the reason."

"Because Richard did a little gambling from time to time," his father said.

"Well, let's attend to the guests, Dad," Dupree said. Dupree and his mother were holding hands together, walking into the dining room to the guests. *Ding dong!*

"I'll get the door!" his father yelled. "Hello! George, come in! Thank you for coming. And who is this lovely lady with you?"

"Do you remember my wife Rosa?"

"Oh yes, it's been a long time. How are you, Rosa?" Jimmy said.

"We've brought you and your wife a ham with pineapples that my wife Rosa cooked. We've come to give you and your family our condolences."

"Thank you, George. So how is the new job plant building going?" Jimmy asked his friend George.

"Well, we've got that plumbing problem all solved, and it was a big job to repair,"

"Thank you for stopping by." They shake hands by the front door. "Good-bye!" George and his wife walk to their Jaguar, and he opens the passenger side for his wife.

She gets in her seat and he closes the passenger door and walks over to the driver side and jumps in and starts the car and drives off.

"I feel for Jimmy and his wife, losing their firstborn."

"Don't they have another son that came to the service?" his wife asked.

"Yes, that was him with golden brownish hair that was sitting next to his mother and father at the service."

"All I ever met in that family was Jimmy," his wife said.

"Oh, that's right," George said. "Maybe a better time for you to meet his wife."

Richard's Repast

"Who was that at the door, dear?"

"A coworker from the plant, George and his wife Rosa. I wanted you to meet his wife, but they didn't stay long," Jimmy said.

Liz gives her husband Jimmy a kiss on his lips; he returns back to his brown leather chair.

Dupree starts thinking about Lisa as he starts walking up the stairs to his bedroom and calls Lisa.

"Hello, Dupree, how are you feeling?" Lisa asked.

"I'm all right. would you like to go out tomorrow evening?" Dupree asked.

"Sure, that would be nice! Could you hold on for a moment? I have my friends on the other line."

"Yes, of course!"

"I'll call you twins back, bye!" Lisa clicked over. "Sorry about that, so where we're we in our conversation?"

"Yes, I remember!" Dupree said. "Talking about why a beautiful young lady such as yourself is single?"

"It's called depending on options, if you know what I mean," Lisa laughed.

"How old are you, Lisa?"

"I am twenty-four years old, and what's your age? May I ask?" They both giggle.

"Well, I'm twenty-six. When is your birthday, Dupree? I like your name too!" Dupree started laughing, feeling a little excited.

"October 16, and your birthday is?

"June 18," Lisa replied.

"So you're a Gemini?" Dupree said.

"And you're a Scorpio?" Lisa said. "Our signs are compatible for lovers. We're a perfect match." Dupree was smiling hard. "So what do you like to do for fun?"

"Go to the clubs with my friends and have a drink or two, and what do you like for fun?"

"I like going out sometimes and sit and watch others act a fool." They laughed.

"You look so beautiful, Lisa." She begin grinning hard.

"And where are your girlfriends?" Lisa asked.

"I don't have anyone special at this time. I'm studying to be an automotive engineer." "That's cool," Lisa said.

"So where would you like to go tomorrow night?" Dupree asked.

"A French restaurant with good food, then over to my place for a drink?" Lisa replied.

"That sounds nice. I'm going to move into my own place one day! Not now while my parents need me around, and which club do you and girlfriends attend? I bet you'll be smelling and looking sexy." Lisa laughs loud.

"This one club called The Sham! My girl friends and I go on the weekends sometimes. It's in the south area on Hall Street. Do you know where it is?" Lisa asked.

"Yes, I've heard of the club, but I've never been there. Dupree, are you there?"

"Yes, I hear you, Lisa," Dupree said in a low sexy voice. *Beep.* "Can I call you right back, Lisa? my mother has a call coming in." Dupree said.

"That's cool," Lisa said.

Dupree answers the other line. "Hello? Is Mr. or Mrs. Oxford home?"

"Yes."

"I'm calling from the American Insurance Company for Richard Oxford. Can I speak with Mr. or Mrs. Oxford?"

"Yes, let me get my mother." Dupree calls his mother to the phone. "Mother!"

"What is it, Dupree?"

"You have a phone call from an insurance company." Dupree hands his mother the phone.

"Hello? This is Mrs. Oxford."

"Hello, Mrs. Oxford, my name is Lee Michaels and I'm with the American Insurance Company and I would like to meet with you and your husband tomorrow, if that's convenient with you."

"What's this concern?" Liz asked.

"The policy for Richard Oxford in American life Insurance Company."

"Yes, can I get the address?" Liz rushed to get a pen and paper.

"The address is 700 Street Suite 3900, and I have an opening tomorrow at eleven a.m.?" Mr. Lee Michaels said.

"My family will be there at eleven a.m. Good-bye," Liz said, with her uncontrolled grieving, and they both hang up.

"Why did that insurance company call for Richard, Mother?" Dupree asked while coming upstairs, eating a piece of fried chicken from the kitchen.

"I forgot about these other two policies. We have paid extra!"

"Mother! Do you have life insurance on me also?"

"Two policies life insurance on all of us. We have to be at the American Insurance Company at eleven a.m.! You're coming with us. Let me go talk to your father about this."

"I wonder which other policies Richard was paying," Dupree asked.

"I don't remember, son." Dupree waits for his mother to walk back downstairs.

"I'm going to return Lisa's call." He rushed to the house phone. *Ring.*

"It's Dupree!" She was looking at her caller ID.

"Back to what we where talking about," Lisa said. They both started laughing.

"So why don't you use your cell phone?"

"It's on the charger today. not so many bars left on it," Dupree said.

"I wanted to tell you that you are a nice-looking guy," Lisa said.

"Well, that's a nice compliment," Dupree said. "And you know, you're a very hot sexy-looking lady yourself. And I like your hair and your legs. I'm a legs and thighs guy," Dupree said. They both laughed.

"So how long have you been single from your last girlfriend?" They both were giggling. "To be honest, about a couple of weeks ago now, but let me ask you a question. Who was your last sexual partner?"

"All up in my business," Lisa shouts. "Um, this black guy named James."

"So you're not a virgin?" Dupree said.

"No! Not an angel! I'm guilty!" Dupree started laughing hard.

"Shut up, stop laughing at me, Dupree."

"I'm sorry. I just still had a little laugh in me."

"Sounds like you're feeling better."

"Oh yes, talking to you makes me feel a lot better," he said.

"So do you have a car?" Lisa asked.

"Yes, I have a white 1999 Acura car that saves on gas, and what about you?" he asked.

"I have a gray Lexus with tinted windows," Lisa said.

"Oh, you go, young lady!" Dupree shouts. "So when can I see you again?"

"Dupree!" his mother yells!

"Yes!"

"Your cousins are here!"

"I'll be there in a while, Mother! I'm on the phone! Sorry, Lisa, for yelling in your ear," Dupree said.

"You are so polite too. I think that's so sweet of you to talk politely to a lady like me," Lisa said slowly.

"Thank you very much, pretty lady," Dupree said with his soft deep voice.

Knock.

"What's up, cousin!"

"What's going on, Keith! Can I call you back later, Lisa?"

"No problem!" Lisa said softly. As they both hung up, Dupree jumps up from his bed to give his first cousin Keith and his younger cousin Josh a hug. Keith grew up with Richard and Dupree from grade school till high school and college.

"How you doing, Dupree?" Keith asked with care, hugging Dupree, walking down the stairs toward the kitchen.

"Is this little Dupree?" his auntie Louise said.

"Oh, come give your old auntie a hug. I haven't seen you since you were like fifteen years old. That's about the time my brother decided to move to the north from the south side."

"Where is Liz?"

"She's in the kitchen." His auntie walks into the kitchen.

"So, Dupree, how you holding up?" his cousin Keith asked.

"I'm still devastated," Dupree said with his low voice.

"Are you both hungry?" his uncle Jimmy asked.

"I'll eat in a little bit," Keith said.

"Dupree, let's go talk outside for a little bit and throw some balls," Keith said.

"We haven't done that in a while," Dupree said.

"I'll be back, Father."

"Okay, watch out for the cars," his father said.

"I got a football in my car," Keith said. They both walk to cousin Keith's car as Keith gets his keys out of his pocket and opens the trunk and Dupree was adoring Keith's 1975 low-rider Cutlass, painted in sparkling red, a two-door four-sitter with a sunroof top. "When did you get this old car with the silver rims?" Dupree asked.

"Check this out!" Keith said and walks over to the driver's side and jumps in and puts the key in the ignition and turns on his music with big speakers in the trunk blasts loud and vibrates with wolf speakers.

"You have a nice ride."

"Get in. I'll take you for a ride."

"All right, this is nice, cousin!" Dupree jumps in the passenger side and shuts the door. Keith starts his Cutlass and puts his gear into drive and pulls off with the loud music.

"I bought this car from one of my homeboys, six months ago for three thousand. This is an old-school vehicle with white leather covers and the steering wheel with fur."

Feeling important with his first cousin, feeling relaxed, kicking back, listening to 2Pac music, Dupree began feeling the beat.

"Don't worry, cousin, we are going to find who did this to your brother and my cousin, but I heard Richard was into all kinds of mischief like messing with a married woman and he didn't give a care! That's how I've seen my cousin Richard, a single man with a good job and a nice car and his own place and did a lot of gambling. He threw his money away all the time on drinks and women and drugs," Keith said.

"I remember when Richard was messing with that bitch! Susan, that's her name and she is married, but Richard wanted her anyway. He wanted her so bad, he would call her on her cell and the bitch would come to him and leave her husband at home!"

"That's crazy!"

"Richard could have had any other single woman he wanted," Keith said. "But now, I'm thinking about her husband. I'm thinking he knew about his wife cheating on him and followed Richard home that night and killed him. Tomorrow night, I'm going to that Bam bar and hang around there and see if I see the bitch and follow her home so I can see what her husband looks like and I bet Richard has seen him before. Are you with me, cousin, on this project of detective work?"

"You know you make a lot of sense," Dupree replied. "And I remember what she looks like. Yes, tomorrow night would be perfect because she should be there with or without her husband because she loves to get drunk and fool around with different men. Her husband must not care."

"If he doesn't show tomorrow night?"

"I'm thinking we'll just follow her home. It's a perfect plan. I'll pick you up around 9 p.m. when the club is full. and we'll go to the Bam club and see if I spot her." Keith said with the look of a detective.

"I'm down with that, cousin!" Dupree said. Keith parks in front of Dupree's home with the music still turned up. His mother walks to open the front door as Keith sees his mother, telling him to turn his music down.

"Auntie, still looks the same."

"You're right about that, my mother is never going to change. She will always be a churchgoing woman. Why don't you come to church with us sometimes? Lots of good woman there, Dupree."

"Maybe that's what I need, church," Dupree said.

"Come on, get out of the car, and play some ball," Keith said. Keith's seven-year-old brother runs out of the house to play ball with his big brother Keith.

"Stay out of the streets, Josh! You remember your little cousin Josh!"

"Hi, Josh, he got big!" Dupree said.

"Can I play ball with you, Keith?" his little brother Josh asked.

"Not now, but I need you to go ask Mom nicely to fix me a plate to take home."

"Okay, Keith." His little brother Josh runs into his cousin's house and closes the front door behind him and goes into the kitchen where it's crowded and squeezes through and sees his mother.

"Mom?"

"Yes, Josh!"

"Keith said would you please fix him a plate to take home for later." Little Josh was taking deep breaths from running into the house.

"Tell him all right. I'll fix him a plate." His mother touched his forehead. "Okay, baby, go play outside with Keith till I'm ready to go." He was wiping his lips.

"We're going home soon," his mother said.

"Okay, Mom." Josh rushed back outside. "Our father is still working, he couldn't make it to the service," Keith said.

"How is Uncle Keith?"

"He's a senior and I'm Keith Junior. You remember when my dad told us to call him Daddy and Uncle Senior. We laughed every time."

"Yes, I remember that!" The two cousins are throwing a football back and forth in the streets.

"It's all right, Dupree, don't worry about a thing. You know you can tell me anything, cousin."

"Just thinking about this young lady, Lisa, I'm supposed to take out tomorrow night,"

"What time do you have to pick her up?" Keith asked.

"Around seven thirty p.m. to take her to this other bar in the south side," Dupree said. "That's cool. After that, we can stop by the Bam bar and sit with a drink and chill out and watch who comes in around eight or nine p,m." He throws the football.

"That sounds like a plan," Dupree said while he catches the football again.

"Keith! Mom said we're leaving in little while," his little brother Josh said with his small baby voice and his light complexion that brings out his black and brown curly hair.

"I'm going to give you my new cell phone number, and you call me tomorrow around seven p.m.," Keith said. "Do you have your cell phone on you now?" Keith catches his football and walks to his car to put the ball in the trunk and walks toward his younger brother who is playing on the sidewalk. "Come on, Josh, let's go into the house where Mom is."

"Josh has gotten tall for his age," Dupree said.

"He's growing tall like our father!" Dupree, Keith, and Josh walk into the doorway and walk to the kitchen where the other guess where eating and talking. "Excuse me, Mother. Did you make me a plate?"

"Yes, I did, son!" Keith and Josh walk back over to Dupree who was standing in the living room, talking to his father's friend Peter.

"How are you feeling, Dupree?"

"I'm doing all right, thanks for asking."

"Hey, little Josh! How are you doing in school?" his uncle Jimmy asked.

"I'm doing good, Uncle," little Josh said, smiling with his little red lips.

"How old are you now, Josh?"

"I'm seven years old and my birthday is coming and I'll be eight years old!" little Josh said while he was wiggling around.

"That's good," Jimmy said while he was feeling Josh's curly hair and looking at him. "You're getting to be tall like your dad, Keith," his uncle Jimmy said, drinking his gin and orange juice. Josh walks over to his big brother Keith. Liz and her sister-in-law Louise walks out of the kitchen, holding two paper plates that's covered with aluminum foil.

"Come on, Keith and Josh, it's time to go," their mother Louise yelled. Keith gives his cousin Dupree a handshake.

"I'll see you tomorrow night, cousin, don't forget to meet me at the Bam bar. I'll call you early tomorrow."

"Right on, man, I'll be there," Dupree said, walking out behind Keith and Josh while their mother Louise gives her brother Jimmy and her sister-in-law Liz a big hug. "I'll give you a call later to see how you are doing," Louise said, walking out the front door toward Dupree's car while Liz was standing in the front doorway waving to Keith and Josh. "Drive carefully, Keith!" Liz shouted.

"Keith drives very carefully with me in this low-rider car!" Louise yelled. Their mother gets into the front seat of the low-rider car and Keith starts his car with no music. His mother puts on her seat belt while waving bye to Liz. Dupree was watching his cousin Keith drive off, and he walked back into the house with his grieving mother. Dupree rushes to his cell phone to call Lisa back while his mother walks back into the kitchen to attend to the other guests. Dupree picks up his cell phone and looks at his two missed calls. No missed call from Lisa. Dupree sits on his bed to call Lisa back.

"Hello!" Lisa answered.

"Are you busy?"

"Not really. I'm just coming back from the mall with my auntie and my sister-in-law."

Alan's Secret Lover

"**S**o where were we in our conversation earlier? So are you going to be ready for tomorrow night?" Dupree said.

"Slow and sexy. Of course."

"It looks like Alan hasn't made it back yet."

"I hope he's all right?"

"Okay, I'm going to fix Patrick a plate, then I'm going home." Josephine walks into the kitchen while Joanna goes into her bedroom to see if Alan had been home or changed his clothes. "Let me give him another call. He better answer his damn phone!" Alan looks at his caller ID. "It's Joanna again." He pushes silent on his phone, not ready to talk to her. While he still lying in the bed with his lover Alexis, he was turning the channels on her cable television. Under the covers, he was nude, feeling her soft nude body.

I really don't have to explain anything to my wife, he was thinking and he looks at the time from the cable television. Seven p.m. "I better get going in another hour or so." He then pulls the cover over his and Alexis's heads and begins their overwhelming sexual appetite. An hour later, Alan gets up and takes a quick shower and gets dressed, watching Alexis sleeping. He sits on her bed to put his socks and shoes on and gives Alexis a kiss on her right cheek. "Are you leaving?"

"Yes, baby, I'll give you a call later." He then picks up his cell phone and puts it into his pocket and he gives Alexis a kiss. He walks out of her brown wooden front door and grabs his keys out of his left pocket and jumps into his '69 Mustang and drives off headed toward main street. "Joanna better not start any problem with me tonight. I'm feeling stress free for the moment, thanks to sweet Alexis."

He then turns left on road 15, feeling a little guilty with adultery, having his mind on his lover Alexis. "She sure makes me feel so free from worries. Why can't Joanna give me that feeling? I don't feel for my wife as much as before, but a lot of her feelings has changed in our relationship. She doesn't like to give me love and passion. She just hangs out at the house and keeps shopping with my payroll. And more issues keep climbing with that noisy Detective Theodore who's looking for a way to trap me with this accidental death. I didn't even check his pulse. I could have saved his life, but I panicked that evening and my thoughts were so confused and I feel so disgusted with myself with endless guilt. I didn't mean to hurt or kill Mr. Johnson. I feel so guilty like a big hole in my heart about this whole ugly nightmare."

A couple of seconds later, he pulls into his driveway. *Vroom! Vroom!* His wife rushes to their front door.

"Are you all right? Why didn't you answer your cell phone?" Alan just looked at her and didn't say anything. He just walked past her and walked into the kitchen.

"Hi, Auntie!"

"Are you okay, Alan?"

"Yes, feeling much better. I just needed to get away for a couple of hours!" Alan said and walks into the living room with a warm fried chicken leg his auntie handed him while Lisa was sitting on the couch talking to Dupree.

"Alan, you're home! Are you all right, brother?" Lisa asked.

"Yes, I'm all right and feeling better." Joanna sits in the dining room chair, wondering where has he been the last few hours and with whom?

He doesn't seem drunk. He looks more peaceful. I just hope he didn't cheat on me. That would cause more issues between us. Maybe he's

been over at James's place watching a game and he seems all right.
Joanna was thinking with her big brown eyes looking straight at
her husband, wondering where he's been while opening a cold
beer from the bar refrigerator.

"Who are you talking to, Lisa?"

"That's my brother trying to get into my business."

"That's good, he made it back safe."

"You're so kind and a real gentleman."

"Thank you."

Alan looks at his sister. "Is that James?"

"So that's where you were over your friend James's place
watching football?"

He kept silent, head down to ignore her question, while he was
pouring himself a drink. *Psychology really works when you want
someone's mind to think otherwise*, he said in his own thoughts.
Lisa looks at her brother with smirk on her face.

"It's none of your business who I'm talking to. Can I have a
beer, brother?" she asked.

"I'll be nice and get you a beer if you tell me who's on the other
line?" He gave his sister a small grin as he walked past his wife
where her mood felt cold as ice. He then walked into the kitchen.

"I have to get home to my husband now, and I have put the
food away. I also washed the dishes."

"Thanks, Auntie." He gives her a kiss on the left cheek. They
both walk out the kitchen while Alan walks past his auntie with
a cold beer.

"I told you he would be all right now. Walk me to my van."

Josephine then gets into her van and starts the motor and
drives off. Alan walks into their bedroom and sits on the bed and
puts on his house slippers and walks back into the living room,
while she was talking on her pink cell phone. He drinks his beer
behind their little bar.

"Thank you for the beer, brother."

"Who are you talking to?"

Lisa gives her brother a smirk.

"Could we have an honest talk?"

Alan walks out of the living room over to where she was.

"What do you want to talk about, Joanna?" Alan said with an attitude!

"About where you were earlier."

"I don't have to tell you every move I make, Joanna!" Alan shouted.

"Why didn't you call me back?" his wife shouted. He walks back into the living room to finish his beer to cool off. Lisa just sits there listening to them argue.

"And if you keep asking me the same damn questions over, I'm going to leave, Joanna! I just want peace of min. Is it a fucking crime, Joanna?"

"What's the hell is wrong? All I ask is the truth from you, Alan." Dupree was listening over the phone.

"I can feel when something isn't right with you."

"We will never argue like these two are doing."

"I would rather talk things out and we go from there. I'm a quiet and charming guy and I would never put my hands on women."

"That's good to hear." Lisa gets up and grabs her purse.

"I'm going home, Alan. I hope you both work things out and don't kill each other," she said while walking out their front door. "Good night!"

She walks to her Lexus car and gets her keys out of her purse and unlocks her car door and gets in and starts it and drives off going west with Dupree still on the phone. Lisa gets her ear piece to her phone from the glove box and puts it into her right ear so she can talk and drive with both hands. "I'll put on some soft music for the both us," Lisa said. "Can you hear me, Dupree?"

"Yes, I can hear you clear. So are you driving home?"

"Oh yes, to feed my kitten Fluffy."

"You named your kitten Fluffy?" Dupree started laughing.

"Why are you laughing? I named her," Lisa said. "She's only six months old with different colors in her fur. She's so little and needs love and care." Dupree continued laughing hard as Lisa had a big smile on her face, laughing with Dupree.

"I have to meet this Fluffy tomorrow night." He was still laughing with Lisa while she was driving up into her driveway and turns off the engine and opens her car door and gets out and locks it and walks to her front door and opens it with her keys and walks in while Fluffy runs to her.

"Fluffy baby." She picks up her small kitten and closes her front door while Dupree laughs. "You love that kitten, don't you?"

"Yes, that's my little Fluffy!" She gives Fluffy a kiss and puts her back on the carpet.

"Can I get a kiss like Fluffy?" They both laugh.

"Maybe if you act right, you can get all the kisses you want."

"I'll be on my best behavior," Dupree replied.

"What time is it?" Lisa asked.

"It's almost eight thirty and people are still here," Dupree said.

"My cousin came by and we are going on a investigation mission. I'll be meeting my cousin Keith tomorrow at 8 p.m. So, Lisa, would you mind him riding with me?"

"No, that would be fine."

"I hear water running in the background."

"I'm going to take a long hot bath."

"Can I take a bath with you, Lisa?" She give a little giggle. "Once we get to know each other better."

"I'm going to hold you to that," Dupree said. "So are you taking your clothes off yet?" "After I get my nightgown out the closet, I'll then be taking my clothes off," Lisa said. "Meow!"

"Fluffy baby!" Fluffy rubs against Lisa's right leg.

"Can I watch you take your clothes off?" Dupree asked. Lisa just laughs.

"You just make me laugh and I'm looking for something to wear for tomorrow night."

"Wear something sexy so I can keep my eyes on you at all times."

"You talk so sexy, Dupree. Let me check on my bath water—ouch, that's too hot!" she shouted. Lisa turns on the cold water to cool of her bath and walks over to her wide mirror in her bathroom and started washing her makeup off.

"Don't drown."

"I won't. I have Fluffy to save me." Dupree started laughing even harder.

"Now that's funny, Lisa!" Lisa started getting undressed to get into her bath water with lots of bubbles. "Meow!" Fluffy walks in, watching Lisa step in her bath, while the cold water was still running.

"Are you in the tub yet?"

Umm, this feels nice."

"What?"

"This hot water with my bubbles."

"That does it! I want to come over right now," Dupree said.

"You might this weekend," Lisa said.

"Are you getting tired, Dupree?"

"A little bit tired," Dupree said.

"Where are you?"

"In my room, waiting for the guests to leave, so I can make sure everything is off when my parents go to bed."

"You're very sweet, Dupree. I mean, so far since we've meet and been talking, I feel you're a good person inside and hurting from your brother's death, and that's where you're going to need love and attention from a woman to make you feel better."

"So you're going to give me that love and attention?" Dupree asked while rubbing his eyes and yawning.

"We've been on the phone for two hours without hanging up with each other."

"Does your brother pick on you a lot? Sometimes?"

"Alan is sweet. He takes me to a restaurant and buys me anything I want! He's my only brother! He bought the flowers that I was holding for your brother's services."

"Lisa, oh, that was nice of you and your brother." Dupree, at this time, was sounding sleepy.

"Dupree, are you sleep?"

"No! Just resting my eyes. I hear you and I hear your bath water splashing."

"Yes, I'm washing my body off. That's how you take a good bath and soak at the same time."

"Umm, I can't wait to see your beautiful body," Dupree said slowly falling asleep. Lisa laughs, feeling good soaking in a warm bath.

"You asleep, Dupree? You want me to let you go to bed?"

"No, I'm awake!"

"What time do you have to be at work tomorrow?" Lisa asked.

"I don't have to go back till Monday because of my brother's service. I get time off for a week. but I'm going back Monday."

"Are you going to be able to concentrate on your work?"

"No problem. I have a couple of cars to work on that's been in the shop a week and the owner already paid in full, but the parts haven't come in yet."

"You sound like you know your work pretty well."

"My brother had a good job while having fun at the same time, but he did pay his bills, but he was greedy for money, and he did what he wanted to do at the time,"

"So you were mad at your brother before he died?"

"No, it's just he would talk crazy to me all the time." Dupree quickly changes the subject.

"Did they ever catch who killed that guy on Road 15?"

"No, but that detective keeps coming by my brother's place."

"Why?" Dupree asked.

"That detective thinks Alan saw something that night, but Alan just got to drunk that night and came home sick from his friend's place and went to bed early. My sister-in-law Joanna called the doctor that evening," Lisa said.

"Really?" Dupree said.

"What time is it?" Lisa asked.

"It's almost nine p.m. Why? Are you going somewhere?" Dupree asked.

"No, silly. I have to go to work tomorrow," Lisa said.

"What street do you work on now?"

"I work on Main Street," Lisa said.

"I'm going to call you and get the address tomorrow so I can come by there and watch you work," Dupree said.

"You're so silly," Lisa said. She turns the hot water on slowly.

"That's water running again," Dupree asked sleepy.

"My bath water was getting cold."

"Let me come over there to keep you warm all night!" Dupree said. Lisa gives a little laugh.

"Meow."

"Fluffy is just sitting there, waiting for me to get out of my bath," Lisa said.

"When I start coming over there, Fluffy is going to start getting less attention from you because I'm going to be getting a lot of attention from you," Dupree said. Lisa was just laughing. "Is that right?" Lisa asked.

"Yes, that's right!" Dupree said. "I'll be getting attention from my woman and I'll be giving her all my attention and that's how it should be."

"Anytime I need attention I will call you at work. Is that alright?"

"Yes, I have a Bluetooth ear piece for my cell phone and I'll have my phone in my top pocket." He then turns the question on her. "Can you talk while you're at work?" Dupree asked.

"Yes, when I'm not with a customer," Lisa said.

"What do you do there?"

"It's a dress shop called Quotable Women dress shop. I help women find the outfit they're looking for or like, and I run the register and answer the phone," Lisa said.

"That sounds cool, baby. Well, if we hook up together, expect greasy blue uniforms with oil and dirt to wash and I have to go to class in the evenings," Dupree said.

"What time do you go to class?" Lisa asked.

"From seven to nine p.m.," Dupree said.

"What time you get off work?" Lisa asked.

"At five p.m. I just come home and take a shower and eat and rest a little and then I'm off to class," Dupree said.

"That sounds like a plan. You just like to stay busy?" Lisa asked.

"Yes, sometimes, but I would sleep better if I was sleeping next to you right now," Dupree said.

Quotable Women's Dress Shop

"That sounds exciting, but I'm going to get out of the tub and dry off and get my nightgown on." She lets her bath water out and steps out of her tub. "Meow! Fluffy baby!"

"Fluffy gets to see your sexy body."

Lisa grins over the phone. Lisa starts brushing her teeth in front of her bathroom mirror after she puts her nightgown on.

"I'm off to bed," Lisa said.

"What time do you want me to call you at work tomorrow?" Dupree asked.

"Anytime after nine a.m., my boss leaves for the day," Lisa said.

"Okay, I'll call you when I get up after nine in the morning," Dupree said slowly. "Good night, Lisa!"

"You get some sleep, Dupree. Good night, love!" Lisa said. Friday morning, Lisa arrives to her job and parks her gray 1999 Lexus in front of the Quotable Women Shop and locks her car and walks into her job and puts her purse behind the counter with a lock.

"Good morning, Ms. Carmen!

"Good morning, Lisa. I'm glad you're here today. We have a fitting for a wedding today.

The young lady will be in around eleven, and Mrs. Hayward want a fitting for her daughter's wedding in two weeks."

"Yes, Ms. Carmen."

"I need you to also take down messages because there's lots of programs and weddings going on," Ms. Carmen

"Yes, ma'am," Lisa said.

"I have a meeting to get to in one hour. Oh, how did the service go yesterday?"

"It was sad, but it wasn't all bad at the end," Lisa said.

"I'm glad you keep a good spirit, Lisa, and you're still young. Now, don't forget the fitting at eleven," Ms. Carmen said.

"I'll take care of everything, and when Wendy comes in, tell her to pull the new items in front by the window and last month's items back more. It's ten after eight the morning. The freeway is packed. I'll drive down Main Street," Ms. Carmen was talking to herself while Lisa was just standing there listening. "Okay, Lisa, I'll be back in a couple of hours."

"Yes, Ms. Carmen, don't worry, it's all going to work out," Lisa said.

"Thanks, Lisa!" Her boss walks out the building to her vehicle, The phone starts ringing. Lisa walks behind the counter to answer. "Quotable Women, Lisa speaking!"

"Yes, is Ms. Carmen there?"

"No, she's not in till after lunch," Lisa said. "May I take a message?"

"Yes, I'm Mrs. Hayward, and I have appointment today and I forgot what time is my appointment."

"Let me take a look!" Lisa gets the appointment book out and opens the pages.

"Your appointment is at two o'clock today!"

"Well, thank you, it's for my daughter's wedding in two weeks. Well, thank you, and your name?"

"Lisa Jones! Yes, I'll be doing your fitting today."

"Okay, I'll be there at two today. Thank you, Lisa, good-bye." Lisa hangs the business phone up and looks at her cell phone to see what time it was for Dupree's call.

"Good morning, Wendy, it's about time you showed up for work today," Lisa said.

"Where is Ms. Carmen?" Wendy asked.

"She had a meeting to go to, and she wants you to put the new items in front of the window and last month's items more in the back," Lisa said. Wendy walks and puts her purse behind the counter with Lisa's purse.

"You know if you keep coming in late, Ms. Carmen is going to fire you!" Lisa said. "So let's get to work."

"Sorry but my car keeps messing up! And I need this job to pay my rent!" Wendy said. "Well, things will get better," Lisa said to Wendy.

"Yes, maybe you're right, Lisa. Well, I better get these clothes and outfits in order," Wendy said.

"We have two fittings today, one at eleven and the other at two p.m., Mrs. Hayward for her daughter's wedding in two weeks. You can take the eleven appointment, and I'll take the two o'clock appointment," Lisa said.

"That's a deal!" Wendy said. Lisa looks at the time.

I should call to see if he is up! she was thinking.

It's eight forty a.m. *Ring!*

"That's my cell ringing. Good morning, Dupree," Lisa said.

"Good morning, so were you waiting for my call?" Dupree asked.

"Yes, and how are you feeling this morning?" Lisa asked.

"I feel a lot better than yesterday," Dupree said. "So are going to give me the address of where your job is?"

"All you have to do is drive down Main Street till you see Quotable Women Dress Shop on the right side across the street from the Brookville Park."

"Okay, I'll be coming to take you for lunch. That's cool," Dupree asked.

"Yes, that would be nice."

"That's because I'm a gentleman, and I enjoy treating a nice-looking lady like yourself out to lunch."

"I'll be looking forward to our first date!" Lisa said. They both started laughing over the phone. Wendy was standing by the clothes rack, looking at Lisa with a curious look on her face.

"I'll see you at noon, I have something to do, Dupree," she said looking back at Wendy.

"Okay, I'll see you in a little while," Dupree said. "Bye." And she closed her cell phone and got up from behind the counter to help Wendy. Lisa's cell phone rings again.

"I'll be right back, Wendy, and walks back to the counter and picks up her cell phone and looks at the caller ID.

"Hello, Alan? So are you and Joanna okay now?"

"Not good," Alan said. "I just called to see how you're doing? And that you left your black jacket over my place. It's on the coat rack, I put it there," Alan said.

"Oh, I left that jacket."

"Yes, you did, sister. Are you coming by tonight?" Alan asked.

"No I'm going out with a friend tonight! I'll come over this weekend." *Beep.*

"Mr. Jones!"

"Yes?"

"Detective Theodore is here to see you!" the receptionist said.

"Send him in please! It's that damn detective bothering me again!" Alan said to Lisa.

"Why does he keep coming to us? He's coming in now. I'll talk to you later." He hung up his office phone. "Detective! What can I do for you today or did you come up with another idea or theory?"

"No! I just come by to tell you that the young man that got killed on Road 15 that the family put a reward out for five thousand dollars if anyone has any information on the hit and run murder of her husband." Alan started feeling sick to his stomach and his face started turning pale.

"If I hear anything, I'll let you know, Detective, but I don't know anything about that!" "Are you sure about that?" Detective asked.

"I'm sure, Detective." He gets up and opens his office door. "I'm very busy, Detective!" The detective looks at him with a strange look. "Oh, another thing I forgot to ask you!

Did you go to the funeral services of Mr. Johnson's? The reason I asked is because there was a car that looks just like the same color Mustang parked about a block away from that service. Just sitting there, but no one got out of the vehicle." Lieutenant Theodore turns his head and looks out the corner of his eyes at Alan and walks out of Alan's office with an unlit cigar in the corner of his mouth. Alan closes his door and walks back to his desk and sits down in his black office chair and began wiping his forehead with his right hand. *He keeps pressuring me like he can see the guilt in me. I can handle this pressure and I will not break for that damn detective!* he thought to himself. *I feel this is between me and God! If Joanna hears about the reward of the man I killed by accident, the greed in her, she may turn me in for that reward money! But if she does that, she loses everything, even our four-bedroom house. She doesn't make enough in a year. She would lose her taxes trying to keep that house. No, I think she needs me around for the money! She can have new outfits and expensive jewelry and sit around with her friends, thinking she's all that! Nope, I think Joanna wants to keep feeling that she's the queen of the Nile! Joanna's not going to say anything unless it benefits her.* He is momentarily feeling good. *Let that detective keep thinking but have no proof! And everything will be all right with this stressful situation, and Richard had enemies and I didn't even realize it!* Alan was thinking to himself. *Poor Richard, I am going to miss him. I wonder who's the new guy that's going to be taking Richard's place and office.* Alan thoughts were roaming. *After lunch, I'm going to call Alexis. I hope she not mad at me for not calling her yet. They did a good job washing my car. But I'm still feeling Alexis's sexual passion. She is very sweet and a great lover. Let me get to work, time would go by faster. I should switch cars, but then, that detective would really think I'm hiding something and I know he's going to be snooping around when I get my Lincoln back. Let me check out this file.* Alan was kicking back in his black leather office chair, feeling like he has everything under control *I am just going to take a realistic approach to everything that's going on now and that sexual feeling for Alexis. She sure is good in bed, even better than Joanna. I'm going back over to Alexis real soon!* he was thinking. *Beep!*

"Yes."

"Mr. Jones? A package has arrived for you," his receptionist said. Alan gets up and walks out his office to get the package. "Here you go, Mr. Jones." The receptionist hands him a yellow eight by twelve package. Alan walks back into his office and closes the door behind him and sits in his black leather chair and opens the package and pulls out the paperwork.

"Oh yes, Mr. Williams' paperwork for his loan that Richard had going at the time before his death. Now I have to sign to finish his last loan," Alan was thinking.

A couple of hours later. "I am finished for the day." He gets up from his black chair. "I'm going to go pick up my vehicle. It's now eleven fifty a.m." He walks out of his office.

"I'm going to lunch. I'll be back in an hour," Alan said.

"Yes, Mr. Jones," his receptionist said. Alan walks to the elevator and pushes the ground floor button to walk to his 1968 Mustang.

"Alan! I'm glad I ran into you! I just want to say sorry about Richard!"

"Thanks, Marv."

"Do the police have any leads on the murder?" Marv asked.

"I haven't heard anything yet!" Alan said.

"Did you go to his service?" Marv asked.

"Yes, I did with my family!"

"I didn't see you there, Alan!"

"I was sitting in the back. I'll see you later!"

"Wow, you're driving that vehicle?" Marv asked excited. "It's nice but a gas eater. You need two paychecks just to keep gas in it!"

"Yes, but it rides nice," Alan said. He gets into his Mustang and starts it up! Marv was watching Alan drive off. Alan pushes on the gas pedal. And shifts it into reverse and then into drive.

Alan blows the horn once at Marv and turns right on Main Street. Toward the body shop, driving slow, feeling that powerful motor, he decided to stop at a Huffy Sandwiches and Hamburger and drives through.

"Welcome to Huffy Sandwiches and Burgers," the lady at the speaker said.

"Yes, may I have a pastrami sandwich and a 7 Up please."

"That will be 3.75 at the window." He grabs his wallet out of his pocket to pull out his money, driving slow up to the window, trying to have the right amount of change. Alan hands the young lady the money; she hands Alan his food. Alan puts his food bag on the passenger side and drives off toward the auto shop.

Fifteen minutes later, Alan arrives at the auto shop and parks his 1968 Mustang in the lot and turns the motor off while a thin man walks up to him. Alan walks into the auto shop looking at his vehicle. "Here are your keys and I'll show you the work on the hood of your vehicle, how we spray over the hood where the dent was." They both walk over to his Navigator. Alan begins to look for any cracks on the hood. "It looks really good, man," Alan said.

"It's all paid for and ready to ride. It was worth every penny, $1,090.27." He pulls out his credit card. "Can I pick it up tomorrow?"

"Sure, you can park it over there," the auto man said. Alan takes the keys and unlocks his car and drives his Lincoln over to a fence and parks it till he takes a cab to pick it up tomorrow.

"I'm going to park into the driveway when I get home or maybe I'll just go over to Alexis. I'll call Alexis and see if she would like some company this evening, and if so, I'll spend some time with her tonight before I go home and have to feel guilty. I sure hope Auntie and Uncle will be there to keep me company because our marriage is on the rocks. It's no fun sitting around, looking at her all night complaining, so when I get off work, I'll call sexy Alexis." Alan was thinking while eating and driving back to work. A few minutes later, he got back to work and parks his 1968 Mustang in his parking space and gets out to return to work. *Ring! Ring!* Alan gets his cell phone out of his pocket and looks at the caller ID.

"Lisa!"

"Yes, I was calling you back!"

"Did you get some lunch?" Alan asked.

"I'll be going to lunch in a few minutes. I'm waiting on someone," Lisa said. "But are you back at work?"

"Yes, little sister!"

"All right have a good day, brother." Dupree walks into the shop; Lisa hangs up with her brother. "Hello, Dupree!" Lisa said softly with a smile.

"So this is your job? Very nice," Dupree said. Lisa grabs her purse.

"Wendy? Are you going to lunch? It's twelve fifteen," Lisa said.

"Yes, let me get my purse," Wendy said.

"I have the keys to lock up," Lisa said to Wendy. "And I'll be back at one p.m." Dupree opens the door for Lisa and Wendy and Lisa locks the door. Wendy turns and walks the other direction while they walk to his vehicle. Dupree opens the passenger door for Lisa and walks to the driver's side and jumps in with a smile and gives Lisa a bright smile. Lisa was looking at Dupree and started touching his eyebrows.

"They're very thick," she said as they were putting on their seat belts. Dupree starts his car and drives off. "So which restaurant would you like to go to, Lisa!"

"Let's go to the salad bar on Bear Street, you've ever been there?"

"No, but I've seen the place," Dupree said while smiling at Lisa. "So is our date still on for tonight?"

"Yes," Lisa said. "So what are you going to wear tonight?"

"A pair of dress pants and a nice clean shirt with some dress shoes." They both laughed. "All right, Dupree," Lisa said.

"You're asking me questions, how about you? What are you planning to wear? I hope something sexy for me," Dupree said. They both laughed.

"I'm wearing my black and light green outfit that brings out my shape so you can get an eyeful! I see the way you look at me," Lisa said.

"And I'm going to keep on looking. You're very pretty and I love your eyes and I would like to keep seeing you, if you don't mind?" Dupree said.

"Yes, I would like that. Come here! I want a kiss!" Lisa said.

"I'm driving." He puts his brakes on as Lisa kisses him. Lisa gets closer to Dupree and started tongue kissing him. The signal light changes, horns where blowing at Dupree, and he began driving and made a left turn into the salad bar restaurant and parks. They continue kissing even harder.

Dupree yells, "Oh yes! That was good!" And he opens his car door and walks quickly around to Lisa and opens her the door and they were both smiling hard at each other. "I have to hide my feelings. Oh, Lisa, I can't walk in there all hard. Till it goes down, see what you did to me! You got my private all hard! It's going down." Lisa's eyes spread wide; she was looking surprised.

I can't wait for tonight! Dupree was thinking to himself.

"What was that?" Lisa asked. They both started laughing hard. "Wait a minute, you are that big! That thing is huge."

"You haven't seen how big it is yet," Dupree said.

"But you're going to make sure I do, right!" Lisa said. He grabs her hand and walks into the restaurant and they both look around.

"May I help you both get whatever you want!" Dupree said.

"The crab sandwich looks good with chips and a drink for 2.95," Lisa said.

"That's what you want?" Dupree said. "Then I'll have the beef on rye bread and chips with a drink." The guy starts writing down their order and went to the cash register. "That will be 5.75." Dupree gets the money out to pay for their food. "Is this for here or to go?" the cashier asked. "For here," Dupree said. They both walk over to a table, holding hands, and sit together. "What time are you picking me up tonight at my place?" Lisa asked. "Around seven tonight. Are you going to be ready for me tonight?" Dupree asked. She started laughing aloud, swinging her golden long hair to her back. "I'll be ready, baby," Lisa said. "I love the color of your hair," Dupree said. Ten minutes later, a waiter brings their food. "The drinks are over there."

"Thank you," they both said. And the man walks away while Dupree goes and gets their drinks from the drinks fountain.

Lisa's New Date

A couple of seconds later, Dupree brings their drinks, and he sits down across from Lisa. "I wanted to tell you that I feel good being around you. I feel a good vibe about you. And you make me feel happy too!" Dupree said. They begin eating their lunch, grinning at each other. Thirty minutes later, Dupree and Lisa finished eating their meal. Lisa gets up. "I'll be right back, I'm going to the ladies room."

"All right, baby. I'll be right here waiting." Dupree gets up and walks to the trash and throws away the napkins after he wipes his hands holding his and Lisa's 7 Up drinks. Lisa walked out the ladies room and Dupree was standing near the door.

"Are you ready?"

"Yes! Let's go," Lisa said with a smile and they both walk out the restaurant to his vehicle. Dupree opens the passenger side door for Lisa and gives him a short kiss. While she gets into her seat, Dupree closes her car door and walks over to the driver's side and starts his vehicle. After he gives Lisa a short kiss and drives off to take Lisa back to work. Lisa holds his right hand while he was looking out for traffic to get back on the main street, driving north. "You enjoyed your meal?" Dupree asked.

"Yes, it was very delicious. Thank you."

"What time do you get off work?" Dupree asked.

"Five o'clock and I'll go home and take a shower alone!" He gives a little smile.

"I'd like to see that!" Dupree said.

"Wait for you to come pick me up tonight!" Lisa said.

"And I'll be there, give me your address."

"Oh, that's right. Let me write it down now so you won't have any excuses," Lisa said. "You don't have to worry, baby. I'll find you!" Dupree said. They both laughed. Ten minutes later, Dupree pulls up in front of 25 Payton Street, Lisa's job. Lisa smiles and gives Dupree a kiss before she gets out of his car and opens the car door and steps out with a smile while Wendy waits in front of the shop for Lisa.

"It looks like someone had a nice lunch," Wendy said.

"It was an interesting lunch," Lisa replied while she walked behind the counter to unlock the cashier.

"Don't forget we still have a fitting at two p.m. with Mrs. Hayward. The eleven o'clock appointment went good and that lady knew what color of dress she wanted."

The phone rings. "Quotable Women dress shop, Lisa speaking."

"Hello, Lisa, it's me, just got out of the meeting, and I'm on my way to do Mrs. Hayward's fitting at 4 p.m. How did the eleven o'clock appointment go?"

"Okay, Ms. Carmen. It went good."

"That's good to hear. Did Wendy finish with the new outfits?"

"Yes."

"I'll be there in a little while," her boss said. While she was feeling a little excited, thinking how cute he looks with his golden hair and his Swiss gray cat eyes, and he has a job! Twenty minutes later, the owner, Ms. Carmen, came walking in her dress shop.

"Good afternoon, Ms. Carmen," they both said. Lisa was standing behind the counter, answering the phone, waiting for the time. Wendy was still rearranging the clothing on the racks. Mrs. Carmen walked into her office till her next appointment arrives.

"It's one thirty p.m., four more hours for closing. She was thinking while her cell phone was vibrating.

"I sure hope it's Dupree."

"Hey, girl. Are you going to the rags club tonight?" her friend Diana asked.

"Yes, with a new friend."

"What time you going? And who is your new friend?"

"You'll see him tonight!"

"So we'll meet you there at seven?" Diana asked.

"I'm going to be looking good tonight!" Lisa said.

"There are going to be some fine guys there tonight!" Diana said.

"Where is Dana?"

"She's watching a movie with my mother."

"I better get off this phone before my boss comes in and catches me. I'll call you when I get home, Diana. All right, talk to you then, bye," Lisa whispered. "Twenty more minutes for that fitting, this day is going by so slow, but we did have a nice lunch together. I feel we are going to be close." She was having her moments of thoughts with a smile.

"Lisa, I need your help!" Wendy said. She stands up from behind the counter while two customers came walking into the dress shop. "Can I help you, ladies?" Lisa asked.

"Yes, I'm looking for a dress, not too loud but casual."

"Over here, we have all new outfits and dresses that just came in," Lisa said to the tall lady.

"Now, this is a nice-looking dress with the purple shade."

"Just a moment please," Lisa said to the tall lady while her boss's appointment walks in.

"Hello, I'm Mrs. Hayward, is Ms. Carmen in?"

"Yes, just a moment." Lisa walks to her boss office.

"Mrs. Hayward is here for her fitting!"

"I'll be right there!" Lisa's boss said, and she walks back to her customers.

"Miss? Do you have the same kind of dress like this one, but in a larger size?" the lady costumer asked. While Lisa was working and thinking about Dupree, time went by. Fifteen minutes to five p.m., Lisa was taking care of the customers behind the cashier.

"That will be twenty-five dollars and ninety-five cents." The customer hands Lisa the money while her boss comes behind her to the cashier, waiting for Lisa to finish with her customer.

"Thank you and come again," Lisa said with a smile.

"I'm finished with Mrs. Hayward's fitting," her boss said.

"Everything went okay?" Lisa asked.

"Yes, it went very well, and she picked out the dress she wants to wear to her daughter's wedding in two weeks," her boss said. "Now, I have an early fitting Monday."

"Thank you, Mrs. Carmen, and I would like to purchase this blue and yellow dress," Mrs. Hayward said.

"If you walk over here, I'll take care of you, Mrs. Hayward," Lisa said. Her boss walks over to Wendy. "Let's close shop for the weekend, Wendy. Close those blinds over there. Thank you, Mrs. Hayward, come again."

It's two minutes to five p.m. Lisa starts getting her purse. "I'll see you both here Monday morning. We have a couple of fittings and you both have a good weekend," their boss said. "See you Monday morning." Wendy walks out of the dress shop and to their vehicles. She starts her car, then gets her cell phone out of her purse to call Dupree. *Ring!* "Hello!"

"Hi, Dupree, are you getting ready?" Lisa asked.

"Not at the moment," Dupree said. "Can I call you back in a few minutes?"

"Sure!" Dupree walks into his house, hearing a different male voice and walks into the living room.

"Detective!"

"You look surprised?" Detective Theodore said.

"Any new leads, Detective?" Dupree asked.

"No! Um, I just came by to ask you a question about that evening when your brother was killed. You said you were with your friends that evening."

"Yes, what's this about?" Dupree asked.

"Well, I couldn't contact any of your brother's other friends, and I was wondering do you know who he was with the last couple of days or where he hangs out with at the Bam club?"

"There's this tall lady Richard was with a few nights ago before he died. But she is also married!"

"Do you know her name?" Detective Theodore asked with curiosity.

"I think Linda? No, Susan Ross! She hangs out at the Bam bar where my brother hung out. I think her husband might be involved," Dupree said.

"Yes, I know where it is. What makes you think that?"

"Well, he may have followed them one night and found out where my brother lived."

"Well, thank you. I think that's all I need for now."

"If you hear anything, Detective, please let us know," Liz said.

"I'll walk you to the door, Detective," his father Jimmy said. Dupree goes upstairs to get dressed for his date.

"Dupree, there's some mail that came for you," his mother said while walking into the kitchen. Dupree had his mind on a nice evening with Lisa, and he rushes to the bathroom upstairs and turns on the shower and walks to his bedroom and opens his closet doors to get his brown dress pants off the hanger and lays them on his bed with his beige long-sleeved turtleneck sweater. He then walks to the hallway and he grabs a towel out the cabinet and rushes into the bathroom and jumps into the shower. Ten minutes later, Dupree gets out the shower with his hair and body dripping wet and grabs his large blue towel and dries his hair off and gets and his muscular body and then brushes his white teeth and puts on his swish men's cologne. Lisa was getting ready, playing music from her stereo in her living room, dancing around her one-bedroom half duplex. Her kitten Fluffy was following her into the bathroom. With a towel wrapped around her small nude body, she danced into the steaming hot shower washing her hair singing. Ten minutes later, she gets out the shower and brushes her teeth and dries her hair. She then walks into her bedroom and starts getting dressed. She walks over to her cell phone: two missed calls.

"Dupree and Diana, I missed their call." She sprays her Far Away perfume on and then her makeup, rushing to put her golden short dress on that matches her golden blonde hair and her black pump heels. She walked over to her big round mirror.

Ding-dong.

"That must be Dupree." Lisa walks out of her bedroom and to the front door and looks through her peek hole. Lisa opens the door slowly. "Hi, Dupree! Come in!"

"Hello, Lisa." Dupree walks in holding a bottle of wine.

"What's this you brought?"

"Well, it's a gift for us. We can drink it later this evening. We can drink it when the moon is full."

"Thank you. I'll put it in the refrigerator. She walks by smelling of far away perfume. "Meow."

"So this is Fluffy."

"Yes, let me get my purse," Lisa said. "Meow." Fluffy was rubbing against Dupree's leg while he was looking around her half duplex.

"Very nice place you have!"

"Thank you. I'll be back, Fluffy." Dupree opens her front door like a gentleman would. "Thank you." Lisa steps out on the porch, holding her keys. Dupree steps out walking to his car to unlock the passenger side for Lisa she walks to his car and gets in. Dupree closes her door for her and walks around the driver side and gets in and starts his car. "What are you smiling so hard about?" Dupree asked.

"I think you are very nice and handsome and you're a gentleman."

"Don't all the guys open the doors for you?"

"Don't date much for that treatment."

"Some guys don't treat a lady like we really should be treated. And those that are married still open the doors for their wives That's right!"

"How do you feel about relationships?" Dupree asked.

"I would like to experience love and spend eternity together, and most marriages last forever and most don't. A relationship is a job itself. I look at other people's relationships. It's the trust and honesty with love and commitment forever," Lisa said.

"That was very nice," Dupree said with a smile and he grabs her hand while driving to the club.

"I have to meet my cousin in a little while over at the Bam club tonight!" Dupree said while driving up to the Ace Club, a red brick building with loud music coming from the inside. People were walking in and out of the bar, laughing and having a good time. Dupree parks and turns off the engine and looks at Lisa and gives her a kiss, and he jumps out to open the door for her. Lisa steps out with her golden purse that matches her golden dress. They both start walking toward the door where there was loud music.

"There's a service charge of ten dollars," the bouncer said. Dupree gets his money out of his pocket and gives the man twenty dollars. The man opens the club door while Dupree has both his hands around her waist, and Lisa was holding his right hand, feeling closer to him. They both walk over to a round table with a lit red candle and a white cloth. Lisa sits like a lady with her legs crossed while Dupree goes and gets her brandy and Coke with ice and him gin on the rocks.

A couple minutes of later, Dupree comes to the table with their drinks.

"Brandy for the lady," Dupree said.

"The music is kind of loud, but it's nice in here," Lisa said.

"Would like to dance?" Dupree asked.

"Yes." They both get up and walk to the dance floor and begin slow dancing to some slow romantic music. Dupree puts his hand around Lisa's waist and Lisa grabs Dupree close to her breast with her left hand around his waist. They both were smiling. He holds her tightly. "You feel so good," he whispers in her right ear.

"So do you," Lisa said. They both were feeling each other's bodies closer with romance in their eyes.

"I'm glad we met!" Dupree said, holding Lisa tightly in his arms. "You are so beautiful, Lisa." They started kissing and dancing slower to a love song. Lisa was feeling like she was floating on cloud nine,

I am slowly falling in love, Lisa was thinking how she's feeling, laying her head on his chest, kissing him with her soft lips, feeling love like never before. He began squeezing on her butt while the trip lights are dim. She starts holding him closer. The slow song had stopped and the lights came on; they stopped and looked at each other with deep breaths, and they both turned around and walked back to their table, holding hands. Lisa gets her drink and takes a quick sip, feeling kind of different sitting next to Dupree.

He's so handsome, Lisa was thinking to herself.

"There's Lisa!" Diana shouted.

"Dupree, these are my friends, twin sisters Diana and Dana," Lisa said.

"Nice to meet the both of you," Dupree said.

"Nice to meet you. Same here!" they both said.

"He's nice looking, girl!" Diana whispered to Lisa.

"He sure is," Dana said.

"We will see you later, girl. Have fun!" Diana said. Thirty minutes later, Dupree and Lisa finish their drinks and get up to leave. "Bye, ladies, Diana and Dana."

"Give us a call tomorrow," Diana said.

"Have fun," Lisa said, and they both walk out the Ace Club together and walk to his car. Dupree opens the car door for her and walks over to the driver side and unlocks his car door and gets in, and they give each other a kiss. Dupree starts his car with a smile.

"Thank you for the good time," Lisa said.

"You're welcome, baby," he said with a soft smile. *Ring.* Dupree gets his cell out of his right pants pocket. "Hello, Dupree. Where are you, man? I'm here at the Bam club, waiting for you," Keith said.

"I'm on my way, cousin, with my girl." He was smiling at Lisa while driving down main street. "I'll be there in a couple of minutes, Keith. There's a police car behind me. I better get off the phone, see you in a minute, cousin," Dupree said. Dupree was looking into his rearview mirror, watching the police car behind him. "Is everything all right, Dupree?"

"Yes, baby! Everything is fine." Dupree begins feeling nervous as the police car passes Dupree's car, and he took a deep breath. A couple of seconds later, they arrive at the Bam club, noticing his cousin Keith was standing by his car, smoking a black and mild cigar anxiously waiting. Dupree pulls up and parks next to Keith's vehicle. Dupree gets out to give his cousin Keith a handshake. "How you doing, cousin?" Keith asked.

"I'm good!" Dupree said. "Let me open the car door for my new girl Lisa." Dupree walks over to Lisa and opens the car door and she steps out of the car smiling. "Keith, this is Lisa. You remember Alan? Richard's coworker?"

"Yes, sure," Keith said.

"This is Alan's sister, Lisa!"

"Nice to meet you, pretty lady. Wow, she's fine!" Keith whispered.

"It's nice to meet you also!" Lisa said. Lisa was feeling like an important lady with Dupree and his cousin, Keith. Dupree grabs her right hand, feeling special with a beautiful lady like Lisa, looking like a new model. Dupree kept his vision only on Lisa with a small grin.

Cousins Investigate

*A*s they walked into the door of the Bam club, three guys were playing pool and others were standing around. Some couples were sitting at tables, drinking beer and hard liquor. A bearded guy who looked like a rough rider was holding a pool stick with a cigarette hanging from his mouth, wearing dark shades and a black vest and old ripped blue jeans. He was looking at Keith, Dupree, and Lisa while they sit at the bar. "Hello, Pete! How you doing?"

"Hey, Dupree. I'm sorry to hear about your brother Richard. We'll miss him," Pete the bartender said.

"Thanks, Pete."

"Is there anything I can get you?" Pete asked.

"Yes, do you know a lady named Susan Ross that's been in here lately?" Dupree asked. "Yes, she and her husband were here last night," Pete said. "I almost forgot to tell you, Dupree, that a detective has been in here asking questions about you and your brother.

"What kind of questions?" Dupree asked, surprised.

"Like what happened between you and your brother that Friday evening and if I saw Richard with anyone. And he kept curiously asking about the Fourth of July evening," Pete whispered. Dupree takes a deep breath.

"Thanks, Pete," Dupree said.

"Would your lady friend like a drink?" Pete asked.

"What would you like to drink, baby?"

"I would like some red wine." She then had two more glasses of red wine. Three hours later, it's eleven forty-five p.m.

"I'm feeling a little tired," Lisa said.

"Ready to go, baby?"

"Sure," Lisa said.

"Thanks, Pete!" He gives Pete a handshake.

"Have a good night," Pete said while Dupree, Lisa, and Keith get up from the bar and started walking toward the bar door. Pete the bartender continued serving his costumers. "It looks like they aren't coming tonight," Dupree said.

"No, we missed her last night, but don't worry, cousin. We'll catch up with her and her husband and find out where they live," Keith said.

"Okay, cousin, I'm going to take her home and I'll give you a call tomorrow," Dupree said.

"All right, cousin. Have a good evening. He gives Dupree a handshake and walks to his car while Dupree gets his keys out of his pocket. They both walked to his vehicle while watching Keith drive off. Dupree opens his car door for Lisa, and she gets in like a lady while Dupree walks over to the driver's side and unlocks it and sits in.

"Are you all right, Lisa?"

"Yes, I'm just a little high now. I need to get home," Lisa said. Dupree starts his car and drives back to Main Street.

It wouldn't be a good time to ask her for one more drink from the bottle of wine in her refrigerator chilling, Dupree was thinking to himself. Dupree drove north to get to Road 20 toward Lisa's place, driving 25 mph, while holding Lisa's left hand, listening to music from his car radio, "I Had the Time of My Life" from the sound track of *Dirty Dancing*. Lisa started singing the song on the radio. "Feeling better?" Dupree asked.

"Yes, much better. I really enjoyed this evening," Lisa said.

"It doesn't have to end so early," Dupree said.

"Turn right here," Lisa said. Dupree turned into her driveway and turns the motor off and opened his car door and gets out and walks around to Lisa and opens her door and she gets out of his car and walked to her front door and pulled her keys out of her purse while Dupree walks behind her. Lisa opens her front door, and they both walk into her doorway. He closes her door and she takes Dupree's right hand and pulls him into her bedroom. Fluffy stands by her bedroom door. "Meow." Lisa pulls Dupree to her bed with a smile. They both fall onto her bed and begin kissing while Dupree lays on top of her as they begin rolling around on her bed, laughing and kissing each other.

"Do you have an extra toothbrush here?" Dupree asked.

"Yes." Lisa gets a toothbrush out the bathroom cabinet that's still in the pack and hands it to him and turns the sink water on to brush their teeth. Lisa was feeling happy with Dupree, feeling close to him already like they were soul mates.

"I feel as if we've known each other for a long period!" Lisa said to Dupree. "Don't you feel that?"

"Yes, I feel that too!" He grabs Lisa with her pink towel wrapped around her nude body and gives her kiss after he brushed his teeth! They both walk back into her bedroom. Dupree puts his underwear on and then his pants and walks into her kitchen and opens her refrigerator door to get the white wine out, then he gets two glasses and sets the white wine on the counter and opens the bottle. He twisted the top off and throws it into the trash and walks back into Lisa's bedroom with the lights dim while Lisa was putting her fresh red panties on and a night shirt on with Betty Boo in front of it. Dupree sets the wine and two glasses on her nightstand. Lisa looks at the time. "It's only ten p.m.," she said. "We have the whole evening to ourselves."

"What's your brother going to think about us hooking up together?"

"I'm a grown-ass woman! And my brother doesn't have anything to do with my affairs!" Lisa said.

"That's cool!" Dupree said.

"And if we wanted to get married, he couldn't do anything about it!" Lisa said. Dupree looks at Lisa with a smile. Dupree pours the wine into both glasses.

"Let's make a toast to that!" Dupree said. Lisa walks over to Dupree and gives him a kiss, and he hands the glass of white wine to her and they click their glasses together.

"Cling to the future!" Lisa said, and they both take a drink. Lisa walks to the living room to turn on some soft music from her stereo while Fluffy walks into the bedroom. Dupree just smiles at the little kitten. "He's growing big."

"How old is he?"

"Six months old now. She has different colors on his fur, and at night, his eyes are amazing. I'll turn the lights off and just have the TV on and his eyes glow different colors," Lisa said.

"That's cool. Now can I some more good sex tonight?" Dupree said, and they both laughed. "You have the most pretty smile and you're so beautiful to me. Your long golden hair, the perfect face and body and your tan skin is so soft." And he kisses her on the lips. Lisa gives him a hug around his neck and kisses him. Dupree takes their glasses of wine and puts them on the nightstand. As they begin to lay on the bed holding each other, listening to the song, "Where Is the Love" by Roberta Flack and Donny Hathaway, kissing through the song, both falling in love with each other.

"I want to make some exotic lovemaking to you tonight."

Lisa gives a little laugh. "Let's do it!" she said. Looking into her green-gray eyes and then taking one more drink before they begin making love again.

They continued making love all through the evening while Fluffy continued sitting by the bedroom door. Lisa had her right leg across Dupree's left leg, kissing and holding each other closely with the covers over their nude bodies. Dupree gets Lisa a glass of wine and hands her glass carefully in the bed. Lisa lays there and sips on her wine, listening to the music with Dupree lying back, holding his glass of wine in his right hand while holding Lisa in his left arm. They both started to feel the red wine; she was feeling more comfortable with Dupree as he was kissing her on her forehead while she was feeling loved. Dupree noticed the remote control to Lisa's color television and grabs it off the nightstand to turn on the television. When it came on, it was a movie channel. Lisa was falling asleep on Dupree's chest. She then puts her glass of wine on the nightstand on her side of the bed. While Lisa was falling sleep, Dupree was changing the channels on her color television to the sports station. He gets up to use the restroom. A couple of seconds later, he returns to Lisa's bed, feeling comfortable lying next to her as he puts her head back on his chest and gets the remote to turn the volume up to hear the preview games that he missed. He gives Lisa a kiss on her face as he pushes her hair back out of her face while she was sleeping the wine off. One hour later, Dupree looks at the time. It's eleven forty-five p.m. Dupree tries to get some sleep and turns off the television.

Soul Mates

The next morning, Lisa gets up to cook breakfast while Dupree continued sleeping. Lisa brings the bacon and scrambles the eggs and hot pancakes with coffee. Dupree smells food in his sleep and wakes up and sits up on the bed, rubbing his eyes and puts his pants on and shirt on and walks to the kitchen. "Did you sleep good?" Lisa said.

"I've slept good." Dupree walks up to her and gives her a hug.

"Breakfast smells good," Dupree said.

"Breakfast will be ready a in a little bit," Lisa said Dupree gave her a kiss on the cheek and walks back into her bedroom to finish getting dressed; he looks at his two missed calls. *I need to call home to see if everything is all right*, Dupree was thinking.

"Hello, Mother. Good morning!"

"Good morning, son! Where are you? I've fixed breakfast for you and your father this morning," his mother said.

"I'm having breakfast here this morning with a friend, Mother, but keep it warm till I get there," Dupree said. "You know I'll still eat when I get there, Mother."

"What time are you coming home?" his mother asked with a little worry on her mind.

"I'm fine, Mother, and I'll be home soon all right! I'll talk to you when I get there. How's Dad doing?"

"He's doing better!"

"Okay, I have to finish cooking. I'll see you soon, son!" He hung up.

"Baby, your breakfast is ready," Lisa said. Lisa was setting their breakfast on her dining table and walks back into the kitchen to get the pancakes and orange juice out the refrigerator and put the juice and the hot eggs sitting on the table with hot bacon.

"Are you ready, Dupree?"

"Yes, I'm coming, baby!" Dupree said, and he walks to the table.

"You're all dressed," Lisa said.

"After we finish eating, I have to check on my parents, then I'll be back before it gets dark," Dupree said. "Are you going to be here by the time I come back?"

"Yes, I'm not going too far, just to my brother's place a few blocks from here, then back here to lie down. I have a little hangover," Lisa said.

"Oh, baby, eat well and get some rest while I'm gone," Dupree said. "I need you rested up for tonight! Because I'm coming to make love to you."

"You did a good job on breakfast. I didn't know you could cook this good!" Dupree said. "Oh yes, my mother and Auntie Josephine said I had to learn when I was a little girl. They love to cook," Lisa said.

"That's good. You would make a good wife!" Dupree said with a smile.

"That makes me feel good to hear it," Lisa said. Twenty minutes later, they finished breakfast. Dupree gets up from the table and gets his car keys out of his pocket. Lisa gets up to clear the breakfast table. Dupree walks up to her and gives her a kiss on her lips.

"I'll be back, baby!"

"Okay," Dupree said. "I'll be back soon you need anything before I leave?"

"Just yourself," Lisa said while hugging Dupree.

"Okay, I'll be back," he said. Lisa walks him to her front door, and they gave each other a long kiss. Dupree walks out to his car while Lisa watches him leaving. Dupree starts his car and drives to the corner and makes a right toward his place while Lisa gets ready to go over to her brother's place and visits the family.

"It's Saturday morning," Lisa said to Fluffy. "I should just sleep a little longer, feeling this way! I sure feel I have a little hangover this morning. I had three drinks last night feeling good, but later, my head began spinning and hurting. I'm going to take a shower and get dressed and drive over to my brother's place later. I have a love hangover." "Meow!"

"I'm going to clean the dishes, then lay down for a couple of hours," Lisa was thinking to herself.

Thirty minutes later, Lisa pulls herself out of her bed to answer the door. *Dupree's back already?* Lisa was thinking to herself and looks out her peep hole on her door and opens the door. "Alan!" She was surprised!

"Good morning, sister!"

"What you doing here this morning?" Lisa asked with concern.

"I just need to get away from Joanna for a while! She keeps starting arguments with me. She just wants to dig up in my nerves to see what's going with me," Alan said.

"Well, I hope things work out! Would you like some coffee? Before I go lie down for a couple of hours," Lisa asked.

"You go lie down. I'll get my coffee," her brother said. "Who did you go out with last night?"

"Alan, don't start bothering me this morning about who I am dating. You sound like Dad," Lisa said. Alan gives a little giggle and walks to the kitchen and gets a cup and pours himself a cup of black coffee with cream from the refrigerator and walks back to the living room and sits back on her light green leather sofa and gets the remote to her color television that's across from sofa. Alan's cell phone rings. He looks at the caller ID. *Oh no!* Alan was saying to himself. *I don't feel like hearing all that shit! Always wanting to know my every move. She's watching me all the time. I hate that she is so damn insecure. She stopped trusting me a long time ago!*

"What!"

"Why are you yelling at me, Alan!" Joanna said.

"Because you keep aggravating me! The same shit over and over! You keep talking about the same thing, Joanna! You just don't trust me anymore!"

"I just want to know where you were last night. Just be honest with me, Alan, because I felt something wasn't right last night!" Alan hangs up on her. Lisa gets up and walks to the bathroom and closes the bathroom door. A few minutes later, she walks to the living room. "What's wrong?" she asked her brother.

"I think I'm going to move out. We need a break from each other for a while!" Alan said. Lisa looked surprised. Alan takes a deep breath.

"Where are you going?"

"To a friend's place! For a while," Alan said. "I'm going to call my friend in a little while." Lisa looks at Alan.

"Well, brother. I hope things work out!" Lisa said.

"Not with Joanna, she just wants what she wants. I thought she wanted just me! But no, I was wrong on that point!" Alan said.

"I cooked some breakfast on the counter if you get hungry, okay?" Lisa said. "I'm going to go lie back down."

She walks to the kitchen first to pour her some orange juice and grab her a piece of bacon from breakfast and walks back to her room and puts the glass of orange juice on her nightstand. *Ring!* Lisa picks her cell phone up. "Hello, Lisa, how you feeling, baby?"

"A little better."

"Are you still going to your brother's place?"

"No! He's here now, he came over a few minutes ago!"

"Oh good, then you don't have to go anywhere," Dupree said. "How's your parents doing?"

"They're fine! They're just relaxing after breakfast, watching television. What is your brother doing?"

"He's just trying to calm down. He's fighting with his wife Joanna So he came over to get away from her for a while."

"All right, baby. How long he's going to be there?" Dupree asked.

"Probably a couple of hours," Lisa said.

"Good, because I'm coming over this evening to spend some more time with you!" Dupree said. "I really enjoyed you last night and this morning!"

"Yes, very nice," she said with a little hangover.

"When I come over, I'll make you feel better, baby," Dupree said.

"Yes, you make me feel better," Lisa said. *Ring!* Alan answers his cell. "What? Joanna!" "You know I'm just trying to help you, Alan! That's what wives are supposed to do!" Joanna said.

"If I wanted your help, I would have asked you!" Alan yelled. "I'm so tired of your attitude, Joanna! You know I have a big problem with that detective and what had happened! So why are you hounding me with the small shit, Joanna?"

"Because I didn't want you to get arrested for DUI, that's all I was worried about last night!" Joanna said.

"No! I know what you're worried about! If I was with someone else all night! Your damn insecurity! Just give me peace of mind, Joanna! I'll call you later!" Alan said. And he hung up. Lisa was still talking to Dupree.

"You can come hold me this morning," Lisa said. Dupree laughed.

"It's Saturday morning!" Lisa said slowly, yawning on the phone. Her eyes were getting more sleepy lying under the covers feeling a love hangover with Dupree.

"It's nine a.m. I'll call Alexis. I hope she answer her cell phone," Alan was thinking. *Ring!* "Hello! Alexis, are you up yet?" Alan said.

"Not yet!" Alexis said. "Why? Do you want to come over?"

"Yes, if you don't mind!" Alan said.

"Come over, baby!" Alexis said.

"Is your sister there?"

"No. She stayed the night over her boyfriend's place last night! So it's safe!" Alexis said. "All right. I'll see you in a minute," Alan said. Alan finishes his coffee and gets up and walks to Lisa's kitchen to put the empty coffee cup in the sink. "Lisa! I'm leaving," Alan said.

"All right."

"Come lock your door!" Alan yells. "I'll give you a call tomorrow." Lisa gets up and walks toward her brother.

"Where are you going?" Lisa asked.

"Over a friend's place! Look, if Joanna calls you and asks you where I went, you don't know!" Alan gives Lisa a kiss on the cheek and opens her front door and walks out. Lisa locks her front door. "Was that your brother leaving?" Dupree asked.

"Yes, finally."

"I can come over and hold you in my arms all day!" Dupree said.

"Can you please stop at the store and get me some aspirins? Please, my head is pounding," Lisa said.

"Yes, I can do that for you, baby! Oh, my baby is not feeling very well. Okay, let me finish getting dressed and then I'll go and get that for you! I'll be there soon, baby!" Dupree said.

"All right, love," Lisa said. Dupree started getting ready to go to Lisa's place.

"Dupree! Dupree! Come quickly!" He comes running down the stairs as his mother yells! "What is it, Mother?"

"The morning news is on about your brother Richard!"

"How is the investigation going on the murder case of Richard Oxford?" the newscast lady shouted. "Detective Theodore! Do you have any suspect yet! Detective?"

"The case is closing in. So far, the investigation is going good," Detective Theodore said. "Do you have any lead suspects in this case at this moment, Detective?"

"Well, I'm still looking into his murder at this time, but we are going to close in on this case!"

"So you do have a suspect?" the newscast lady asked.

"Well, I can't say anything at this time," Detective said.

"Thank you, Detective! That was Detective Theodore who's working on the case of Richard Oxford's murder! This is news Channel 65 live! Cut!" the newscast lady said. The news cast walks back to their van to load up their equipment.

"They must have recorded it yesterday!" his mother Liz said.

"They said they're closing in on the case," Dupree said. "Well' I'm going to finish getting dressed. Where's Dad?"

"He's lying down for a while," his mother said. *Knock*. Liz walks to the front door and looks out the window. "It's the detective," Liz said and opens the front door.

"Good morning! Detective Theodore, come in!" Liz said. "I just saw you on television." "Um, I'm sorry I came so early! And on a Saturday morning! But I would like to speak to your son again."

"Sure, Detective, he's upstairs. I'll call him!"

"Dupree!"

"Yes, Mother!"

"Detective Theodore needs to speak to you!"

"I'll be right there!" Dupree said. A couple of seconds later, Dupree comes walking down the stairs. "Good morning, Detective!" He gives the detective a handshake. "What can I do for you, Detective?"

"Well, I haven't found that lady you told me about yesterday. Do you have any idea where she lives?" Detective Theodore asked.

"Somewhere near the Bam bar with her husband."

"Why are you looking for a lady? You think she has something to do with Richard's murder?" Liz asked.

"Maybe, Mrs. Oxford, I'm just fishing right now, and have you seen Curtis lately, Dupree? The reason I asked is because I think he's involved with the murder of your brother!" Detective said.

"That guy!" Dupree shouts. "He's a wimp of a guy, Detective! I don't think Curtis could kill a worm! He's too scared." The detective gave a little laugh." I know what's he's like just a little from what my brother told me that he was trying to help Curtis, but I have to say that the two were close friends and who else would do it?"

"What he did to Richard's private parts—"

"Hush, Detective! I don't want my mother to know about my brother! It would kill her if she found out!" Dupree whispered.

"Oh, okay! Well, I guess I'll be going now! Sorry to bother you this morning." Detective Theodore was walking to the front door.

"I'll walk you out, Detective."

"Sorry about that! I thought your folks knew about your brother and his friend Curtis?" "No! And I don't want them to know ever," Dupree said. Detective Theodore puts his cigar into his mouth and looks at Dupree. "Well, what if they do find out the truth about Richard?"

"It would crush their hearts and spirits more because they looked at Richard differently!" "Oh, what do you mean?"

"Well, Richard was their firstborn! And they wouldn't imagine Richard with another male in a sexual relationship. It would crush their hearts even more!" Dupree whispered. "And I don't think Curtis would hurt Richard if he really cared for him!"

"Maybe you're right! But I still have to look into it! If you get that lady's address that Richard was seeing at the time, I would appreciate it!" Detective Theodore said.

"I sure will try, Detective!"

"Thank you. It would help a lot!" Detective whispered to Dupree. "And if you get it! Call me at the station!" The detective walks to his car and starts it and drives off! Dupree turns around and walks back into the house and closes the front door.

"Did the detective leave?" his mother asked.

"Yes, Mother."

"Now what lady was he talking about? I want to know, Dupree!" his mother shouts in aggressive way. "If it's about Richard, I need to know!" his mother said.

"The detective thinks this lady Richard was seeing is married, and he thinks her husband maybe involved!"

"A suspect! And who is Curtis?"

"Oh, Richard's friend!" Dupree said and ran back upstairs while his mother was sitting there, thinking about the man that could have killed her son. Dupree grabs his keys and jacket and walks down the stairs to give his mother a kiss on the cheek.

"Don't worry, Mother! Things will be okay! I'll be back later!"

"Be careful, son!" Dupree walks out the front door toward his car that's parked in the driveway while the detective sits across the street watching the Oxford's residence, waiting for Dupree to drive off so he could follow him. *Maybe he's going to that lady Susan Ross,* the detective was thinking to himself. *Because I have to admit the kid has something there. Maybe he could become a good detective someday like me. Well, let me see where he is going. I'll just follow him for the day! And I know who killed his brother. The gay guy Curtis. I don't have any proof to give to the judge yet! As soon as I find the knife he used, and I bet it's in his house! He probably washed it and reused it to cook with, because he seems like that type who would do something like that! But I need evidence. Some kind of DNA, maybe the fiber from the carpet. I'll call them Monday and see what they came up with,* Detective Theodore was thinking. *And his DNA would be in there. But then again, he may have been going over to Richard's for them to be lovers. But I have this gut feeling that Curtis killed him out of jealousy and having his feelings hurt by Richard cheating on him or someone else is involved, but who? Maybe Susan's husband? Come on, Dupree, let me see this woman, so I can find her husband. That's another clue that he may be the one that's involved. Curtis could have paid Susan's husband to kill Richard because Curtis is hiding something big! I felt that first day I met him or her and how he tries to point the finger at Dupree by telling me about what went down that night with Richard and Dupree. I don't think Dupree would hurt his only brother for money! But Curtis on the other hand would viciously kill Richard like that, so now I need to find Susan's husband. I think that could be the link to this case that would point to Curtis. I just have this gut feeling about Curtis.*

Dupree stops at a market to get Lisa some aspirins. Dupree parks in front of Zee's market and gets out and walks into the market. A few minutes later, Dupree returns to his car while Detective Theodore watches parked four cars away. Dupree is not paying any attention, not noticing the detective following him. Dupree starts his vehicle and puts it into reverse and backs up and puts the gear into drive. East to north toward Lisa's place, Dupree turns on his radio. "The reward is now twenty-five thousand dollars on any information on the hit and run and bury case that killed a city worker three weeks ago! If you have any information, please call the local police station near you! Now back to the music."

I remember that accident on Road 15 that killed that worker, Dupree was thinking. Driving closer to Lisa's place a few minutes later, driving the speed limit, he arrives to Lisa's and parks his car in front of her place and turns of the ignition and gets out and locks his car with his remote and walks up to her front door while the detective drives by looking hard and wondering, *Why is he going to Alan's sister's place? Now, I'm confused. Let me park down the street so he won't see my car.* The Detective was thinking with a lit cigar in his mouth. *Maybe they're dating? Or just friends! This case is getting better every time!*

Parking four cars down, he turns off his ignition and lays low for a while.

Lisa, she sure is a pretty young lady! With her shining golden hair and pretty complexion and a nice-looking body. Hey! I'm nice-looking young man. I could go for a woman like that. I have nice brown hair and thick brown eyebrows and sideburns with a fade with a small beard. I think I'm very handsome myself. I would like to arrest her my way for just one night! Detective was still thinking about Lisa.

Engagement Plans

*I*t's only eleven forty, almost lunchtime and I'm off today. I just wanted to poke around today, and today is very interesting! Detective Theodore was thinking to himself. *Yes! I think they're more than friends. He hasn't come out yet, and two hours went by already. I'm going to get something to eat, but I'll be back later to see if his car is still here.*

Lisa and Dupree spend time together. Dupree's showing attention to Lisa while she has a love hangover. Dupree lies next to her dressed. She lays her head on his chest with her arms wrapped around him. He gives her a kiss on her forehead. "You ready to take an aspirin?" Dupree asked.

"Yes, baby."

"So you can feel better." She rose up while Dupree gets up and goes into the kitchen. He opens the refrigerator for some cold water; he pulls out the water container and gets a glass from the cabinet and pours the cold water into the glass. He then puts the cold water back into the refrigerator and closes the door and walks back to Lisa and gets the aspirin out the bottle and hands two aspirin to Lisa and hands her the glass of water. "Now you will feel better," Dupree said as he lies back down next to Lisa and gives her a kiss on her lips. She smiles and puts her left arm around him. He grabs her and holds her with love. Six weeks later, Dupree and Lisa get engaged and Auntie Josephine plans an engagement party.

"She's having the party at a hall near Main Street downtown. She rented the hall, and there is going to be plenty of food there because my auntie loves to cook and my mother and father are coming to the party. I can't wait for you to meet my folks." Lisa rushes to jump on Dupree's hips as he grabs her butt, holding her tightly. She puts both her arms around his neck. Dupree had a big smile on his face, laughing. "Are you happy, Lisa?" "Yes! Very happy!" They give each other a long kiss. "My ring is full of diamonds!" Lisa said. "And I love it!" Dupree looks closely at his engagement ring: a 14k gold band! "Where did you get it?" Dupree asked.

"At Bills Jewelers. I got it for half price."

"This ring is cool! I love it!"

"Because I love you and you're going to make a good husband," Lisa whispered while they continued kissing each other. Both are feeling love in the air.

"Are your parents coming to the party?" Lisa asked.

"Oh yes, I'm driving them there to make sure," Dupree said. "And my cousin Keith is coming also. I talked to him yesterday. you've met him at the Bam club!"

"Oh yes, when we went out on our first date," Lisa said.

"How did your brother take it that we are engaged?"

"He's happy for us both, he said. He'll be there! You have to get to know Alan. He's the quiet type, keeps a lot to himself. Lately, he and his wife aren't getting along, so Alan moved out of the house to get away from her, and I hope they don't get a divorce. That wouldn't be good because Joanna, my sister-in-law, is full of greed. She would get everything and leave Alan penniless. Thank goodness, he has a good job," Lisa said. They both were lying back on Lisa's leather sofa relaxing at her place, with the television on. "So now that we are engaged, when are you going to move in?" Lisa asked while lying on top of his chest with his right arm around her small waist.

"How about this weekend?" Dupree said.

"That would be great because the engagement party is next weekend," Lisa said.

"Better yet! How about Monday when I get off work? I'll just grab my belongings and move in," Dupree said while Lisa had a big grin on her bright face. She gives him a kiss on his lips. "Now that I'm the man of the house, Fluffy, you can't get all that attention from my wife-to-be," Dupree said to Fluffy as they both laughed.

"Meow."

"Oh, Fluffy, come on, let's go cook dinner!" Lisa gets up from Dupree's chest and body and walks to the kitchen. "We are having spaghetti with meatballs and Ragu sauce with basil." She's talking to Fluffy.

"Baby!"

"Yes!"

"I'm going to give you a hundred dollars to go shopping for food or anything else you need tomorrow morning before I go to work," Dupree said.

"Oh yes! What kind of food do you want me to buy?" Lisa asked. She pulls out the ground beef and gets out the onion and green pepper and gets a knife to cut up the onion and green pepper as she grabs the salt to make the water boil faster.

"I eat any good cooked meal. Get some steaks and potatoes and chicken, and I love shrimp and crab meat."

"Dupree, me too. I love it too," she said and pulls out the skillet and turns on the fire. To start cooking the ground beef, Lisa pours a little cooking oil in a silver skillet and starts breaking up the ground beef in the hot skillet. Dupree starts hearing the ground beef sizzling and the smell of ground beef began hitting Dupree's nose. Lisa puts her seasoning on the meat and started cutting up the onion and green pepper, watching the water boil for noodles. She grabs the spaghetti noodles from her white container and puts a few into the boiling water and continues frying the ground beef and cuts up the onion and green pepper. "It smells good," Dupree yelled.

"Dinner will be ready in about another twenty minutes, baby. I better get the garlic bread in the oven to get dinner ready. She turns her oven on and gets the bread out the refrigerator and puts it on a flat cooking pan and sticks it into the oven. Lisa grabs two plates and sets them on the table with their silverware and napkins. "You want me to go get something for us to drink with our meals?" Dupree asked.

"No, there's orange juice in the refrigerator. You don't need to go anywhere." She sounds like a new wife in control. Lisa hears her cell phone ringing and walks to her bedroom and picks it up and looks at the caller ID. It's Joanna.

"Lisa, is Alan over there?"

"No, he's not here," she said.

"All right. I'll try his cell again!" Joanna said.

"Okay, bye." Lisa walks back to the kitchen to finish cooking dinner. Dupree was watching a sports station. Joanna had insecure thoughts rolling. *I've should've followed my husband this morning with his damaged ass! Cheating again, he said, he was going over to Lisa's place. I just have this strange feeling that Alan is with someone else right now!*

Ding-dong! "Alan and Joanna!" Josephine was yelling at their front door. Joanna gets up and answers. "Good morning, Joanna!" Josephine said.

"What's wrong?"

"I have to use the restroom right away!" Josephine rushes through the dinner room down the hall while Patrick was getting the groceries out their car. Joanna went outside to help him carry the groceries inside the house. "Where's Alan?" Patrick asked.

"He left this morning," Joanna said. "I've been calling his cell, but he won't answer it!" They both walk into the house. Patrick closes the front door while Josephine comes walking from the hallway. "Did you get all the groceries out the car, Patrick?"

"Yes, my dear!" Patrick said, being in a good mood!

"Where's Alan? Did he have to work this morning for the fire department?" Josephine asked.

"He left this morning!" Patrick said.

"What's going with him? It's Saturday morning, and I came over to make the best breakfast this morning!" Josephine said.

"That all sounds good," Joanna said. "You can start cooking. Maybe he'll smell your cooking and maybe come running through the door!"

"Yes, so let me get started." Josephine grabs the groceries and walks into the kitchen.

"Do you need any help?" Joanna asked.

"Yes, I do need your help!" Patrick walks over to the bar and fixes him a light drink with gin and orange juice on ice and walks around the living room looking for the remote to their big screen television. He noticed it was lying on the couch between the pillows, and he sits on the sofa and turns on the screen TV to the sports station. He begins watching a football game while Joanna was helping Josephine in the kitchen cooking breakfast.

Thirty minutes later, they sat around the table eating breakfast.

Joanna can't help but watch the front door as she wonders why Alan her only true love hasn't returned home.

Fifteen minutes later, they all finished eating breakfast. Patrick gets up and goes into the kitchen to wash his hands and walks back into the living room while Josephine and Joanna were still sitting at the table finishing their coffee. "Did you try to call Alan again?" Josephine asked Joanna while she had a worried look on her face. "Don't worry, Joanna, he'll be all right! Maybe he had to go do something important." But Josephine knew she was lying to herself because she knows how Alan was when he was a young man, just doing what he wanted to do! *He was spoiled like that,* Josephine was thinking to herself. Joanna was calling Alan again. "He's not answering his cell. It went to voice mail. Alan? Your aunt Josephine cooked breakfast for us and your uncle is waiting for you! Give me a call when you get this message!" Joanna said and closed her cell phone. "No answer?" Josephine asked. Ten minutes later, Alan calls back. "Let me speak to my auntie please," Alan said.

"He wants to speak to you, Josephine!" Joanna hands her the cell phone.

"Hello! Alan?"

"Hi, Auntie, you cooked breakfast?"

"Yes, we went to the market this morning."

"Where's Uncle?"

"He's in the living room watching a game!" his auntie said.

"Tell him don't drink all the liquor," Alan laughed. "Okay, I'll be there soon!" "Okay, I'll see you when you get here!" Josephine said.

"Oh, Auntie, keep my plate warm for me," Alan said. "Okay, I'm on my way, give me thirty minutes."

"Okay, nephew, I'll see you!" Josephine hands the phone back to Joanna.

"Alan! He's gone!"

"He said he wants me to fix him a plate and keep it warm. He's on his way home," Josephine said. "Why didn't he want to speak to you, Joanna?".

"We've had an argument earlier. Alan stayed out all night! And all I asked him was where he's been all night! But he pays no attention to me! He just walks away from me and keeps silent!"

"Baby, never ask him questions like that! When he's ready to talk to you about what's bothering him, he will! Because it's not getting anywhere with the both of you mad at each other! For example, when he walks in, just say, 'Good morning, Alan!' Like nothing is brothering you! And he'll feel more relaxed and maybe he will stop leaving so much," Josephine said, rubbing Joanna's left shoulder. Joanna gives Josephine a hug!

"Thank you for the advice, Aunt Josephine!"

"Anytime, Joanna! One more cup of coffee for me," Josephine said while Joanna gets the coffee pot and pours her and Josephine another cup. "Patrick! Alan is on his way home! And he said, don't drink up all his liquor! And he means it!"

"Well, he better hurry up before it's all gone, every drop of liquor will be gone!" Patrick said. Joanna started laughing at Patrick with his big belly, holding his glass of gin and orange juice and gets up and walks toward the kitchen for more ice. "And where is Lisa? Let me call that girl!" Josephine said.

"I talked to her earlier and she didn't say much!" Joanna said.

"Let me get my cell phone out my purse!" Josephine said while Patrick came walking out the kitchen.

"Who you calling, your ex-boyfriend?" She gives him a crazy look while Joanna was laughing hard at her uncle-in-law.

"You are crazy! He's just messing with me! Here's my cell phone." Josephine sits back at the table to call Lisa. "I might be thin, but I can keep on trucking. I'm not like that big old lazy man over there on the couch, watching TV," Josephine said, picking on her husband Patrick. "Lisa! How are you doing this morning!"

"We are doing good, Auntie. Where are you?" Lisa asked.

"Over your brother's, but I called to tell you that I have all the food set up for your engagement party for next weekend. And I wanted to know what color do you want the cake I'm buying for your party!"

"Baby! What color of cake do you want?"

"White with strawberries in the cake. I love strawberries," Dupree said.

"Okay, Auntie, make it white with strawberries and a lot of white frosting. Are you getting ice cream also, Auntie?"

"Yes, if that's what you both want!" Josephine said.

"I want lots of balloons with different colors, and what about the music?"

"Don't worry about the music. I'll get the music," Dupree said.

"Oh, Auntie, Dupree said don't worry about the music, he'll handle the music!" Lisa said with laughter.

"And we rented the hall. Downtown at the hall where they do the grads for the kids!" Josephine said.

"What time do we get there Saturday?"

"At one p.m. till seven p.m.," her auntie said.

"Thank you, Auntie!" Lisa said excited.

"You can eat and dance!" Josephine laughed. "This gift is from the both us! So are you and your future husband coming over later? So we can get to know him better!" Josephine asked.

"Yes, Auntie, we'll be there in a little while. Okay, we'll see you when you both get here, and we can plan more things for the party," Lisa said, feeling excited.

"Sure, Lisa, see you soon," Josephine said. Twenty minutes later, Alan walks into the house and notices his auntie Josephine yelling at Patrick. "Stop drinking! Oh, good you made it home, Alan!"

"Good morning!" he said.

"Good morning! How you feeling, Alan?" Joanna asked politely with a little smile. Alan was looking at her weird. "I'm doing fine, Joanna!" he said with a smile. And he walks into his living room. "Hello, Uncle, you didn't drink all my liquor up yet!" They both laughed. "Not yet, but I'm on my way drinking it all up!" Patrick yelled. Alan started laughing at his uncle. "How you doing, Uncle? Auntie hasn't killed you off yet!" Alan said laughing softly.

"No! Her aggressive ways are going to kill me off!" They both started laughing louder. Josephine just looks at Patrick, holding a fork in her hand, aiming at him.

"I would come over there and kill you off now, Patrick, but you don't have enough insurance for me to kill you off!" Josephine said with a little attitude.

"You know it's amazing how you too get along after all those years. Wow!" Joanna said. "Well, it takes a lot of work to keep a relationship together. It takes two to pull together. No matter what you go through together, keep the faith!" Josephine said.

Alan was paying no attention to what his auntie and Joanna was saying, making himself a gin and grapefruit juice behind his bar with no ice in the bucket. Alan walks from behind the bar and walked past Joanna. "Auntie, is my breakfast ready?"

"Yes! Let me get it out the oven!" Josephine walks fast into the kitchen, and Alan follows behind her to get some ice.

"It's warm and ready for you."

"Okay, Auntie. Thank you." She grabs his plate out the microwave after he grabs the ice out the freezer and walks back into the dinner room and walks past his wife, keeping silent and walks into the living room and puts his glass and plate down on the coffee table that's sitting in front of the couch.

"You want me to make you a drink while you eat your breakfast?" Patrick asked.

"Sure, Uncle, if you feel up to it!"

"I'll make you a good strong drink to where you can catch up with me!" Patrick said.

"Oh, Alan! Oh, nephew, Lisa and Dupree are coming over later!" Josephine said.

"Oh really?" Alan said. "I like Dupree, he's so quiet!"

"Yes, a very nice young man. Who's his family?" Patrick asked.

"Richard's brother. Remember the one who used to work with me who got killed in his house! The service we went to a month and three weeks now, almost two months, and here is Lisa engaged to his brother. This world is too small!" Alan said.

"No, it's what a small world we live in!" Patrick said, making Alan's drink behind the bar. "Now don't make my drink too strong, Uncle!" Alan gets up and walks toward Joanna. "I'll take your plate into the kitchen for you!" Joanna said nicely and gets up from the table and walks into the kitchen while Alan goes and washes his hands in his bathroom.

"Yes, I've have met Dupree once, right, Josephine?"

"Yes, Patrick, you met Dupree, he's a very handsome young man and he works! He's not lazy!"

"Yes, he seems like a bright young man," Alan repeated, walking out his bedroom, feeling Joanna's eyes watching him.

"And their engagement party is next weekend. Josephine set it up!" Patrick said while Alan was walking toward his uncle to get his drink. Patrick hands Alan his drink and he takes a drink from his glass. "Uncle! This is too much gin and not enough juice! Trying to get me drunk fast?"

"Yes, so you can catch up with me! I told you that!" Patrick said, laughing at Alan.

"I thought you were just talking!" Alan said with a sour look on his face. Patrick was laughing. "You should see your face right now!" Patrick said. Alan goes behind the bar to fix his drink better. *Ding dong!* "Oh, that must be Lisa and Dupree!" Josephine said, jumping up from her chair and walks to the front door. "Hello, Lisa and Dupree!" Josephine said. "Come in! Come on the both of you!" Lisa and Dupree walked in together. "Hello, everyone!" Dupree said.

"Dupree, you can go into the living room where the men are!" Lisa said.

"I'm so glad you are here!" Josephine said.

"Hi, Alan and Uncle Patrick!" Lisa said.

"Hello, Dupree. How are you doing, soon-to-be brother-in-law!"

"Feeling good!"

"Hello, Dupree, do you remember me, Patrick?"

"Umm, Lisa's uncle, right?"

"Yes, would you like a drink, Dupree?" Alan asked.

"Sure, something light!"

"How about a Coors beer?" Alan asked.

"Yes, that would be fine," Dupree said. Alan goes into the kitchen to get Dupree a cold beer out the refrigerator. "So, Dupree, what kind of work do you do, son?"

"I'm going to the university to become an engineer and also I'm working as a mechanic at a big George garage."

"Well, that's sounds like a plan!" Patrick said while Alan returns to the living room with a Coors beer for Dupree, looking at his sister with a grin on his face.

"What, Alan?" Lisa asked politely.

"I just can't believe my baby sister and only sister is engaged to a good man like Dupree over here."

"Here you go, brother!"

"He seems like a good man! But what I can't figure out is what is he doing with you?" Alan said, joking with Lisa. "Because he knows a good woman when he sees one," she replied to her brother. "That's right, Lisa," her auntie said. "Don't worry, Dupree, these two go at each other like this all the time! This is their relationship!".

"Oh, it's okay," Dupree replied with his soft voice.

"So, Dupree, are you excited you're gaining a wife soon? Just take very good care of my sister!" Alan said.

"Oh yes, for sure, man! And would you like to be my best man at our wedding, Alan?" "Yes, for sure!"

"Thanks, man!" Alan gives Dupree a handshake and a hug, feeling happy!

"Dupree, I'm so sorry about your brother," Patrick said, feeling tipsy.

"Patrick!" Josephine yelled. "Don't talk about that! His heart and soul is still healing! Don't talk about sad occasions at this time!"

"All right, wife!" Patrick said with a little attitude. Alan and Dupree were drinking. "Who's playing today?" Dupree asked.

"Lisa, he seems very nice," Josephine said.

"Yes, and now you're gaining a husband!" Joanna said with snarky attitude. They both looked at her when she said that!

"I am so happy with him. He makes me feel like all my problems are gone!" Lisa said. "And that's a good feeling," her auntie said. "And that's when you know its real love! And you're in love, girl! I've seen that sparkle in your eyes and that's why you and Dupree can't stop looking at each other."

"He came from a respectful family! I can't wait till you meet his parents. They're really nice people and his cousin Keith! I've met him and he seems very nice too!"

"I notice Dupree is a very quiet person. Anyway, I'm really glad you are happy, Lisa! You're finally getting married soon!" Josephine said. "And you're still young. That's a good thing! Now about the party next weekend, I want to discuss. We are getting paper plates and cups and forks and spoons, that's on the check list!"

Engagement Party

"Our engagement party is going to be nice!" Lisa said. "Auntie has everything set!"

"And I want to tell you two nice young men are coming to help out with the decorations! I am giving them dinner and fifty dollars to come help with the cleanup also!"

"Wow! That was really nice, Auntie! I wonder what the wedding is going to be like?" Lisa asked.

"You both are going to have a very nice exciting wedding with lots of pictures and food and celebrate the love you and Dupree feel about each other, which is matter of the heart!" Josephine said. "I remember when Patrick and I got married!"

"Auntie! We're supposed to be planning the party!" Lisa said. "Not go into deep memories." Lisa started laughing a little at her auntie. "You do this all the time, Auntie! And the cake is going to be white with strawberries around it," Lisa said. "What about decorations?"

"We can go by that store Happy Party Place on Main Street," Josephine said. "I'm going to do all this before Saturday."

"Thank you, Auntie." Lisa gave her auntie a big hug.

"And your parents will be here Friday morning! My sister said don't start the party without her." Josephine and Lisa were laughing while Joanna was sitting there drinking her coffee and cream listening to Lisa and Josephine talk.

"So you and Dupree are staying for dinner, right?" Josephine asked.

"Yes, for sure. Can't pass up your cooking!" Lisa said. "Let me tell my soon-to-be husband." Lisa gets up from the dinner table and walks over to Dupree. "Baby! My auntie wants us to stay for dinner! She's the best cook in the world! And that's who showed me how to cook!" Lisa said. "And you love my cooking already, don't you?"

Alan was noticing how happy they looked, Lisa talking to her soon-to-be husband.

"Yes, baby, for sure, we can stay for dinner! Anything you want, baby, you know that!" Dupree said. As they both kissed each other in front of everyone, they all were smiling at Lisa and Dupree. Lisa turns around and walks back over to her auntie and Joanna sitting at the table while Lisa had a big smile on her face. "Come over here, lover guy! Let me fix you another drink," Alan said with a grin on his face.

"Oh, Auntie, what about invitations?" Lisa asked.

"I'll start mailing some off tomorrow and hope everyone gets them in time," Josephine said. "But most of them I'm going to call because I would have to drive to the post office and put stamps on all of them. I'll get on it when I get home tonight," Josephine said. "You can call all your friends tomorrow and that would speed things up with the guest list."

"I have a lot of friends and I'm going to need to send invitations also," Lisa said.

"I'll pick some up while you're at work Monday."

"Thank you, Auntie, that would help a lot!" Lisa said.

"So what are you going to wear at the party, Lisa?" Joanna asked.

"I don't know. I might buy me a new outfit from the Quotable Women's Dress Shop. I get retail price because I work there!"

"That is great, Lisa," Josephine said.

"I'll be down there at your shop by Wednesday to buy me an outfit for the party," Joanna said.

"Great, sister-in-law, and I'll be there to help you find the right outfit and have you looking sexy." Lisa was feeling excited.

"So what do you all want to have for dinner tonight?" Josephine asked.

"Pork chops and Rice-A-Roni with applesauce. That sounds good!" Lisa said. Joanna just looks at Lisa. "This girl eats anything," Joanna said while grinning at Lisa.

"Then that's what I'll go and get from the market really quick and get back here and cook. The both of you come ride with me?" Josephine asked.

"Sure, Auntie!"

They get up from the table. Lisa walks back over to Dupree. "I'll be right back, Dupree. I'm going to the market with my auntie and get some pork chops and applesauce for dinner," Lisa said.

"Hurry back, baby, give me one of these wet lips before you go!" Dupree was feeling good. Lisa puts her arm around Dupree, and they give each other a big kiss while Joanna walks over to her husband.

"I need some money for the market, Alan?" Alan goes into his wallet and pulls out fifty dollars and gives it to Joanna. "Just don't spend it just on dinner tonight! Get some meat that will last a few days," Alan said to his wife.

"I've already given Joanna fifty dollars to get the pork chops. You don't have to keep spending your money on us, Auntie!" Alan said. "Get what you need for dinner tonight and tomorrow night." He is watching Joanna as she walks toward the front door with Lisa. They walk out to Joanna's silver Tahoe Hybrid Chevrolet with tinted windows, and they all get into her car. Joanna starts the vehicle while they fasten their seat beats on and she puts it into drive and pulls off slowly. Josephine sits in the front seat and Lisa in the backseat. Joanna turns on her radio. Slow music was playing. "I always play an oldies station on my way to work," Joanna said.

"Did Alan have to work this weekend with the fire department on the corner?" Lisa said. "That's where James works too, Auntie."

"Oh really, so that's where Alan's second job is," Josephine said.

"He hasn't been there. There haven't been any fires lately," Joanna said while she turns left, going into town going a few blocks to the market. The signal light turned red. They were listening to Phil Collins' "Take a Look at Me Now." They were singing while they were waiting for the green light so she can continue driving to the market.

Ten minutes later, Joanna drives up to the market and parks. Lisa opens her car door and gets out the car and closes her door to help her auntie Josephine out the car.

"I might be thin and a little older than you, ladies, but I can handle anything," Josephine said.

"You're thin enough, Auntie. You're size 3. You can fit in my and Joanna's clothes. We are all the same size," Lisa said. They were walking toward the front sliding doors at the market. They made it into the market. Auntie went looking for the meat department while Lisa went with her while Joanna grabs a basket on wheels to shop around. Joanna follows Lisa and Josephine. They hear a little music in the market; they were looking around. Josephine walks over to the meat department and started looking at the pounds of pork chops. These pork chops looks healthy, and there are twelve in the pack for eight dollars," Josephine said. "Go look for the applesauce. Get two cans, baby!" Josephine said. "All right then. I'll be right back, Auntie." Joanna was looking at the chicken and beef steaks, and she gets the two packs of beef steaks and two chickens.

"And I need some more rice and flour and black pepper." Joanna was talking to Josephine.

"Yes, you need those things to cook," Josephine laughed. Lisa was returning back with the applesauce and she puts it into the basket. "I need to get Fluffy some more food. I'll be right back," Lisa said. Her shining golden blond hair caught a couple of guys' eyes. Lisa noticed both guys flirting with their eyes and their smiles, trying to get her attention while she walks down the pet food lane. The two guys follow her like they were looking for something for their pet. But they don't have a pet; they just want to try to get closer to Lisa to look at her closer. Lisa grabs a small bag of cat food and walks back to Josephine and Joanna still over by the meat department. "Okay, that will be it," Josephine said.

"I got some chicken also for next week," Joanna said.

"Oh, Lisa, I'm cooking four chickens for your party next weekend and a tray of appetizers and cut them up into chicken nuggets, so everyone can have a taste of my famous fried chicken with my secret seasoning," Josephine said.

"Lisa! There are two guys looking at you," Joanna said.

"And they have been following me around the store."

"It's time to go now before I say something to hurt their feelings," Josephine said.

"They're just looking at us."

"Let's go to the aisle and get out of here," Josephine said. As they all walked to get into line, Lisa picks up a magazine and starts flipping pages while standing in line.

Few minutes later, they came walking out the market to her vehicle, carrying a couple of brown bags. While other cars was passing them by them, they started walking to her car. Joanna opens her trunk to put their groceries in and closes the trunk and walks around to the driver side while Lisa helps her auntie back into the car. Josephine gets in and fastens

her seat belt and locks it in while Lisa fastens her seat belt. Joanna has her seat belt on so they won't get a ticket. Joanna starts her vehicle and puts it into drive and drives off going east to get back on the freeway toward north.

"Did you guys see those creepy guys? I think they were up to something like stealing out the store," Lisa said.

"Whenever they were, I'm glad I'm out of there with those guys looking at us strangely!" Joanna said. "We're almost home, but I need to make a stop and put some gas in this car before we'll be pushing it to the gas station," Joanna said. She noticed a gas station on a corner and turns into the station to a gas pump to get ten dollars of gas. Joanna turns the motor off and gets her wallet out of her purse and gets a ten dollar bill out and opens her car door and gets out to walk into gas station and store to pay for the gas and walks back out the store to the gas pump and grabs the pump and puts it into the tank. Lisa gets out to get her some gum while Joanna was holding the pump, looking at the price moving to the amount a few minutes later. Lisa comes out the gas station store with her gum while Joanna puts the pump back, smelling strong gas fumes, and they both get back into the car to drive home.

Several minutes later, they arrive at Joanna's place and pulls up in her driveway. Alan hears her driving up and gets off his cell phone, where he was talking low so no one could hear him. Patrick and Dupree were watching a football game while the women walked into the house to start cooking.

Josephine puts the groceries on the table while Lisa rushes to Dupree to tell him about the two men that was following her in the market.

"Were they good looking?" Dupree asked with a smile.

"No, baby! They were young guys trying to get at me!" Lisa said.

"Hey. They like what they see, a pretty face with golden hair and a nice shape and pretty legs. I would follow you too!" Dupree said, laughing with his sense of humor. Lisa smiled. "Don't worry. Don't worry about it!" He was hugging her tightly! "I missed you while you where gone!" Dupree said.

"I missed you too." They were holding each other tightly with their lips locked to each other. Alan was looking at them, smiling.

"I told your brother he was going to be the best man, if that's okay with you, Lisa!"

"Sure, that would be great!"

"Keith will be the other best man!"

"That sounds great, baby!" Lisa said.

"Let my new brother-in-law enjoy the rest of the family." Alan was feeling a little tipsy. They give each other another tight hug before Lisa goes into the kitchen to help cook. Joanna and Josephine were getting dinner ready. Josephine had the pork chops in a strainer, washing them off before she cooks them. She got the flour out and the seasoning and then she gets the skillet out from the oven and turns on the first burner and pours cooking oil into the skillet with the fire down low while Lisa opens up the two cans of applesauce and puts it into a bowl and puts the applesauce into the refrigerator. "Lisa, get that bag sitting there and make the salad for me, baby," Josephine said.

Joanna begin flouring the pork chops. "What do you have to drink for dinner?" Lisa asked while she gets the salad mix out.

"We have soda and red Kool-Aid and coffee and tea," Joanna said.

"I'll make the Kool-Aid," Lisa said.

"That sounds good."

"Where is your sugar, Joanna?"

"Over there on the third shelf."

"I got it! Thank you," Lisa said.

"You're welcome, sister-in-law, who is soon to be married. I would never thought you would be getting married this soon. I thought you were going to wait till you got a little older and have your fun now," Joanna said. "Let me shut up because I did the same thing with Alan. I was just twenty when we got married, but I'll admit I was fully in love with your brother when we met and we decided to buy this house together."

"Why didn't you two have any children?" Josephine asked.

"I guess we didn't try hard enough to have children," Joanna said. "I would have loved to have one child!"

"That would be nice and maybe you too will get along a lot better!" Lisa said.

Dupree Meets His Fiancée's Family

Forty-five minutes later, lunch was ready. Lisa was putting the plates and silverware on the table with the white paper napkins while Josephine and Joanna were walking out the kitchen with the hot pork chops and the green salad. Lisa walks back into the kitchen to get the applesauce. "Dinner is ready! Come on, guys," Josephine said. "Patrick put that drink down!"

Alan and Dupree walk over to the dinner table. "Dupree, you can sit here next to Lisa," Josephine said.

"Everything smells delicious," Dupree said. Lisa walks out the kitchen with the bowl of applesauce and sits next to Dupree while Josephine says a meal prayer. After the short prayer, Lisa began Serving Dupree pork chops and green salad.

"Would you like some applesauce?" Lisa asked.

"Sure, a little," Dupree said.

"Alan, why didn't you go to the fire station tonight?" Lisa asked.

"No fires tonight!" Alan said.

"Lisa didn't tell me you were a fireman!" Dupree said.

"Sometimes on the weekends, I volunteer. I started out with a close friend. Lisa, you remember James?" Lisa looks at Alan like she wants to sock him!

"Stop it you two! You two are like peas in a pod! Can't get along!" Alan started laughing. "I'm just kidding with her," Alan said. Lisa rolls her eyes at her brother.

"I told you about James, baby, the African American guy we've talked about!"

"Yes."

Thirty minutes later, they were all finished eating lunch and the men get up and walk into the living room to get fresh drinks and finish watching the game while Josephine gets up to clear the table and put the rest of the food away and sits back at the table after eating.

"That was good. I'm so full," Lisa said. Joanna was grinning at Lisa.

Two hours later, the football game was over. Lisa and Dupree get ready to leave. Alan and Patrick give Dupree a handshake.

"Thanks for coming, Dupree! We enjoyed your company, Patrick, and thanks, Dupree, for making me the best man! We will be seeing a lot of each other! Baby sister! I love you!" Lisa gave her brother a smirk.

"Love you too, Alan!" Lisa said.

"You guys have a good evening."

"I'll call you, Auntie. Be good, Uncle Patrick!"

"You make sure you come back over, Dupree, we are going to be family!" Patrick said. Alan walks them to the door and opens it.

"Okay, Auntie, I'll call you," Lisa said.

"And thank you for the lunch," Dupree said. Alan shuts the front door and walks back into the living room and picks up the remote and looks at Joanna and his auntie sitting at the table. Josephine gets up and walks to the bathroom while Joanna walks into their bedroom and closes the door behind her while Alan continues drinking his gin and juice with his uncle Patrick.

"Dupree is respectful young man. Lisa got a good man, and he's not bad looking!" Patrick said. "Do you know any of his family besides his brother?"

"Yes, I met his parents at Richard's services. They seem very nice," Alan said.

"We'll be meeting his parents at the party Saturday," Patrick said.

"Yes, you will, Uncle," Alan said, taking a drink with a sour face.

"What did you just drink?" Patrick asked.

"Straight gin that time," Alan said.

"Give me a straight shot without your auntie knowing," Patrick whispered while Alan pours his uncle straight gin.

"One shot all right, Uncle?" Alan said. "Now I'm ready for anything," Patrick said with a sour look on his face.

Patrick hears his wife walking back into the den.

"The sun is bright today!" Josephine said. "Yes, Lord. The sun is bright today! I'll make a fresh pot of coffee." She walks into the kitchen while Dupree and Lisa make it to her place, and he parks his car and they both get out and walk into her place and to the bedroom to relax with each other. They're feeling love and passion for each other. Lisa closes the bedroom so Fluffy won't come in. Lisa and Dupree started taking off their clothes to make some passionate lovemaking. "Meow!" Fluffy was standing at the bedroom door. The next morning, Dupree gets up from the bed to get ready to go and get his things to move in with Lisa. Dupree is thinking about what his parents are going to think when they hear that I'm moving out and in with Lisa! *I think they will love it! Then they can have the house to themselves! It's about time I move out the nest anyway. I'm twenty-four years old and still at home with my parents. Yes. It's time to move out and with my soon-to-be wife! I have to think about buying Lisa an engagement ring that will shine for her!* "Baby! I'll be back." He gives Lisa kiss on her lips while she sleeps. He grabs his car keys and walks out the front door to his car and jumps in and starts it up and puts it in drive and drives off toward his place. It's eight thirty a.m. "Come on, sun! That's too bright this morning!" Dupree was talking to the sun, rubbing his eyes from waking up, trying to see clear through the sunlight. A couple of minutes later, Dupree arrives to his residence and parks his vehicle in the driveway next to his parents' car and turns off his engine and steps out his car and walks up to the front door and opens the door.

"Hello, Mother!"

"You're back!" she said.

"I have to talk to the both of you about something. It's great news!" Dupree said. "Lisa and I are engaged to get married!"

"Oh, Dupree, we are so happy for you! When is the wedding?" his mother Liz asked. "We haven't made a date yet but soon!" Dupree said.

"Congratulations, son!" His father gives Dupree a hug and pats him on his back!

"Thanks, Dad, and both of you are just going to love Lisa!"

"You mean Richard's friend Alan's only sister? The pretty tall young lady?"

"Yes, Mother. That's her!"

"Well, son, you are lucky to have her. She's nice looking!" his dad said.

"Thanks, Dad! Saturday is the engagement party her family is giving us! And you both are coming to our party!" Dupree said.

"Yes, can't wait!" his father said. "Where is the party going to be?"

"The hall downtown Lisa's auntie rented for a few hours for the party Saturday at one p.m. till six or seven p.m."

"This is good news! I have to call my brother and let him know that my son is getting married," his father said. "Can the family attend?"

"Yes, for sure, Dad, call everyone." His mother had a big smile on her face.

"Hurry up with your call, so I can call my sister and family too," Dupree's mother said. "Mother can use my cell phone while I go up and take a shower, and, Mother, I'm going to be moving in with Lisa."

"When are you moving out?"

"Lisa wants me to move in right away!" He was walking up the stairs to his room while his parents made phone calls.

"I can't believe it! Our son is getting married!"

"You realize we lost our oldest son in death, and now God is blessing us with a daughter-in-law," Liz said while Leroy was calling his older brother. "It's good to see my Parents happy again!" Dupree was looking down at his parents standing at the top stairs, looking down, walking to the bathroom to take a shower.

"I'm really sorry about what happened to you, Richard, but it's time I make our parents happy now!" Dupree was thinking to himself, walking into the bathroom and closing the door behind him. "Hello! Is my brother Leroy there!" Jimmy was talking loud.

"Hello! Guess what, Louise! Dupree is getting married!"

"What! Who's the lucky girl?" Louise asked.

"Do you remember Richard's friend he worked with? His name is Alan Jones. I told you about him a long time ago! The tall guy! The very nice-looking guy that worked with Richard?"

"Oh yes, he's very handsome," Louise said.

"Yes," Liz said. "Dupree is marrying his sister! Her name is Lisa Jones. I've met her a month ago! The dinner for my son Richard. It just breaks my heart every time I think about my son that was murdered," Liz said.

"Well, he's in a better place," Louise said.

"Yes, with the Lord. Oh, Louise, I almost forgot to tell you that Lisa's Auntie Josephine is having an engagement party Saturday at the hall downtown, and I'm going to ask if they need any help with the party, like if they need help with food or anything they need, because after all, we have to pay for the wedding!" Liz said. "Don't worry, Dupree will help pay for his wedding."

I'm so happy, Louise, but still standing strong for Richard and still healing," Liz said. "Jimmy! Listen to this, Louise, Jimmy, guess what? I just thought of something."

"What!" Jimmy yelled. "I'm on the phone, Liz! What is it!"

"We have to pay for the wedding!"

"What? Oh, that's right. We are the groom's parents! Hold on, brother, for a second. Let me think for a moment. How much is it going to cost?" he whispered to his wife Liz. "When you're finished talking to your brother, we will talk about it then, Jimmy,"

Liz said. Jimmy picks his house phone up to finish talking to his brother Leroy. "What's wrong, Jimmy? You have to pay for your son's wedding. Now that's when you have to go into your savings and put up most of it. A wedding costs a lot."

"I'm about to fall out!"

"Well, I'll call Dupree down and see what he says. Come down here for a minute, son!" "He's in the shower, Jimmy! Tell Leroy about the party Saturday at the hall!" Liz said, feeling a little excited.

"I forgot to tell you about Dupree's engagement party Saturday at the hall downtown by the Bam club, the one we used to go to on Main Street together," Jimmy said.

"I remember those days. We used to get down at the Bam club back in the days before we got married!" Jimmy and his brother started laughing harder.

"It's good to hear you laughing again, Jimmy!"

"Yes, but it's a rough road what me and my family is going through together!"

"Yes, my prayers are with you and Liz and my nephew Dupree," Leroy said.

"Thanks, big brother. So what suit are you wearing to your nephew's engagement party Saturday?"

"I don't know yet, maybe my blue dress suit," Leroy said. "Let me know if my nephew needs anything for his wedding, I will help you all out!"

"You know, brother, you're too damn cheap!"

"You've always been that way, just like our father was. Just be ready Saturday! You can talk to your nephew now since he's coming down the stairs. Dupree! Come over here and sit with me and your uncle, Leroy wants to talk to you on the phone." Dupree takes the phone from his father and sits next to him, dressed casually wearing a pressed black shirt and Wrangler blue jeans with a gold chain hanging from his left pocket with the smell of aftershave lotion and his reddish brown hair combed back with one diamond earring in his left ear. "Uncle!"

"Hey, Dupree, congratulations, nephew, you're getting married!" His father looked worried. Dupree looked at his Dad's face. "What's wrong, Dad?"

"Can I ask you a question, Dupree? How much is this wedding going to cost us?" his father asked.

"Dad is worried about the money! Don't worry, Dad, everything is covered with you and mother and Uncle's help and her family also! Everyone can pitch in on the wedding, so don't worry, Dad. It's good!"

"Your uncle Leroy had me worried."

"Why? What did Uncle say?"

"Ask him, he'll tell you!"

"Uncle! What did you tell my dad to have him worry?"

"That he had to clean out his savings to pay for the wedding. It's only traditional that the groom's father has to pay for the wedding," Leroy said. Dupree started laughing.

"Don't worry, Dad! We will all pitch in together and, Uncle? Don't be having my father worry!"

"Oh no! I wasn't making him worry. I was just telling him the truth!" Leroy said.

"Okay, Uncle."

"Tell me about your engagement party, nephew!"

"It's this Saturday at one p.m. at the City Hall on Main Street. Uncle, all you have to do is show up. As a matter of fact, just drive over here Saturday morning, then you can ride with us. And you won't have to worry about paying for parking. So don't worry, Uncle," Dupree said.

"That sounds great."

"Uncle, just be ready Saturday."

"Son, you're moving out!" his father asked surprised.

"Yes, Dad, I'm moving out this afternoon."

"Liz! Why you didn't tell me that our son was moving out today? Things are moving too fast. Just a month ago, we buried our oldest son, and today, our youngest son is moving out and getting married in the near future."

"Dad, everything is going to be all right. Stop worrying. We'll call you later, Uncle!" Dupree hangs up the house phone and gets up and walks into the kitchen.

"Mother dear, you are the best cook in the world. Just don't tell Lisa I said that." They both laughed while he looks at the kitchen clock. It's almost 9 a.m. "Let me take a look in the oven. Bingo! Buttered biscuits with baked sliced ham and fried potatoes. Oh, yes." Dupree was hungry for his mother's cooking. He felt his cell phone vibrating in his pocket and he looks at his caller ID. "Hello. How is my soon-to-be wife feeling?"

"Queasy and nauseous with morning sickness."

"I'm feeling that way sometimes too. I'm going to grab some of my things, and I'll be home soon, baby."

"I love you, Dupree."

"The feeling is mutual." They both hang up, feeling love. Lisa lies back down with the covers over her thin body and falls asleep.

Dupree grabs his plate of food and walks to the dining room table and sits down and begins eating his breakfast with his mother. "How is Lisa feeling?"

"A little queasiness and nausea."

"How do you feel about becoming a father?"

"Overjoyed! And thank you, Mother, for your famous breakfast." He gives his mother a kiss on her cheek and rushes up the stairs to his room to pack a few of his things along with his dirty laundry while his mother was talking on the phone and his father went to take an early nap on the couch. A few minutes later, Dupree comes down the stairs with his things in a small box. "I'll be back later."

"All right, son, be careful and tell Lisa, I hope she feels better."

"I will, Mother." He gives his mother a kiss and walks out the front door and closes it behind him and walks to his white Acura car and puts his things in his backseat and jumps into the driver seat quickly and he drives off going south. Couple of minutes later, he stops at a corner store to get a power drink and, for Lisa, an orange juice.

"Hey, baby, I stopped to get us something to drink, and I'll be there in a couple of minutes."

"Okay, love." He then fasten his seat belt. Dupree noticed a police car passing by going north. A couple of minutes later, he turns right on Lisa's block and turns into their driveway and parks next to Lisa's Lexus and turns off his engine and opens his car door and steps out and locks his car door and walks up to Lisa's front door and uses his new key to unlock the front door. "Hi, baby!" Lisa said. Dupree gives Lisa a kiss. "I have some of my things in the backseat of my car. I just wanted to bring in the drinks and see how you're feeling, baby." They both were hugging each other by the front door with her head on his shoulders while he hands Lisa her drink and turns around and goes back out to his car to get his things.

The Love Nest

*D*upree returns from his car with a large box with his work boots and change of clothes for work and a couple of outfits and walks into Lisa's bedroom to hang up his suits in her closet.

"I'm going to start lunch for us, baby!"

"Let's get something from that restaurant we went to and they deliver," Dupree said.

"Do you know the number?"

"Yes, I have it in my cell phone. I'll get it in a minute after I put my things away," Dupree said.

"Let me help you!" She helps Dupree put his things away.

"Thanks, my soon-to-be wife!" And he grabs Lisa and picks her small body up. She laughs and he gives her a kiss.

"Did you eat breakfast yet?"

"Yes, I had some Cream of Wheat this morning. I'll order us some lunch so you won't have to cook today." Dupree reaches for his cell phone to call a restaurant to order a couple of roast beef sandwiches.

"Would you like some corn chips with your sandwich?"

"Yes, that would be fine," Lisa said. "Meow!"

"Not for you, Fluffy, girl," Dupree said.

"Meow!"

"Fluffy, what do you want to order?"

"Meow!"

"Okay, I'll tell them." They both laughed.

"Hello? Yes, I would like two orders please. Okay, I would like two roast beef sandwiches with corn chips."

"Would you like any drinks with that, sir?"

"No thanks."

"Just two roast beef sandwiches? And what's the address there, sir?"

"Lisa baby, what's the address here?" Dupree asked.

"2233 Centric Court Drive, Brookville, California."

"That's correct."

"Okay, it will be ready in twenty minutes."

"Okay, that's fine."

"And the total is eight dollars and twenty-five cents."

"It will be cash," Dupree said. "In twenty minutes, our food will be here." He then picks up the remote from the nightstand, feeling comfortable, sitting up on the bed, facing her color television, turning channels. She was putting his dirty clothes into the hamper to wash.

"Baby, you need any help?" Dupree asked.

"Of course, you can help carry this heavy hamper into the garage for me. It's kind of heavy for me." Dupree jumps up and drops the remote on the bed and walks down the hallway and picks up the heavy clothes hamper while she opens the garage door from the kitchen. Dupree walks into the garage and sets the hamper in front of a Maytag washer and drier.

"Baby! I could make this garage into a workshop for me!" Dupree walks up to her and puts both his hands around her small waist while looking at the empty cabinets in the corner of the garage.

"I can do wonders in here!" Dupree said.

"That would be great. It will keep you busy when you're at home." He gives Lisa a long kiss.

"Honey, let me get this laundry into the machine." She begins separating the colors from the white clothes. While Dupree was thinking of ideas about making a tool shop in this corner. "And I can start building a tool holder on the left side, and I would put a piece of carpet on this concrete floor so no oil would mess up the floor. When I get off work every evening, I'll start working on my new project. I'm sounding like a real husband." She had a grin on her face. While she puts the colored clothes in the washer, Dupree heard the cold water running from the washer. Lisa was putting the laundry detergent in the washer around the clothes and closes the lid and walks to Dupree and puts her right hand around his neck, hugging him. "Your eyes are so sexy to me and your brownish curly hair just turns me on!" Lisa said. Dupree had a bright smile on his face as they were hugging each other.

"I like working on cars' engines. And don't worry about the oil dripping, I'll get some carpet for the concrete floor, and I'm going to use this left side of the wall to build a tool wall."

"That's very creative!"

"Thank you, baby! That's a compliment." And he gives her a wet kiss on her lips. "I plan to get right on my project after I get off work on Monday evening, and of course, give my baby some attention every evening when I get home, and we need to sit down and work out our income together before we get married because my father is kind of worried because my uncle told him that he had to clean out his savings for our wedding, but I told him that everyone was going to pitch in on the wedding. I've told my father that he can relax and I'm not going to let my father pay for the whole wedding that wouldn't be fair to him, you know, and we both can put in our part! Because this wedding is for the both of us and it's really our responsibility anyway!" Dupree was explaining to his wife-to-be.

"That makes a lot of sense, honey! I wouldn't want your father to pay for the whole wedding."

"All right and get some paper and a pen and let's figure things out in the finance department of the Mr. and Mrs. Dupree Oxford family!" Dupree said, smiling hard at Lisa. She walks over to her brown desk and got out a piece of paper and grabbed a blue pen and walked over to her dining room table and sat next to Dupree. He gets the paper and blue pen.

"Okay, I'm going to ask you some questions for the both of us. Here we go!" he said with deep voice and sits in a brown wooden chair that matches the table. "When do you want to get married?"

"Today's date is October 16, 2000. Okay, let me think for a minute—how about now!" And she gives Dupree a kiss. "No, but seriously, let's get married in two weeks. November 9 is on a Sunday," Lisa said.

"Um, I get paid before the thirty-first," Dupree said. "Okay, you want a church wedding?"

"Yes, for sure. I don't know what church? Oh, wait a minute! My auntie Josephine's church! We can get married there!"

"That's good. Give her a call to make sure." Lisa gets up to get her cell phone. Dupree was writing down some ideas. "A church wedding won't cost much, but there's her ring. That's a thousand right there and then she can pick out her wedding dress, and I would have to rent a tux and then there's the limo and the food and a band at the reception party. I think things are going to work out in Tthe finance department in this family because I like to manage my money." Dupree was thinking. Lisa comes and sits back next to Dupree.

"Okay, Auntie. That sounds great! I'll call you later!" Lisa gets off her pink with diamonds Samsung cell phone. "Get this! My aunt Josephine said that preacher at her church would probably not charge us too much, like a hundred, for his services."

"Hey! That would be great! Because I was just thinking about our finances and I want to tell you something about me! I went to school to become an accountant also and I'm good at counting money!" Dupree said. "So let me handle the bills, with your help!" "That's great, having an accountant in the house!"

"Baby, it feels a little chilly in here. Can you make a fire please?" *Ding dong!*

"That must be the food!" Dupree walks to the front door.

"Hello, Mr. Dupree?"

"Yes, here is the money," Dupree said and hands the money to the deliveryman.

"Thank you very much, sir!"

"You're welcome." Dupree closes the door behind him and walks into the kitchen. Lisa gets up and walks into the kitchen. "Let me get two plates for us," Lisa said.

"Okay, baby. I can't wait to start on the project I have in mind and I'm so excited! And you know the good thing about our relationship? We are compatible."

"They call that soul mates!" Lisa said.

"That's right, baby!" Dupree said and they walked back to the dining table and sat together and started eating their lunch. Lisa gets back up and opens her refrigerator and gets her orange drink out and closes it back and walks back and sits back next to her future husband.

"Okay, back to the list!" Dupree said. "I've put down the food and the band and your wedding ring and my tux and your dress, but I'll let you get any dress you want and I'll pay for it cash!"

"Oh! Thank you, baby!"

"Because I want you to be happy from now on," Dupree said to his future wife and they kissed. "Now what I have figured out came to three thousand dollars wedding and the reception party. Is that cool, Lisa?"

"That sounds about right, baby!" While eating her roast beef sandwich and opening up her soda, she said, "I can put up one thousand for your ring and tux and you have to pay for my ring and dress. That's what my auntie told me if I ever got married to tell my future husband that." Lisa gave a little laugh.

"And you know what, she's absolutely right about that!" Dupree said. "Okay, everything is set for our wedding, and now, I want to finish this sandwich!" he said.

"You forgot something!"

"What, prayer?" Dupree said.

"No, the fire!" Dupree puts his sandwich back down and gets up from his chair and walks over to the fireplace and starts putting the wood into the fireplace and grabs the box of matches and lights one and puts the fire under the wood with newspaper that's already under the wood. As the fire began burning the paper and wood, he put the iron rod in front of the fireplace and walks back to his sandwich and sits down and says grace in his mind before he takes a bite of his sandwich and they both started looking at the fire.

One hour later, Dupree and Lisa were lying on the bed together, watching a movie together. Lisa and Dupree were holding with each other and began kissing that led to making love to each other; the day was moving into the evening. The next morning, the alarm goes off at seven a.m. Dupree and Lisa get up to take a shower together for work. They were washing each other's backs and bodies. Fifteen minutes later, they get out and dry each other off to get dressed for work. They both walk back into the bedroom to put their clothes on while Lisa rushes to the drier and combs her hair to fix breakfast: two eggs and two pieces of bacon for the both of them. She puts on the coffee, still buttoning up her white silk blouse while Dupree had on his uniform and puts on his brown work boots. Lisa was pouring him a hot cup of coffee and hands him his cup of coffee while the eggs and bacon were cooking. Lisa looks at her clock on the kitchen wall.

"It's seven thirty in the morning," Lisa said. "And this weekend is our party! Okay, baby, breakfast is ready. She gets two plates down, and they sit at the table and eat their breakfast. Five minutes later, they both get up and rush getting out the front door. They both give each other a kiss. "I love you and have a good day, baby, and I'll call you on my lunch break." They get into their vehicles and start them up and Lisa pulls off first and then Dupree pulls up behind her. Lisa has her left blinker on, and Dupree follows Lisa into town, driving down Road 15 into town. Ten minutes later, they make it to their jobs. Friday evening came. Lisa was excited for their engagement party. Lisa bought Dupree an engagement present to bring to the party and Dupree went shopping for Lisa and to check out the price on a rented tux and went to buy himself a pair of black dress shoes and a pair of black socks and a nice-looking blue silk tie that matches the white tux. Then he walked two doors down to the diamond jewelry store to take a look at ladies' wedding rings. Dupree was looking into a locked glass case.

"Excuse me! Can I take a look at that gold-plated ring with the diamonds around it?" Dupree asked. A tall Caucasian male steps over to Dupree. The man gets his keys out of his pocket and opens the glass case and gets the diamond ring and hands it to Dupree and he takes a closer look at the ring.

"How much is this ring?"

"One thousand dollars!"

"Cool, I'll take it with the case!" Dupree said. The man was in a little shock and started wrapping the case in colorful paper. Dupree goes into his wallet to get his Visa credit card out and hands it to the man and uses his machine for the credit card.

"And will that be all, sir?" He hands Dupree back his card.

"Yes, that would be all." And Dupree puts his Visa card back into his wallet.

"Thank you, sir!" Dupree said and walks out the door and walks toward his car parked by a coin meter, and he unlocks his vehicle and gets in before the light changes for cars to pass him. Dupree starts his vehicle and waits till the light changes so it would be safe to pull off. Dupree was looking into his rear mirror to watch the traffic stop. Dupree now pulls off going west to get on Highway 12 to get closer to home. "I can hide her ring now. I have paid for the tuxedo for one day, got the ring, and I gave Lisa the money for her dress, so everything is going good so far," Dupree said to himself. "It's just six thirty p.m. I need to go by my parents' place really quick and see how they are doing and to make sure they will be dressed nice and call Uncle Leroy to remind him also." Dupree was thinking to himself as he was driving closer to his parent's home. Forty-five seconds later, he arrives and pulls up into the driveway and turns off his engine and opens his car door and steps out with Lisa's wedding ring that's in a black velvet box. Dupree gets his spare key and opens the front door and notices his mother was sitting in her brown velvet chair and he walks over to her and gives her a kiss on the cheek while Jimmy was watching a John Wayne western movie.

"Hi, Dad, how are you feeling?"

"I'm doing good, son! I was just taking a nap."

"I have something to show you both!" Dupree opens the little black velvet box and shows them a sparkling diamond wedding ring.

"Wow, Dupree! A really nice diamond ring!" his mother said. His father gets up and looks at the ring. "Let me see closer, son!" He puts his reading glasses on to see better. "Oh yes! She is going to love this ring," his father said. "She is going to fall in love with this ring! Very nice, son, you always had good taste in things and you have a very pretty young lady too! We want to get to know her better. So you have to start bringing her around us more, you know, she will be our new daughter-in-law!" His father was feeling excited for Dupree. "Yes! Your father is right, Dupree!" his mother said.

"Mom and Dad, please be ready tomorrow afternoon and let me call Uncle too!"

"Yes, son, we will be dressed and ready for your engagement party," his father said cheerfully.

"And I went out today and I bought a gift for you and Lisa from the both of us," his mother said.

"Thanks, Mother!" Dupree said. "I'm calling Uncle really quick! Then I have to go."

And suddenly he is on the phone. "Uncle Leroy! It's Dupree. I called to see if you are going to be ready tomorrow afternoon?"

"Yes, I'll be there at noon!" his uncle replies.

"Okay, I'll talk to you tomorrow." Dupree hangs up his phone and stands up.

"Okay. Remember, dress nice! I want to be impressed by you guys, okay, because I want her to love you both, like I do!"

"Thank you, son," his mother said.

"Thanks, son." His father gets up and gives Dupree a hug.

"And we love you too."

"Well, I have to go now. I'll see you both dressed and ready by noon!" Dupree walks out their front door. The next day at noon, Dupree arrives at his parents' place at noon. His mother and father and his uncle were standing in the doorway, waiting for Dupree. They all walk to his car while Dupree locks up the house. They arrive fifteen minutes later at the party, and he parks his car to help them out the car and into the party. "Oh, everything looks nice," his mother said as they all sit at a long table covered with red cotton cloth. Dupree calls Lisa. "Hey, baby, where are you?"

"I am on my way with my aunt Josephine and uncle Patrick is riding with me and my mother and father is driving behind me and Alan is driving his car," Lisa said. Dupree's mother gets up to look at the food and cake that reads "Happy Engagement, Lisa and Dupree." Dupree walks over to his mother and notices the cake sitting there and all the different food: four hot boxes of fried chicken and mustard greens with corn bread and last salad that Josephine had cooked. The family arrives and the guests walk in and find them all a seat. "Wow. This is a lot of family and friends of Lisa and Dupree." Lisa drives up. "Dupree, I'm here, baby. Come help me with my family please." Dupree walks outside to help Lisa. They all walked into the hall as Dupree introduced his mother and father to Josephine and Patrick. "Mother, this is Lisa's family, her auntie Josephine and Patrick."

"Hello!"

"And you remember Lisa, Mother and Father?"

"Yes, of course, how are you doing, Lisa? Congratulations!" Liz said.

"And I'm so happy that you're going to be in the family," his father said. "Congratulations!" Patrick said. They continued enjoying themselves till closing time.

Wedding Ceremony

"Oh, Lisa, you look so beautiful!" Joanna said while her aunt Josephine was fixing the bottom of her dress. "Thank you, Auntie! I'm so excited! I'm finally getting married? Please, Joanna, tell me this isn't a dream!" She twirled around in her strapless silk pearl white dress designed with white pearls making a floral pattern, and her long golden blond hair was pinned up in a bun with her loose curly blond hair dropping past her thin nose. These were complemented by her white short pearl veil over her brown eyes. She was smiling with pink glimmering shining lip gloss, and her brown eyes with natural-looking makeup. She looks like Cinderella rather than a normal bride. "The wedding is about to start, sweetie, let's get going." Joanna smiled and took Lisa's hand, leading her gently to the door where her soon-to-be husband Dupree waits anxiously on the other side of the door, along with a lot of guests constantly staring at the bridesmaids who were throwing flower petals on the floor as they were walking down the lane in anticipation of the new bride. It hit Lisa with a slap in the face; her knees begin to shake, and soon, her whole body was filled with trembles and butterflies. "Oh, Joanna, I don't know if I want to do this anymore!" Joanna took Lisa's face in her hands, and she looked straight into Lisa's eyes. "Listen to me, Lisa, you're getting cold feet and it's okay! Almost every bride feels this way before their wedding. You agreed to marry this beautiful handsome gentleman, right? This is what you been waiting for. You want this man, Lisa. Everything is going to be beautiful!" Lisa smiled and nodded her head. "Yeah.

That's right. I do love this man!" The music begins and the doors opened. The church seemed much bigger this day rather than any other day even though many people filled all the seats to see this wedding. Dupree stood handsomely at the altar in his white tuxedo and maroon tie. "Wow, she looks beautiful!" he thought to himself. She immediately knew this would be the longest walk of her entire life and the tunnel vision kicked in at the first step down the aisle. Guests were looking surprised. Lisa's lifetime flashed before her at the time of her happiness. "What is this flashing before me? What is this warning I'm sensing? This is supposed to be the happiest day of my life…oh, just shake it off, Lisa, it's just wedding day jitters. It all just happened too quick." Lisa was walking down the aisle closer and placed herself next to Dupree as they were holding hands while saying their vows and putting their rings on each other. Happy tears were running down Lisa's face.

At that moment, they both felt like a dream, and before they both knew it, they were saying, "I do until death do us part. The guests were smiling and clapping as they sealed their marriage with a kiss and began to walk back down the aisle, both smiling bright, walking to the white stretch limousine to their reception party. It was more than Lisa could imagine. "Is this really happening?" Lisa shouted with excitement, kissing Dupree on his left cheek. Dupree attended to her every need. Dupree had his left arm around her shoulders. "Are you as happy as I am, sweetheart?" Lisa asked. "Yes, I am, wife!" And they both kissed in the limousine. "Let's make a toast before we get to our guests."

Dupree gets two glasses and pours Lisa a glass of champagne and then poured himself a glass, and they both made a toast that they will be together always. They both sip from their glasses and give each other a kiss. Five minutes later, they arrived to the hall. The limousine pulls up to the hall. While everyone was getting out of their cars and into the hall, some guests were waiting for the bride and groom step out of the limousine. The driver walks around the limousine and opens the right side door of the long white stretch limousine. The bride steps out first and then the groom. Most of the guests were taking pictures of the bride and groom standing together while everyone was feeling happiness for the both of them. The bride and groom walk into the hall together, holding hands while photographers were flashing with laughter and joyful noise was echoing in the reception hall. Lisa and Dupree noticed all the different flowers and color balloons flowing on the walls and the floors and the decorations on the tables are so colorful. Yellow and blue tablecloths, punch bowls full of red punch, and a silver bucket sitting by the tables and on the floor, with three cases of different beers and wine coolers so the guests could enjoy themselves even more. The wedding cake was covered with white icing and strawberries trimming around the edges of the four-layered cake with the bride and groom sitting on top of the cake. "There is so much food here, Auntie!"

"Yes, and look how many guests have come!" Josephine said while Lisa and Dupree were walking around the table, looking at all the different appetizers. The live band began playing soft music from the stage. Lisa grabs Dupree's hand and pulls him to the middle of the room and begin dancing slowly to soft and romantic music. "I love you, Mrs. Lisa Oxford," Dupree said. Family and other guests were enjoying themselves, dancing and eating. The detective and two other officers walked into the reception hall. Detective Theodore was looking around for Dupree. With a white piece of folded paper in Detective Theodore's right hand, he walked over to Dupree and Lisa, where they were fast dancing on the floor. "Dupree Oxford!"

"Yes!"

"You're under arrest for the murder of your brother, Richard Oxford! This is a felony warrant and drug conspiracy!" Detective Theodore was reading his rights and the music stopped. The two officers grab Dupree. "Please put your hands behind your back, sir," the officer said, holding silver handcuffs.

"Wait a minute. This is a mistake!" Dupree yelled while the family members and guests were looking surprised. "Detective! This is a mistake!" Dupree's mother Liz shouted.

"It's okay, Mother. It will be all straightened out, Lisa baby!" Dupree shouted while Lisa was looking shocked. Her mother and Auntie Josephine walk over to her right away, hugging her. Lisa was looking shocked.

"I'll bail you out, son!" his father said. "Detective! Do you have proof that my son did this crime?"

"Yes, I do. You can come down to the station if you like, Mr. Oxford, but I'm taking your son!" Detective said aggressively, walking behind the two officers that put Dupree in the backseat of their black and white unit car. Dupree was looking angry while Lisa was running out the hall door, watching the officers close the backseat door. Lisa's eyes were pouring down with big tears. "Dupree, I love you!" Lisa shouted as the officers and the detective drives off with Dupree. "I'm going to the station," Lisa said. The guests were gathering their things and leaving. Liz and Josephine grab their purses, and they all leave the reception hall to the Brookville County Jail. They arrived ten minutes later. Lisa runs into the county jail. "Where is my husband, Dupree Oxford?" she shouted. Her mother and Auntie Josephine follow behind her. Officers walk by her and look at her in her wedding gown. "Miss, you'll have to wait!" the officer said behind the counter. "Then where is Detective Theodore? I want to speak to him right now!" Lisa shouted. Detective Theodore walks out of his office and toward Lisa. "And I need to speak to the family in my office please," Detective Theodore said. Lisa and her family walk into Detective Theodore's office, and he closes the door behind him. "You all can have a seat," Detective Theodore said. "Now, Detective, you know in your heart, my son did not kill his brother Richard!" his father Jimmy said. "Well, I have something here I want you all to read in this diary that belongs to Richard's friend,

Curtis, the gay guy, who I also arrested," Detective Theodore said. He hands the diary to Jimmy to read aloud.

"On August 31, I had a visitor, Dupree Oxford, who knocked on my door for a delivery to me. Some cocaine, that's what Dupree does for Richard. Dupree gave me an offer I couldn't refuse. Five thousand dollars to kill his brother for the humiliation and embarrassment Richard gives Dupree. So I took his offer and I killed Richard two nights later. I also wanted him dead for cheating on me with that Linda and many other females he had. I admitted that I was jealous of Richard, so I left a message from his body. I cut off his private for revenge of the hurt and pain Richard had given me through the times we spend together in bed. He knew I loved him very dearly and I had to finish this memorable relationship we had together for two years. I had that feeling he never told anyone about us. That's another thing that pisses me off. I thought we were going to be together forever. Curtis." Teardrops were coming out of Lisa's brown eyes. "Can I see him, Detective? There is a surprise I need to tell him," Lisa said. Detective Theodore looks at Lisa with pity in his eyes, feeling for her. "Sure, this way. I'll let you all visit him for a little while, okay!" the detective said. As they all get up and follow Detective Theodore out of his office and walk down the hallway and then down to the stairs, they hear gate doors clicking, officers talking to the prisoners. "Hello, Officer. Could you bring out Dupree Oxford! Please!"

"Sure, sir!" The officer gets his large keys out to open the jail gates. Five minutes later, Lisa notices Dupree walking toward the two-inch windows where the black jail phones are for visitors. Lisa looks at Dupree wearing an orange jumpsuit with big lettering on the back: Prisoner. "Lisa! I'm so sorry about this, baby! But I did not do this crime! Lisa, I love you very much. You have to believe me, baby!" Dupree said. "Stop it, Dupree! I saw the diary that Curtis had. It says you went over to this guy Curtis's place and you paid him five thousand dollars to kill your brother,

Richard!" Lisa breaks down and cries loud! Lisa was holding the phone receiver. "How could you do this, son!" his father yells and grabs the phone receiver from Lisa. "How could you kill your brother? He gave you everything!"

"No! He did not, Father! He used me and humiliated me and embarrassed me many times! But I did not kill him or pay to kill my brother!" Dupree shouted. Lisa's nose was red, runny with her tears. "Dupree! I have something to tell you! It was going be a wedding surprise for us!" Lisa said while his father was holding the phone next to her. Both were sitting on two silver stools and looking through the thick glass. Dupree had a guilty look on his face.

"I'm going to have our baby!" Dupree's eyes widened.

"Baby, that's great news! And I'm going to get out of here to be with you and our unborn baby." Lisa just looked at him with pity and sorrow. A few minutes later, Dupree watches his new wife and his mother and father leave. Dupree had guilt running down his spine and soul and his heart while walking back to his cell with an officer. "That plan was a big mistake in my life, drug trafficking, and wait till I see Curtis in here! I'm going to kick his butt for snitching on me. I should not have went over to Curtis's place that night! I wouldn't be in the small cold cell now! But in court, I'm going to tell everything that he made it all up that night. He was mad at Richard. Curtis called me one evening and he said that he had a problem with Richard, and I asked him why is he telling me this? Curtis sounded upset that night! What did Curtis write in that diary?"

"He verified what he said."

"Officer! Can you call Detective Theodore to come see me please!" Dupree yelled while other inmates yell, "Shut up!"

The officer who was walking past his cell said, "Sure! I'll give him the message." Dupree then lays on his thin strip mattress with a gray wool blanket and a flat pillow and a mirror on the wall and a white toilet stool and a small sink. "What happened? I was happy one minute, getting ready to enjoy the rest of my life!" Dupree said. "Oh, God! Help me out of this situation now! My new wife!" Tears were rolling down Dupree's eyes. Crying hard in his heart, feeling broke and lost from happiness with Lisa. "I want to go home to my new wife and my baby on the way, Lord! Please help me, I didn't do this crime. Lord, show me the way out of here!" Dupree was praying with thick tears. "I didn't kill my brother, Lord! And you are my witness, please be the judge, Lord!"

Alan's Mortality

Lisa's mother was hugging Lisa around her neck while they were leaving the jail.

"It will be all right, baby!" Lisa's mother said. "We will help you in every way and is the baby okay?" Lisa 'smother Lynn said. Lisa just shook her head while her tears were getting heavier and thicker; her heart felt crushed.

"I just can't believe this has happened on our wedding day!" Lisa said in shock. "How could that detective believe that gay guy Curtis could have made all this up and wrote it down! I think he was mad at Richard and blamed Dupree! Because Richard broke up with Curtis and he wanted Richard dead! So he blames my new husband!" Lisa starts to shout. "That is the answer!" Her mother and Josephine agreed. "And I'm going to find a way to prove it to that damn detective!" Lisa said. Her tears were dropping with her broken heart. "And if my husband can't ever get out, I'm filing for a divorce in a year!" Lisa said with anger and lays her head on her auntie Josephine while her mother was driving her little neon car to Alan's place where Josephine and Patrick's car was parked. Twenty minutes later, they arrive to Alan and Joanna's place and Lynn pulls up in front and turns off the engine and everyone gets out of the car and walks toward the front door. Joanna was home, but Alan was gone somewhere. "Come in, all of you!" Joanna said. "Oh, Lisa, you poor baby, I'm so sorry this happened and you look so beautiful today!" "Let me put some coffee on for us," Josephine said. Lisa was still crying her heart out. Patrick and Lisa's father were standing behind her, rubbing her back as her father was giving her a big hug. "You're going to be all right, baby," her father said and gives her a kiss on her forehead and turns around to the living room. "Come on, Patrick, let's make a drink because I'm upset about all this shocking mess Dupree put her through and his family and our families," Lisa's father said. Lisa's cell phone rings. "I can't talk to anyone right now!" Lisa shouted and lets her cell phone ring! A few minutes later, Josephine comes out the kitchen with three cups and a hot pot of fresh coffee steaming in the air and pours Lisa and her sister Lynn a hot cup of coffee and takes a seat. "You know what we need to do is pray and pray hard that your new husband gets out of jail so he could see his baby born," Josephine said.

"But if Dupree didn't kill Richard, then he shouldn't be charged with murder!" Lisa yelled. "Do any of you have Detective Theodore's number? I want to call him and tell him that my husband is innocent!"

"And you're right, Lisa, this sounds like a set-up! And that Detective Theodore will find the truth! And that diary won't stand up in court because that could be made up, the judge will say!" Lisa's mother said.

"And your new husband will be home in no time, just keep the faith, Lisa," Josephine said. Lisa gets her cell phone and calls Detective Theodore on his office phone.

"Detective Theodore speaking!"

"Detective! I need to talk to you right away!"

"Who is this? Mrs. Lisa Oxford, Detective, it's very important that we have figured it all out about that guy Curtis."

"I'll be right there." The detective hangs up his office phone and grabs his coat. "It's a little chilly outside and walks out his office door and out the building rushing to his light blue 1998 BMW and starts it and drives off fast to the Jones's residence.

"Detective, I'm glad you're here! We believe Curtis set Dupree up! Could you look into it please?" Lisa asked sadly.

"Yes, right away," Detective said. "Tell me the information you have on Curtis!"

"We know that Dupree was set up by Curtis! He put that in the book because Dupree told me over the phone that Curtis set him up for the murder because he knew that Richard was having affair with a female, Dupree told me this, Detective, and I believe my new husband!" Lisa said. Two weeks later, Joanna walks to the front door from her bedroom to answer the front door.

"Detective! He's not here!" Joanna looked surprised. "Would you like to come in and have a cup of coffee, Detective?"

"Yes! That would be nice!" Detective Theodore said and he takes a seat in the dinner table, looking around. A couple of seconds later, Joanna walks back into the dinner room with a pot of fresh coffee. "You take black or with sugar, Detective?"

"No, just black would be fine!" He was looking at Joanna with some terrible news.

"Mrs. Jones, when was the last time you saw your husband today?"

"Earlier, why, Detective? What's wrong? Is he in jail?"

"No! No! I'm afraid it's worse than that! He's been murdered, Mrs. Jones," Detective Theodore said, feeling confused. Joanna puts both of her hands over her face, shaking with her head down with little tears falling from her wide brown eyes. "I'm sorry, Mrs. Jones! But I had to come and tell you personally before it got out to the papers."

"Where was he, Lieutenant?" Joanna asked, holding a white tissue to her face, wiping her dry tears. "Behind the Bam bar, out on Main Street in the back alleyway. Someone noticed him lying there bleeding and called 911, and it was your husband, Mrs. Jones," Detective said slowly.

"Oh my god!" Joanna yelled.

"I'm so sorry to ask you at this time, but do you think you can come to the morgue to identify the body tonight! Or even better in the morning, if you'll feel any better," Detective Theodore said. "I could come pick you up!"

"No. I'll go tonight, Lieutenant! I'll get my things and we can go," Joanna said while she was still wiping her dry tears from her eyes, walking to get her coat on and purse and opens the front door and walks out with Detective Theodore to his vehicle. He rushes to unlock the passenger door for Joanna, and she gets in and the detective drives off slowly. Joanna was looking upset and nervous with her fake watery eyes and her hands were shaking nervously. "Oh God! I just hope it's not him!" Joanna said to Detective Theodore. He looks at her with pity. Ten minutes later, they arrive to the city morgue and park two blocks down the street from the police station. They both get out of his vehicle and walk slowly toward the front door of the morgue. Detective Theodore opens the single glass door and they both walk into the front office. "May I help you both?" a lady behind the counter asked. "Yes! I'm Detective Theodore." He shows his badge to the young lady. "We would like to see Mr. Jones's remains."

"Yes, sir, it would be a couple of minutes." The lady behind the counter makes a call.

"Yes! There is a Detective Theodore for Mr. Alan Jones's remains," the lady said. A few minutes later, a tall Caucasian male walks out wearing blue gloves and a black rubber apron tied around his waist with bloody stains on the apron and a blue and white trim paper hat on his head. "Hello, I'm Dr. John, the medical coroner examiner, and you're here for the remains of Mr. Alan Jones, who just came in a couple of hours ago. If you both step this way," the medical examiner said. They all walked between two swinging doors, Joanna was feeling fearful and frightened.

They both walked up to a thick glass window, looking at a white sheet covered over the body. The coroner examiner pulls the white sheet from over the head of the body.

"Oh my God! It's my husband!" Joanna yelled. "No! It can't be Alan! No!" The medical coroner examiner covers the body back up and pushed the body out from the wide window and to the back room for an autopsy.

"I'm so sorry about this, Mrs. Jones, are you all right? Let's get you back home," Detective Theodore said and grabs her by her right arm to help walk her out the morgue and to his vehicle. Joanna had her head down while the detective goes into his pocket to give her his handkerchief. She takes it and wipes her runny makeup as they both get into his vehicle and puts their seat belts on. He starts his car and drives off toward main street. "Are you all right now?" the detective asked in a kind way.

"No, not really, but I'll be all right," Joanna said sadly. Detective Theodore was driving northeast freeway to get to Joanna's place faster. Detective Theodore was looking at Joanna and watching the traffic carefully, driving 45 mph, trying to figure out if she really set her husband up for murder. The detective was thinking to himself while watching out for other drivers. "Mrs. Jones, were you and your husband all right before he left? I mean, was he upset?" Detective asked. Joanna looks at the detective and takes a deep breath. "Detective, I'm going to be honest with you. Me and my husband had a hot-tempered steaming argument before he left tonight!"

"What was the argument about?" Detective asked. Joanna looks at him. "I believe Alan was cheating on me with someone," Joanna said. "And I had this strange feeling that night he didn't come home that he was with someone else."

"Mrs. Jones, now I'm going to be honest with you! I know for a fact that it was your husband that hit and buried Mr. Johnson on the Fourth of July! That was his last name, but your husband, he kept it silent! I believe he told you what had happened that night." The detective was looking at Joanna ready for her to confess what she knows. "And when he told you everything you knew, he was damaged to you and I believe you had him set up tonight, but I have no proof," Detective Theodore said. "And you knew I was closing in on your husband for murder with evidence of the facts of the tire cast, the dent on his vehicle! So you decided to get rid of him for good, so you won't lose everything you worked for! Am I close?" Detective said. Joanna just looks at him with sadness and anger. She keeps silent as he exits off the northeast freeway and drives closer to her neighborhood. "A couple more blocks, I can't wait to get home." Joanna was wiping her runny nose, thinking to herself.

A couple of seconds later, he drives up into her driveway. She opens the car door. "Oh, Mrs. Jones, the case is closed, and I hope everything works out for you!" Detective said with a smile. "Thank you, Detective," Joanna said and closes his car door and walks to her front door. "Joanna! Where have you been? We were worried," Josephine asked. Joanna looks at Josephine and Patrick and takes a deep breath with tears.

"Alan is dead!"

"What! What happened?" they both asked panicky. Joanna was looking sad with dried-up tears. "He was killed behind the Bam bar tonight, and that's why the detective came over tonight for me to identify his remains and it was Alan! He was stabbed multiple times! I believe something happened tonight in that bar and Alan was involved," Joanna said. "That's what the detective thinks." Joanna knew she was lying to herself and to them both. "Oh, Joanna, I am so sorry," Josephine said, with tears coming out her eyes.

Patrick was feeling sad with a drop of a tear or two, standing next to his wife for support. He puts his left arm around his wife to let her cry on his shoulders. "This is a mess," Patrick said. "I have to call Lisa and let her know that her brother is dead! That he was murdered," Josephine said.

"Calm down, dear, before you call Lisa," Patrick said. Josephine turns and walks to the kitchen to call Lisa while Joanna goes into her bedroom and closes her bedroom door and sits on her bed to think things out, feeling guilty like Alan, her husband, was feeling. "I'm so sorry, Alan! But I had to do it! You were damaged!

And you would have damaged me! And I couldn't have that!" Joanna was talking to Alan's spirit as she gets up to take a shower with her guilty feelings.

Joanna turns on the shower and gets undressed and steps into the shower, feeling the death of her marriage as the hot water pours over her head and body with her eyes closed, trying to get rid of the guilty feeling!

"I know how Alan was feeling now, hoping this feeling will go away soon," Joanna was thinking to herself as she stands under the shower water for ten to twelve minutes, hoping that the guilty feeling would wash away. Joanna steps out of the shower and looks into the steaming mirror, and she wipes the steam off the mirror and takes a long look at herself, feeling ashamed that she did this crime in her heart. "Now things have to change," Joanna was thinking to herself, looking at herself, wiping the steamy mirror again and wraps her pink towel around her nude body and pulls out the hair drier and plugs it up and turns it on. She was drying her long brown hair.

A few minutes later, Joanna gets dressed and feels better about herself, but the real guilt won't go away. "I'm just going to try my best not to think about this tragedy, just try to put it behind me, so others won't notice. That's what I used to tell Alan when he told me the truth about that night, and he was looking guilty." Joanna was thinking hard to herself while she was getting dressed in her black silk nightgown and her white sparkling little diamonds, white slippers with short heels, holding her white napkin walking out her bedroom, looking down. "Lisa said she's coming by," Josephine said in her sad voice. "How is Lisa doing with her pregnancy?" Joanna asked.

"I guess she's doing her best, the way she's feeling, it's been only two weeks, and she is feeling really blue about Dupree getting life in prison, and Lisa has to go through this pregnancy alone without her new husband. She is feeling really down," Josephine said. "Now she wished she never married him. I bet that's what she's thinking. The poor girl and I am going to help her in every way with the baby." Suddenly another thought crosses Josephine's mind as tears start rolling down her cheeks. "Oh, let me call my sister Lynn and break the bad news about her son." Joanna walks over to Josephine and gives her a hug, feeling deep down in her heart. Josephine gets up from the dinner table and walks to the kitchen and picks up the phone and dials her sister's number. "Hello! Lynn!"

"Hi, Josephine, what's going on?"

Josephine couldn't say anything yet, she had to pull herself together for a moment. "Lynn, something bad has happened!"

"What happened? What is it? Josephine! What happened?"

"It's about Alan." Josephine breaks down and starts to cry.

"What happened to him? Is he all right?"

"No, Lynn! He's not all right! He was murdered tonight!" Lynn was yelling over the phone. "What happened? Where was he? Who did this to him?"

"He was at the Bam club tonight, and that's all we know for now. Detective Theodore dropped Joanna off. They had just came from identifying his remains."

"Oh my Lord, we need to come out there right away, Leroy! Come right away!" Lynn yelled. "What's wrong!" Lynn begins crying hard. "What happened?" her husband asked in a panicky way. Lynn looks at her husband with big tears. "It's our son, Alan, he was murdered tonight. Oh God, no!" She yells as her husband grabs her and gets the phone from her. "Hello! This is Josephine. Is she all right?"

"Yes, I have her. What happened out there?" Leroy asked. "Your son was murdered earlier this evening."

"Oh God!"

"You both need to come into town right away," Josephine said.

"We'll be there in about an hour," Leroy said and hangs up the phone and holds his wife Lynn, who is not taking it too well.

"Come on, honey, we have to go!" her husband Leroy yelled.

"I can't right now!" his wife said, sitting on their green sofa, crying her eyes out, feeling a mother's pain of loss. "Okay, I'll get things together and put them in the car, and I need you to put your shoes and coat on, and I'll be back to get you," her husband said. Leroy was rushing, getting their things ready to travel.

"I better get my wallet and keys and get my shoes and coat on and get my wife together." He goes into their bedroom to grab her coat and shoes and their change of clothes. "No telling how long we are going to be out there!" Leroy was thinking to himself. Lynn was feeling strong to get up to help her husband to get their things together. "Feeling a little better, honey?" her husband asked. "Not really," Lynn said with her puffy red eyes. "I need to put our dinner away before we go and pack some snacks for us and eat something on the road."

"Yes, dear." They both were feeling devastated and confused, rushing to put things in their car. "Honey, grab a blanket. It gets cold at night there," Lynn said to her husband. They both were ready to leave and get on the road to go see their deceased son Alan.

"Oh, I should have called Lisa. I know my baby is worried and still upset about what had happened at her wedding, and she is having his baby," Lynn said to her husband. "Yes, I know, dear, let's get going," her husband said, and they both get into their white van and drive out their garage and on a long highway road to the I90 freeway to Brookville, California.

Family Mourners

One hour and forty-five minutes later, Lynn and Leroy arrive to their son's residence. Josephine hears a car door slamming. "It's my sister!" She hurries to the front door and rushes out to her sister. They both grab each other crying as Leroy had his head down, looking devastated. Josephine and her sister Lynn were walking back into the house, hugging each other with sorrow, and Leroy walks behind them, carrying a suitcase into the house. "Where is Joanna?" Lynn asked. "She's resting," Josephine replied. "And where is Lisa?"

"She hasn't come over yet, and she's feeling down about her husband. I know how she's feeling Confused and lost," Josephine said sadly. "I'll call her and let her know that you both are here!"

"Did you tell her about her brother yet?"

"Yes! I called her earlier," Josephine said. Lynn takes a deep breath. Joanna walks out her bedroom door with her head down. "Hello, Lynn!" They gave each other a loving hug. "I miss him so much!" Joanna said to her mother-in-law and gave her a hug. "Yes, we all are going to miss him! Come sit over here, so we can talk," her mother-in-law said. "I'll go put some coffee on," Josephine said and walks into the kitchen to start the coffee. "Hello, brother-in-law," Patrick said to Leroy. "This is devastating!"

"Yes, heartbreaking to us all."

"I'll fix you some Seagram's dry gin on ice," Patrick said while Leroy was looking confused and devastated." Joanna, did you identify his remains?"

"Yes, Detective Theodore came by to take me to see if it was him. He was beat up badly." She breaks down crying. "I'm sorry we had a big argument before he went out slamming the front door and that was the last time I saw him alive!"

Joanna pretended to cry loud." I know it's heartbreaking," Lynn said, hugging her daughter-in-law when Josephine came walking out the kitchen with a pot of hot coffee looking at Joanna and Lynn crying. "Now, pull yourselves together. This is not what Alan would want right now, and we have to start thinking about Lisa and the baby coming," Josephine said. "Yes, let me call her right now to see where she is?" Lynn said. *Ding-dong.* Josephine opens the front door. "Lisa! Your mother is here! She was about to call you. How are you feeling, baby?"

"I'm all right."

"Oh, baby girl."

"Mother! I'm glad you're here!" Lisa said. Her mother was looking at her stomach.

"Are you having morning sickness, Lisa?"

"Yes, sometimes. Oh, Mother! I miss Dupree so much, and I believe he didn't do this crime," Lisa said.

"I know, baby! Well, have you tried to talk to him?"

"Yes! He calls every night, and he said that Curtis is setting him up because of his brother and Detective Theodore doesn't believe him. What can I do to get my husband back to me?"

"Lisa baby, it's now up to the judge," her mother Lynn said. "Deep in my heart, I feel he is innocent! All you can do now, baby, is pray and keep the faith, and if it's right, he will come home to you."

"Oh, thank you, Mother," Lisa said. "Have you seen a doctor yet, Lisa?"

"Yes, Mother, I have another appointment next week to see how the baby is doing. So far, the baby is doing good and the doctor told me if I don't stop stressing, I could lose the baby," Lisa said as her mother gives her a big hug. "Come sit down, Lisa," her mother said. "Would you like something to eat or drink, Lisa?"

"Yes, green tea. Please, Auntie."

"Yes, right away, sweetheart." Josephine goes back into the kitchen to make Lisa a cup of tea. "There's your father standing over there."

"Hi, Daddy."

"Lisa baby, how are you doing?" Lisa gets up to give her father a hug.

"Oh, baby. Everything is going to be all right!" her father said while hugging her, then gives her a kiss on her forehead. "Thank you, Daddy." She walks back to her mother who is giving her comfort and support that she needs. "I feel so bad about my brother,"

Joanna sitting down in the dining room, no fear of guilt, no real tears flowing from her heedless heart, sipping on her black cup of Coffee. Pretending she has a real soul to help compose herself from losing her mate.

Five days later, it was Alan Jones's service. Everyone was coming out of the church, wearing black. Driving to the cemetery, his wife and his family has prepared to bury him at the Brookville Cemetery. Everyone arrives and gets out of their vehicles to Alan's grave. Walking on wet green grass, Joanna noticed the fake green grass was covering a plot of dirt. Joanna and Lisa and her mother and father were walking with Josephine and Patrick. They sit down in the brown chairs that's in front of the grave. They were looking at Alan's white with gold trim closed casket while the minister begin saying the last words. "Let us bow our heads now with silence." A few seconds later, it was over. Joanna was looking at Alan's casket, going down into the grave. "Good-bye, my love." Wearing her black veil over her face, all the mourners were throwing the yellow flowers into the grave while the casket was being lowered. All the mourners turned around to walk back to their cars while Joanna was still standing there, looking at the grave. Lynn pulls off her coat, and Joanna begins walking with Lynn and Lisa while Josephine and Patrick rush to get into their vehicle. The weather feels a little chilly in November.

"The wedding was really nice till Detective Theodore came and ruined our reception party by taking my new husband to jail where he doesn't belong!" Lisa began feeling anger again. "Baby, it's going to be all right," her mother said while holding Lisa around her waist, walking back with her grieving parents. They all get into her parent's van, and Lynn starts the van up and drives off when it was clear from other cars driving slowly out the cemetery and onto going traffic, driving northwest to get to her son's home. Joanna was just looking out the passenger window from the left side backseat while Lisa was sitting next to her and gives her a hug. Joanna puts her arm around Lisa as Lisa lay her head on Joanna's shoulders, holding a white tissue, wiping her nose that was still runny, feeling a knot in her stomach. "I am four weeks pregnant!"

"It will be all right, Lisa, we all are going to help you," her sister-in-law said. Fifteen minutes later, they arrive to Joanna's place. Lynn parks their 1997 van in front of the house and unlocks her seat belt and opens the sliding doors on the right side of their van and walks around to help her husband out the car and closes the car door. Lisa and Joanna get out and walk up to the front door. Josephine and Patrick were already there, waiting for everyone to eat dinner that was delivered from friends and family members as all the other family and guests have just arrived to sit and eat with the mourning family for a couple of hours. Joanna was waiting for all this to blow over so I can go handle some business at the bank.

The next couple of days while her house was full grieving of people with lots of food and drinks where all the men were standing by the bar laughing talking about Alan past and how he had a great sense of humor with laughter. and how he made the football bets, and lost most of the times, as the men was laughing on the good times of Alan Jones as his employees were laughing that knew him from work, as [Note: Please rephrase this.] There was a knock at the front door and then the doorbell rang. "Oh, let me get the door," Josephine said. She opens the front door. "Hello, James, I'm glad you could make it to the services today," Josephine said.

"Come on in, James." Lisa's eyes lit up, noticing James. "Hello, everyone," James said while taking off his black leather coat and hands it to Josephine. She takes it to the back room with the other guests' belongings. James walks over to Lisa and gives her a kiss on the cheek. "I'm sorry about Alan, he was a good person," James said.

"I'll introduce you to my mother! Mother! This is James, Alan's friend from the fire station," Lisa said.

"Oh yes, I've heard about you. Alan used to talk about you all the time."

"Your daughter uses to date him," Josephine said, looking at Lisa with care.

"Well, I'm going to step over to where the men are. Will you all excuse me?" James said. "Yes, of course, it was nice meeting you, James," Lynn said.

"Hello, everyone," James said, walking over to the gentlemen hanging around the bar area.

"Hello, how are you doing, James?" Patrick asked.

"Feeling devastated," James said.

"Yes, my boy. I'm Alan's uncle, you should remember me!" Patrick said, feeling a little tipsy. "Would you like a drink, James?"

"Sure."

"And what would you like to drink?" Patrick said.

"I would like a rim on ice," James said. Guests were sitting at the dinner table eating and talking about different things. Lynn was sitting with the guests and other family members who were laughing and eating. "Do you remember when Alan was a young boy and kept wanting chocolate all the time, he was in love with

candy! And that's why he had a lot of dentist appointments."
Lynn was laughing with her grief, trying to compose herself from
mourning so hard while her eyes were still red and puffy.
The family and friends were surrounding Lynn and rubbing her
shoulders and her back while trying to cheer her, and Lisa was
sitting next to her mother.

"Oh, good news, everyone!" Lynn shouted as everyone's ears
came to attention. "Lisa is going to have my first grandbaby!"

"Oh, that is wonderful news." And family members said,
"Congratulations, Lisa!" "Thanks, everybody," Lisa said quietly,
drinking her lemon tea slowly. "Lisa, you want another cup of
tea?" Josephine asked. "Yes, Auntie, please. That was good tea."
Lisa was rubbing her belly as her mother grabs her hand and
gives Lisa a kiss on the right cheek. Her mother was still talking
about what to get the baby. "Oh yes, I love to shop for newborns.
Their clothes are so little and precious."

"So when is the baby due, Lisa?" her cousin Gail asked…

"Um, the doctor said around August next year."

"Do you know what you're having?" Gail asked.

"No, not yet, hoping it's a girl, and if it is a girl, I'm going to
name her Destiny Oxford." "I want to tell you that your wedding
was really nice."

"Thank you, Cousin Gail. Yes, it was nice until Lieutenant
Theodore came and said that Dupree paid his brother Richard's
lover. Curtis wrote in a diary that Dupree paid Curtis to kill
his own brother. Dupree loved his brother. He wouldn't have
done that! I'm going to call Detective Theodore and tell him
that Curtis set my husband up for that murder," Lisa said with
aggressiveness. "Lisa, don't get yourself all worked up. Remember
when you get upset, your baby does also. She feels everything you
feel!" her mother said with a smile.

"Our wedding was on the second of this month and my
brother gets killed two weeks later and my husband's been in
jail two weeks too long." Lisa gets up and walks to the kitchen

to call Detective Theodore. She calls information. "Hello, yes, I would like Detective Theodore's number please." The operator gives Lisa the number. "Thank you." She hangs up and dials the number. *Ring.* "Detective Theodore speaking!" Detective Theodore, this is Mrs. Lisa Oxford."

"Oh yes, how you doing?"

"Not good, Detective! I miss my husband." She began crying. "Please, Detective, let my husband go free! Because I know for a fact that Curtis set my husband up! Curtis made all that up." Lisa stops talking for a moment.

"Mrs. Oxford? Are you all right?"

I'm taking it hard, Detective! My husband is in jail and my brother is deceased! And I heard Curtis was really mad at Richard! Not Dupree!"

"Well, we will see what the judge says Monday at eight thirty a.m. department 108, maybe they will drop it! Maybe," Detective Theodore repeated, "because Curtis admitted that he killed Richard Oxford and there isn't any real proof that Dupree paid Curtis two thousand dollars, so don't worry, I'm going to talk to the DA and see what they say about that diary all right! So don't worry, Mrs. Oxford, I'm sure everything will be all right," Detective Theodore said.

"All right!" Lisa said sadly. "Thank you, Detective!"

Lisa hangs up the kitchen phone and rushes back into the dinner room, looking more positive with a little smile. "What did Detective Theodore have to say?" her mother asked.

"He said not to worry that Dupree's case may be thrown out of court because there's no hard evidence against Dupree!"

"That's great news. See! Just keep faith in God," her mother said.

"I'm going downtown to visit Dupree tomorrow! He doesn't know about Alan yet!"

"You want me to go with you, Lisa?" her mother asked.

"No thanks, Mother. I need to talk to him in private," Lisa said.

"Okay, baby! And you're right. You need to talk to your husband alone and make sure you tell Dupree that we are here praying for him to come home to his pregnant wife!" her mother said and gave Lisa a loving smile. "Here you go, Lisa. Your hot tea with lemon and a little sugar," Josephine said and puts the cup of tea in front of Lisa.

"Thanks, Auntie."

"You're welcome, baby!" Josephine walks back into the kitchen while Patrick was talking loud, feeling drunk. His wife and everyone else could hear him. His wife walked out the kitchen fast over to her husband. "Patrick! Patrick! You could wake the dead loud as you are talking! Now keep your tone down. His wife was looking at him as a drunk. "Oh, woman, go back into the kitchen and cook something!" Patrick said.

"I'll cook you in five minutes." All the guests started laughing at Patrick. "And she will too! I remember when Alan used to tell you to control your wife when she gets mad at you?" James said.

"Not that woman! She will tie me up and hang me for days to dry out like a chicken." Everyone in the living room, some standing by the bar, were laughing hard at Patrick. His face grew long. "That woman has always been the boss," Patrick said. "Look how mean she is! All she has to do is sit on me and I give in!"

"And she only weighs 120," Patrick said. All the men in the living room by the bar were still laughing at Patrick. "See, I'm like Alan."

"Do you have any control over your wife, man?" James asked.

"Not really. Josephine even made me say I do when I didn't want to say I do!" All the men were laughing with happy tears at Patrick, loud, with their drinks in their hands.

"Patrick, you have to put your foot down on her!" his friend Bill said.

"I don't see you controlling your wife! You're in the same boat with me, friend," Patrick said as the men were laughing at Bill. "You, too."

"Yes, but not like Patrick's wife!" Bill said. The guys were now laughing at the both of them. "See, we have control of our wives," one of the guests said.

"And how did you manage that one?" Patrick asked.

"Well, it's like this: give her what she needs and she is always right in suggestions. Just agree with her, and the arguments will be prevented. That's the rules in marriage," one of Alan's coworkers said. All the gentlemen in the room were agreeing together.

"That's what Alan would have told me!" one of Alan's coworkers said.

"Are you hungry? Maybe you need something to eat, Patrick!" James said.

"Okay, James. Will you get something for me out the kitchen please," Patrick asked.

"I'll be right back!." James puts his drink on the corner of the bar and tries to get past the other guests to go tell Josephine that Patrick needs something to eat. James goes to Josephine. "Mrs. Josephine! May I speak with you?" James whispered over the table as Josephine gets up from the table and walks into the kitchen. James follows her. "What is it, James?"

"Your husband needs something to eat, and I wouldn't mind taking it to him because he's kind of drunk."

"Yes, I'll fix him a plate, and thank you, James. I had a feeling it was time for him to eat right about now while he's in there getting his head full of liquor, by tomorrow he is going to have a good hangover and that's the time to hang him out to dry!" Josephine said. James had a grin on his face as Josephine was fixing Patrick's plate with some turkey and dressing with gravy.

"I'll fix your plate later, James."

"Okay, yes."

"Thank you," James said.

"You're welcome, James!" The evening was late, and the guests went home. A couple of days later, Joanna gets out of her bed to get ready to go to the bank. She was making plans with Alan's bank account. "I am going to transfer all his money into my account before they find out that he's deceased and close his account. But I don't think they can touch it without my permission. I'm his wife, so let me get downtown and take care of it." She rushes to get dressed, and it's Monday morning. "What time is it?" She looks at the time and makes herself some breakfast. "I need to make a couple of phone calls before I leave." She continued eating her breakfast. She began thinking about the changes that's coming. "I need to also call the insurance company and see when they are going to send the insurance check. It's been a couple of days now since Alan's services, and I know it takes time, but not this long, so I can pay the funeral home for their services." Joanna was thinking to herself. *Knock-knock.* "Who is it?" Joanna gets up and walks to the front door. She opens it.

"I have a letter for you to sign for, Mrs. Jones," the Postman said as Joanna took the signature card to sign it.

She then turns and closes the front door and walks over to the table where she had a cup of coffee. She sits down to open the letter. "It's from the insurance company, this is what I've been waiting for." She reads the letter. "Look at all the costs he owes his car insurance! Four hundred and twenty-three dollars for the month of October and November. What the hell was he doing with his money besides drinking? And there's the cost of his service: seven thousand dollars! Oh, no! There's no money left for the bills!" she yelled. "And I have to pay the remains of his bills and close them out! That bastard! I just hope he has money in his account! Let me get there now! I'm so damn upset!" She grabs her coat and brown leather purse and her car keys and opens the front door. "Oh, wait, I need to use the restroom now."

Alan's Assets

Joanna arrives to the bank of Brookville and parks and walks in and takes a seat to wait for a bank clerk to come to her. "Hello, Mrs. Jones, how can I help you today?"

"I'm here to close an account."

"Sure, just step over here to my desk and have a seat, and which account would you like to close today, Mrs. Jones?" the bank lady asked. "My husband's account. Here is his certificate of death." Joanna hands the lady. "Do you have his account number?"

"Yes!" Joanna hands her deceased husband's account number. The lady was putting in the numbers and was looking into his account. "Mr. Alan Jones has a balance of three thousand dollars and fifty-five cents in his account."

"Can you transfer it all to my account please?"

"Yes, of course. If you would just sign here that his account is officially closed. Oh, yes one more thing, here it says that he also has a safe box in his account."

"Safe box?" Joanna repeated.

"Yes, when we are finished here, I'll walk you to the safes for private use." She signed her name right away and gave the lady back the signed card and pen. "Now, all his assets have been transferred over to your account, and now, I'll show you the safe deposit boxes." She gets up from her chair and follows the bank lady through a short brown door and uses a key to open another brown wide door. They both walk to the back of the bank to the safe boxes. "I'll get the key to his safe if you would take a seat here please and

I'll be right back." Joanna was looking at all the silver locked safe boxes. A few seconds later, the bank lady came back with a key with the number 121 in the back. "Here is the key, just knock on the door when you're finished."

"Thank you." She gets up from the chair and starts looking for the number. "I wonder what Alan has in the safe box. Because from my understanding, it's very important to lock up!" Joanna was thinking. "Box 121, where are you? Where is 121? Here it is. I can't wait to see what's inside." She then pulls out a long thin gray box and sits at a private table and opens the box. Her brown eyes widened. "Where did he get all this?" She then closes the safe box right away and locks it and put what was in the safe box into her purse and walks to the door and knocks twice. The bank lady opens the door to let her out. "Thank you." She walks with a causal smile. "Everything all right, Mrs. Jones?" "Yes, everything is fine and thank you very much!"

"You're welcome." The bank lady walks away and Joanna walks out her bank and to her vehicle and unlocks her vehicle and steps in and takes a deep breath and starts her vehicle and drives off on to main Street, feeling a little surprised. "Where did he get this money from?" she was thinking while driving toward her place, feeling nervous about what was in the safe box. "I wonder what the hell Alan was into? I just hope he didn't steal it from somewhere or robbed someone? Alan was a kind of a sneaky guy, and why would he hide this large amount? I don't know, but now I have the money! And I was just thinking about his unpaid bills! And now I can pay off his bills and close them and I plan to move! I've always want to move to the west side of town where it's peaceful, no family members around, well, not his family. I love them all, but I can't stay in that house any longer because it reminds me of him and our relationship that went to hell! But it all turned out just great! I have no remorse or guilt feels for our love. It had faded away and the great feelings are moving in." She smiled while she was driving closer to her unloved home.

She then turns on the radio to listen to some soft music. A song was playing!

This is a woman's world! but I am still feeling no grief for losing her husband and lover! A stubborn husband where things went great for the first few years and, and then he changed a lot by drinking more and having a relationship with another woman, and all that time he was with me. I felt it in my soul and heart, but all I could do was nothing! He made sure if I even asked him where he has been all night, he would keep silent and would stare at me like he wanted me to know that he was in love with someone else and he knew I didn't want that! Because I didn't want to get my heart and spirit broken, again like the first time he cheated on me. I loved Alan very much for eleven years but he took me for granted.

Joanna drives up into her driveway and turns the engine off and just sits there for a moment, taking a deep breath and unlocks her seat belt and grabs her purse and gets out and locks the doors with her remote and walks up to her front door with her keys. "I hope no one is here. I don't see Josephine's car."

Joanna opens her front door and walks in right away and closes the front door and locks it and walks to her bedroom and puts her purse on her bed and pulls out the money! "Oh my goodness! How much is this?" She started counting the money: five stacks with white rubber bands around the stacks of money! "Maybe Alan was planning to leave me with this money and moving in with Alexis or someone else? No! I don't actually know, but I wouldn't put it past him, only if he was still alive. Wow, it's about twenty thousand dollars here! It's all mine! I feel I deserve this money from all the pain Alan caused me through the years. I have to hide this money, and then, I'm going to start looking for another place right away and move from this house with memories, and I would have more money and less stress will appear. I can feel it, and when I move into my own home, I'll feel a lot better. I don't have to keep soaking these memories of us together.

I'm just going to think of the good times we've had and try to move on, and with this money, I can help Lisa and the baby. I'll buy her a baby bed or something that the baby can use after the baby is born. I'll buy her a stroller for the baby. It should be warm weather by then and she can walk the baby to the park, and I hope her husband gets out of jail to help her. It's a shame how things turned out for Lisa, and at the end, it all turned out for the best. Twenty thousand dollars in cash! And now I know how much it is, I'm going to put this money in my pink suitcase till I buy a lock safe tomorrow and have it delivered." *Ring*! Joanna looks at her clock. It's eleven forty a.m.

"Hello. did I leave my gray gloves over their last night?"

"I don't know, Lisa, I'll take a look around the house and call you back." She hangs up her phone receiver that's sitting on her nightstand. She then walks to her closet to get her traveling suitcase and drops the suitcase on her bed and rushes to open the traveling case and picks up the stack of twenty thousand dollars and puts it into her pink traveling suitcase and locks it and puts it back into the closet and closes the closet door and walks around the bed feeling excited and then she walks out her bedroom and into the living room to see if Lisa's gloves are in the living room and looks around on the bar. She walks to the dining room table and sees her gray gloves sitting to the table. Joanna picks them up and goes into the kitchen to call Lisa back.

"Hello! Lisa, I found your light blue gloves that feels like crushed velvet, nice-looking gloves."

"Thanks, Joanna!"

"I'll put them up till you come over next time, and, Lisa, don't worry about getting the baby things. We will go shopping soon so the baby will have everything she needs because you will always be my sister-in-law, and I love you, Lisa, and I feel Alan would want me to help you and the baby."

"Did Alan know I was having a baby?"

"Yes! I told him and he was happy for you both when he heard the news and he really liked Dupree and then he was disappointed when he saw Dupree get arrested! His face went from happy to disappointed. We all were surprised, Lisa. Don't worry, he'll be back with you soon."

"Thanks, Joanna."

"And if you want to come over and eat leftovers your aunt Josephine cooked. You can warm it up in the microwave, and there's also iced tea," Joanna said. "I'll be over in a little while and maybe we can go shopping to cheer us both up."

"I'm missing my brother his ways and his laughter."

"I miss him too, but he would want us to stay strong, especially for the baby. So why don't you get up, Lisa, and drive over and call Auntie Josephine and see if she will cook for us because she can cook better than the both of us!" Joanna said.

"I'll call her and she can cook lunch and we'll go shopping," Lisa said.

"I'll be over, sister-in-law." Lisa gets up from her bed with her puffy eyes

"It's Sunday, and Auntie Josephine loves to cook on Sundays, and she's the best cook in the world and I am so hungry. Good morning, my Fluffy. I'm going to go see my husband today, Fluffy!" She was rubbing Fluffy's furry hair and gives her a kiss on the top of her head. "I miss my husband. No more tears, get it together. I know my heart is bleeding and my spirit is broken, but it will all heal when Dupree gets home. "You miss him too, Fluffy."

"Meow!"

She walks into her bathroom to turn on the shower. She continues rubbing her belly, feeling pregnant, walking back into her bedroom to get her things together. "I still feel so depressed. Missing my brother. What happened that night, Alan?"

"Meow!"

"Thanks, Fluffy, but that isn't the answer I was expecting." Fluffy looks at Lisa while licking her palms.

She starts getting undressed to get into the hot steaming shower, where she prays it will wash away the pain of missing her only brother Alan, and her new husband Dupree!

Oh, God! Please bring my husband home and make it all right, God! And she starts crying from her heart and soul with big tears rolling down her thin face.

Move Forward

*F*our days after Alan's funeral services, Thanksgiving was around the corner.

"I know Joanna can't cook that great, and I know Lisa can cook better than Joanna. Joanna can microwave and Lisa cooks on the top stove. I remember when Alan asked me to come over anytime to cook and he meant it! He misses my cooking and his mother's cooking especially! And that's why he asked me to always come over and cook for him every day. Alan had told me that Joanna couldn't cook! Why did he marry Joanna? Maybe he was deeply in love with her and didn't care about food at the time. But Joanna knows how to dress. I'll give her that and the most expensive clothing and fur coats. Alan wanted his wife to always look good in front of us, and she dresses sometimes like a model." *Ring*! "Hello, Auntie?"

"Lisa, are you all right?"

"I'm okay, Auntie, what do you have planned for Thanksgiving Thursday?"

"I am planning to cook here, and you're more than welcome to come over with Joanna. That's funny because I was just talking to Patrick about Thanksgiving."

"Thank you, Auntie, and we will be over there, but what are you planning to cook tonight?"

"Oh, child, you want me to cook you something. What are you craving for?"

"Baby back ribs with potato salad and corn chips."

"I'll have it ready around five p.m."

"Thanks, Auntie, I love you so much.

"See you when you get here."

"Okay, Auntie."

Lisa was rubbing far away body lotion on while her pink cell phone was ringing, and she looks at the caller ID. "Private?"

"To collect this call, press 7. This call is from Dupree Oxford." Lisa gets excited and presses 7 to receive his call.

"Hello, Dupree. I miss you so much!" Tears began to fall from her brown eyes.

"I know, baby," Dupree said.

"Oh, I want to tell you that Detective Theodore said that there's no real crime against you and that you may get out!" she said excited.

"Did he say when?"

"Yes, Monday morning at eight thirty in court. Keep the faith, Dupree, and pray to come home tomorrow."

"I missed you so much, Lisa! I cry for you," Dupree said sadly. "Did you hear about Alan!"

"No! What happened?"

"My brother was killed behind the Bam bar two weeks ago and his service was Thursday. Oh, Dupree, I can't stop crying."

"I wish I was there with you to give you support, baby. How's the baby doing?"

"Just growing and I been having morning sickness and just been feeling down. Still grieving about Alan and missing you dearly. You need to get out of jail and come home," Lisa said, crying over the phone as Dupree had a couple of tears from his eyes.

"I love you, Lisa, so much and I will call you tomorrow after I see the judge all right, baby! Just keep praying for me! I have to go now, Lisa baby, I love you! And I'll see you soon, baby." She continued crying, feeling more depressed and devastated. Lisa gets up to get some tissue for her runny nose and wipes her tears. "Oh, let me stop crying so much! Just making my eyes swallow and puffy more than they are. I better call Joanna, and tell her that we are having dinner over my auntie's house." Lisa rushes to finish getting ready to go shopping. It's almost ten a.m. She was still feeling depressed.

"It was so good to hear from my husband, and now, I'm feeling a little better, but not about my brother. I can't cry anymore. I've been crying for weeks now!"

She grabs her things and opens her front door. "Meow!"

"Fluffy, watch the house, okay? And I'll be back home soon." She locks her front door and walks to her white 1999 Lexus.

She is struggling to maintain her composure because of her brother's Death, and her husband's Arrests. She only wants to focus on the changes in her life! *A baby on the way and that's the best joy and love to have. I'm sure Dupree feels the same way. I can't wait for court Monday. I know in my heart and soul that my husband didn't commit that crime. He wouldn't try to kill anyone, he's the shy type, and I don't think Dupree would get that mad at his brother... that lying Curtis just wants to put the blame on my husband.*

She, suddenly, bashes her fist against the steering wheel. *I think Curtis probably tried to get Dupree for himself and that's the reason he's blaming Dupree for the crime, that sluggish gay bastard! Dupree would have assault charges for trying to kill Curtis's pathetic lifeless ass while he's in that awful jail! That would hit the newspapers for sure.*

She was thinking hard while she pulls up into her deceased brother's driveway, listening to a slow love song. She then turns the ignition off and opens her car door. Joanna rushes to her front door. "Hello, Lisa! How are you feeling?"

"Just a little morning sickness, but it's normal, the doctor said. I was trying to call you, Joanna, that Auntie invited us for dinner today and we are also invited over for Thanksgiving Thursday. Hope my husband comes home? We will be spending some quality time together. So are we going shopping for my baby?"

"Of course! Just give me a minute and let me get my things," Joanna said while they both walk into the house. Lisa closes the front door and walks over to the living room.

"It's quiet in here. It feels like Alan's spirit is here." Lisa was rubbing both her arms, looking for Alan's spirit. Joanna came walking out her bedroom, wearing her blue sweater that matches her skirt and her blue high heels.

"What's wrong, Lisa?"

"It feels lonely here now since Alan's gone. I felt his spirit." Her wandering eyes were looking around. "Come on now, Alan is not here!" Joanna said and walks toward her front door. Lisa follows Joanna out the front door. Joanna locks her front door. "Whose car are we driving?" Lisa asked. "I'll drive my car," Joanna said. "All right," Lisa said as she was feeling weird, leaving her brother's house, like a cold wondering feeling. "Are you all right, Lisa? You look spooked like you've seen a ghost or something!" Joanna said. "I'm all right."

A lot was going through Lisa's head. She was feeling spooked. *I can't wait to tell my auntie Josephine about this spooky feeling I've felt, like Alan's spirit was there when I was standing near the living room. I'm still feeling a strange chill.* Joanna was driving twenty-five speed limit toward the north side of the ocean near Brookville Hills area where Josephine and Patrick live.

Two minutes later, they arrived for lunch. Lisa gets out of Joanna's car and walks up the glass screen door. Josephine opens her front door. "Lisa baby, you've both made it! Come in!" Joanna walks behind Lisa. Joanna then closes the front door behind her and looks around. "Hello, Lisa and Joanna!" Patrick said. "Everything smells nice," Joanna said while Lisa and her auntie were giving each other a hug. "So did you hear from Dupree yet?"

"Yes, and he will be going to court Monday and I'm going to be there at eight thirty in the morning!" Lisa said. "Good for you! Oh, I made you a chocolate cake with different color sprinkles. Lunch is almost ready after the fresh bread is finished baking and then we all can sit down at the table and say grace and then eat," Josephine said. "Joanna, you can come sit at the table. I haven't forgotten you, baby! How have you been holding up without Alan?"

"Lonely!" Joanna said. "Oh, I'm so sorry." Josephine walks up to Joanna and gives her a hug. "Well, he's in a better place now," Josephine said. "And we all miss him dearly." She then turns to her husband. "Patrick, go wash your hands. It's time to eat."

Lisa and Josephine are putting the dinner on the table. "Everything looks good," Joanna said. "I know you both miss my cooking," Josephine said and she gives a little laugh and walked back into the kitchen while Lisa was bringing in the fried chicken and mashed potatoes with a bowl of brown gravy and sets the food on the long brown oak wood shining table with a white tablecloth covering.

Patrick came walking in to sit down for lunch, smiling. "Everything looks nice and smells delicious," Patrick said. "Thank you, Patrick, you say that every night," Josephine said. "And that's why you never left me!"

"That's right, your cooking kept me with you all these years," Patrick said and gave Lisa a wink from his left eye and a smile. Lisa and Joanna began to smile while Josephine comes out the kitchen with green salad and sets the salad bowl on the table and sat down to say a prayer. "Thank you, Lord, for the blessings of this food we are about to eat. Amen!" They all said together and begin to eat their fried chicken while Joanna was serving herself and Lisa also.

"Oh, let me get the iced tea out the refrigerator." Josephine gets up from the table. Joanna was feeling more guilty around Alan's family, not recognizing that it was her who had Alan killed! "This fried chicken and crab salad," Patrick said while Lisa and Joanna started laughing. Josephine enters with a pitcher of iced tea with the ice cubes floating on top. Lisa picks up her crystal drinking glass so her auntie could pour her tea first. Josephine then walks around the table and pours Joanna and Patrick a glass of iced tea and then pours herself a glass of iced tea and takes her seat and begins serving herself. "Everything tastes delicious, dear," he said while he was eating. "Yes, Auntie, it's all good!"

"Thanks, niece."

Joanna was sitting there wondering, just picking at her salad with her fork, thinking hard about where Alan got that twenty thousand dollars from.

"Joanna!'

"Oh, sorry, my thoughts wander off."

"I can understand that!" Josephine said. "I just wanted to know what's your plan now?"

"I thought about selling the house and moving to the west side of town into a smaller place because the memories of me and Alan in that house is breaking my heart every day."

"Poor Joanna, I'm sorry, we all miss him dearly too," Josephine said.

"Oh, Auntie! I have something to tell you that something strange happened to me! I was standing near the living room, waiting for Joanna and then I felt this chilly feeling came past me and I felt it like standing next to me."

"It was probably your brother missing you!" Josephine said.

"No, really, Auntie! I felt someone for real! I have never experienced anything like that before."

Dupree's Court Date

"I'm ready to move if Alan's spirit is living there," Joanna yelled. "And I'm alone in that house."

"He doesn't want to hurt you, Joanna. He's just missing you."

"I'm just waiting for tomorrow. I'll call my boss lady and tell her that I have an appointment."

"Yes, that would be wise," her auntie said. An hour and thirty minutes later, they all finished eating their lunch and washed their hands to get ready to leave for the afternoon shopping. "Oh, I almost forgot your chocolate cake to take with you, Lisa, and give a couple slices for Joanna."

"Thank you, Auntie!" They all give each other kisses. "Bye, Uncle Patrick, and don't eat all the food," Lisa said, joking with her uncle. "Talk to you both later," Josephine said while she shuts her front door. Joanna drives off going north toward Brookville mall to shop for the baby. Next morning, Lisa wakes up and rushes to get ready for her husband's court date. Twenty minutes later, she locks her front door, feeling nervous about what the judge was going to say.

She jumps into her white 1999 with gold trim Lexus and puts it in reverse and drives out her driveway and to the corner stop sign and puts her left blinker on to drive downtown of Brookville, California, on Court Street.

"I never thought I would ever enter that court and jail building," she was thinking while driving downtown to Court Drive. Ten minutes later, she parks in front a meter and turns off her ignition and gets her purse to get some change out, feeling nervous but more excited to see her husband and step out of her car, and she puts six quarters into the meter for at least three hours, and she walks toward the court house, wearing her white long-sleeves blouse and her long white and green skirt and her short heels. She enters the court house. An officer was standing near the swinging doors.

"Your ID please?" the female office asked.

"I'm here for Dupree Oxford's court date."

"Just go straight down the halls and you will see the numbers on the doors." The officer hands Lisa her ID. Lisa started walking toward the court room doors, looking for 108. "Here it is." And she opens the court room door and walks in slowly to find a seat close to where she can see Dupree and to make sure he notices her. Others in the court room were whispering. Lisa looks at the sign: No Talking in Court Room. "All rise," as the judge came in wearing his black gown and takes his seat and started calling names from case files. The judge was calling case numbers: "Two-forty-five, Mrs. Timber, you are charged with drinking in public. How do you plead?" the judge asked. "Guilty, Your Honor," Mrs. Timber said. "You can pay the fine on your way out!" the judge said. "Next case, number 275, Mr. Dupree Oxford." An officer walks Dupree into the court room with handcuff s behind his hands, standing behind a brown wooden stand. He started looking around and he noticed his wife and smiled and gave her a wink, a little worried that the judge won't let him go. "I have to say that this note in Mr. Curtis Leo's diary is totally unacceptable! There is no evidence that Mr. Oxford did this crime. You're free to go, Mr. Oxford. Charges against you are dropped," the judge said. "Next case!" Tears of joy came rolling down her face and she gets up and asked the officer, "Where would I wait for my husband?"

"You can wait for him in the waiting room toward the front," the officer said.

"Thank you," she said, wiping her tears of joy from her brown eyes as the officer was watching Lisa walk toward the waiting room. "Very nice looking," the officer thought to himself. Lisa walks into the waiting room where there were six to seven other people waiting for their loved ones. Some got bailed out and some were released. Lisa walks over to the counter where there was an female officer on the computer. "May I help you, miss?" the officer asked. "I would like to know how long will it be before Dupree Oxford will be released?" The officer looks him up. "He just had a court date and the case is dropped and he's being released!"

"Yes! I know all that!" Lisa said with sarcasm. "How long does it take for him to get dressed?"

"Around thirty minutes to an hour." She then lowers her aggressive attitude, rolling her eyes. "Why is she behind that counter? She does not know anything about computers. I know I can type better and faster than she could." Lisa was thinking and walks over to a seat and wait like the others. As they all were looking at her and her shining face and long golden hair that hangs to her lower back while she was smelling of far away perfume, holding her keys. "I'm glad I locked my purse in the car, then they would have to search all in my purse. It's not that I'm hiding anything. I just don't like people touching my things," Lisa was thinking. "Like that lady getting her purse searched. I have my identification and my keys." She was still thinking to herself. "It's only been ten minutes." Lisa was looking at the clock on the wall of the court house, having her legs crossed. A little black girl was looking at Lisa's shoes and outfit. Lisa gives a wave at the little black girl who looks fifteen months old or so. Lisa was thinking. She takes a deep breath and sits like a lady. People were walking past her; the people in the waiting room had their eyes fixed on Lisa and it grabbed her attention as she was waiting for Dupree to walk out the wide gray iron door that has thick bolts surrounded with a red light. Forty-five minutes later, she continued watching the wide round clock, waiting anxiously. She heard a loud door open, and she noticed five other prisoners walking out, and suddenly, she noticed her husband! She was excited, holding both her hands across her mouth, like she was about to say a prayer. She felt like shouting his name. Dupree was trying to rush through the gate after he noticed Lisa, feeling free. He tried to walk faster, wearing his tuxedo from their wedding day.

"Lisa!" They began hugging each other tightly. "Oh, Lisa, I'm so glad to see and feel you again!"

He was hugging his new wife tightly, walking out of Brookville Courthouse kissing each other.

"Where are you parked, baby?"

"Down a block by the parking meters on the streets." They were hugging each other side by side, walking fast to her vehicle. A couple of minutes later, they makes it her 1999 Lexus. Lisa gives her husband the car keys, feeling overjoyed.

"That was the longest two weeks I have ever experienced."

"It was a long nightmare for the both of us. We both were lonely and depressed for each other."

"So how is the baby doing?"

"Eating a lot and growing bigger. I see you're getting bigger in the belly." They both were feeling overwhelmed while he was feeling on her little pudgy stomach. "Now that this mess is over, we can go on our honeymoon that I promised you. That's my baby!" He was talking to his unborn fetus.

"It's a boy! And if it's a girl would you love her more?"

"I love girls too, but I can teach my son football!" Lisa began laughing with joy. "That's right, baby! We have a baby coming," he shouted out. "And we are almost home and my car is still sitting in the driveway.

"Yes, and the tuxedo store has been calling."

"What did you tell them?"

"We get a chance to bring the tux in, and he said that the bill is almost two hundred by renting a day. So tomorrow, you take it back."

"No, today!" Dupree said.

"And I would have to go to the bank and get the money out to pay them and apologize for keeping it so long."

"Yes, you're right. After we make love," he said with a smile, still rubbing his unborn baby. "A couple of more blocks, baby, and we are home!" He was feeling excited.

"Lisa, baby, I really miss your fried chicken and tacos. Guess what they eat in jail?

Imitation food! That's not real food they're eating, baby."

"What would you like for me to cook for lunch?"

"Fried chicken and crab salad with corn on the cob. I haven't eaten lately, baby, and I am so hungry!" He pulls up into their driveway and notices his car. Lisa opens her door and steps out while Dupree turns off the engine and jumps out, feeling happy and closes the car door and locks it with the remote and walks to the front door, following his new wife. Both were feeling excited, and suddenly, she begins kissing him while he unlocks the front door, and they walk in into their one-bedroom apartment and lock the front door.

"Meow."

"I hate to say it, but I even miss Fluffy." And they both laughed, hugging each other. "She is a house kitten, and I never let her out the house." Lisa pulls her new husband into their bedroom and leaves the bedroom door open. "You get undressed. I want you fully undressed," Lisa shouted while she goes into the kitchen and into the freezer and grabs four chicken legs.

"I'll put the chicken under cold water and make the crab salad in a little while."

House for Sale

*M*eanwhile, Joanna was at the realtor's office, making a deal to sell her home.

"Your home will be on the marketing list in one week."

"Thank you very much." She then walks out the realtor's office and was on her way to their lawyer's office for the insurance and his will and trust fund. Joanna carries her deceased husband's death certificate to prove to the insurance company that her husband is deceased. She gets into her 1999 Tahoe Hybrid car and drives down on Main Street going south.

"The address must be that tall brown skyscraper," thinking to herself. She then drives into a parking lot where there's a stop at a white rail to pay to park. She grabs a valet parking ticket and parks her Tahoe Hybrid and turns off her car and opens her door and gets out and locks it with a remote and started walking toward the front two glass doors, and she walks into a nice-looking business building. She walks to the elevator and pushes the down button. As the elevator door opens, Joanna walks on to it and pushes the seventh floor to the lawyer's office. She then walks off the elevator walking with a twitch in her hip, looking and smelling good. "Yes, may I help you?" a lady asked. "I would like to see Mr. Howard."

"And your name?"

"Mrs. Jones."

"Just a minute," the receptionist said. "Mr. Howard, there's a Mrs. Jones here to see you!" "I'll be right there!" And he gets up from his desk and walks out of his office to meet Joanna.

"Mrs. Jones!" He shakes her hand. "We can talk in my office." They both walked into his office together. "You can have a seat," Mr. Howard said. Joanna sits down slowly like a lady.

"Hello, Mrs. Jones." They shook hands. "What can I help you with today?" Joanna pulls out Alan's death certificate and hands it to her lawyer. "My husband passed away two weeks ago and I would like to see our will and trust fund amount."

"First, I want to give you my condolences for Mr. Jones's passing." He began reading the death certificate. "My husband was killed two weeks ago at a bar." She grabs a tissue feeling like crying in front of the lawyer. "Take it easy! And I'll get whatever you need, Mrs. Jones. I'll just be a minute."

Joanna nodded her head. "Yes, of course." Looking around the lawyer's office with her eyes that never had moist tears drop. Mr. Howard returns and sits down in his big black leather chair with a folder. "Why, yes, you have an amount for the insurance and the trust fund you both had opened a few years ago, and it amounts to twenty thousand dollars, and his life insurance amounts to twenty-five thousand dollars."

"Wow! That's forty-five thousand dollars! You can sign them both over to me with a cashier's check in my name please."

"Yes, of course, Mrs. Jones. I just need you sign this card to close the account." And he hands her a writing pen and she begin to sign. "And this will close your account for your husband also," her lawyer said. "I'll be right back with your check, Mrs. Jones." Mr. Howard walks out of his office. Joanna was feeling excited that her plans were moving along even more! "I'll have close to fifty thousand dollars and the money Alan had in his safe and the insurance money and the trust fund and sell the house. I'll be close to being rich. This is too good to be true." She was thinking to herself. "And I have plans to buy myself a new house and travel and enjoy spending his money that he had in the bank safe."

A couple of minutes later. "Sorry about the wait, and here you are, your full amount of forty thousand dollars and eight cents." He hands her the cashier's check. "It was nice doing business with you, Mr. Howard."

"And my deepest sympathy to you, Mrs. Jones."

"Thank you. and have a good day." Joanna walks to the elevator and pushes the ground button. The elevator door closes as she watches the numbers going down to get to her car and to the bank to put the money in her new account.

The elevator doors open. She rushes to her Tahoe Hybrid vehicle to get to the bank, then to her job. "I'm late for work. I told my boss that I would be a little late, but now I'm really thinking about quitting my job for a while so I can move out that house and manage my money. I'll give Lisa and Josephine some money before I move from this area." Joanna was thinking while driving to the bank of Brookville. While she was driving, she decided to turn on some music. "So I can keep her mind off Alan! It's like he is hanging around me twenty-four hours a day!" Joanna was feeling his spirit all around her. "I'll feel much better when all this is behind me!"

Collecting her thoughts, listening to some soft jazz music, she then pulls up to her bank and parks her car and turns off the engine and gets out with her black leather purse and locks her car door and walks into the bank to put the cashier check's into her new account. Joanna was waiting in line for a teller.

Few minutes later, she walks up to the teller. "Hello, I would like this cashier check into my new account, and here is my Visa bank card."

"Okay, wow," the teller said. "Forty thousand dollars, just sign here and it will be deposited into your checking account, and here is your balance of sixty thousand dollars and you're all set."

"Thank you," Joanna said and walks out the bank with a big smile.

"Now I'm going to get the newspaper and start looking for a new place to buy till the house sells and that's more money, and the more, the merrier," she said to herself while she was getting into her two thousand silver Tahoe Hybrid. With a big grin on her face, she starts her Tahoe Hybrid. "Find a realtor also and find me a new place to live right away. I don't even want to be there any longer. It's so lonely there since Alan's been gone. I keep feeling his spirit around me, and I wish he leaves me alone and I know he's not because he really loved me once. Getting back to work will keep my mind occupied and having this weird feeling off me. It feels as if Alan knows the truth, but it's too late to do anything about it, Alan Jones! Go rest in peace. Our relationship is over!" Joanna shouted. "Go rest in peace!" She was yelling at his spirit. "It's almost noon, I better stop and get something to eat before I go back to work," she was thinking and she pulls up to the Jack in the Box drive through. "I feel so rich to where I can do anything and move to wherever as long as I get out of that damn house! It has too many memories, and I need to move on with my life and stay single for a while. It feels really good to be single, and maybe next year, I'll meet a new friend. I'm feeling very single, ready to date right now! And it feels great with no husband now, no tagalongs," she was thinking to herself.

"Can I take your order?"

"Yes, I would like number 3 please."

"Anything to drink with that?"

"Iced tea with a lemon and sugar." Joanna was talking to the speaker.

"That would be 5.95 at the window."

"Thank you." Joanna pulls up to the window to pay for her food as a young lady comes to the window. "Five ninety-five please." She grabs her wallet and a twenty dollar bill,

Destiny Arrives

*L*isa goes into labor. "Push harder, baby!" Dupree said. Lisa continued pushing for three hours, and Destiny Oxford was born. "Six and a half pounds and eight ounces born at seven twenty p.m., the twenty-first of August 2000. Our baby is so small," Dupree said and gives Lisa a kiss while a nurse was cleaning the baby. Dupree had a little tear in his right eye, waiting to hold his new daughter. Lisa was feeling proud to be a new mother. The nurse walks up to Dupree and hands his newborn daughter in his arms.

Dupree began feeling like a father and was feeling graceful and proud and steps closer to Lisa and hands their new daughter Destiny, who was still sleeping wrapped in a pink blanket. Lisa started touching her silky straight black hair on her little head and looking at her little pink lips and white Caucasian face and little tiny ears. Dupree couldn't stop looking at his new daughter, giving Lisa a kiss. "Thank you, baby, for our daughter."

"It was all that good lovemaking or our baby wouldn't be here," Lisa whispered. "And she looks like the both of us." They both kissed each other. "How long will it be before I can get some?" Dupree had a sexy look on his face. "Not for six weeks, the doctor said,"

"I can hang in there, but nothing wrong with a little you know what," Dupree said as Lisa started laughing. "It hurts when I laugh, baby!"

"Sorry, my love," Dupree said. "I can't stop looking at her." *Knock.*

"It's feeding time, and then I'll bring her back in a little while." The nurse picks up Destiny Oxford carefully. "We have to do the birth certificate. Do you have a name for her? Yes, you write it on the sheet of paper and I'll be right back!" the nurse said. Lisa gets a pen to write their daughter's new name. "I am so proud of you, Lisa." And he gives her a sweet soft kiss. "I love you so much, Dupree, you need to call everyone and tell them the good news!" Lisa said. "Yes, baby."

"Use this phone, just push 9 for an outside line."

"How are feeling you now, baby?"

"A lot lighter and flatter now."

"You will feel better soon." They give each other a kiss. "Call your parents and tell them that they are grandparents now!" They both laughed. "They are going to get a kick out of that one!" Dupree said, and he began dialing his parents' number. *Ring!* "Hello! Dad! Guess what! You and mother are grandparents now!"

"What! She had the baby! Liz! Lisa had the baby!" Liz came running to the phone and grabs it from her husband. "Dupree!"

"Hi, Mother!"

"She had the baby? What did you have a boy or girl?"

"Slow down, Mother! I am the father of a baby girl!" Dupree said calmly.

"Where are you? I want to come see our grandbaby," Liz shouted. "Jimmy! Get your things together, we are going to meet our new granddaughter! They had a girl!"

"I am a grandfather of a baby girl!" Jimmy said, feeling proud.

"Dupree! What's the baby's name?"

"Destiny Oxford! Come to the Brookville Hospital on the fourth floor, ask the nurses when you get here! I have to make another call, so I'll see you both when you get here, Mother!"

"We are on our way, Dupree! Tell my daughter-in-law we are on our way!" Liz said. "All right, Mother!" He hangs up.

Dupree had a happy smile on his face. "What's your auntie Josephine's number?"

"573-9658," Lisa said. "It's ringing." Dupree hands Lisa the receiver.

"Hello! Auntie! Guess what? I had a girl!"

"What! Where are you?" Josephine asked. "At the Brookville Hospital? We're on our way! Patrick! Lisa had the baby! Let's get ready to go meet our new niece! I'll see you all in a little while." Josephine hangs up on Lisa, rushing to get her things together. "Come on, Patrick! Oh, I need to call my sister and tell her that she is a grandmother and to get out here! Lisa probably called her." Josephine grabs her purse and keys and her husband out the door and to their van, while Patrick was feeling very proud to be a new uncle! "All right, which way is Brookville Hospital? Turn left to go into town?" his wife asked, feeling excited while Patrick was trying to concentrate on what to buy the baby.

Twenty minutes later, Dupree's parents arrive proudly and walk into Lisa's room. "Hello, Lisa, how are you feeling?" Liz asked.

"I'm so proud of the both of you." She gives Dupree and Lisa a kiss. "Which way is the nursery? I want to see my granddaughter!" Liz said. "Her name is Destiny Oxford, you can go see her in the window of the nursery," Lisa said. "We will be right back," Liz said. Dupree's parents walked down the hall and noticed all the newborn babies through a thick glass. "Oh, there she is! Oh, how beautiful she looks and she's not a crier, She's just lying there, sleeping peacefully," Liz said as they were just looking at their new granddaughter. Dupree walked up to his parents, putting his left arm around his mother, while his father was just looking at his new granddaughter. "I am so proud of you, son, and congratulations, she looks healthy and strong," his father said.

"Thanks, Dad. I needed that!"

"She looks like you, son!" his father said. Dupree still hasn't for gotten how his father wasn't on his side when he went to jail for a crime he didn't commit.

Dupree was feeling different about how close they were. "And now I differently about my father not having faith in me." Dupree was thinking. "But we put it all behind us. Lisa and I are closer than my father and I are now, and I will love my father always." Dupree hit a little memory while Josephine and Patrick walk up to Dupree. "Congratulations, Dupree!" Josephine said.

"Thank you! Lisa is in that room." He pointed. "Oh, let us see the baby first! Which one is she?"

"Right in the middle of the crowd!"

"Destiny Oxford. That is a sweet name for her, and she is just sleeping," Josephine said. "Oh, Mother, you remember Lisa's Auntie Josephine and her uncle Patrick?"

"Yes, I remember. How have you both been?" Liz asked while Patrick and Jimmy were shaking hands. "We are so proud of them both!" Josephine said.

"Oh, let me go see about Lisa." While they all just stood there looking at the babies.

While Josephine and Lisa were hugging each other, Patrick came behind her. "Hello, my niece! I'm going to the gift shop and get you and the baby something really quick," Patrick said. "I just wanted to say I am very proud of you. I'll grab Jimmy and take him with me, so I won't get lost in this hospital." With a little laugh, he leaves the room and walks toward Dupree and his parents. "Jimmy! let's go to the gift shop and get Lisa some flowers and a gift for the baby," Patrick said. "That sounds good, let's go," Jimmy said and gave his wife a kiss. "We will be back, stay with Dupree and the baby!" They both began to walk down the hall to get on the elevator to another floor where the gift shop is on, the main floor. Seconds later, they both walk off the elevator and to the gift shop where they both bought some flowers and a newborn baby pink gown for a gift, both feeling so proud and happy, and makes it back to Lisa's room with gifts and flowers. They both give the gifts to Lisa and Dupree. "Thank you both." He gives them both a handshake. Just seconds later, a nurse walks in with the baby. Everyone was excited and wanted to hold the baby, and the nurse hands Lisa her daughter, Destiny. "She's so tiny!" Josephine said. "I forgot to call your mother and tell her the good news!" "My mother doesn't know yet?"

"Not till I call and surprise her. Let me get my cell phone out my purse and call her and tease her. She is now a grandmother! When we were growing up, your mother betted me that she would never become a grandmother. Here's my cell phone." Dupree was sitting next to his wife on the corner of the bed. Everyone was gathering closer to get a good look at the baby who was stretching to wake up. "She's a little wiggly thing. Let me hold her for a minute," Dupree said. Lisa hands Dupree his daughter. "She is so small," Dupree said while Lisa was smiling. "Let me get my camera and take a picture of this," Liz said.

"Lynn? Guess what?"

"What, Josephine?"

"You're a grandmother now! I wanted to break the news to you!" Josephine was laughing.

"What! Lisa had the baby!"

"What did she have?"

"A baby girl! And her name is Destiny Oxford."

"Oh my goodness! Tell Lisa we are on our way!" Lynn said." Let me talk to Lisa really quick!" Lynn rushes to put her shoes and gets the car keys. "What happened, Lynn?" her husband Leroy asked. "You're a new grandfather! Lisa had a baby girl a couple hours ago! Let's get ready and drive out there!"

"Wow, we're grandparents! Let's get my coat and shoes," Lisa's father said. "She made us grandparents." Leroy was feeling a little excited, getting his things ready to travel for an hour and a half. "Honey, get your things and lock everything up while I start the car!" Lynn said, rushing to their car.

"Here we go to meet our newborn granddaughter I bet she looks just like Lisa," Leroy said. "Our daughter is married and has a family of her own now. I sure do miss Alan."

"I know, baby. I miss him too! And it would be a good time for him to be here and meet his new niece," Lynn said.

Fifteen minutes later, Lynn makes it to Brookville Hospital to meet her new granddaughter.

New Edition

The next evening, Lisa and Dupree arrive home with their new baby. "You know we have to think about moving into a bigger place now," Dupree said.

He rushes to the front door to unlock it and open the door for Lisa and his new daughter. She carefully walks in the doorway as Dupree closes the front door and locks it behind them, while Lisa walks into their bedroom to put the baby in her new pink and white with yellow little flowers bassinet with padding all around it to make sure she doesn't get hurt as the new parents were watching her very closely from hearing about other babies with crib death.

Sunday morning, August 22, the family was gathering gifts and food to take over to Lisa and Dupree's place. Both families came over at noon to cook and serve Lisa and Dupree and spend time with the new addition to the families while the guys went out to get a drink for Dupree to celebrate that he's a father. Now his father began giving him advice

that it's a big job to be a father and husband.

Dupree starts his car and drives out his driveway and he then turned left to the store. "You will learn soon and I know this is your first child, and it's a experience in life when you bring a new life into the world," his father Jimmy said. "Dupree? What happened about you getting charged on that murder!"

"The judge dropped the case. I didn't do any crime!"

"Take it easy, son! I just was asking."

"Yes, take it easy, Dupree, he didn't mean anything by it!" Patrick said.

"Good, we made it!" Patrick said and unlocks his seat belt and opens the car door as they all get out the car and walks into Jake's liquor store off main street as his father-in-law puts his arm around his shoulders. They walk into the liquor store, noticing all different liquors up on the shelves as Patrick walks up to the counter with his mouth juicing even more for all that whiskey and gin and rim with brandy.

Patrick felt he was floating in liquor heaven while licking his lips. "Yes, may I help you, sir?" the store clerk asked. "Yes, you can give me a half pint of gin with the white label." "This one, sir?"

"Yes," Patrick said. Dupree came walking behind Patrick with one liter of 7 Up and a gallon of milk, smiling at Patrick. "Why are you smiling like that, nephew? Come on tell me," Patrick said. "It's nothing! Just feel like smiling," Dupree said with a hard grin, putting the milk and 7 Up on the counter. "Patrick, are you going to get a chaser with your drink?" Dupree asked. "I never have and never will. I drink it straight up!" Dupree begins laughing at Patrick while paying the clerk. His father walks up with a six pack of Bud light beer and some chips and dip.

"Here I go!" Jimmy said, listening to Patrick talking about his liquor.

"That will be 5.27, sir," the clerk said. A couple of seconds later, they walked out Jake's liquor store and started walking toward Dupree's vehicle, and they all get into his car and buckle up. Dupree starts his vehicle while Patrick begin to sing to his half pint of gin. "I can't wait to open and drink you all down! And make me feel the way I'm supposed to feel very happy with you, gin! But I have a wife that don't like you, but that's her problem, Mr. Gin!" Dupree and Jimmy gave a little laugh. "He does this all the time?" Dupree said. "But only when his wife isn't around, it's his best friend, Mr. Gin! who is with him." They both laughed, getting closer to Dupree's place.

"I hope my wife is cooking because I want to eat before I drink!" Patrick said. "Don't worry, Patrick, I hear you have the best cook in the county, Mrs. Josephine, and she is a good cook! Lisa's mother is a damn good cook also!"

"My wife loves to cook," Leroy said. "As a matter of fact, they all were raised to cook from their mother and be very independent and loyal and respectable women. We have the best women in the county. They never think negatively!" Dupree just looks at him and listens to him, making Dupree feeling even prouder to be married to Lisa. Dupree pulls up into his driveway and turns off his engine.

Dupree couldn't wait to get into the house to be with his wife and new daughter, Destiny. He gets his keys out of his pocket and puts it into the door lock and turns it and walks in, smelling some baked chicken and baked potatoes. "Hi, Josephine." He gives her a kiss on the right cheek. "Is he drunk yet?" Josephine laughed a little not yet, but he said he needs something to eat before he gets started on his Mr. Gin, he calls it! They both laughed. "He's coming in with Jimmy! Let me go see my new family."

Dupree was excited and walks into their bedroom and closes the bedroom door while Patrick and Jimmy walk into the house giggling while Josephine had her hands on her hips, waiting to see her husband Patrick. "Are you hungry?"

"Yes, my dear," Patrick said. "Now, you haven't been drinking yet, have you?"

"No, dear! Smell my breath!"

"No! Get back." She gives him a swap with the kitchen towel. "Oh, give me a kiss on my lips." Patrick was playing with his wife as she snatches his gin with a brown paper bag. "What are you doing, woman?" Patrick yelled with a loud tone.

"I am going to hold your bottle of Mr. Gin till you eat!" his wife said.

"That's cool! But it's Mr. Gin, baby!"

"Get back!" his wife said, holding a fork to stab Patrick if he tries to take the bottle for her. "Now get out of this kitchen and let me finish cooking!" Patrick walks into the living room where Jimmy and Liz, Dupree's parents, were sitting. "So, Patrick, how do you feel about being a new uncle?" Liz asked while she was sitting on the couch, drinking a bottle of fresh spring water. "He was in shock when I told him that's how nervous he was." Dupree comes out the room with his daughter while Lisa takes a shower. "Oh, let us see her!" Liz said.

Destiny was wrapped in a soft warm pink baby blanket while her father was holding her close to his heart, and he gives his new daughter a kiss on her forehead and hands his newborn daughter over to his mother. Destiny continued sleeping soundly, feeling comfortable in her grandmother Liz's arms. Dupree was standing guard over his new daughter, watching his mother sit with her new granddaughter, talking baby talk to Destiny.

She opened her gray eyes for a second. "Destiny! It's Grandmother Lynn, wake up! She feels soft like thin tissue," Lynn said. "Here! Let me have her for a minute!" Dupree's father said anxiously. "I'm feeling proud and she looks like her grandfather."

Suddenly, Lisa walks out of the bathroom from her shower, rushing to get dressed to get back to her newborn daughter. "Open your eyes, little one. Her name is Destiny," Liz said. "Hello, Destiny, my little granddaughter."

"Can I have my new daughter now, Dad?" His dad hands Destiny over to her father with a smile. "Oh, I just saw her smile, she's dreaming or she has gas," Liz said. *Ding-dong*, the doorbell rings. Josephine rushes to the front door.

"It's about time you both arrived. Lisa, your parents are here! Hello, everyone!" Lynn and Leroy said. Lisa walks out her bedroom, smelling fresh and clean and walks toward Dupree and her newborn daughter.

Lisa was touching her baby's soft hair and gives her daughter a kiss.

"Hello, sweetheart! How are you feeling?" her mother asked. "Say, we're doing really good, Grandmother." Lisa was speaking for her newborn daughter. "Can I hold my granddaughter now?" Lynn asked. Lisa takes the little blanket from over Dupree's shoulders and puts it on her mother's shoulders, and then she takes her daughter and lays her daughter's little body on her mother's shoulders while Dupree was busy watching his daughter closely. "Relax, Dupree, she's not going to drop your daughter!"

"Yes, I know, Dad. I just have this overprotective feeling towards my daughter"

"And that's good! But you can't protect her all her life!" his mother-in-law said.

"Well, I'm damn going to try my best to protect her much as possible till she's grown and beyond!" Dupree said excited. They all grinned at Dupree. "Oh, let me see my new granddaughter," Lynn said and gets the baby from Liz, Lisa's mother-in-law.

Brother's Death

*D*upree was standing out on balcony of the hotel. "I still carry a little guilt. I feel more committed to his death," Dupree was thinking to himself!

"Baby! It's so nice out here," Lisa said, walking out on the balcony, standing next to her husband, looking at the evening half moon and a little fog over the moon. "How are you feeling?" Dupree asked his wife. "Feeling better, kind of sobered up from the wine, but I just want to enjoy the evening," Lisa said. They begin hugging and kissing each other. "Well, I'm going back to finish the movie and you come with me and eat a little and get some rest while I watch the movie," Dupree said, standing with his hands in his pants pockets, watching the view, feeling a little lump in his throat, taking a deep breath, and they both walk back into their honeymoon suite. Dupree closed the curtains of the sliding door to keep a little breeze of air coming through and walks over to the dinner table to finish their dinner and a movie for a couple of hours. It's eleven o'clock. Dupree begin yawning. "That was a good movie." He looks over to his wife and noticed she was sound asleep. Dupree was kissing her on her right cheek, pulling her golden hair out her face while she was sleeping. He then just turned over to his side of the bed with his right hand on his right side of his face to hold his head up while he begin thinking about how things were when his brother Richard was alive. "Richard, I loved you as my big brother, but things just got out of hand with you, and I still can't believe you were gay! I was shocked to find out about you! So embarrassing to the family that you were gay! And our folks are still in shock about you! I'm sorry, brother, that things didn't go right for you! Like the gay thing with Curtis and the drugs you were using and used me to deliver the drugs and not showing me the right things in life! You were living the fast life, and you fooled a lot of people that thought you were living right with a good job! But the job was just a cover-up and Dad made you go get a job when you were twenty-one! Remember that! I was only three years younger than you and I knew my time was coming soon to go and get a job! That was something, but Dad just wanted to raise us decent with morals and values, and that's what he give us but you wanted everything. I feel that it was God's will to end what you had going on, which was not in his will. It was you willing to do the wrong thing. He knew you were using me hard and disrespecting me and that you were having sex with the wrong sex partner, a male! That is disgusting! Thinking about something like that and when Curtis cut your penis off and put it into your mouth, that was a message to you. He knew you were cheating on him with a female. You had a lot going on in your life, brother! Wow! That's a brutal murder! And how Curtis tries to set me up for the murder! That bastard! And how he showed up at the services dressed like a hoe that turned my gut upside down! I could never be a gay guy. I wouldn't know where to start!" Dupree was continually thinking deeply to himself.

"I felt thoughtless at the time. I was angry at you for using me and treating me like a rat, I hated you at the time! But now, I kind of miss your company when you were a real gentleman. Most of the time you were, but then you always thought you were the man! Because you got a job of seventeen dollars an hour! A huge company hired you through a friend. That's the only reason you got the job! And what pisses me off about you! You really had Mom and Dad believe in you more! You were clever, I'll give you that much! You had them eating out of your hands, hungry elders, because you give them money all the time! And you had a female lover also! Brother, you really had it going on! And she is married! I hope she used protection! What was her name?" He snapped his two left fingers. I can't remember her name!" Dupree was thinking out loud while Lisa was turning her body over closer to her husband.

Dupree then lays her head on his left shoulder and was feeling comfortable with his wife. He continued feeling relaxed, clearing his mind about his thoughtless fear that I carry in my soul if I confess the way I felt before maybe this fear would fade away. I feel inside my soul betrayed secrets, and I feel it in my heart that guilt! I have to confess, Lord, for this feeling of betrayal of honor and love to my brother! That's because I looked up too him in many ways, and he turned more against me and others also! He just changed! Got more angered with devilish ways. He embarrassed me in front of his friends, and they all just laughed. Instead of protecting me, he went totally against me! Like he hated me in his heart for what reason? He used to give me brotherly love when we were young, but people change like you, Richard! I named you a dysfunctional psychotic at the time I was angry with you! And I believed that because you had a lot going on with your gay lover Curtis, who is doing life! But what I don't get is why? I did not give him two thousand dollars to kill my brother? I need to go see him and ask him who paid him two thousand dollars because Richard was too cheap to give him money and Curtis didn't work! He was getting disability! And Curtis is afraid of his own shadow. So why would Curtis just lie about that statement! Curtis might be gay! But he says things that mean something Richard told me. I don't think it was Curtis that killed my brother Richard. He's not that smart! But he had strong love for Richard! And he had a jealous rage toward Richard also. So the question is who paid Curtis that money? Who is he covering for? I need to call Keith! And we'll do some investigation ourselves! I'll call Keith tomorrow when we get back and let him know I've have it all figured out! Maybe Curtis paid someone to kill my brother! I'll contact Detective Theodore about this! But first, I have to really look into this closer before I notify the detective!" He looked the clock on the nightstand. It's one thirty a.m. He then turns off the television with the remote volume turned down and turns over to his wife and puts his both arms around her body and holds her tight and kisses her while she was sleeping. He then begins kissing her on her neck, but she continued to sleep the wine off. She is a light drinker and falls asleep fast!

Dupree was thinking to himself as he began falling asleep. "Lord, forgive me and forgive my brother Richard for his sins. Dupree was praying to God to take this unwanted feeling away while he was falling asleep slowly.

Dupree Solves the Case

*D*upree jumps into his blue jeans pants and puts on his white t-shirt and his blue slippers. Lisa walks out dressed in her yellow and pink blouse and her long white cotton pants. "Today, we are going home to our daughter," Lisa said. "I can't wait to talk to my cousin Keith."

"What is it about, guy talk?" Lisa asked. "Something like that?" Lisa gave a little grin to her husband. "I'm going to call and check on our daughter while we eat breakfast and tell them that we will be home this evening."

"No, baby, we are leaving before that so I can get ready for work tomorrow."

"Yes, husband, this place is really nice!"

"And that's why we are going home before you really fall for this room," Dupree said while eating his breakfast.

"You're so silly, Dupree!"

"Push 9 to get an outside line."

"Um, this breakfast is good, baby! Good morning, Auntie."

"How are you feeling?"

"I'm feeling good! And how is my little angel doing?"

"She is an angel! Now, your uncle Patrick is a job!" They both laughed. "But he's your baby too!" Lisa said to her auntie Josephine. "I just fed her and lay her back down, she is so small and still smells like a newborn," Josephine said.

"Dupree? Can we go home in couple of hours? I miss our daughter," she said sadly.

"Let's get ready after lunch!"

"Auntie, we'll be there after lunch. Have you cooked breakfast yet?"

"Oh yes, before Destiny woke up!"

"Thanks, Auntie! We'll be on our way soon! I'll call you before we leave," Lisa said.

"Okay, dear, see you when you both get here." And they both hang up.

"How's our daughter?"

"Sleeping again. Auntie fed her this morning and she went back to sleep!"

"That's our newborn daughter!" Dupree said. Lisa sits next to her husband and began eating her breakfast. "Um, this bacon is good and the eggs look good also," Lisa said.

"You ordered breakfast?"

"Yes, earlier while you were sleeping."

"Well, it's delicious." They give each other a morning kiss to the fullest in their honeymoon suite. Dupree was watching the news while finishing up his breakfast. "Look at that! Wow, what an accident!"

"Where is it!"

"On Highway 18, the over path of our place, you know that freeway going north by our place! Look at that rig turned over on its side and these people from that car that's upside down."

"What's the name of that car, Dupree? Since you said you knew all the cars in the world!" Dupree started laughing! "That's a blue Volkswagen Jetty lying upside down!"

"So you do know all cars?"

"I should, much as I worked with cars through the years!"

I need to call Keith while my wife is in the bathroom, Dupree was thinking. He looks for Keith's number.

A few seconds later, "Hello! Keith, it's Dupree. I need to talk to you. Meet me at my folks' place at two p.m. today. I've figured it out! I know who really killed Richard!"

"I'll be there."

Dupree gets into his white 1999 Acura car and starts it and drives off going east. It's ten minutes till two p.m. "I made it back just in time to meet cousin Keith, then we are going to Detective Theodore and give him the layout that it wasn't Curtis. But I know who the killer is! Why didn't I think of this before? Because when it comes to Curtis, he couldn't kill a crawling bug. He would scream like a bitch! He's too damn scared to hurt anyone!" Dupree was thinking while he pulls up into his parents' driveway next to Keith's red sparkling 2000 Cutlass and turns the motor off and gets out right away and walks over to his cousin Keith's Cutlass and jumps into the passenger side. Dupree begin laying the facts out on Richard's murderer. "We were right! I knew it. Stay here, I need to get that detective's number from my mother. I'll be right back," Dupree said and he jumps out of his cousin's car and rushes up to the front door of his parents and knocks on the door. "Mother, open the front door!"

"Dupree! When did you get here? How was the honeymoon and where is Lisa and the baby?"

"We had a great time, Mother! Lisa and our daughter is over her auntie Josephine's for a couple of hours. Mother, do you still have that detective's number?"

"Yes, it's in the kitchen on the refrigerator door! Why?"

"I can't explain it right now, but I'll bring Lisa and the baby by tomorrow evening when I get off work, okay?"

"All right, Dupree."

"Thank you, Mother. Where is Dad?"

"He's at the poker game over his friend Kevin's place!"

"Okay. Thanks, Mother, and we'll come by tomorrow." Dupree then walks over to Keith's Cutlass and gets in and closes the car door and grabs his cell phone. "Detective Theodore, this is Dupree Oxford. I have something that you might want to hear. Can we meet you somewhere in the next twenty minutes?"

"Yes, where?"

"How about the Bam Club on Main Street?"

"Yes, I'll be right there!" Detective Theodore hangs up and rushes out of his office and to the parking lot to a patrol car that has a silver antenna on the hood of the trunk for radio frequency. Detective Theodore rushes with his sandwich hanging from his mouth, trying to get his seat belt on while eating at the same time and starts the patrol unit car and puts it into drive and drives off toward main street, heading east from the Brookville police station one block away. The detective stops at a red street light for sixty seconds and finishes his ham sandwich and opens up a can of root beer soda and begins driving from the stop light. "The Bam club is about ten to twelve blocks from here," Detective Theodore was thinking. "All these street lights are going to make it slow for me, but I'll get there," he was thinking to himself. "I wonder what Mr. Dupree has in mind to call me. He told me he wanted to be a detective. It better be good and not waste my time. He knows Curtis is in jail. What could it be that this young man came up with? He said he has something for me. I'll see what's going on when I get there." *Beep! Beep!* Detective Theodore got aggravated and thought to himself, "This traffic is heavy. Why can't they all just be behind a desk and not on the streets!"

A few minutes later, Detective Theodore arrived to the Bam club to meet Dupree. He parks two cars down and gets out of his car and noticed Dupree and Keith standing next to Keith's Cutlass. "Detective Theodore!"

"Hello, Dupree!"

"This is my cousin Keith!"

"Hello, Keith! What do you have for me?"

"Richard's married lover! I figured it out when Curtis lied on me about the two thousand dollars, and then it dawned on me that Curtis can't hurt a bug or fly! He's a bitch that screams if he even sees a bug or fly!"

"What's your point?" Detective asked with anguish.

"Richard's female lover, Mrs. Ross. Curtis paid Mrs. Ross to kill my brother!"

"How did you come across all this?" Detective asked.

"The things Curtis was saying and I remember what Richard always told me since he and Curtis have been friends: to listen closely to the things Curtis says and I asked him why? And he told me that the things Curtis says means something always important! Even in the clubs, when he drinks, the truth always come out and that's why he doesn't have too many friends," Dupree said to the detective.

"And you think it was Mrs. Ross that killed your brother? Well, it does make a little sense on this and about Curtis not hurting a fly, but what's her motive to kill Richard?" Detective asked.

"HIV, Detective! He gave her HIV because Curtis told me my brother had it and that's the real reason I was mad at him! He had the virus and give it to Mrs. Ross. Check it out! I know it's embarrassing to the family, but it's the truth, Detective Theodore! And please don't let my wife know about any of this, she will freak out and she's so happy now."

Detective looked straight at Dupree. "You could be the next future detective someday. You know I was just looking into your brother's file, and I was thinking the same thing about Curtis and you're right. He couldn't hurt a fly, and I believe this all may be true! Is she inside the club?" Detective asked.

"I don't know. We didn't go inside to look around," Dupree said.

"Okay, Dupree, stay out of that club and I'm going back to the chief and get a search warrant, and if all goes well, you deserve a medal for this and you should become a detective and you both should take a class and see where your future is bright."

"I'll do that, Detective!" Dupree said.

"Okay, I want you both to go back to your homes and wait for my call so you can identify her! Because I've never seen her before and I know the both of you have been playing detective." Keith and Dupree look at each other with a little pride. "Don't worry, I think the both of you are a team together!" Detective said, giving them both a compliment in playing detectives and solving the case before Detective Theodore figured it out on time on who is the real killer of Richard Oxford. "I was right the first time, I had a feeling it was her and that feeling is still with me," Keith said, feeling all excited in front of Detective Theodore. "Now you said you had a feeling it was her!" Detective asked.

"Yes, and at the time my cousin was murdered! I had that feeling," Keith said. "And I believe God will find a way and the truth!" Keith was preaching to Detective Theodore. "You both may become our next future detectives."

"When I write my mystery book, you're the detective in my novel!" Keith said. Detective Theodore felt flattered while walking to his patrol car.

"Thanks for the complement! Remember, Dupree and Keith, wait for my call." And he jumps into his dark blue patrol vehicle and drives off.

"Come on, Keith." And they both rush back to the green Cutlass vehicle with his loud pipes and turns on his rapping music, following Detective Theodore down main street going from the west to north freeway driving back to the police station. while looking in his side view mirror and noticed Keith is one car behind him.

"This is Detective Theodore, could you look up a Mrs. Susan Ross? A white female, aged thirty-three. She lives in the County of Brookville."

"I have a Mrs. Susan Ross, once convicted on assault charges on her husband Mr. Ross in 1992, and that's all I have on Mrs. Susan Ross," an officer said.

"What's her height and weight?"

"Her height is five eight and her weight is 240. Big girl!" the officer said over the intercom.

"And what is Mr. Ross 's weight and height?"

"He's 175 and his height is five eight, and I think she could hurt him before he hurts her," the officer said over the intercom.

"What's the address of Mrs. Susan Ross?"

"149 Walter Way, Brooksville County."

"Can you have that information ready for me?"

"Yes, Lieutenant."

"I'll be right there." The detective hangs up the car phone and continues looking out his rear view mirror and changes lanes driving closer to the station while he watches Keith turn right toward Dupree's place. "Now, let me hurry up before the captain leaves for the day." Detective drives a little faster, going 25 mph to beat the street lights and catch his captain. "Wait till I tell him this story! He'll probably tell me that the case was closed and now it's back open! I will tell him with the clues and the motive. He would consider reopening the case," the detective was thinking before he faces his captain. "And I think he would let me get that warrant for the address, 149 Walter Way." Detective parks in reserved and turns off the engine and opens the car door and jumps out and rushes into the station. "Lieutenant! Here's the information on Mrs. Ross."

"Thank you very much. Is the captain in his office?"

"I suppose."

"Captain! I need a favor right away. I need a search warrant for a Mrs. Ross who killed Richard Oxford."

"What! I thought that case was solved!"

"Listen to me, Captain! Curtis did not kill Richard Oxford! He paid Mrs. Susan Ross two thousand dollars to kill Richard Oxford!"

"And why would she have done this murder for the money?" his captain shouted!

"Just a moment, Captain! Officer John?"

"Yes, Detective!"

"Could you get me the medical file on Richard Oxford for me please? It should be true that Richard Oxford had the HIV virus."

"Here you go, Detective."

"Now let me see if I'm right." He started laughing. "Dupree Oxford was right! He hit it right on the button."

"What is it, Detective?"

"Richard Oxford had the HIV virus. It's in the autopsy report and he gave the virus to Mrs. Ross and this was the missing piece. That's the reason I need that warrant on Mrs. Susan Ross and I know for a fact that she killed Richard Oxford. I knew there was something nagging me about this case that it was not completed, but today, if it's God's will to find a way and bring out the truth. I heard that from someone who wants me as his character in his book and wants to become a detective like me." His captain looks at him with a grin.

"Okay, Theodore! I'll get the warrant in about an hour, and I would have to say good job!"

"Thanks, Captain!" And he walks out his captain's office smiling. "That young man is good and listens very well from what his brother told him. Now, I'll wait on the warrant for Susan Ross."

"Detective?"

"Yes, Captain?"

"What's the address of Mrs. Ross?"

"It's 149 Walter Way!"

"That will be all, thanks." His captain walks back to his desk while talking to the judge.

"I would like Dupree and his cousin Keith there. I'll call him and let him know what's going on with the warrant," the detective was looking in his address book for the number. Detective was dialing Dupree's cell number.

"Hello, Dupree. This is Detective Theodore."

"Oh yes, Detective."

"My captain is calling for the warrant now and I would like you and your cousin to be there when I go in and arrest Mrs. Ross for the murder of your brother Richard!"

"Yes! Detective, we'll be there!" Dupree was excited. "What's the address?"

"Just meet me at the Bam club when I call you."

"All right, Detective Theodore, we'll be there! Cousin Keith, this is it!"

"What did he say?"

"He said he wants us to meet him at the Bam club and we are going to watch him arrest Mrs. Ross for the murder of my brother Richard."

"This is great man!" *Ring!*

"Oh, shit! Hi, baby, what are you doing?" Dupree asked.

"I'm calling to see what my husband is doing?"

"Keith and I are just sitting on the bench for a moment before we start playing ball again." Dupree was trying to stay calm.

"Oh, okay, we're missing you, and Auntie said she's keeping your plate warm."

"Okay, baby, I'll be there soon!"

"Say love you, Daddy!"

"Love you both too." And he hangs up. "Let's go play some ball till the detective calls back!"

"That's cool, let's do this."

"I'm so anxious and can't wait for the big finale, then I have to act cool around my wife and new baby. What about the newspapers and the news on television? We both might be on the news?" Dupree's eyes had widened. "And I think Lisa would go off on me for not telling her about this."

"Why would she do that? We've solved the murder case for Richard."

"You know what? You're right, cousin, we are really heroes and we've solved my brother's murder case together," Dupree shouted. "And I think Detective Theodore knows the reason he wants us to meet him and we both are going to take a law enforcement class together and make that big money like Detective Theodore. And we will become detectives with a badge, working in a detective building, solving cases and we are going to be top detectives because we have a bright future ahead of us and we are still young," Dupree said.

"I was just thinking about the big bucks we will be making in just one year, and the income tax will be sweet!" Keith said.

"Yes, and I can buy me a Mustang like yours, cousin, but my Mustang will be sparkling apple green color."

"That would be sweet and have the loud pipes and spinning rims."

"No, Cousin Dupree, that's only for the players and you're married unless you're still looking for that other woman?"

"No, Cousin Keith, nothing like that anymore. I've stopped being a player the day I met Lisa and she has the smoothest skin and good loving."

"You are so lucky. But not as lucky as I am," Keith said.

"What do you mean?"

"I can get more women and more sex then you can Cousin?"

"And when are you going to find a good woman and settle down and get married?" Dupree asked with concern.

"I'm almost ready, cousin, because what you just said makes a lot of sense. And you do have the potential of becoming a detective, Dupree. We'll keep our day job and take a law enforcement class in the evening," Keith said.

"It sounds exciting to become a detective," Dupree said. Keith pulls up and parks his Cutlass and they both jump out! Keith pops the trunk open to get his basketball out and they both walks to the basketball court to play some hoop ball. Couple of hours later, Dupree's cell phone rings. "Hold up, my phone is ringing." They both were breathing hard from playing ball. "Hello. I got the warrant for your brother's killer and I thought you and Keith would like to see the action."

"Sure, Detective. Where do you want to meet?"

"A block from the Ross's residence in about twenty minutes."

"Okay, we'll be there, Detective!" Dupree was feeling excited to see the action.

"Cousin Keith, we have to leave!"

"What's up, man!" Keith asked anxiously.

"That was Detective Theodore." Dupree taps Keith on the stomach. "We are in with Richard's murder case!"

"Really?"

"He wants us to meet him in twenty minutes to watch the action!"

"Let's go, man!" Keith yelled. "Things are looking up for us already!" He was getting his keys out of his pocket to unlock his Cutlass's door to let Dupree in, while he opens his trunk of his car to put his basketball away and he jumps in and starts his Cutlass. "Where are we going?" Keith asked.

"A block from Mrs. Ross's residence in forty-five minutes."

"We are going to make a quick stop to the gas station first because I have to pee," Keith said. "There's Circle K store, they have a bathroom. I'll pull over by the water and air." Keith rushes into the Circle K store to get the key and rushes into the bathroom. "Hurry up, man!"

"I have to piss like a fountain!" Dupree said. A few seconds later, Keith comes out the men's bathroom. Dupree rushes in. A few seconds later, Dupree walks back into the Circle K store to return the key that is on a large wooden board. Keith was walking to his Cutlass and noticed his cousin Dupree rushing back.

"Are you ready?" Dupree asked.

"Yes, I'm good!" Keith starts his car and they both snap on their seat belts to go meet Detective Theodore. "What time is it?"

"It's almost eight p.m.," Dupree said. Keith was driving east toward the Bam club just four blocks from the Ross's residence. "Detective Theodore said to park a block from the Ross's residence in ten minutes."

"We are going to have the best seats up close."

"How, man? Detective Theodore won't let us get too close," Keith asked. "Maybe? But we are going to park across the street from her house, but not directly across but a little way down where we can see as clear as the next person," they both said together, feeling excited. "We are coming close to the block. Do I turn down that block?"

"No, turn around and go down the next block, and we'll be closer to see the action!" Dupree said. They were feeling excited about the arrest of his brother's killer!

The Fatal Truth

"That's Detective Theodore car parked on the corner," Dupree announced. Keith pulls up behind Detective Theodore's dark blue vehicle. Detective Theodore noticed a red Cutlass. "That must be Dupree. Are you guys ready?"

"We sure are, Detective Theodore!" Keith said.

"Wow, five police cars. That's a lot of police cars," Dupree said excitedly.

"Keith, follow me and park behind my vehicle and stay in the car and don't get out of this car. My captain doesn't know you both are with me." He winks his right eye at Dupree and Keith. "We have to keep it silent, guys."

"For sure, Detective!" they both said while they were feeling anxious to see live action up front while Detective Theodore rushes back to his car and gets on the car radio.

"Let's do it!" he yelled over the dispatch radio to the officers that came speeding from around the corner and parks their police cars in front of Mrs. Ross's residence with weapons while the detective parks across the street from the residence of Mrs. Ross. Keith then drives up and parks behind Detective Theodore's dark blue police patrol vehicle. They both were feeling excited, waiting for the police to run into Mrs. Ross's residence. They both jump out of Keith's car to watch the action closer. The police had loaded guns. *Bang, bang.* "This is the Brookville Police Department!" Two officers kick the front door open. "What the hell!" Mr. Ross jumps off his brown couch.

"Get on the floor and put both your hands on your head! Check every room in the house," Detective Theodore said.

"Get the hell out of my house!"

"Mrs. Ross, you're under arrest for the murder of Richard Oxford. Put your hands behind your back." The officer rushes a pair of silver cuffs on her thick wrists.

"You have the right to remain silent. Anything you say can be held against you in the court of law."

"Susan!" Mr. Ross yelled with shock. "What's going on?" She turns around to face her husband. "I'm sorry, husband, I had cheated on you with Richard Oxford and he gave me his HIV virus, and I killed him! Now you know the truth!" she yelled while in handcuffs, with big tears flowing. Dupree stares at Mrs. Ross with shock about his brother, and she looks at Dupree with shame. Mr. Ross felt darkness under his feet that their marriage was a big lie while he watches the officers put her in the police car and close the back door. While Keith walks over to Dupree who was standing across from Mrs. Ross's residence, feeling disappointed in his deceased brother having the HIV virus.

"Come on, cousin. It's over now." Dupree had a little tear in his left eye. Detective Theodore walks over to Keith and Dupree. "Well, it's over, guys, and I hope you both learn something from this. And, Dupree, I know it was a shock for you to hear the truth about Richard and I just wanted you both to get a little taste of becoming the next future detectives. Well, I want to thank the both of you for your help in this case, and I have to say the both of you did a great job on this investigation and good luck to the both of you." Detective Theodore gives them both a handshake.

"Good-bye." He gets into his blue unit car and drives off toward the police station to do his report on Mrs. Ross's case while Keith and Dupree head home feeling proud.

"I feel we have achieved a better future. I was a little surprised to see how heavyset she was," Dupree said. "She looked like she can take the both of us with her muscular body." Both began laughing for Dupree to feel better. "Lisa will be shocked when it hits the papers tomorrow that we solved my brother's murder case. She will be excited that she has an intelligent smart husband as the next future detective," Dupree said.

"Good night, Cousin Keith, and thanks for being by my side on this case."

The Great Sense of Humor Story

*I*t was the year 2005. I was rushing to my doctor's appointment when I had crossed the streets of harbor, and I came to the corner bus stop and I passed a man that was sitting there. "Excuse me, miss," the voice of a man who looked like he haven't had a meal or a bath in months. The man yelled, "Miss! Do you have a cigarette?" I kept walking when my heart hit me, and I happened to stop and turned around and said to the man. "I'm so sorry." I handed him a basic menthol cigarette and said to the man, "I should be ashamed of myself. God will punish me if I don't share my blessings," I said. The man tried to give me a quarter. "Oh no, mister! You keep that!" And he stared in my eyes and said, "God is going to bless you soon." Then he threw the shining quarter into my open purse. I just stared into his eyes and an overwhelming feeling came to me. I then turned to walk away, and I happened to look back at the man, but he was gone. That incident was puzzling to me and I will never forget that day. The year of 2005, on an early evening, I felt tired, so I lay down for a short nap. When the front door had opened wide, there was a bright shining light coming from the living room where there were a gathering of people all in white gowns with their huge wide wings that were spread out. God's angels! I had stood up from my bed to see what was going on and why my front door was open, and I walked toward my front door, and there was a man with white wool hair standing in front of my front door in a brown trench coat that looked like he was homeless, and I just stood there looking at the white wool-haired man until I looked deeper into his eyes and recognized him, then I got excited and started running down my hallway, but I didn't get very far. With quick thinking, I had turned around and looked into his eyes and I shouted, "Oh my God. It's Jesus Christ, our Lord and Savior with his great sense of humor." It was also Jesus Christ, our Savior, at the bus stop, looking poor and homeless, knowing he's the shine to us all! God has a great sense of humor, and we have our moments of laughter together. Our Lord Jesus Christ comes in all disguises. When another male approached me, he told me that God has a special gift for me. I have never seen this person before in my life. God was sending messages to me in any every form I passed. So I stopped and looked at the heavens and said, "I hear you, Father, and I understand!" God will speak to you only if you listen to his whispers.